W9-BGY-514

Exiles of Dal Ryeas

Paula Kalamaras

Strategic Book Group

Strategic Book Group
P.O. Box 333
Durham CT 06422
www.StrategicBookClub.com

ISBN: 978-1-60976-206-3

Printed in the United States of America

Book Design: Rolando F. Santos

Contents

Dedicated to best friends and family.

Prologue

And the legend goes:
"Far beyond the limitations of space and time, in the folds of eternity, the Creator sat in the garden of his wife, Divine Wisdom. There, amidst the greatest of his creations, he sat and contemplated the ordered rows of her philosophies and contemplated his future triumphs. He determined the paths through the voids; he painted the mists of eternity and fixed time. He pondered his creations and began to mold from the clay of his wife's garden, creatures to rule his new domains. These he whimsically called humans and he gloried in the different shapes, colors, and styles of his newest creation. Serene, contemplative, aloof, the Creator sat isolated in his glorious splendor forging the universes from the void.

It was here, in the midst of his wife's peaceful garden, that the arguments of his offspring reached him. The energy and fury of the young gods as they argued with his eldest son, spilled into the blissful quiet of the Garden of Wisdom. Chaos, though long banished from the precincts of the eternal, threatened again to overwhelm the garden. And Wisdom, sensing the total destruction of her garden, called out to her husband for assistance.

Majestically, furiously, the Creator rose and overrode the angry shouting of his children, "Silence!"

The young gods fell silent, fearful of their father's fury. The Creator surveyed his numerous offspring with a censorious eye. Even his eldest Son and his twins, Sarama and Saevirg, squirmed uneasily under the stern paternal gaze. No one spoke until the

1

Creator, turning to his wife, said, "What am I to do with them?"

"Increase their duties. It is time for them to assist you," Wisdom replied. A moan, small as a breeze, escaped the young gods. Their mother smiled suggestively at their father. The Creator, in a flash of insight, nodded and spoke his decrees.

"Your Mother, my sons and daughters, is right. Too long has your idleness rung the corridors of Heaven with discord!" The Creator glanced at his children.

"I set before you my newest creations. My universes are in need of populations. I had intended to populate them myself and then give them as gifts into your care. Instead, I give them to you now, to shape as you please. My only stipulation is that these," here the Creator indicated the rough unfinished forms of man and woman he had sculpted from Wisdom's clay, before his offspring had so rudely interrupted him, "are the dominant life forms in all of your worlds. You may have others with souls, but I want these to be the rulers. Other worlds will have other life forms, but these new ones, which will glide along the paths I have created — these are to be the dominant. The rest I leave to you. You may scour my workrooms for ideas. You may use your own thoughts and projects. The freedom of choice is yours - and when you are finished I will walk the paths that I have set between your universes and breathe life into your worlds."

"May we do whatever we please in our universe?" asked Saevirg, the boldest of the god-twins.

"Yes, of course. But you may not interfere with any of your siblings' worlds. You may visit as a guest. A brother or a sister may borrow that which you create, but you cannot introduce anything unwanted to another's world without permission. These are my prohibitions. Otherwise, you are free."

The excited and happy young gods dispersed to choose their building materials. As their voices faded away, the serenity of Wisdom's garden felt restored.

Then the Creator turned to his wife, intent on restoring his own marital harmony. Instead he saw that she was troubled and pre-occupied. He waited for her to speak.

"It is not altogether wise to allow them such utter freedom. They are young and ambitious. I fear for your lesser children." She pointed to the unfinished models before her. "They will suffer from these enthusiasms." Wisdom sat beneath her favorite fountain allowing the water to embrace her. The Creator watched his wife surrounded by the waters of creation and was pleased. He loved it when she, who was often so reluctant to use her powers, became involved in his projects.

"Although I have no wish to interfere with your plans for the children, I will bestow on each world a gift — a Talisman — which can be used by the wise and strong among your lesser sons and daughters to protect and keep them. This Tal will guide the rulers and give them a touch of magic. Yes. That is what I shall do." Wisdom declared emphatically. "But for your younger children to use it effectively I will hide it until the strong, the brave, and the wise among them discover its presence and delve its power." And Wisdom smiled and embraced the Creator beneath the waters of her fountain.

And from the thoughts of Wisdom, came the Tals, hidden on all worlds, safeguarding all from the excesses of the gods . . .

PART ONE

Chapter 1

"Have you had any word at all?" Lila Harrison poured another cup of tea for her friend and neighbor Lauren Olenteas.

"No, not even a message through my parents - and the longer Ric has to wait, the unhappier he becomes. I know that he is trying hard not to show me, but I know he's just waiting for a summons to go home. He won't just desert me, I know that, but he is forever hoping that the situation will change so he can go home with some honor intact."

Lauren grimaced. "I think that he's waiting for something that will never come. I've told him to go, but he won't. Maybe now that we are here and you are so close, he will." Lauren was an attractive woman in her early thirties, with long luxurious dark hair and penetrating, cold brown eyes. She seemed cool and aloof, removed from her surroundings. This caused casual acquaintances to think her haughty, arrogant, and uncaring; that is, until she smiled. On those rare occasions when she did smile, it had dazzling warmth that lit up her entire face, making her almost beautiful.

Lila Harrison smiled at her guest. "Perhaps you will be summoned. I always thought that this was a temporary situation."

Lauren laughed bitterly. "I hardly think so. I am about as popular as the Ebola virus or swine flu. Nope, there's no going home for me." Lauren looked around and deftly changed the conversation. "So tell me, where did you get the mini-blinds that color?" She noted her friends new forest green kitchen shades.

Before Lila could answer, a commotion spilled from the hallway into the kitchen. Lila rose to deal with the fuss, when her son, accompanied by her two daughters, burst into the room.

At once her younger daughter Lisa, a petulant thirteen-year-old, started crying, "Mom, make them take me with them. They are going to the mall and *he* won't let me come along." The girl stuck her tongue out at her older brother Mark. She was a small girl, with straight strawberry blond hair cut to her shoulders. Her blue eyes were red rimmed and furiously focused on Mark as if he were the cause of all the trouble in her life.

Mrs. Harrison tried to reason with her 20-year-old son, "Mark, why won't you take Lisa to the mall with you? Is it so much to ask that I be allowed to entertain a guest without having to do extra time as a U.N. Peacekeeping force?"

"Mom," Mark answered patiently. "She wants to go to the mall and annoy us. I'm only dropping Diana off there to meet Jim and then I am going to Scott's to play pool. No one is going to be around to play with the baby." Mark finished sarcastically.

Lisa grew red in the face and was about to retort furiously when Diana, the older girl of 18, interjected, "Don't worry Lisa, we'll go shopping tomorrow."

Lisa's face crumpled into tears and she ran from the room screaming, "That's what you say now! Nobody wants me around!"

Diana exchanged a long look with her mother. Reluctantly, Diana followed her sister from the room. Lila looked after her elder daughter in undisguised pride. Not only was Diana a beauty with her lovely chestnut hair and dark eyes, but she possessed a calm temperament and keen insight into people. At times she seemed so much older than her years. If only ... and Lila Harrison quickly stopped that line of thought. Instead she turned her attention to her son.

Mark Harrison was trying to appear untroubled by the scene that recently enacted before the new neighbor. He really wanted to get to know Lauren Olenteas, and was glad that his mother was renewing an old acquaintance. He was furious that Lauren had seen the latest childish and embarrassing drama and knew that he had come off badly.

It was all Lisa's fault. She needed control and discipline, but no one except he ever seemed to see that the indulgences the girl had received as a young child, due to severe health problems, had created a monster. As a soon-to-be college junior, Mark felt that his parents should have consulted him about their child-rearing techniques. Diana was fine. In fact, he was looking forward to having her join him at the university during his senior year. Lisa, on the other hand…ugh.

Mark leaned against the doorframe watching his mother and her friend. He was a tall, strapping young man, nearly six foot two inches tall. He towered over his sisters and used his height to his advantage. His dark hair and blue eyes were set in a healthy tanned face. He knew he was fairly good-looking, but that did not affect his relations with other people. He was warm, friendly and trusting, with an easy-going temperament and keen, intelligent wit... except with Lisa. With her, the charm and manners that had made him popular and secure vanished in one ill-spoken word.

"Now, Mark" said his mother in fond exasperation, "why didn't you just tell her these plans?"

"She never gave me a chance. As soon as I asked Diana if she was ready to go, Lisa started making demands! I just lost it."

"Honey, I want you to promise me that when we leave in a couple days, and you are in charge, you'll control the way you always "lose it" with Lisa. She's younger than you are and at an awkward stage. You're going to have to be able to control your temper, because she won't be able to control hers. Lisa acts on passion and doesn't always think through her actions. She needs guidance, not censure. Now promise me that you'll try to deal fairly with her." Lila Harrison pulled her tall son into a warm embrace.

Mark's muffled voice, reluctant and embarrassed, emerged from the area of her shoulder saying, "OK, I promise." Lila smiled and let him go, amused at the red-faced young man standing before her.

Lauren, who had remained silent throughout this strange interlude, added, "It's lucky that we moved in when we did. If you have any trouble, Ric and I are right next-door. We'd be more than happy to help out in any way."

"Thanks" Mark said, unenthusiastically. While he appreciated

Lauren's offer, he was leery of Ric, her whatever. Ric was a huge man, with ice blue eyes and the chiseled features of an ancient Viking. He was at least 6 inches taller than Mark and built on heroic lines. Even though he was an artist who sold his paintings and sculptures in the small shop Lauren owned in town, there was something very different about him, something that reminded one of a caged wild animal. Mark could imagine those large capable hands swinging a two handed ax rather than sculpting intricate and delicate artwork. Mark was nervous any time he was around the older man.

Lauren grinned wickedly, as if reading his thoughts, "Well, the offer stands. Lila, I know you have a ton of stuff to do. I hope you have a great time. You and Ron deserve it. I am certain Ron Jr. and the new wife will be thrilled to have you for an entire month - and in Europe no less! We'll have you over for dinner when you return to hear all about your trip."

With that, Lauren rose, gave Lila a warm embrace, and went home. Mark watched her cut through the backyard to her own. He was puzzled as to why instead of walking straight across the lawn, she made a half circle and avoided the middle of the grass. Before he could think of mentioning it, his mother asked him a question and he forgot about it.

* * *

Mark and Diana rode home in silence after dropping their parents off at the airport for their trip to Europe. Mark felt the enormity of his responsibility crashing in on him and making him feel glum. He was in charge of the house and the girls. Diana could take care of herself, but Lisa.... She was feeling so sulky and irritated that she didn't even go to the airport with them. She claimed she was sick and the parents believed her, as they always did. It was going to be a really long month.

He found himself hoping that Lauren Olenteas's offer to help was sincere. Lisa seemed to like her and especially Ric. Maybe, if he was lucky, he could palm her off on them for most of the month. Of his sisters, Mark had never really gotten on with Lisa. She had always been the favored pet of her parents and had little time for her older brother. And he had even less time for her. Mark realized that he had not spent any time alone with Lisa since she was a little girl sick in bed, and he had read stories to her.

"Lisa hates me," he announced to Diana about seven blocks from home, breaking the silence.

"No. She doesn't. She just doesn't know you as well as the rest of us." Diana tried unsuccessfully to reassure him. She had her own doubts about Lisa's response to Mark's authority. Although a bright and pleasant girl to her sister and her parents, whenever Lisa was near Mark for any extended period, she turned into a screaming little witch. It was no wonder Mark thought that she was an unreasonable brat. This month was going to be a living hell, Diana decided, and hoped that she could escape to her boyfriend's house most evenings.

"She hates me that is why she doesn't know me. It's why she wouldn't come to see Mom and Dad off. She's pretending to be sick just to avoid the moment when I was put in charge." Mark asserted. "You have to help me Di, or we're going to have a monstrous month!"

"Sure, Mark," Diana tried to soothe his anxiety. "Besides, she's preoccupied with the neighbors." Diana spoke in a low quiet voice, trying to calm him. A nervous Mark could only mean trouble when faced with a belligerent Lisa.

"Let's hope the Olenteas' keep their mystique throughout the month then." Mark said as they turned into the driveway. As they got out of the car, they could see Lisa emerging from the house next door and start for home. Mark waved and received a blank stare in return.

"See? She doesn't even acknowledge me." He murmured as he slammed the car door. By the time Diana had gotten out of her side of the car, Lauren had joined Lisa in the yard.

"Hello!" she called. "Did your parents leave without too much fuss?"

Mark grinned nervously. He liked Lauren quite a lot, but suddenly felt uncomfortable with her being so near, especially without the restraining influence of his parents. "Yep. They're winging their way to London as we speak! We're on our own now!" He grinned with the bravado of the nearly-twenty-one.

Lauren grinned back. "Good luck. We'll be here if you need us. I don't envy you your task."

Mark pulled his earlobe and shyly muttered, "Thanks."

Lisa, who was talking to Diana, looked at Lauren in puzzlement

11

but did not say anything.

"Actually, Ric and I were wondering if all of you could join us for dinner tonight. You've been busy seeing your parents off and you don't need the added burden of cooking, not on your first night."

"Hey thanks. We'd love to come!" Diana accepted eagerly. "I have the feeling that I'm going to have to do most of the cooking and I don't really want to have to start before I have to!"

"OK. How about seven, then?"

"Sounds great! See you then!" Diana put her arm around Lisa's shoulders and went inside. Lauren returned to her house, leaving a glum Mark standing on the drive outside. He sighed, straightened his shoulders, and went in, dreading the coming month.

At five minutes to seven, the three Harrisons met in their foyer. Diana and Lisa were dressed in good trousers and dress tops while Mark wore khaki pants and a good shirt. It was their first "formal" dinner party without their parents and they wanted to look as adult as possible. Silently they approved their sartorial choices and strolled next door.

Both Diana and Mark felt a sense of mild anticipation as they went to meet these friends as adults for the first time. They had not been inside this house since the Olenteas's had moved in and they wanted to see what they had done with the old place. The house had been empty for nearly all their lives and considered a haunted house by all the neighborhood children. Rumors of murder and satanic rituals whispered at sleepovers and strange lights and whirling leaves when there was no wind contributed to the spook factor. It was almost with a sense of disappointment when the house sold and the Olenteas' renovated.

Now it had a warm and inviting look to it and they were glad that they finally had neighbors who were fairly young and exciting. Lisa was excited at the prospect of staying up late and treated as a "grown-up."

Ric opened the door. As always, Mark felt a mild shock at the man's sheer size and overpowering physique. The tall blond man smiled and said in his deep baritone. "Greetings, young Harrisons. Enter freely always."

His words, spoken with a slight unidentifiable accent, and

the curiously formal half-bow that he gave them seemed highly ritualistic. Mark paused to allow his sisters to enter first, receiving a laugh and shocked look from Diana as a reward for his chivalry.

Lauren emerged from the kitchen, wiping her hands on a towel. She smiled gaily, "Hello. Dinner will be ready in a few minutes. Let Ric take you into the living room for a bit."

Diana and Mark barely heard her. They were staring at a painting hanging on the staircase wall in the center hallway. It was an unusual seascape: a green sky, gray-black waves crashing over yellowish rocks. Above them rose a cliff of white rock. At the summit was a huge black fortress. Strange birds were circling the sky. In the foreground at the edge of the cliff stood a huge gray horse rearing over a young woman seated on the ground seemingly oblivious to her danger. Fascinated by the power and the odd quality of the work, Diana and Mark never heard Ric return from the living room for them.

"Do you like it?" he asked quietly. "I only hung it today. I decided it was time to see it again - outside of my dreams."

Slightly startled, Diana blurted out, "Yes I like it. But I don't know why."

"It's a little disturbing. I painted this about five years ago, from a memory. Although I suppose things have changed since then."

"From a memory?" Diana asked. She had never seen birds like that or any indication of that kind of cliff. On the table below the picture, there were some unusually shaped and colored crystals arranged in an interesting pattern. She was about to pick one up when her attention was reclaimed by her host.

"Uh, I meant a memory from a dream." Ric added quickly, and changed the subject. "Would you like to see the rest of the house? I spent the day putting out some of our more interesting belongings.

"Now that all the renovations are done, we felt it was safe to do this. Lisa helped us while you were at the airport." The big man guided them to the living room and away from the painting and the crystals.

The living room was really more of a great room, dominated on the north wall by a huge fireplace. Over the mantle hung two swords; one was a large blade, the proper size for Ric while the other was smaller and better suited to Lauren, Diana thought.

Somehow she never considered these two as candidates for a medieval role-playing group, but then you never really knew your neighbors.

As Diana looked around the room she saw many other strange and unusual items. On a small table was a tubular vase filled with unrecognizable glass flowers. An odd needlepoint abstract design, a tiny ceramic animal with a cat's face and curved horns, and another set of multifaceted crystals were scattered throughout the room.

"Wow!" exclaimed Diana, "Where did you get all these things? They are so cool!"

"Thanks. I have a lot more, but these are the ones that are helping me establish my presence in this room," Ric said modestly. "Otherwise, Lauren's asceticism would dominate in plain walls and modern gadgetry."

His presence *was* felt, in the large comfortable furniture, the warm wall color and the artwork scattered throughout the room. Very little of Lauren seemed to be part of this great room. Before she could ask Ric why, Lauren came to the door and announced that dinner was ready.

Ric herded them into the large and elegantly appointed kitchen. Diana suspected hidden laughter lurking beneath the man's usually somber exterior. She had a sudden wild urge to make her host laugh aloud, right then and there. Only she couldn't think of a way to do it.

Dinner was an odd collection of everyone's favorite foods: pizza, salad, hummus, chicken, ribs, hamburgers, hot dogs, and fries. Mark was stunned. "But there're only five of us!" he blurted out when he saw the amount of food spread before them.

"You haven't seen Ric eat. And anyway, you all look hungry." Lauren grinned maliciously at the large man across the table from her. Ric scowled but said nothing. Within minutes after sitting down, they realized she was right. Everyone ate as if he or she hadn't eaten in a week.

For a while no one spoke, the awkwardness of strangers falling over each of them like a curtain, until finally Mark asked a question that had been plaguing him since they first met. "I don't mean to be rude, but where are you really from? I've never actually known."

Ric looked up from his food and grinned at Lauren as she replied. "We've lived around a lot, but most recently we are from England."

Mark replied, "I've always wanted to go there. I've been studying History at school. I've always felt that I should have been an Englishman from the early middle ages. I feel that I was born in the wrong time.

"Or the wrong place?" Lauren asked, intently staring at the young man.

"I don't understand what you mean."

"I do." exclaimed Lisa. "Like a fantasy book. You know, being from another place or dimension and trying to fit into our world."

"What are you talking about?" Mark snapped. "Lauren didn't mean that. She meant like being born in Twenty-first Century America instead of Ninth Century England. Right?"

"Sure, whatever." Lauren exchanged a look with Ric who shrugged and continued to eat.

Mark became uncomfortable and tried to return to the previous topic. "Anyway, England always has been my favorite topic. So what's it like?"

Lauren started to describe life in northern England and the area around York. "It's rather misty and gray, but when the sun does come out over the moors, it's magnificent. Somewhere Ric has a series of sketches of life on the moors."

"Remember when we went to that 12th Century church?" Ric asked with a laugh. "The one they were excavating? Where you got stuck?"

"Thanks for sharing that." Ric grimaced at Lauren. The Harrison watched them, not sure if they were joking or not.

"Well it's true! Ric was going into a small tunnel and got stuck. The archaeologists had to dig around him to get him out. He at least speeded up the operations!" Lauren laughed.

Ric grinned nastily at her. "What about you at the bottom of the Roman well?"

"What?" exclaimed three voices, eager for the story, and Lauren and Ric spent the remainder of the evening in story-telling all about their travels. The evening flew by and before they knew it the clock struck eleven and it was time to go home.

After the Harrisons returned home and Lisa stumbled up to bed, Mark turned to Diana and said, "Did you notice that in the entire conversation tonight, neither Lauren nor Ric said anything about their childhood or their relationships to other people? Isn't it strange?"

"In fact they never mention their childhood. Just like Mom." Diana mused, "and isn't it funny that they knew Mom many years ago and just happened to move into the haunted house next door?"

"It's odd. Very odd," Mark concluded as he headed up to bed. "I really wonder what their childhood was like."

"I wonder what Mom's was like," murmured Diana.

As the month progressed, the Harrisons fell into the habit of visiting their neighbors at least once a day. Diana and Lisa found myriad reasons to visit next door. Diana liked to watch Ric work on his unusual carvings or paintings while Lisa delighted in the variety of strange objects that Ric had scattered throughout the house. One day, Lauren opened a trunk of "fancy dress clothes" and the three spent an afternoon trying them on and laughing at their appearance. They even wore these clothes to dinner and startled the men with their beauty.

Mark enjoyed talking to Lauren while having tea at her kitchen table. He asked her advice about how to handle his new responsibilities and often followed it. As the days went by, however, he felt guilty that they were beginning to impose on their neighbors' good natures. Lauren tried to reassure him that Ric and she enjoyed their visits and not to worry about it, but he refused to listen to her.

Mark was honest enough to admit to himself, if to no one else, that his guilt was tainted with a slight jealousy about his own hard-won position as "head of the house". He realized that his zealous protection of his neighbors' privacy had personal motives as well. He irrationally blamed Lauren and Ric for his loss of control. But he steadfastly refused to acknowledge that it was Diana's company he missed, or that his chance to know Lisa was slipping away. He decided to control the number of visits to the neighbors. Two weeks after his parents left, Mark decided it was time to assert his authority.

While putting the dishes away from the dishwasher Lisa

announced to Diana, "I'm going next door. Lauren went out today and bought a new mystery game. Want to come?"

"Can't," said Diana, "I'm going out with Jim tonight. He should be here in a little while."

Mark, who was rinsing the dinner dishes, spoke up, "It's eight 'o clock. You have to stay home, Lisa."

Lisa looked at him and said in a tight, controlled little voice. "Why? I'm only going next door for an hour or so. Come on Di, just for a little. The game looked fun."

Before Diana could answer, Mark declared. "I said no. It's too late and too much of an imposition. Don't you think that Lauren and Ric have better things to do than play with a little girl all the time? You're wearing out your welcome. I'll play chess with you if you want."

"Who died and made you Attila the Hun?" Lisa was stung by his accusations and his insult to her age.

"Mom and Dad. That's who. I don't want you going out. It looks like rain and I think you ought to stay home."

"Diana's going out."

"Diana's 18 and not under my control. You're 13 and I'm responsible for you."

"It's not my age. You just don't like Ric and Lauren. You're jealous. Ric is Diana's new idol and I like Lauren. And they like me, which is more than you do." Lisa yelled, throwing a pot explosively into the sink. Water went everywhere.

"Clean that up." Mark said through clenched teeth. "And I don't want to hear another word about Ric and Lauren liking you or not. You're not going."

"*I AM, I AM, I AM*" Lisa screamed. "You can't stop me!" The girl was working herself into a hysterical frenzy.

"Christ, Mark," said Diana, "You sound like Dad on one of his bad days!"

"You stay out of this. You're no help. All you do is undermine me." Mark snarled at her.

Shocked, Diana said nothing but as the fight escalated, she quietly texted her boyfriend and canceled her date. She felt someone had to pick up the pieces once the battle was over. Frightened at the ferocity of the raging battle, she thought of calling Lauren to help diffuse the situation, but thought better of it.

Lisa was screeching now. "All my life, all you've ever done is ignore me. Now suddenly you're interested in what I do? Who the hell do you think you are?"

"I never ignored you. You hated me from the start. If I came near you, you cried. Even when you were sick and I read to you, you were thrilled when I was finished. You couldn't wait for Joe or Alexis or Ron Jr. to visit to ditch me! Well that's too damn bad, because I'm in charge now and you're going to hear me out!" Mark shouted more loudly than Lisa screeched.

The fight continued for what seemed like forever. After an hour or so Diana, unable to find a quiet place in the house, went out the front door and circled around to the backyard. It was one of those rare still nights in June. The stars were clearly visible and seemed endless in the night sky. All was quiet except for the screams between Mark and Lisa.

Diana sat on the back steps trying not to hear the fight, but it kept intruding on her consciousness. She said to herself, "It's been coming a long time. They have to get it out if we're going to survive the rest of this month." But as the voices inside escalated in volume, she realized it had been going on too long. They were starting to say some really unforgivable things. "I'd better get some help".

Resolutely, she crossed through the short hedges to the neighbor's yard and approached their back door. She knocked tentatively and Ric, dressed only in jeans, answered the door. The rippling muscles of his chest and stomach stunned Diana, who had never seen him without a shirt. She was unable to speak for a second. Finally, she stammered out, "Ric... Mark and Lisa are in a huge fight. I don't think it's going to stop on its own and I don't know how to get them to stop."

Without turning his head, Ric called out, "Lauren, I think our charges need help!"

Lauren appeared behind him. She was casually dressed in jeans and a t-shirt. Beside Ric, she looked almost frail, although Diana had seen her lift boxes weighing over a hundred pounds easily. "What's the problem?"

"It's Mark and Lisa. Can't you hear them?" Diana was stunned, as Lauren seemed oblivious to the chaos erupting next door.

"I thought they'd explode eventually." Lauren said. "They're

18

too much alike. It was inevitable."

"Oh, ya think ..." However, before Diana could angrily retort farther, a strong wind suddenly appeared from nowhere. It violently blew all around the house and slowly swirled into a small cyclone of flower petals and cut grass, creating a whirling curtain of red and green as a dark path formed in its center.

In a shocked voice Ric whispered, "Maelstrom."

Chapter 2

Lauren whirled and ran into the house. As soon as she had, Lisa burst from the back door of the Harrison's house with Mark close behind her. Wildly looking around, Lisa saw Diana and Ric on the porch next door. She sprinted across the lawn towards them, oblivious to the strange phenomenon revolving in her path. All she wanted to do was get away from Mark.

Mark, seeing her head directly for the whirling petals, felt a sudden chill and immediately forgot his anger. He ran down the stairs to grab her and pull her away. As he reached her, the wind whipped out misty tendrils and grabbed her. Mark was pulled in after her, and they found themselves trapped within a wall of swirling wind.

Ric was in motion before either of them could cry out. He reached them just as the wind began to fold inwardly, pulling them into oblivion along a dark path that had opened below their feet. Mark stretched his hand out of the twisting mass and Ric grabbed for it. With muscles straining against the force of the wind, Ric braced himself and tried to free the trapped pair by sheer brute strength. It was not enough though and the powerful man felt Mark's grip slipping rapidly.

Lauren, holding the two swords from the living room, raced past where Diana stood motionless, like a department store mannequin, her eyes wide, and mouth open.

"Alaeric!" Lauren cried and threw him his huge sword. Even in her shock, Diana was awed by the accuracy and length of the throw.

Glancing for the sword's location in the air, Ric caught the weapon one-handed. Holding it high above his head, he shouted something in a strange language. The swirling wind began to slow, but even as it did, Mark's hand began to slip away.

"Lauren! They are drifting. Blood me, anchor the place!" Alaeric shouted, desperately trying to maintain his hold on Mark. He gripped Mark's wrist with all of his power but the wind's strength was stronger.

Lauren grasped Ric's arm and cut it with the edge of her own sword chanting in the same language in which he had shouted. A streaming trail of his blood swirled in the vortex and wrapped itself around Mark's arm. Still straining mightily, Ric kept trying to pull Mark back from the path below his feet. He felt dragged into the maelstrom himself and shouted for Lauren to help him. She grabbed his waist and pulled. Ric's arm, now dripping blood profusely, entered further into the vortex before she could wrest him away. Diana heard a great cry of "No!" as Ric finally lost his hold on Mark and the small whirlwind closed in on itself, disappearing into a cold mist. Lisa's scream abruptly stopped and there was silence.

Lauren, pulling back on Ric, lost her balance and they fell together sprawling on the grass. The wind was gone; the petals were drifting slowly towards the ground. The moon was bright and it was once again a still June night, except for the sound of Ric's rasping breath.

In a shaky voice, Diana asked, "What happened? Where are they?"

Slowly, Lauren looked up not recognizing the girl for a moment. Then as realization of who Diana was dawned, she sighed. "This is going to take a while to explain. I have to get Ric bandaged. Come inside."

"I asked where Mark and Lisa went!" Diana demanded in a shrill hysterical voice.

"We will explain." Ric growled from the ground. "Now come inside before I bleed to death." He started to rise, cradling his wounded arm. Blood dripped in a scattered pattern on the ground.

Diana rushed him, screaming, "Where are they, damn it! What have you done to them?" She knocked Ric off balance and he fell

21

again, but not before her belt buckle caught the cut on his arm, ripping it further. He cried out in renewed agony.

Before Diana could inflict any more damage on the wounded and bleeding man, Lauren grappled her from behind and brought her to her knees. She held Diana in an iron grip and was unmoved by all her struggles. Unable to break Lauren's grip upon her, the girls' agitation eventually lessened. Diana began to cry quietly. Lauren, sensing no further struggle, left her and went to Ric, who was clutching his arm in silence as the blood flowed between clenched fingers.

"She will be all right?" he said, nodding at Diana.

"Fine. But we had better get inside and decide what to do. Diana," she turned to her, "come inside. We must talk."

Then without caring if the girl followed, Lauren turned to Ric and helped him to his feet. "Come on, cousin. I have to get you patched up. This place might prove very bad for those of our blood."

Swaying dizzily, Ric leaned on Lauren. They slowly made their way towards the house, with Diana following close behind. She only hoped that these strange and frightening people knew what happened to Mark and Lisa.

"Do you think that you could hurry with that? I am liable to bleed to death by the time you put a bandage on me." Ric complained as Lauren washed the cut on his arm.

"Don't be such a baby." Lauren sighed as she rubbed, "The infections of this world may kill you. I have to make certain to clean it properly. I do not need to lose you too."

Diana watched them warily, her hands gripping the arms of a chair. Each time she felt compelled to speak, a quick look at Ric's strained and pale face, and then the great sword leaning against the armchair dripping blood, silenced her.

Eventually Lauren looked up from her task. A crisp white bandage covered Ric's arm. "I hope this will control the bleeding," she said in a worried voice.

Sensing her deep concern, Ric said gently, "You did not have a choice. We needed an anchor. Otherwise how could we follow them?"

"Well, if you die, at least it will be for a good cause." Lauren remarked bitterly. "And how am I supposed to follow them if you

22

are dead?"

"Well I am not dead yet," Ric snapped. "And with any luck, I will get you there before I drop. How does that sound?"

"And how do —" but before Lauren could complete her sentence, Diana spoke up in a soft plaintive voice, "Please. What happened? Where are Mark and Lisa?"

Ric covered his face with his good arm. "They have been caught up in a trap meant for us, I suppose. We will do our best to get them back as soon as possible."

"That's not good enough!" shouted Diana. "What the hell is that supposed to mean ' a trap meant for us'... who the hell are you?"

Ric sighed. "No, I suppose that is not a good explanation. Only I do not know exactly how to go about this. We are very hard to explain, especially here. I guess the best way to explain what you saw is told in our legends." Rising slowly, he walked to the front hall and retrieved an octagonal crystal from the hallway table. Then he opened a drawer and pulled out a book-sized box that rather looked like a Kindle. He dropped the crystal into the box and handed it to Diana. "Listen to this. Uh... It will give you an operational framework so that you can understand, um. ..things. When you have heard it, we will try to explain what happened."

Suspiciously, Diana took the box from him and gripped it tightly. Ric touched her hair gently and looked at her with a great sadness in his eyes. "I am so sorry." Then he touched the top of the box "Begin."

A light alto voice began to speak as pictures formed on the surface of the box.

"Far beyond the limitations of space and time, in the folds of eternity, the Creator sat in the garden of his wife, Divine Wisdom..."

When Diana had heard the entire creation myth, she put down the box and looked at Ric and Lauren, her expression cold and distant.

Lauren met her stone gaze. "What you saw this evening was one of the Creator's paths. Someone was trying to lure Ric and me onto it. There was a deliberate manipulation of the energies of the paths and that means someone was looking for us in particular. Unfortunately, it snared Lisa and Mark instead. Somehow we are going to have to go after them and bring them back."

"Are you serious?" Diana was aghast. She stood up shaking in rage. "You're telling me fairy tales and my brother and sister are missing?"

"Your mythology is my reality." Lauren replied coldly.

In a serious, pain-filled voice, Ric said, "Sit down, girl. Lauren and I are not lying to you. Sometimes a myth explains notions that are difficult to comprehend. Your world has very few paths leading here, so you get few visitors from the coreworlds, and this edgeworld easily seals... That is why we were exiled here."

"Exiled?" Diana asked, confused. "Edgeworld? What the hell are you talking about?"

"It is a long and complex story. For now just understand that our King was obligated to send us into exile for a rebellion in which we had no part. This place is on the edge of the universal pathways. Only those very skilled in pathfinding can locate such a hidden place." Lauren's expression was grim as she looked over at Ric.

"Perhaps it was someone very skilled, someone like a master sorcerer?" Ric murmured.

Lauren looked at him in growing alarm. "A master sorcerer would be a dangerous opponent."

"What are you going to do about getting Mark and Lisa back?" Diana demanded. "I really don't care about all this mumbo-jumbo. All I want are my brother and sister returned safe and unharmed. Right now!"

"When Lauren slashed my arm, my blood dripped onto Mark. It is a rather primitive rite of associative magic but we were pressed for time. We will be able to follow my blood and in turn follow them onto the path."

"What if they're not there?" Diana half-believed them. She saw the maelstrom suck her brother and sister into oblivion and was almost ready to believe whatever she they said.

"Then we will search for them." Ric answered, looking at his bandaged arm. "Lauren, it appears that I am still bleeding. We had better go soon, before I am too weak to give you a focus point. Association is chancy at best. We will only be in the vicinity of their arrival as it is."

Lauren shook her head, "You need some rest. Otherwise you

will not make it at all."

Diana was staring at Ric's arm, horrified at the crimson bandage. Somehow this blood, more than the story or even the disappearance, made her believe what they were saying, even as she tried desperately to think of rational explanations for the evening's events.

"I am going with you," she announced.

Lauren and Ric exchanged a long silent look. Then Lauren turned to the determined young woman. "All right, I would not want you to stay here alone in any case. If they came here once looking for us, they might come again. If you got caught without any sort of anchor, you might wander the paths forever lost and we could never find you." Lauren paused. "My only concern is that I do not know how long this is going to take. I hope not too long, but it may take weeks."

"I'll leave a letter for my parents. They won't believe it. I hardly believe it myself. But at least I'll tell them what you have told me."

"You would be surprised what they would believe." Lauren muttered.

"What?"

Lauren put a comforting arm around her and shook her head. "Nothing. Anyway, we will leave tomorrow. We have to gather supplies, close the shop and I want Ric to get some rest. I suggest you stay here tonight."

Diana agreed and the two went into the kitchen. Lauren made some tea for everyone and served Ric, still seated in his chair in the great room. The big man seemed to be concentrating on his cut arm and did not join in the planning of the supplies. Once the list was made, Lauren showed Diana to a spare room.

Before Diana entered the room, she turned to Lauren, "I don't know why I believe you." Her voice made thick from unshed tears. "Maybe because I grew up reading fantasy and wanted to go to Narnia and marry King Peter. Maybe because of what I saw tonight or just maybe because I trust you. I hope you're right. I hope that we can find them soon and come home and forget this ever happened." She paused, tears welling up now, "I think that I have to trust you. Only I don't know why."

Diana entered the bedroom and closed the door.

Lauren, her own eyes glistening, said softly to the closed door, "Oh my dear, if you only knew."

The sun was low in the afternoon sky by the time Lauren decided that they were ready to follow the path. Ric had rested all day and although very pale and easily tired, he was finally ready to make the transition. Lauren had kept Diana busy all day buying food, camping equipment, and packing their belongings, keeping Diana from dwelling morbidly on the unknown fate of Mark and Lisa.

Ric dragged himself about making his own preparations. Lauren kept a watchful eye on his arm throughout the day. Although the blood had slowed to a trickle, Lauren feared that the accumulated loss of blood and the chance of infection would lessen Ric's chance of withstanding the stress of pathwalking. Inwardly she cursed herself for not being empowered with a stronger skill, like healing or translocation. Her only alternative was to keep Ric from exerting himself too much before departure. Between Diana's anxiety and her own worry over Ric's weakness, Lauren found her own state of mind beginning to fray by the departure time.

Near sundown, almost the same time that Mark and Lisa were sucked into the maelstrom the day before, Diana emerged from her house and met Lauren in the backyard.

Lauren was pleased to see that the younger woman was dressed in a tank top, with a long sleeved shirt over it tucked into sturdy jeans. She was carrying a jacket, a backpack, and a flashlight. "Almost ready? Are you frightened?

Diana nodded. "A bit. I'm not terribly imaginative sometimes. I used to regret it, but now I think I like the idea. This way I can't imagine what's going to happen." She chuckled softly, but then somberly asked, "Do you think that they're all right?"

"I really do and Alaeric thinks so as well."

"Alaeric?"

"That is Ric's full first name. It does not sound all that edge-like so he shortened it. So did I actually. My full first name is Laurenthalia. But since I was a little girl, I was always called Lauren. If anyone called me by my full name, I usually found a reason to give them a black eye." Lauren grinned briefly.

"How are you guys related? We thought you were married

when you first moved here, but you don't share a room. Are you siblings?"

"Cousins, actually. At first we pretended to be married, but that never worked since Alaeric is already married, so we reverted to making people guess if we were siblings or lovers or whatever. That has been one of the few pleasures we have had in the past five years."

"Oh." Diana paused, taking this in, then asked. "Please tell me why you've been exiled here." She was intensely curious. Part of her wanted to know if she was going off into space with homicidal maniacs or not.

"Well, as we told you, for some reason, there are fewer natural paths leading to this edgeworld."

"What is an edgeworld?"

"It's a technical term used to describe the worlds on the fringes of the universes, mostly devoid of operational sorcery and not subject to the same laws and philosophies as are the coreworlds or even the otherworlds."

"Otherworlds?"

"Places we cannot reach, that have no known paths to them, but that we suspect exist. We think that these are where the Creator has placed his other life forms and...." she shook her head. "Look, we do not have a lot of time for me to go into detail. I promise someday that I will explain fully or at least get a qualified sorcerer to do it, okay?"

"Okay. So why were you exiled?" Diana persisted, returning to her original question.

Lauren sighed, "Because our fathers betrayed the King. They effectively ruined our lives."

Engrossed in their conversation, Diana and Lauren never hear Alaeric arrive until he said, in his deep soft baritone. "Are we ready?"

Both women jumped. "Do not do that!" Lauren exclaimed. "You could take years off a person's life! Yes, we are ready."

Alaeric bent to the collected luggage, found his sword, picked it up, and unsheathed it. "Do your tricks, Oh Princess of the Mountains."

"Stop that! Do not call me that," Lauren snapped. "I am nervous enough. It has been five years since I have done anything like this." She drew her sword and pointed the tip towards the ground.

As Diana listened to the cousins talking, she began realizing something else was odd. Their accents were more pronounced than before, and their English more formal. Before she could enquire further, Alaeric interrupted her thoughts.

"Diana, please come here. Pick up a couple of the packs. Then make certain that all the rest are touching each other and then touching you. Once you have done that, grab my belt and hold on. When Lauren is ready, she and I will touch swords and we will begin moving onto the path."

"What about the wind?" Diana asked nervously, remembering the cyclone from the night before. "There will be only a slight breeze. Last night was an aberration, a deliberate spell. Lauren possesses a skill we call 'pathfinding'. She has the ability to open ways that are marked, as we did with my blood, and follow them. She can also take people and things with her. The other advantage is that once she has been to a place, she can always find the path back."

"You mean, like here? She can always get back here?"

"Sure," Alaeric motioned for Diana to come near him. Quickly the girl shouldered two packs and put the others between her legs and Alaeric's. She then grabbed onto Alaeric's belt and anxiously awaited the transition. Once Lauren saw that her companions were set, she began her focus.

Unlike the wild winds of the night before, only a gentle breeze swirled about them as Lauren spoke a short chant, more like a poem. In a fluid movement she held up her sword. In her other hand she held a small undulating beam of silver light that came from a small green crystal ring on her hand. Alaeric brought up his great sword to clang against hers. Lauren tossed the light into the center of the breeze, and shouted one word.

Twenty-first century earth vanished; the houses, the trees, even the comfortable sun were gone and only a gaping dark path lay before them. Lauren took a step forward and the others glided along behind her. She followed a small trail of crimson as other paths forked away from the one on which they traveled. Distant stars and nebulae swirled around them.

Diana found herself gripping Alaeric's belt with both hands

28

and screaming as they vanished into the void. Then it was over and the three were standing on a carpet of high grass. Day instantly had turned to gloaming.

Alaeric and Lauren immediately unlocked their swords. Both were wearing black harnesses and they sheathed their weapons at once.

"How is your arm?"

"Lauren, it got us here." Alaeric winced, "The bleeding is stopping." He looked around them. "So, any idea where we are?"

"It seems familiar, but I am not sure. I do not think I have ever been here before, but if nothing else, it does have the feel of a core world. I sense many paths. But somehow this place seems... empty." Lauren's voice trailed off in confusion.

"Empty?"

"Uninhabited then," Lauren looked around her, feeling a sense of disquiet she found hard to put into words. "It is late. We should set up here and you should get some rest. I will check out the place a bit."

"What about—"Diana started, still shaky from the odd journey.

Lauren smiled reassuringly, "And if we do not find Mark and Lisa at once, we will begin to search in earnest once Alaeric has rested. They should not be too far."

Reluctantly Diana agreed to this plan. She helped Lauren set up the tent and camp stove, and got out a sleeping bag for Alaeric to rest on. The big man was frighteningly pale and Diana could see why Lauren wanted him to rest before they began to walk around.

Lauren spent most of the rest of the strange day scouting the perimeter and calling out for the missing pair, but was not able to locate them. She returned as the sun and fully set and it was preternaturally dark.

"They have probably gone to look for help," she told Diana. "We will look for them in the morning."

Diana, staring at the alien night sky, agreed. There was no point in trying to search now. Lauren made a quick dinner, changed Alaeric's bandages, and tried to comfort Diana as best she could. She was exhausted, but knew neither the worried young woman nor the wounded man was able to keep watch. She found a rock and sat on it before the dying camp stove's fire.

As Diana fell asleep under a strange purple sky, she saw Lauren silhouetted against the night, keeping watch. Somehow, she felt strangely comforted.

Diana awoke with a start. Disoriented, she felt frightened and confused when she saw the huge silver green trees and the dark purple grass instead of her backyard. She scrambled out of her sleeping bag, trying to decide what to do. As she turned she saw Lauren seated crossed-legged on the grass, a naked blade by her side, gently stroking Alaeric's hair as he lay asleep, his head pillowed on her thigh. Lauren looked up at Diana and calmly put a finger to her lips for quiet.

"Good morning, Diana. I hope you feel rested." Lauren said softly, "I am really sorry, but we will be experiencing a slight delay before we can start our search. Alaeric's wound ripped open and he started bleeding very badly in the night. I have only now gotten it under control but he needs to rest for a bit. He insisted that he could do the second watch and I believed him." She grimaced, "I was not thinking clearly."

"What about Mark and Lisa?" Diana demanded angrily. "It's been two days since they disappeared. They could be anywhere!"

"Without Alaeric's blood, we would not even be in the same universe with them." She replied coolly, "I suggest we try to keep him alive."

"You mean he could die?" Diana asked in a horrified whisper, realizing suddenly how pale and still the big man appeared.

"Not if I can help it," said Lauren. "He lost a lot of blood, and the infections of your world are really dangerous for him." A derisive snort escaped her, "He also insists that as the hereditary war leader of the Olenteas, he can go on forever. I managed to pull rank on him and forced him to rest."

Diana looked at Alaeric's still face. She didn't really understand what Lauren was talking about, but she could see that her friend was worried. Alaeric seemed unconscious rather than sleeping.

As if sensing that Diana's confusion was growing, and understanding how she must feel suddenly thrust into a strange new world, Lauren asked, "So, do you have any more questions about us and what has happened?"

Diana made herself comfortable in the grass next to them, "What happened? Why were you exiled?"

"It is a long story. I only gave you the merest sketch of it yesterday."

"I want to understand, but all you do is talk in cryptic half-sentences and assume that I know more than I do. Please just tell me what is happening, who you are, where we are. You know everything."

Lauren sighed. "Alright, I will give you a slight history of events and maybe that will help. A little exposition will pass the time while he rests anyway."

"As I told you last night, we are cousins." Lauren began, still stroking Alaeric's hair tenderly, "Alaeric's father and mine are brothers. We are also the eldest born children of the Olenteas Clans of Dal Ryeas, our world.

"For many years Clan Tadiak ruled the kingdom. In the early days of the kingdom of Dal Ryeas, Queen Rikara bore nine children: Tadiak, Pyramus, Olenteas, Cynthea, Leantas, Sylva, Tersa, Bilateas, and Bogeas. From the families of these nine children sprang the great clans that settled the different parts of Dal Ryeas. Each clan was named for its founding parent and all of us to this day take the clan name to identify us to others, no matter what our individual family names are.

"Anyway, Queen Rikara encouraged loyalty and affection for her land in each one of her children. Being a wise mother, as well as a Queen, she gave her sons and daughters vast lands to rule under the over-lordship of the crown. She found them worthy mates and assisted them to recruit loyal followers to help them develop their lands. For her eldest child, her daughter Tadiak, she kept the crown lands and the lands around the City of Tadia. Pyramus, her second child and oldest son, got the sea coast lands while her son Olenteas was given the Forest Mountains that overlooked the sea. The other six children each received lands in the interior of the country.

"For years the crown kept a loose reign over the clans. Every King or Queen knew the power of the clans and called on them only in times of dire need. And then the clans rose and defeated all opponents to the Kingdom of Dal Ryeas." Lauren looked towards the woods surrounding them and in her imagination saw the mustering of the ancient clans.

"Fierce in their loyalties," Lauren continued, as if she were reciting a well-known epic. This reminded Diana of the ancient Greek poetry and she wondered if Homer sounded anything like this. "They repelled all invaders. Great deeds and much glory covered their names. For five hundred years all the clans thrived until a plague came and wiped out the desert clans of Bilateas and Bogeas. Only a scattered few clans' folk survived and they were given refuge within the other clans. Soar of Bilateas wed Rorick Pyramus and Maron Bogeas became husband to Lucia Olenteas. And the original nine became seven while Pyramus and Olenteas increased in lands and power.

"A hundred years later, Clan Tadiak began to falter. For countless years, against the advice of their doctors, councilors and enchanters, Clan Tadiak chose their mates only from within its dwindling kinship. Intermarriage brought strange genetic disorders and the Crown of Dal Ryeas was under the control of weaker and weaker rulers. Tadiak was letting go the reins of power and chaos was becoming the norm throughout the land. The last Tadiak King, Philos, was insane by the age of twenty-five. He was the culmination of Tadiak's perverse breeding program and had inherited its congenital madness. In your world he'd be diagnosed as bi-polar and psychopathic. In ours, he was watched warily, but nothing was actually done. He was crazy, but not stupid.

"In a cunning power-play, the King invited each of the clan lords to send him children to foster at court. The clans, answering an age-old custom, and never dreaming he would use these children for ill, complied and sent their sons and daughters to court. Philos then attempted to consolidate his power and essentially become an autocrat instead of an overlord. He used the children as hostages for their parents and subsequently their clans' good behavior. When he suspected a problem with a clan, or if someone disagreed with his new policies, Philos would punish the hostage child.

"At one point he suspected Clan Pyramus of plotting sedition and decided to take action to stem any thoughts of revolution. He killed Leas Pyramus' daughter in a gruesome public ceremony that was supposed to squelch any thoughts of revolt. Instead, Leas Pyramus went ballistic.

"Clan Pyramus, lead by Leas, exploded in violent rage and the Tadiak lands ran with blood. Other clans sided with Pyramus, for they too had lost children. Leas Pyramus led Cynthea, Olenteas, Sylva, and Tersa to victory. When the bloodshed was over, the throne stood empty. King Philos fled his kingdom, taking with him his young daughter Killia and his enchanter Sindelar with him. In his haste, however, Philos forgot the one great weapon in his arsenal, the one thing that could have restored him to his power - the Tal. The stone that wisdom assigned to each world to protect it and that focuses the power of the world in the hands of the ruler. I am certain that Sindelar was livid when he found out that Philos had left it behind." Lauren chuckled a bit.

"After the defeat of Philos and clan Tadiak, the clans elected Leas Pyramus as the new King. He ruled fairly and well for fifteen years and then abdicated the crown to his son Tyrmandos. For the next seventeen years Tyrmandos maintained the peace and brought prosperity and calm to the kingdom. A hunting accident ended his life at the age of sixty and brought his son Tarq to power." Lauren closed her eyes. Diana suspected her of hiding tears.

"What happened to the exiled King?" Diana asked, trying to change the focus of the story.

"Sindelar kept Philos and Killia hidden. He is a formidable sorcerer and understands the magic, path making, and the coreworlds as few others do. So, even though Leas and Tyrmandos tried to find the renegade Tadiaks with the full power of the Tal, Sindelar was able to hide Philos, his child, and his loyal followers from detection.

"If you think about it, it was an incredible use of power and energy. The exiles were able to travel the paths undetected and well camouflaged. They were safe from the vengeance of the new King and especially the clans, solely guarded by the powers of Sindelar. Travel along the paths is an uneasy business, as you saw, unless you hold a Tal and let it guide you or you have an exceptional sorcerer to assist you. Or you can do as we did and mark the path with blood, but that can be messy." Lauren shook her head.

"During the reign of Tyrmandos, after there was some distance between the rage that overtook the clans under Leas and the calm of the new reign, Sindelar got in secret contact with the clan lords of the Olenteas. The Olenteas lords were harboring grudges against the new rulers, thinking that the new kings, in spite of their assistance, had slighted them after the revolution. They sent Sindelar a bride for Philos to marry and to help him raise Killia. Once Philos went completely mad and had to be restrained, Sindelar and the Olenteas stepmother turned their attentions to grooming and training Killia. The Princess became the focal point of hope for Tadiak's restoration.

"Her stepmother lobbied for Killia to marry Prince Tarq, Tyrmandos' oldest child and heir, thereby becoming Queen and widening Tadiak's gene pool. Negotiations commenced when the children were about six or seven years old. I do not think that the King was serious about saddling his son with a wife with her genetic predisposition to madness, but as long as they kept up the charade that the two would marry, no active revolution would take place. It was a good ploy but about ten years ago, King Philos and his wife were found in what appeared to be a murder-suicide."

Diana shivered a bit, that last hitting her like a sudden bucket of ice-cold water.

"Sindelar petitioned King Tyrmandos to allow the former King and his wife to be brought to Dal Ryeas for burial. Because there were still so many followers of the fallen tyrant, the King allowed Killia to bring her family home. I think that the King reasoned that the murder-suicide by Philos would convince the people that they were better off with Pyramus' sane calm rule rather than mad Tadiaks.

"Instead, all they saw was a beautiful brave young woman bearing the grief of her father's madness and deeds stalwartly. They saw her as alone, frightened at coming to the planet she thought she should rule. In that one clever public relations ploy, Sindelar was able to make the people forget the reigns of terror under Tadiak and the justice of Pyramus, by creating a living martyr. The Olenteas lords fell right into his trap and joined him to assist Killia's bid for power.

"Olenteas always has two lords who must be in accord for

major policy changes. Usually it takes forever to get them to agree to anything, but this time they fell all over themselves in coming up with plans to lull Pyramus into a false sense of security, while they were secretly plotting the return of Tadiak. They had already sent Prince Ertlan's son, Alaeric, and Prince Kir'san's daughter, Laurenthalia, as pledges of their faith to King Tyrmandos for fostering to further their bid for power, so it was not much of a stretch for them to plan to use these two in their nefarious plans for domination. They figured that they could rule Tadiaks once Killia regained the throne."

Diana looked at Lauren in surprise. The older woman smiled sadly and continued her story.

"We were about ten or so when we arrived at the capital city, Tadia. King Tyrmandos took us in with open arms and showered us with love and attention. He sent us to school and to play with his own children, Prince Tarq and Princess Tayaela. Tarq and Alaeric were inseparable and Tayaela became my best friend.

"When Tyrmandos died, we mourned him more than we would have our own fathers. We had pledged everything to Pyramus never realizing that our families were secretly in Killia's camp. What is so insidious was that under the guise of friendship and loyalty, in the persons of their own children, the Olenteas lords were plotting with Sindelar. They arranged our marriages to Tyrmandos' children without blinking an eye.

"I mean, we always knew that this was what the fostering arrangement was for, so when Tyrmandos announced our double engagement, no one was surprised. To be honest, Alaeric and I did not really trust our father's motives. Every time we went back to the mountains to visit, conversations dried up and furtive looks cast in our direction. We knew something was up, but no one was talking. And we were always happy to go back to Tadia.

"Anyway, Alaeric and Tayaela were married almost as soon as the engagements were announced. For Tarq and me, it was almost a year before we were able to hold the wedding, what with all the fuss and circumstance that accompanies the marriage of the heir to the throne. I really hated that and envied Alaeric and Tayaela's simple ceremony and wonderful reception for friends and family, but I had no say in the matter, except to delay the day when I lost all privacy and become Tarq's queen.

"We finally settled on a date and Clan Olenteas and Clan Pyramus poured into the city from their own seats. Tadia filled, overflowing with my father's and Uncle Ertlan's followers. And all of them were itching for a fight, feeling very up on their muscle and belligerent. More like a brawl than pre-wedding celebrations, actually. One week before the wedding, the King's First Minister, the enchantress Carr, discovered our parents' plans to use the wedding as a cover for a counter-revolution to restore Tadiak to power. She brought indisputable evidence given to her at great risk by her own half-sister of the plot. As I understand it, she also told the King that she suspected that I was involved as well, since I so conveniently kept putting off the wedding." Lauren's mouth was set in as grim straight line. She seemed to be biting the inside of her cheeks.

"On the morning of the wedding, the pre-planned violence erupted, but the King's troops were ready for the revolutionists and suppressed the coup almost at once, with minimal bloodshed. The guardsmen captured all of the conspirators, except for Sindelar and Killia, who were invited to the wedding in a graceful gesture of peace. Sindelar vanished, taking his princess with him. But he left my father and uncle behind to face the King's wrath.

"King Tarq released the common soldiers with an admonition not to meddle in royal politics again and sent them home. The Tal stripped those enchanters who participated in the rebellion of their magic powers. Then they were assigned to do useful work among the needy of Tadia's neighborhoods under the supervision of the High Priestess of the Twins. My father and uncle, along with their more devoted co-conspirators, were sentenced to an indefinite period of imprisonment in the Crimson Tower in the Wastelands until and if the King ever decides to release them.

"Then it was my turn. Try as we might, even swearing on the Tal and by the gods, Alaeric and I were unable to convince the King's ministers that I was innocent. They kept telling me that by my silence, if not my active participation, I had betrayed the King and the Kingdom. I guess every time I thought that my father was unhappy with the King, I was supposed to tell on him. I had no evidence but vague suspicions, and for that I was supposed to report on my father and uncle.

'Since Alaeric was already married to Tayaela, he was above

suspicion. He had fought for the King, while I was getting dressed for my alleged wedding and they held that against me as well. They always neglected the fact that I delayed the wedding as incontrovertible proof of my allegiance to the conspiracy and not merely cold feet.

"Carr felt that my continued presence in Tadia and even on Dal Ryeas would only invite more trouble. She convinced the other ministers that I was dangerous and they in turn pressured the King to send me away. Carr thought that even if I were an innocent victim, I would harbor grudges and become a new focal point for revolution. She considered Killia enough of a focal point in her estimation. Even though Princess Tayaela begged for clemency and the King was obviously reluctant to carry out the sentence of the ministers, Carr was able to prevail. She wanted to have me exiled and that was what she was going to get.

"Her evidence was compelling, if absolutely false, and I was to appear before the court for sentencing. There was nothing the King could do. Considering the precarious state of the nation, King Tarq could only comply with his councilors, who represented all the clans. He had to put the best interests of the Kingdom above his own desires."

For a long time Lauren was silent. Diana, unable to meet her eyes, looked down at Alaeric's recumbent form. She realized that he was awake and listening to Lauren's story. She wondered how long he had been listening.

Lauren continued, not realizing he was awake. "I remember it as if it were yesterday and not five years ago. I was brought to the throne room on a bitter winter day. The snow outside the windows created bizarre shadows from the shape of the pennons reflecting on the floor. All the court assembled to hear the King's decree. Tayaela and Tarq were not in the room yet when I was brought in, but Carr was. She was standing next to the throne and appeared to the entire world as calm and collected.

"I noticed that her hands were clutching at her skirt in nervous anticipation. Alaeric was standing on the other side of the throne next to Tayaela's chair, confident that I would be freed from blame and suspicion. I found myself looking at his rock-steady face for reassurance.

"I can still hear the herald striking the floor three times with his staff. The whispering and betting became hushed as the King and Tayaela entered from a small door behind the throne. Usually a tapestry of Queen Rikara creating the clans hides this door. I still dream of them standing there. They were dressed in black, except for the silver circlet binding back the king's hair. Tarq seated his sister on a chair next to the throne. She resolutely was refusing to look at Alaeric.

"Then the King turned and looked at me. I could tell he had been weeping. Without prompting and with a clattering of the chains that echoed, I fell to my knees before him to receive my sentence.

"Angrily, Tarq motioned for me to rise and be unchained. 'She is as much a victim of this vile plot as I am. Unchain her at once,' he demanded. The guard quickly removed the chains, and I stood before him free of the physical bindings that had separated us. For a moment, I thought he was going to go against the clans and ignore their decision, but the King, if nothing else, was the representative of law and if he broke it for his own personal gain, he would be no better than the tyrants who were trying to overthrow him.

"I can close my eyes and still see that scene. Tarq was trying to save my feelings by appearing cool and remote, but I could feel his heart breaking nonetheless. I knew what he had to do, but I knew that it would be agonizing for him to do it. I see him standing there, unrelenting in the white winter light; tall and rigidly correct, as if any slight relaxation would cause his collapse.

"Sometimes in my dreams I see his blue eyes scanning the room, seeking an ally and the only one he can find is me. I felt the tension in him; I saw the muscles straining the coat. I mourned his face, once open and boyish, now closed and grim. I want to cry at the change that in him, but I know it would do no good. They would think I cried for myself and I would not let them see me weep. That's Killia's trick, not mine. So I drew my overweening Olenteas pride around me like a cloak and listened with dread to the voice I loved most in the world announce my sentence.

'Know now that my minister, Carr, will read the decree of exile for Princess Laurenthalia of Clan Olenteas. The decree is, as is the custom of the land, a proclamation by the Council of Clans and carried out by the power of the Tal. The wishes of the King have no moment in this decision.' He motioned for Carr to read:

My loyal subjects of Dal Ryeas hear then the decree of the Council of Clans regarding the fate of Laurenthalia, Princess of the Clan Olenteas. Know that by the sedition of her father, Laurenthalia, henceforth shall walk in exile among the edgeworlds and be hereby exiled from the realm of Dal Ryeas until the King with the advice of his council rescinds this decree. Further let it be known that in protest of this decision, that Alaeric, husband to Princess Tayaela, Prince of the Clan Olenteas and war leader of the crown — has chosen to accompany Princess Laurenthalia into exile for five years or until the princess is recalled to Dal Ryeas. He does this for his honor and his own share in the collective guilt of the Olenteas for its actions against the Throne, albeit he has never been involved in the revolt and protests the innocence of his cousin Princess Laurenthalia.'

"I looked at Alaeric who nodded and Tayaela who smiled through her tears. I knew what a sacrifice they were making. I almost lost control at that moment. However, Alaeric came to stand by my side and supported me through the rest of the ordeal. Carr looked livid as she finished the decree. Tarq, while still looking grim, glanced at Carr in triumph. He had found a way to thwart her plan to humiliate me by sending me off alone into exile as an example to others.

"I am sorry to say, that my reaction was to think that I would not be alone, a stranger in a strange world. Alaeric and I were cousins. Although we had grown up together, we were not as close as we could have been. When we arrived at court, he was swept up into Tarq's sphere, and I was close to Tayaela. Then was when he fell in love with Tayaela and I fell in love with Tarq, we were again busy with our own separate concerns. But my heart burst with love for them at that moment for their sacrifice. I knew then that I could never repay them for all the time that they would lose, if they were ever reunited.

"Even though I was in my own personal hell, I realized that Tarq was watching me. For a long silent moment, our eyes met and held. I guess we were trying to memorize each other since who knew when and if I could ever return. I suppose he is married now and has children, but for that moment we were alone in a room filled with strangers trying to imprint our love on each other for all time.

"It finally became too painful for us to continue looking at each other, so he turned away and broke the spell. The guards escorted Tayaela to Alaeric's side and we all went behind the throne to the small room to say our goodbyes. Tarq led me to an alcove until all was ready. He did not speak since Carr, who was reluctant to allow the King a moment alone with me, accompanied us with a guard. There was nothing he could say. Alaeric and Tayaela embraced passionately and we all pretended not to watch. As they emerged I heard her say. 'I'll keep working to get this rescinded. Then I'll come find you.' He kissed her again with a longing that made everyone cringe at the thought of their separation. My guilt over this nearly knocked me to my knees again, but only my pride kept me standing.

"Then Tarq claimed my attention. He ignored all the others and took my hand. Carr looked angry but said nothing. He kissed my hand and then drew me into a strong embrace. He had the guard hand me a package. 'These are some crystals and a reader. They will help you in your resettlement. Use them sparingly, since you will not be able to get new ones if they break. They are story ones and some letters from me and ...' His voice trailed off. He kissed me again and whispered, 'I love you, and as soon as I can, I'll bring you home.'

"I took the book and crystals, but found myself unable to reply. Although the intellectual part of me knew that what was happening was according to law, the emotional part of me hated the situation and Tarq for letting it happen.

"I stood mute. I wanted to answer, but I was frightened and resentful. So I let him go without a word. Carr stepped forward, bade us farewell and invoked the blessings of the Creator and our local gods Saevirg and Sarama. Then she opened the predetermined path, but with so many random twists and turns upon it; no one could follow it without the Tal or the rebels, and sent us along it, until we landed on Earth. Since earth is such a backwards place, we did not have too many options. But I guess that is Carr's revenge. Since she was against Alaeric's voluntary exile, she chose a place where we would have to start from scratch.

"Our skills were limited on your world, but since there were other exiles from Dal Ryeas there, we were assisted in learning the ways of the world. Carr also did not know about my pathfinding ability, so she is unaware that I could always send Alaeric home, even if no one else could find us. She also did not know that my father, even from his prison, was able to get word to me of where the other exiles were on earth who came here from the time when Leas took the throne from Philos.

"We found them and they helped us to adjust. We were fairly content on Earth although Alaeric here," she looked down at her cousin who was smiling faintly at her and ruffled his hair, "was ready to go home to Tayaela the minute his five years were up."

"What makes you think I would leave you alone in exile?" Alaeric frowned.

"Tayaela." Lauren smiled at him. "Besides I am able to function on my own now. Just keep sending me the artwork for the shop."

"Oh, do not be such a hard-ass. I have heard you crying for Tarq in the middle of the night." Alaeric struggled to sit up.

"My feelings for Tarq were my business," Lauren snapped. "It does not change my exile. You are free to return whenever you want. Now drop the subject."

"Alright, alright," Alaeric smiled and tried to stretch. Clearly his arm was feeling better. "Besides, even though I try to understand his actions, I still have a hard time accepting why he did it. Sometimes I can almost comprehend them."

"Do you really? Then explain them to me," a voice said from behind them.

41

Chapter 3

Diana watched, amazed, as Alaeric was galvanized into action. One moment he was sitting, leaning weakly against his cousin's arm, the next moment he was standing, a naked sword in his hand, facing the strangers who had emerged from the woods behind them.

Lauren was only an instant behind him, rising up, turning, and grabbing her sword. Then as she realized whom the stranger was who had spoken, she dropped the sword and slowly sank to her knees, her head bowed.

"M…my King," she gasped, old habits dying hard. Alaeric followed but held his sword upright between his hands.

"Get up." Tarq said.

They rose but Lauren continued to stare at him in shock. "What are you doing here?

"You're on Dal Ryeas," the King answered.

"Dal Ryeas? What are we doing here?" asked Alaeric, "Where on Dal Ryeas are we? I do not recognize this place."

"The empty lands beyond the Pyram Sea," replied the enchantress Carr, from behind the King. She was much the same as when Alaeric had last seen her. Tall and slender with chocolate brown skin, large luminous brown eyes and short curly brown hair highlighted with red glints. She appeared to be about thirty years old, which was many years less than her actual age. Her attention focused on the blood-stained bandage covering Alaeric's arm and so never saw his frown as she approached him.

"Prince Alaeric, I see you are hurt. May I help?" She stared at the cut beneath the bandages.

"No need, Lady Carr," Alaeric replied coolly, as he looked beyond her to the meadow and the woods "Lauren and Diana have been excellent doctors."

"I am certain they are," Carr replied, "but if you'll pardon my saying so, you look like you're going to fall over. So, at least sit down." She gently pushed him and he fell, sitting down heavily in the grass. The King was trying very hard not to look at Lauren by keeping his attention on Alaeric.

"That's better," Carr cleared her throat and addressed the King. "Your Majesty ... there are things we must discuss concerning this new situation."

"Yes," growled Alaeric, "like why you brought us here and the whereabouts of our companions. Where is my wife?"

Why did you decide to come?" Carr pointed at Lauren. "Why did she break her exile?"

"Look, Carr," Alaeric snapped, "it takes a first-rate talent to create an opening the size that swept our friends onto the path we saw. So what did you do with the pair you inadvertently grabbed? Is this a deliberate attempt to get Lauren into—?"

"Sire," Lauren interrupted him, "What are you doing here?"

"I was brought here by fluctuations I saw in the Tal. You were brought here by force?"

"No, we followed the brother and sister of our companion here. May I present to you Diana Harrison. Diana, this is King Tarq of the Kingdom of Dal Ryeas and Lady Carr, First Minister of the Crown." Lauren hid her surging emotions behind the veil of formality.

Before Diana could reply, Alaeric demanded again, "Where's Tayaela?"

"She left two years after you." Tarq replied. "She left a letter stating that she was going to try and find you among the paths. She felt that she betrayed you by not going with you and that she needed to find you and get your forgiveness."

"For what? I never blamed her for your stupidity." Alaric snarled at his best friend and King.

Tarq replied, unruffled. "I know, but she blamed herself for not trying harder to stop me or for not getting more clans ministers on your side. I've searched for her but you know that when someone with skill wants to hide in the paths, or on the cores or edges, a person can. She even hid herself from the Tal." His voice became softer as he caught Alaeric's look. "Don't worry, we'll find her. Come on, let's go to our camp, and try to decide what to do about everything."

As they walked, Alaeric explained what had happened the night before. Tarq proved a good listener as he gave Alaeric his strong right arm to lean on, and made some suggestions as to how to trace Mark and Lisa.

"First, we must find these missing ones. We will send out scouts to search," he said as they reached the royal camp. "Alaeric, once Carr has your arm healed, will you organize it?" Surprised, Alaeric agreed.

The King escorted the bemused party to his tent. Quietly, he ordered a guard at his tent flap to take some soldiers and bring back the Prince's belongings. It was large, roomy, and comfortable although sparsely furnished. Alaeric was led to a bed in the far corner behind a curtain where Carr began to attend to his wounds.

"Is he all right?" Lauren called out, in a worried voice.

"He has a little infection and he needs rest," came the terse reply from behind the curtain.

"You know," the King began, "I don't want to be an alarmist but, I begin to suspect the long-fingered hands of Sindelar are responsible for your presence here. Maybe he thought to distract me from his real aims if he lured you back."

"No trouble with that." muttered Lauren.

"What?"

"Nothing. Go on."

"We think that he as an invasion plan ready and I am afraid of what that implies. He must be stronger than we realized." The king pounded his fist on the table, which sprang from the floor, unsettling a number of maps and papers.

"What do you mean?" Lauren was still trying to understand the situation after an absence of five years in a few sentences. "Explain this to me."

"Ever since the rebellion, strange creatures have been marauding throughout Dal Ryeas. While we have been able to capture or kill many of the worst, there always seem to be more.

There have been so many, in fact, that the Tal is clouded at times from path manipulation and the energies that it creates so that we cannot see beyond our borders at times."

"Why do you suspect Sindelar?" Lauren asked. "Could it be anyone else?"

Carr joined them from behind the curtain, and spoke before Tarq could answer. "Sindelar's talents combined very high-level sorcery with unmatched crystal manipulation of maelstroms and traveling the paths. Only a holder of a Tal is greater or more focused. Sindelar may be on the wrong side, but he is brilliant and incredibly skilled. My own powers dim before his."

"After Tayaela left," Tarq continued, "there was an immediate increase in path activity. We thought that because she was agitated and upset, she was inadvertently using her skills as a pathforger, and opened too many paths at once from here during her search, or that she was tapping into the Tal to find other pathlines to Alaeric. We knew that she was searching the worlds for Alaeric and when she vanished we thought that she had found you. We thought the creatures were debris from her forging."

"Then these monsters began to manifest. For three-and-a-half years my fighters and I have battled them. It's now even worse than it was in the earlier surges. The new ones are harder to destroy. We've driven most of them off, but we know that they're still in the wastelands and the mountains. Then, it stopped for a year: no new monsters, no new activity, nothing.

"About six months ago, while I was trying to enhance a spell for a University sorcerer, there was an incredible power surge in the Tal. I was holding it and someone tried to grab it from me. Since it was in my hand the attempt failed. As soon as I pulled it back into my control, I got the image of Sindelar with Killia. After that we've been monitoring every flux and shift in the world openings, in the Tal and in various spells to determine their scope and purpose. We know they want me dead and the throne returned to Tadiak, but it's how they are going about doing this that has us worried at this time."

"A few weeks ago we saw too much energy gathered around here, in what should be an empty place. The Tal could not penetrate these energies, so we decided to investigate in person. We have some troops and advisors along with us, as many as Carr could transport without draining herself." The King smiled at his first minister, who looked back at him with a troubled expression.

"Two nights ago, there was a tremendous maelstrom focused here. The energies it displayed were similar to other disturbances that I've seen recently in the Tal. We were nearly here so we were able to pinpoint the area in which it occurred, and set up the Tal to analyze any others. The only difference in the shift is that we sensed an anchor that led us here. We arrived just before you did and then Carr shifted my first battalion here."

"You two are a battalion? " Diana blurted and then blushed, regretting having said anything. Tarq looked at the girl and smiled. "Oh no, Carr and I were searching for the radius of the whirlwind when we found you. The rest of the troops are scattered in the woods, hidden from prying eyes. We were trying to figure out which way the path to Sindelar was heading. Something or someone is preventing me from seeing clearly with the Tal."

"What is this Tal?" Diana asked.

"It is our world talisman," replied Lauren, "the protection given by Divine Wisdom. I told you that"

"I thought that was a myth in the crystal stories?"

"My reality is your mythology." Lauren smiled and repeated what she had said two nights before. "A Tal in the hand of the ruler possesses great power and greater responsibility. Every world has one." She fell silent and looked at Tarq, who was now avoiding her eyes.

"Ah," said the King before the silence became awkward, "here comes supper. Let's eat and think how to find your brother and sister. I am sure they must be frantic by now". He smiled. "I have some of my finest trackers here so not to worry, we will find them. In fact, we'll send out a second set tomorrow and Prince Alaeric will lead them. We should have you home in no time!"

Diana felt comforted by the King's words. Things seemed so much better than this morning.

Chapter 4

Mark woke at dawn, stiff and sore, to find he was lying on a pile of leaves and dried flower petals with Lisa curled up in a ball next to him. He sat up, looked around at the unfamiliar and vaguely hostile forest surrounding him, and suppressed a rising sense of panic. Reaching out, he shook his sister.

As she came awake, Lisa screamed and clung to him, giving a voice to his fears as well as her own. Her red hair, tangled with leaves, covered part of her face, but he felt her terror in her trembling body. Not knowing what to do, she held onto him. Mark tried to comfort her, immediately taking the wrong approaches.

"Stop crying now. It's not doing any good. We have to figure out what to do..."

Stung with wounded indignation, Lisa pushed him away, "Oh right, first you get us into this mess and now you have to be in charge and order me about?"

"Me? How did I get into this?" Mark exclaimed. "Look I don't know what kind of stunt your friends—"

"My friends?" Lisa shouted. "What do you mean my . . . Oh my God! Look!" she screamed, pointing to his blood-stained arm. In the growing daylight, the dried, caked blood covering Mark's arm shone with a dull gleam. "A-are you hurt?"

"I'm not cut, if that's what you mean, but my shoulder hurts like hell." Mark muttered. "Whose blood is this?" He stared at his arm as if it belonged to someone else.

"I'm sorry, Mark." She got up from the leaves and looked

around. "So do you know where we are?

"No," Mark said shortly, still staring at his arm, "I don't have a good feeling about this place."

Sniffing slightly, but her hysterics under control, Lisa agreed to that. She turned in a half-circle and said, "Don't the trees look funny?" She pointed to the woods looming around her. The colors seemed wrong, a deeper green with an undertone of dark purple.

"Yeah." Mark answered, "Hey look, a path!"

Lisa faced his direction and saw a clearing through the woods. "Maybe it's a way out." She began to run past him but Mark pulled her back sharply.

"Wait a minute! Don't be in such a hurry. Let's mark this place. You never know, we might have to find this meadow again."

Agreeing but anxious to leave the woods and find clear unobstructed daylight, Lisa paced impatiently as Mark built a small stone cairn as a guide."This way, if we go in circles, we'll know we were here before."

Lisa looked at him in disgust. He was always so meticulous it drove her crazy! "Come on Mark, we got to get home. Diana must be going insane by now."

Mark looked at her. She seemed so young. Her long red hair was tousled and dirty. She was thin, almost fragile-looking. How could someone like that be such a pain?

"Lisa, we don't know where we are or how we got here. It's like Dorothy in Oz or being in Narnia. Only here there's no yellow brick road to follow or a friendly faun to show us the way. There's just this path. We have to figure out our way. So calm down and don't be so anxious to run off!"

Lisa glared at him but said nothing. She didn't like his preemptory orders but his harsh voice brought her back to the present situation and she reluctantly admitted to herself that he was right.

Finally satisfied with his cairn, Mark held out his hand for his sister to take but Lisa, mindful of her budding maturity and resentful of his unwitting patronage, ignored the hand, and strode past him.

Scowling, he followed her.

They walked for hours. Mark's watch was no longer working

so they didn't really have an idea as to how long they wandered. The sun, a golden honey colored ball unlike the clear yellow of Earth's sun, rose in the sky. As the woods lightened, Mark and Lisa noted more differences in the trees and animals, especially how different the animals seemed. At one point, an elk-sized horned creature surged across the path, closely followed by a canine-type animal the size of a pony. Mark quickly yanked Lisa from the path and they hid behind a large fallen tree until prey and predator were long gone.

Another argument broke their uneasy peace a few hours after the walk began. It was approaching mid-day and Lisa, tired and hungry, saw what appeared to be a fruit-bearing bush. Eagerly she darted from the path and picked a ripe looking one. Before Mark could protest, she started to take a bite from the ripe, red pear-shaped fruit. Mark knocked it from her hand and shook her.

"Are you crazy? It could be poisonous!" he shouted.

Lisa screamed back, "Then at least I'll die eating! I won't starve to death!"

"Oh right," Mark, replied sarcastically. "Well, make sure you crawl into the bushes to do it. I hate being around dead bodies."

"You are so damn self-righteous, it makes me sick!" Lisa retorted. "How can you stand being near yourself?"

Before Mark could answer, a voice said, "It's not poison, young sir, but you are wise to be cautious in a place you do not know."

Mark, still holding Lisa, whirled towards the voice and thrust his sister behind him. He stood defiantly, as Lisa shifted nervously from foot to foot.

A dozen people dressed in uniforms were standing on the path behind them.

"Welcome." The speaker said. She was a tall woman with short-cropped black hair and green eyes. Her uniform was a dark forest green with black bands that blended into the forest perfectly. "Please come with us."

"Who are you?" Mark demanded, trying not to show his terror.

"I am Captain Rhea Volta. If you will come with me, I'll take you to Lord Sindelar." The woman's smile was devoid of warmth, but her offer seemed to calm the pair.

"Who?" Mark asked, puzzled.

"Princess Killia?" Captain Volta asked, trying another name.

"I'm sorry, I don't know these names." Mark replied, politely. "My name is Mark Harrison and this is my sister, Lisa. Where are we? What are you talking about? How can you speak English?"

Lisa, becoming more agitated with each question Mark asked, finally broke free of his hold, and approached the Captain. "I don't know who you are, but please take us to this Lord Sindelar person. Maybe he can tell us what's going on."

Captain Volta frowned, "Sindelar means nothing to you? Killia? Dal Ryeas?"

Lisa shook her head. "Nope, sorry."

"Orado," the Captain called to a sergeant behind her.

"Ma'am?" the veteran answered, stepping forward.

"I think there has been a major error. They're not ours." Captain Volta said softly. "Escort them to camp. I think my lord and the Princess need to be apprised. There may be more who slipped through."

Captain Volta turned to Mark and Lisa. "There seems to be some sort of mix-up. We'll take you to our camp and get you some food and try to straighten everything out." Volta's tone was very cool, but the authority of her manner comforted Lisa, as her brother could not. She felt as if she had found a protector.

Lisa started to accompany Volta, leaving Mark to stare at her in amazement.

"She's going to get me killed someday, if she keeps doing this," he thought, sizing up the group in front of them.

"Please, young sir," Sergeant Orado interrupted Mark's reverie, "Come along, I am certain that the sorcerer will know what to do."

Realizing he was surrounded by a troop of armed soldiers, Mark followed his sister and her new friend, feeling more uneasy than when they were alone. He turned to the sergeant walking at his side and asked, "Why do you speak English if we're in another world?"

"What's English?" the sergeant asked innocently, "We are speaking Ryean, the main language of the world Dal Ryeas. But since you've obviously just traveled a long path, Sindelar must have lifted the language barriers when he sent out his summons.

I mean, it would be very inconvenient if the pathways didn't have the mechanism to supply a dominant language to a traveler, it they want it, don't you think?"

When Mark didn't respond, the Sergeant continued, "You must come from an edgeworld or something, not to understand the barrier spell. I bet you have multiple languages on your world as well. I've heard of places like that."

"What's a pathway? What's an edgeworld? What are you talking about?" Mark felt adrift in the sea of information Orado was imparting.

"I think we'd better let Lord Sindelar explain," Orado replied, with a quick glance at the Captain and Lisa.

"Who is he?" Mark's voice began to take on a harsh edge.

"Easy, young sir," Orado fingered a long dagger at his side, "No need to get hostile. I assure you, you are in no danger. At present."

Captain Volta stopped the discussion then. "We will go on in silence. There have been strange readings from the paths and I'd rather be careful. Keep your eyes open for more strays." Her last statement was to her troops.

Orado eyed Mark speculatively and it made the young man feel uncomfortably like a side of beef being checked for tenderness. There was something repellent about this entire situation, especially with Volta and Orado, but Mark was unable to put his finger on it. All he knew was that they were in these troops' power and escape for the moment was unrealistic.

For the next hour the only sounds were natural forest sounds. In a short time they had become familiar to Mark and it was oddly comforting for him to hear them. He remembered all the stories he had heard about strange disappearances at home: the Bermuda Triangle, Judge Crater, and the Marie Celeste. He wondered if he and Lisa had just become another unsolved mystery.

Eventually they reached a large clearing. It was an almost perfect circle, with huge trees sheltering it from prying eyes. All around the clearing stood many tents. Hundreds of people were moving about their business. Corrals of horses and other animals vaguely resembling Earth species were scattered around the campsite. In the center of the circle, two large pavilions stood side by side. On one flew a flag of forest green with a flying bird

51

rampant. The other had no pennons or flags, but in front of it was a hastily constructed platform. Seated on this dais was the most beautiful woman Mark or Lisa had ever seen.

Killia Tadiak, exiled Princess of Dal Ryeas, and ward of Sindelar, was tall, with strikingly large and cold green eyes, cascading blond hair bound by an intricate circlet of gold, diamonds, and pearls, and was possessed of an aura of aloof royalty. Even in her field uniform, a green velvet tunic banded with lighter green satin ribbon, green leggings, and leather boots, she appeared every inch the princess. Around her neck hung an heirloom pendant of dark flashing emeralds set on a heavy gold and platinum chain. Her long, graceful hands lay quietly in her lap unadorned by any jewels except a small thin diamond band belonging to her father. Her attention was riveted on her companion on the dais.

Lisa was so busy staring at the woman and wishing that she looked like her, she barely felt Captain Volta's hand on her shoulder signaling her to stand still. Mark, coming up beside her, poked her in the arm to get her to pay attention to the speaker.

"And because you, my loyal companions in exile, because of you we will break Tarq's evil hold over our beloved country and restore our Princess to the throne rightfully hers!" The Princess on the dais acknowledged the cheer that arose with a graceful nod of her head.

"Together we will triumph. This usurper has refused our peace offering, our compromise that would have averted war. He refused the hand of our Princess. For five long years, I alone have harassed this Pyramus King to avenge this slight to our lady. I have sent him the creatures of nightmare: griffins, dragons, manticores and as many other dreads as I could conjure. I have traveled the paths through the coreworlds and the edgeworlds. I found our exiles and I have brought you home. My maelstroms will end our disgrace. Here, and at our camp at Morsea, we are amassing the finest armies in all the universes."

A cheer again went up again. To Mark, they could have been at a sporting event and sitting close to the field, so loud the voices had become.

"We will defeat Tarq and reclaim the Ryean Tal for Tadiak. Killia shall reign in Dal Ryeas and you will all feast with her at her royal seat in Tadia!" The speaker held wide his arms as the cheer arose for the third time.

Mark glanced at Lisa and saw that her attention had shifted from the Princess to the speaker. Sindelar was a tall slender man with dark brown hair and swarthy olive skin. He looked about forty but was addressing the crowd with the energy of a man half his age. Mark watched, feeling that every gesture, every expression, was carefully rehearsed and choreographed.

As the speaker turned to the Princess, his hand outstretched, he presented her to the crowd, and she rose from her seat to speak. "Lord Sindelar, our most loyal and puissant wizard speaks for me. I invite you to feast with me in Tadia, when we have conquered this demon King!" Killia smiled and sat down again.

In the brief silent confusion that followed the Princess' short and unrevealing speech, Lisa exclaimed, "Oh Mark, isn't she beautiful!"

From her seat, the Princess heard the girl's comment. Glancing over the crowd she saw the slight young girl standing next to a young man only a few years older. As the crowd finally realized that the gathering was over and put up another ragged cheer, she said quietly to Sindelar in amusement, "Are your maelstroms calling children here now, Sorcerer?"

"Children? What are you saying?" Sindelar looked confused, "Tyrmandos and even Tarq allowed those with families to pay fines and return home. No children are out there."

"Then," the princess indicated Volta and her charges, "how did she get here?"

Sindelar frowned as he saw Lisa.

"Volta, bring them to my tent!" he snapped. Sindelar then jumped down from the platform and stalked away in fury. Killia followed, laughing quietly, looking as if she were leaving a throne room on her way to a royal progress.

Captain Volta escorted Lisa and Mark to the pavilion directly behind the dais and had them sit on a low daybed. Lisa, suddenly very frightened by the way things were happening so fast, huddled against Mark, who unconsciously put a comforting arm around her.

Volta tried to engage them in small talk, but had no clue as to what to say to these strange exiles from the edges. They were such odd-looking youth. Their clothing was faded and torn. The trousers were of the same heavy dark blue material and the styling was the same for both. Only their tops differed. The girl wore a short sleeved pullover top of bright colors while the boy was wearing a dark collar-less shirt and a jacket of the same material as the trousers. Volta determined that they were in a uniform of some kind and that the maelstrom had caught them only half dressed.

"Your uniform, what type is it?" she finally asked Lisa.

"My uniform? What uniform?"

Volta tried again, "The uniform you and your companion wear. Do the different shirt colors indicate different specialties or branches of service? Perhaps a trainee vs. a veteran fighter?" She looked at the heavy materials and continued, "And it must be a very cold place where you come from."

Mark and Lisa exchanged bewildered looks and didn't answer. Volta, feeling foolish and hating it, did not speak again for the remainder of the time they spent waiting. Before the silence became too awkward, sounds of activity were heard outside the tent. Volta surged to her feet and stood at attention. Mark and Lisa rose slowly, still huddled together.

Killia entered first, followed by Sindelar. Carefully the magus showed the Princess to a seat and motioned for Volta to leave. Without a glance at the children, the Captain saluted the magus, bowed to the princess and left. Suddenly bereft of the only person they knew, Mark and Lisa tightly held hands.

Up close Sindelar was even more attractive than he had appeared on the dais. He was a tall man, with dark brown hair and deep blue eyes. His smile was cool and never quite reached his eyes. He nervously paced around the tent, playing casually with small items scattered about. He never looked directly at Mark or Lisa, but seemed intimately aware of their every move and gesture.

Princess Killia was seated in a high backed canvas chair. Mark and Lisa thought her beauty was breathtaking. Her hair looked spun from gold. Her green eyes were a true emerald color. Her long-fingered hands were clasped loosely in her lap. Lisa was enthralled to be near her. Fairy tales and stories of beautiful damsels raced through Lisa's head, as she gazed with sudden intensity at the princess.

Killia smiled at such scrutiny and raised a languid hand. "Come here, child," she beckoned Lisa.

Breaking her hold of Mark's hand, Lisa approached the Princess. She tried to curtsy, as she had seen people do on television. Killia found this amusing and laughed softly, but Lisa colored, a bit embarrassed. Seeing this, Killia sobered quickly and asked, "What are you called, girl?"

"My name is Lisa Harrison," she paused and added, "Ma'am" since it just seemed right somehow. She had heard Orado say that to Volta and it seemed that if he could say it to the captain, she should say it to the Princess.

The princess reached forward and grasped a long red lock of Lisa's hair. "Look at this, Sindelar. Have you ever seen such a lovely color?" Killia stared in fascination, until Lisa's blush almost matched her hair.

Throughout her life, Lisa had been subjected to comments and attitudes about the fierce red of her hair until she had become quite blasé about them. But Killia's intense fascination was at once exhilarating and embarrassing. Lisa felt that she wanted to please this Princess above all else. Her timidity and fear of this new place were forgotten, and she impetuously gave her complete trust to the beautiful woman seated before her.

Mark, sensing that Lisa was experiencing an instant case of hero worship, felt her drift further away from him physically and emotionally. He turned to the enchanter and held out his hand, "I am Mark Harrison, Sir," trying to get Sindelar's attention, which was focused on Lisa and the Princess. The magus shifted his hard gaze to him suddenly, and Mark felt even more distant. "S-sir, where are we and how do we get home?"

"I am sorry, young sir, but you and your lovely sister here have inadvertently been ensnared in a maelstrom path. I give you my heartiest apologize for having snatched you from your home."

"I don't understand."

"What don't you understand?" Sindelar asked, a bit testily.

"What is a maelstrom path? What is going on? Where are we?"

"Where are you from?" Sindelar asked patiently.

"The United States."

"The what? No, I mean what world? Is it a core or an edge?"

"Core? Edge? I don't know what you're talking about!" Mark's frustration was boiling over.

"Saevirg! They come from the very edges!" Sindelar marveled, suddenly pacing again, "They have no contact!" He stopped and looked at the boy a bit more kindly, "Well, Mark Harrison, the paths are the ways we travel through the universes of the Creator. Right now, we are on an uninhabited part of a world called Dal Ryeas. Many other places exist at the whim of the Creator and his children and all have paths leading to them. Since you are from an edgeworld, there are not so many paths or people who wish to travel them. Obviously on your world, they have fallen in to disuse. From a guess, I'd say that strong sciences are your mainstay and that sorcery is not a factor on your home world. I venture to guess that this is your first brush with magic."

"Uh... yes" Mark stammered. "How do you know that about our world?"

"You are obviously unused to pathwalking, which is a good indicator," Sindelar grinned, but like Killia's expression, his smile didn't touch his eyes. "We here all know that the laws that cover the core worlds do not apply to the edges quite the same way as they do here. Your overlords seem to encourage science over magic. It's a matter of choice actually. I've walked the edges enough to recognize an inhabitant when I see one," he smiled a dazzling and cold smile "or in this case two."

Mark still looked confused but Sindelar laughed. "Enough of this. We'll talk about this more later. After all, you will be here a while."

"What do you mean by that? Can't you just magic, or whatever, us home? That's how you brought us here, isn't it?"

"I wish it were that easy," Sindelar chuckled ruefully, "But you see, I am rather stuck."

"Stuck? How?" Mark felt his stomach start to churn.

"I am unable to return you to your home at this time. If I tried to without specific understanding from where you came, I could cast you adrift along the paths, possibly forever."

"Then how did you get us here?" Mark could feel his temper rising and his face stiffening into an angry mask. It was just like talking to Lisa, he thought bitterly. Every question asked resulted in only more confusion.

"My apologies, children, but three years ago, I set in motion a spell to call the exiles home."

"Exiles?" Mark was reaching total exasperation by this time.

Princess Killia interjected, "Lord Sindelar had been helping me gather my scattered forces from the edge and coreworlds. A battle will return me to my rightful place as Queen of Dal Ryeas. We are trying to overthrow the usurper Tarq and regain the Ryean Tal." The princess looked lovely and her husky breathless voice was mesmerizing.

"What is the Tal?" Once again Mark felt lost in incomprehensible explanations.

"It is the focus. Simply put, with the Tal, one may manipulate the magic of the universes to create a path specifically to a distant location. The Tal embraces the power of any spell and aids the magic of even the feeblest sorcerer. Only the very best, like Lord Sindelar here, can ever thwart the power of the Tal when the one holds it that is consecrated to it. It has endless uses. It could even help us locate the proper path for you to go home."

Mark brightened a bit, still gazing at the princess.

"However, our pathfinders and pathforgers would need very precise information from you. With the Tal, we wouldn't have needed it. What Sindelar did was circumvent the Tal and raise the storms for three years. With the Tal, it may have taken three hours. He has no idea which world you come from and without the Tal we can't be sure."

The Princess felt sorry for Mark as she caught his look, and continued gently. "Pathfinders are people who can travel the already established paths between the worlds. A Finder can return to any world once he or she has been there. A pathforger can also follow the established paths, but is also able to create new ones, locate safe places, like little pockets, within the voids of the universes, and shield them. These are very useful talents and can be done without the aid of the Tal. But with the Tal, the anointed and bound, and their magic workers, can change worlds." Killia's voice took on a dream-like tone, perhaps thinking about possessing the Tal herself.

"What does the Tal look like?" Lisa asked.

"The Ryean Tal is beautiful," the princess replied in a hushed voice, as if sharing a secret. "It's a stone of deep purples with greens and other shades singing in it, wrapped in silver wire. It has an inner power and the music of the gods travels through it."

"Poetic," Sindelar smirked, "but essentially accurate."

"Where is this Tal?" Mark asked.

"With Tarq for now," Killia's voice took on a vicious sneering tone. "But I will regain it, fear not. Tadiak will rule once more!"

"Be patient, my Princess," Sindelar urged. "It will take time." He turned to Mark and Lisa. "Until then, you are our guests. Our tents are yours. Once we hold the Tal, we will send you home."

Killia rose and held out her hand to Lisa. "Come child, you must be tired and hungry. We will go to my tent and get you settled. I think that I will make you one of my ladies. And get you some new clothes."

Mark watched as the Princess led his younger sister to her tent, chatting comfortably with the girl. He saw Lisa trust this stranger as she had never trusted him and it hurt him immensely. Sindelar watched Mark from the corner of his eye and saw the frown line between his brow and the distrust and anger in his eyes.

"Come, Mark," the magus interrupted the young man's bitter thoughts; "I'll find you a place to stay. I know another young man here who spent much time in the edges. You two will be able to talk." Sindelar felt vaguely sorry for Mark, a boy suddenly torn from everything he knew, and thrust into a fight not his own. How did the maelstrom catch them?

Chapter 5

"Well, Mistress Diana, you seem subdued." Carr was standing next to the camp stool where Diana was sitting morosely, staring into the evening gloom of the forest. It had been almost two weeks since her arrival at the camp of King Tarq. During that time, Lauren was out hunting daily for Lisa and Mark, and as soon as Alaeric had recovered his strength from his loss of blood, he had joined her. It made her happy to know they were looking for her sibs, but without Lauren and Alaeric she felt lonely and afraid. They were her only link to home.

Carr felt sorry for the girl. She tried to imagine how it felt to be taken from her own world, her family scattered, thrust into the middle of what was at best an insurrection, and having to accept everything she was told, all the while being consumed with anxiety over a missing brother and sister. Carr was already quite impressed with Diana's composure.

"I suppose, Lady Carr. Everything is beginning to, well, hit home," Diana sighed, "I've been sitting here trying to sort it all out—"

Carr smiled, "Having any luck?"

"No, not really. I know you've tried to explain everything to me, but I'm still up in the air. And I don't understand why Lauren and Alaeric can't find my siblings. And what is the "Tal'? And why doesn't the King talk to Lauren? Why don't you and Lauren like each other? Why would anyone name a child Laurenthalia? And, oh, a zillion other things!" She threw her hands up.

Carr laughed and knelt down next to her, placing a hand on her shoulder. "I think we've let you be on your own too long. You're going to drive yourself crazy. Come to my tent and I'll try to answer your questions. If I can't, then I'll at least give you a cup of tea."

The girl felt more at ease with the sorceress than with anyone else. She was secretly happy that someone was paying some attention to her. In the past weeks she had learned that Tarq's army was scattered in small clusters throughout the forest. She really didn't know how large the force was and this met the King's objective.

Diane followed Carr past a group of soldiers dressed in midnight blue uniforms. One, a young woman named Maril Zan, whom Diana had met earlier, was cleaning an advanced-looking arrow gun that ran on a spring and wheel principle. They watched her for a moment and then continued to Carr's tent.

The sorceress lived in a gray tent isolated from the others. A cheerful cooking fire had a kettle was boiling furiously on it. "No magic needed," she answered before Diana could ask. "I always keep a kettle boiling. You never know when you need hot water."

"Oh," replied Diana, taking a seat. "How do you keep it full?"

"Well, that's a small deviation," Carr smiled. "It's not too difficult."

"The only magic at home is sleight of hand."

"But you have science. Surely that's just another form of magic." Carr bustled about setting out some plates and cups.

"Why am I so miserable?" Diana asked, abruptly changing the subject.

Carr turned to her, "You're homesick, feeling helpless about your brother and sister, and you have nothing to do. The only people you know are suddenly not who you thought they were. You're far from home and you're confused. It's all very natural. But whatever happens, I'm certain Laurenthalia and Alaeric will do their best to reunite you with your family and take you home."

"Is Alaeric all right?"

"He's fine now. The King allowed me to use the Tal to pull the taint from his bloodstream. It was necessary to cut him to create an anchor to your brother and sister. Still, cutting him opened his skin to the dangers of your world and infected his blood. He's strong again, which is good in view of the coming times."

"Coming times?" Diana asked, becoming worried.

"There has been a war for over thirty years. It quiets down at times, but it's been going on since King Tarq's grandfather overthrew the mad King Philos and took the Tal for his own. Our great families are divided in their loyalties. Look at your friends Lauren and Alaeric. No matter who wins, they lose. They've been pawns all their lives. The Olenteas clan lords never took oaths to Tarq's family. The Princes felt this lapse justified plotting and rebellion.

"They sat secure in their mountain strongholds, and raised bands of fanatics to fight for them by creating a secret and pseudo-holy order dedicated to restoring Tadiak to power. They're cunning, these Olenteas Princes, after all, they raised their two eldest, Laurenthalia and Alaeric, in complete ignorance of their subversion. Then they sent them as decoys to quell the suspicions of the Pyramus rulers. For years, the children served as tokens of loyalty while the fathers plotted treason. Alaeric's marriage to Princess Tayaela and Lauren's engagement to Tarq were ploys to allay fears."

Diana spoke up, "You mean the marriages were fake?"

"Yes, in the minds of Prince Kir'san and Prince Ertlan it was all a hoax, a ruse to dull the suspicions of the King and his loyalists. Tarq and Lauren's wedding was the sign for the revolution to begin. But some Olenteas' clan folk felt torn about the coup. Not all felt that the reign of Pyramus should end in the return of Tadiak. I was slipped information and we were able to prepare a defense and keep casualties to a minimum." Carr paused, remembering the days of strife and turmoil as if they were yesterday and not five years distant.

"So you don't like Lauren because of her relationship with Tarq?"

"I have nothing personal against Princess Laurenthalia. I even admire the way she went into exile without causing a fuss. But she was never able to explain why she kept postponing the wedding or why she refused to take the blood-oath to the King, as did her cousin. Alaeric went into exile for the sake of his cousin's honor, and all that gesture accomplished was destroying his family life."

She caught Diana watching her intently and shrugged, "I don't know, maybe Laurenthalia is a casualty or perhaps she was a participant in the revolt. Her actions were not explicable. It was my duty to urge the King to banish her. The views of the country as well as my own are still mixed. Only Laurenthalia really knows the truth about her actions."

She turned back to finish setting up, continuing, "But now you've heard the story. For the last five years, he's been trying to heal the breach the rebellion caused in Dal Ryeas."

"Is he going to be able to do it?"

"We hope so. The fact that he pardoned most of the traitors helped. Who knows?" Carr shrugged. "There's one major solution to the entire problem, but Tarq won't hear of it."

"What's that?"

"Tarq could marry Killia and unite the two houses," Carr stated.

"But I thought you said she was crazy?"

"Well, we could control that."

"What about their children? They'd be crazy too." Diana protested, "That will only prolong your problems."

"It is possible to ensure she has none and that Tarq has one with someone else." The sorceress was beginning to feel the pressure of the girl's indignation.

"That's awful!" Diana was shocked at that notion.

"I know. But it's a solution." Carr poured more tea and looked speculatively at the girl. She seemed very bright and alert. As long as the stalemate continued, the enchantress decided it might prove a worthy diversion to train a girl again.

"You have a keen mind and a strong personality," Carr smiled at Diana. "I can't comprehend all of your problems, but I may be able to alleviate some of your boredom. How about if I give you lessons in magic?"

Diana agreed eagerly, "Oh yes! I'd love to learn. I'm so tired of feeling useless around here."

"Alright," Carr grinned, pleased to see her enthusiasm, "Tomorrow, I'll give you a series of tests to determine to which areas you are best suited. And if you like, you can stay in one of the unoccupied tents. Having a tent alone might give Laurenthalia a chance to decide whether to reveal her true objectives to the King."

Diana grinned, "There are a lot of questions she needs to answer, especially about her feelings for Tarq. Also my being here would give the King a chance to see her without an inconvenient chaperone."

"You noticed that? You are quick." Carr smiled approvingly.

"Well, I saw how carefully they avoided being alone with each other."

"They have a lot of mixed emotions to work out. I think I'll also have Alaeric teach you some fundamentals of fighting with the bow, so you can protect yourself…"

The two talked far into the night. When she finally retired to her tent, Diana began to feel more comfortable with her situation and not neglected anymore.

Prince Alaeric grinned as Diana ungracefully ran the series of exercises she had been given.

"You really have to start understanding the concept of flowing movement if you are going to be an adequate fighter." With a groan, Alaeric hoisted himself to his feet and held out his hand for the short sword Diana was using.

"Remember, now," he said crouching down. "You make," he rose slowly, "Each action," then spun lightly on one foot while thrusting with his sword, "Count." He firmly placed his other foot forward into a half lunge.

"Now, you try it." With steady hands, Alaeric guided Diana's movements until she began to feel the rhythm.

"Ric," she said excitedly. "It's like a dance!"

"Good. Think like that." Alaeric smiled. "It will help you focus. Once you understand the fluidity of movement that exists in close fighting, you will be able to trust your body to fight with you, not against you. And you will not trip over your own feet when it behooves you to be steadfast."

"Let's do another one!" Diana said eagerly.

Before Alaeric could reply King Tarq, who had been watching them for a while, spoke up. "Easy on your teacher, Diana. He's recently been on his sick bed."

Alaeric smiled, "I am a little stiff, true."

"Come on Diana, I'll teach you a Pyramus fighting exercise. It won't do if all you know are the Olenteas' exercises." Tarq grinned and came forward, putting out his hand. Alaeric handed it to him with a bow and mocking smile, and then sat down on a bench to watch.

Unaware that Carr had joined Alaeric; Tarq removed his shirt and tossed it to the ground away from the practice area. As he turned to face Diana, the girl gasped.

"What is it? Are you ill?"

"Uh, no sir." Diana stammered, unable to take her eyes from the four parallel scars that ran diagonally down the King's chest, disappearing into the top of his breeches.

Tarq smiled wryly. "If you think my front's bad, you should see the other side." He turned so that she could see that the same lines continued halfway down the King's back. "It was a very nasty creature called a griff. We thought it was extinct from Dal Ryeas, but some years ago Sindelar reintroduced it to our world. I was lucky to come away with only these scars."

Carr spoke up softly, "The King threw himself in front of the beast to save a fallen companion. The animal raked his front for him as a reward. When he tried to crawl away, it raked his back. He was indeed fortunate that the beast's strength was nearly spent, or we might not have saved the King from its clutches."

"And where were you during this, wizard?" Alaeric turned to her, speaking harshly.

"I was the fallen companion." Carr answered quietly. She was inwardly pleased to see the prince's stone gaze drop.

"It is ancient history," the King dismissed the subject with a wave of his hand, "Come, Diana, this is how the Pyramus fight."

Alaeric and Carr watched appreciatively as the King taught his young guest. No one noticed that Lauren stood in the shadows of the tents, watching Tarq with a sad, haunted expression. Slowly, tears welled in her eyes and streamed down her cheeks. After a time, as she listened to the merriment of the training, the wit and warmth of the King and her cousin's laughter, she felt a sense of loneliness, which even during her years of exile had never possessed her so strongly. In the midst of a camp of her own people, near the person she loved most in the universes, she felt like a stranger. Frightened at the rise of these suppressed feelings, she turned and fled into the dark, anonymous presence of the forest.

Only Diana glimpsed Lauren standing in the shadows and vaguely sensed her distress. Before she could speak and welcome her however, the Princess had fled.

Lauren ran past the camouflaged tents of Tarq's army, through the dark looming trees, heedless of her direction. A great sorrow consumed her. Creatures from her worst nightmares had attacked Tarq and she was not there to help him. On she fled, never escaping the sorrow and sadness of her thoughts, until exhausted; she fell to her knees and wept a heartbroken, unrelieved cry of pain.

For many hours she sat in an unknown part of the wood, lost in her thoughts. Once her life seemed so simple, she swore her oath to her King, she loved him, and she was to be his queen. Her goals and ideals were all focused and clear.

Now they were all confused. At times, even in the misery of exile, she experienced a freedom she had never before known was possible. She had reveled in an unmonitored life, knowing that others never analyzed her words and actions for hidden depths or obscure conspiracies. They belonged only to her. The haughty Olenteas Princess Laurenthalia, heiress to her ancient family, had become Lauren Olenteas, next-door caretaker to three young people. She enjoyed this mild challenge and appreciated the strangeness of her edgeworld.

While Alaeric and she traveled, learning about the harsh world they had entered, she had intentionally buried any recollection of the raw passion and majesty of her own world. She had forgotten its hold upon her heart. And now, once again home, its hold reasserted itself.

"For five years," Lauren thought, "I've lived a new life, a free life. What do I do? He hasn't lifted the prohibition to allow me to go home. Do I want to go home? How can I? How can I see him and know it's all different? What do I do?"

Bound by love and especially by her honor, Lauren knew she was unable to flee her responsibility in finding Mark and Lisa. After that was done, what then? She just could not determine what later would bring.

Finally, under a cold, starless midnight sky and overcast by trees that stood like protective hulking giants, Lauren rose and began her trek back to the King's camp. As she looked around her to get her bearings, she realized that this was an unknown part of the forest. Lauren knew the scouts who were ranging deep into the unknown seeking the lost pair. They were thorough and competent. She had even accompanied a team, but this area was unexplored. Concerned by the oversight, Lauren tried to determine what had caused her sudden realization. Only her wild flight away from Tarq's camp had brought her this way, her mind turbulent and unconcerned by earthy bounds. This was the only variation in her search patterns, she concluded.

With the delicate touch of a lace-maker, Lauren mentally felt for the telltale tendrils of a spell. She only had the skills of a pathfinder to aid her. She was, however, a highly skilled pathfinder and as such was able to feel the sheerest wisp of magic, even if she was unable to undo it.

It was a very subtle spell, the almost-untraceable work of a master. Touching only the very edges of the spell, she quickly pulled her thoughts back to ascertain if any trace of her presence was noticeable. When she was certain of her safety, Lauren backed away slowly from the artificial spell wall.

As she reached the relative safety of fifty feet from the affected area, Lauren noticed a slight shimmer between the trees. A moment later, a man stepped from behind a tree. He was wearing a green and black uniform and carrying another in his arms. Checking to see if he was alone, he then began to change.

Lauren, hiding behind the trunk of a mighty tree, watched as he carefully removed his clothing and hid them in a prepared hole beneath a small natural-looking rock formation. The man carefully replaced the stones and then began to dress.

Lauren drew her dagger. Silently she moved back through the trees until she was only a few feet from the man. He was nearly dressed when she reached him. She timed her attack as he pulled on his leather over-tunic. The moment his head disappeared beneath the tunic, she leaped on him, throwing him to the ground. In a second, she pinned him with her knife against his throat.

Carefully, she cut the tunic that was hiding his face. A shock of recognition ran through her when she realized that this man was one of her Olenteas clansmen, Merrick Dracos.

Before she could speak, the man gasped, "Laurenthalia!"

"Hello Merrick," she snarled. "Still working for the bad guys?"

"Is the King with you?" Merrick asked nervously.

"What is it to you?" the point of her knife gently flicked his cheek.

"On my honor, Lady," Merrick said. "I need to talk to him alone. Please, let me up."

"Right, Merrick, as soon as I do, you'll try to kill me. I'm not entirely stupid." Lauren was sitting on his chest, both feet stepping on his wrists, her razor sharp blade pointing at his throat.

"Lauren, I'm a spy for Sindelar. He sent me to see if Tarq would accept me as a clansman of Lady Carr and try to work my way into your graces. I've been to your camp four times. I've see you, Alaeric, the stranger, and I've never revealed this to him."

"Why not?" Lauren asked suspiciously.

"Because Killia is crazy and I don't want Sindelar to win."

"Give me a break, Merrick."

"A what? Why should I want to break something on you? I want you as a friend."

"Never mind, Merrick, it's an expression from the edgeworld where I was exiled. Why should I trust you? I ought to take you to camp, tell the King you tried to ambush me and watch them kill you."

"Lauren, I-I'm your kin," Merrick turned pale.

"That is what is so ugly about this war." Lauren sadly replied, flicking his cheek casually with the knife. "Kin against Kin."

Merrick flinched slightly, remembering Princess Lauren's swift and brutal temper from long ago. "There are reasons why I'm working for Sindelar."

"Because you are a good son to your father, and I am the King's bitch, the Olenteas whore who would sell her father for a crown." Lauren repeated the statements that circulated throughout the Olenteas clans about her.

"My father is dead," Merrick said coldly. "He died, broken, in exile."

"And for this you hate the King." Lauren sneered, "After all, he was the cause of the revolt."

"No. I hate Killia," Merrick retorted. "Her arrogance cost me my home and my family. We don't need a mad queen." His face became flush with emotion.

Lauren understood the emotional upheaval of exile and felt a slight twinge of sympathy with her clansmen. "I'm sorry about your father, Merrick. Were you with him?"

"Yes, my brother Ferrel, and I went into exile with him. He died within the first year. We were trapped on an edgeworld."

"I see." Lauren felt a vague regret for her cousin, Merrick's father. "I am sorry. The first year is the worst. If you can survive it, you can survive anything. He was fortunate to have you with him. What of your mother?"

"She stayed here, loyal to her Pyramus kin. She disowned us for going with father. Can you imagine disowning an eleven-year-old boy who just wanted to be with his father?" Merrick shifted and found the knife very firmly pressed against his throat. "I give you my pledge not to run or attack or anything if you let me up."

Lauren considered this a moment and released him. She motioned him to sit on the ground while she sat on a nearby rock, pulling her sword out and placing it near her hand. Her dagger firmly in her grasp, pointed directly at him.

Merrick slowly sat up. As soon as he was seated with his hands clasped around his knees, Lauren again questioned him. "When did you come back?"

"We were brought along a path about three months ago to Morsea. At first I worked closely with Sindelar training soldiers, until he discovered my talents at spying. He is a very status-conscious man, and my father's close kinship with the Olenteas overlords raised me to exalted heights in his eyes. Being the half-nephew of the great Pyramus Sorceress Carr didn't hurt much either.

"Killia doesn't trust me much. She considers me too closely connected to the King — and to you. Whenever your name comes up, she practically hisses. At one time Sindelar wanted to contact you in your exile and recruit you and Prince Alaeric to Killia's cause. She told him that if he so much as spoke to you, she'd have him executed. Whatever did you do to her?"

Lauren shrugged. "I supposedly had something she wanted. Go on with your story."

"At first I was on their side. It had been my father's side, but now," he looked at Lauren pleadingly, "now I know that she is ruthless and he worships her. They'll destroy Dal Ryeas if they ever rule."

"So what are you doing in this uniform?"

"They've trapped me."

"Now that I find hard to believe, just defect to the King. Your Aunt will be able to test your loyalties," she laughed mirthlessly, thinking of Carr's sorcery and her ruthless way of protecting the King's interests.

"I can't," Merrick said miserably.

"So, now I have to know why, I suppose?" Lauren was skeptical concerning his tale. She thought it an excellent ruse to gain her trust.

"They're holding Ferrel hostage. Oh, they don't call it that, but he's there, held for good behavior — my good behavior. They keep silken prisoners, this pair. Sindelar holds another boy too, a stranger, not of Dal Ryeas. He makes Ferrel share his tent with him. I believe his name is Mark. Lisa, the girl with him, waits on Killia. I don't understand why they're being held. But they'll never get away from here."

"Mark? Lisa?" Lauren whispered. "You know them?"

"Yes?" Merrick said, a little warily.

"I've been searching for them," Lauren replied. "Are they well?"

"The girl is a pet of Killia's. She's well on her way complete seduction by the oh-so-beautiful Princess. The youth... I fear for him. From what Ferrel said, there is a deep distrust in Mark for Sindelar, Killia, everything. And sharing a tent with Ferrel will only increase his inward disturbance. No...I fear he will not be safe."

Lauren contemplated his remarks carefully. Mark and Lisa were at least alive, if trapped. She had to inform the others of Merrick's report. She was wondering whether or not to believe him, when he spoke again, "What are you going to do with me?"

"Take you back. And keep you with us." She answered curtly.

"If you do, you'll be killing Ferrel. Sindelar sent me out to search. There have been signs of infiltration behind the spell wall and whoever has done this doesn't want discovery. Sindelar wants to know who has the power to hide like that and he expects me to find out the answer."

Merrick leaned his head back against the tree and closed his eyes. "And I'm to report back by first light or he'll see to it that Ferrel suffers." Lauren could see the glimmer of a tear at the corner of his eye.

"Merrick, how can I trust you?" Lauren began. "You admit to being a spy for my enemy." Merrick opened his eyes and stared directly at her. She met his sad gaze with her own cold, unflinching one. His next words stunned her.

"I'll swear an Olenteas blood-oath to you." He said with the finality of a condemned man.

"Do you realize what you are saying?" Lauren was aghast. "A blood-oath? Have you taken leave of your senses? Do you have any concept of what that entails?"

"I may have been an exile for years, but I do know the significance of the oath."

They fell silent as Lauren wrestled with his offer. The Olenteas Blood-Oath - its origins shrouded in ancient mystery and intrigue. It was the ultimate test of loyalty - a simple oath that consisted of mingling blood, and speaking a few carefully chosen words that blended power, loyalty, and kinship into an irrevocable bond. The oath went past a pledge, past the binding of liege and vassal. It created between the bondholder and the bonded a tie so strong that if the bonded betrayed the holder, death would be considered a blessing. It began and ended with honor, loyalty, and duty, and transcended them all. It was said that even death did not sever the oath, but that if needed, the dead would rise to fulfill the bond.

"Merrick, even if you came to hate me and mine, you'd still be bound to the oath." Lauren felt touched by his confidence in her, and frightened of the responsibility the bond entailed.

"I know. Lauren, I need this oath and you need eyes in Sindelar's camp. This is my only hope of redemption." Merrick pleaded.

"What of Ferrel?" Lauren asked. "How will he feel about your bonding yourself?"

"I'll save him this way. You will not regret it. I need a liege, and you are still heir to my father's clan. I have the requisite bloodlines.

Once I have rescued him, he'll give you oath as well."

"So, I get Ferrel as well?" Lauren smiled, and then became serious once more. "Merrick, if you betray me, the oath will kill you."

"I know. But without it I'm only half a man." Merrick grimaced.

"I'm not usually a very trusting person. But, maybe this time my blood is calling to yours. Somehow I believe you. I think you mean what you say and I'll hold your oath."

With that Laurenthalia, Princess of the Clan Olenteas, pulled up her shirtsleeve, took the knife she had been holding on Merrick, and deftly nicked a surface vein in the crook of her elbow. The blood welled and began to slowly course down her arm. She wiped off the blade and handed it to Merrick, then watched as he did the same to his arm. Carefully, he placed the knife between their arms and Lauren concentrated on their combined blood dripping onto the knife. As their blood mingled on the knife, it changed to a bright luminescent blue.

As the blood glowed and swirled on the knife handle, Lauren and Merrick exchanged oaths, reciting simultaneously the words every Olenteas child learned to utter as soon as they could speak but never thought to use.

"I pledge my honor, my life and beyond life to the holder of my bond. Never will I betray my bond. I am sworn beyond eternity." Merrick stated.

Lauren replied, "I hold this bond, and pledge to honor my bonded with my trust, my honor and my life. I will swear beyond eternity to keep this bond a surety for his honor." As Lauren's final words were spoken, the co-mingled blood exploded into a rainbow of sparks and vanished. They stared at the knife handle that lay between them, never before witnessing this ritual. They knew, however, that their bond was accepted.

When it was over, they sat on the ground and bandaged each other's arms.

"What now?" Lauren asked.

"I go back to Sindelar with no evidence of infiltration. I'll tell him it's a rumor. I'll see Ferrel and tell him what we've done."

"If you see Mark, let him know we're going to try and get to him — get him out of there." Lauren paused, "You'd better go, and I should, too. I'll tell the King what we've done. Try to get information to us. We'll give you what we can."

"So now I'm a double agent," Merrick sighed, getting up. "And all I ever wanted to be was a country squire."

"We all do what we must," Lauren said, turning to go. "Good luck, my bonded," she bid him goodbye.

Merrick raised his arm and returned through the shimmer of the spell wall. Soon he was gone.

It was late when Lauren returned to Tarq's camp. Most of the troops were asleep. As she approached her own tent, she was surprised to find a light shining. Diana must be up late, she thought. Warily, her sword half-drown, she pulled back the tent flap and looked inside.

Seated at the table on a campstool absurdly small for him, Alaeric sat sculpting a small soapstone figurine. Suppressing a laugh at the sight of his huge form on such a tiny stool, she entered the tent silently.

Unsurprised by her entrance, Alaeric looked up at her and said, "How goes the search for the Harrisons?"

"Poorly." She sat on her cot and began removing her soft leather boots. "Your scouts have been unable to find any trace of them, and neither have I, really." She thought briefly of confiding in her cousin about the evening's events, but thought better of it, deciding to report directly to the King concerning Merrick and his conversion to Tarq's cause.

Alaeric watched her closely. Uncomfortable by his scrutiny, Lauren decided to share a half-truth with him, thereby forestalling whatever the real reason for his late night visit.

"I do have one thing to report though. There has been a compulsion to avoid the Northeast. None of your scouts go that way. Even I felt it today." She looked at Alaeric. "Mention it to Carr, will you? It's probably a spell."

"Why don't you talk to Carr? Or are you still avoiding her?"

"I go out again in the morning," she yawned, deliberately ignoring his question. "If you will excuse me?" she hinted pointedly. "I would like to change and go to bed."

"That's alright. I used to take baths with you, when we were little. You can change with me here." Alaeric grinned maliciously.

"What do you want, Alaeric?" she said bluntly.

"To know what the hell you're doing? We've been here two weeks and you're out there more than you are in camp." Alaeric indicated the dark woods with a wave of his hand, "You are never here. Gods, you are a Princess of the Olenteas, not a foot soldier. You have one of the best trained minds of our generation and you're out there playing scout!"

"We promised to find Lisa and Mark," she reminded him sternly. "Or did suddenly finding Tarq make you forget your word to Diana? We're exiled, or rather, *I'm* exiled from Dal Ryeas, or have you forgotten? We are Olenteas, children of traitors. Somehow we are responsible for two innocents being lost out there, or have you forgotten that too? Well I have not, and I swore to Diana that I would find them. I for one will not be foresworn."

"Look," she continued in a reasonable tone, "I know you have been hurt and have only begun to search. You are still not up to long distance hunts, so why don't we just split things up. You stay here, as the King's advisor, and I'll look for Lisa and Mark. Then we will all be happy."

Alaeric rose silently, his head bent to avoid hitting the canvas roof as he walked to the door. With one hand on the tent flap, he turned to face his cousin. "I'll probably never know happiness again, Laurenthalia, as long as Tayaela wanders the edges, but at least I'll somehow help her brother. You loved him once and you believed in him. He needs your help. You can't avoid him forever."

"I will help him while I fulfill my oath. My scouting serves his purpose." She fell silent.

For a long time they stared at each other, their thoughts locked away and secret. "Things change, Alaeric," Lauren spoke quietly, "Not everyone can be as stalwart and loyal as you." She sat on her cot and began to undress as Alaeric left.

Lauren reflected on the events of the evening as she sat alone and isolated by her hidden sorrow. She wept to herself for her lost youth and the lost innocence. Then she rose and exited the tent. She had one more report to make before sleeping.

Chapter 6

Mark heard rumors from his tent mate Ferrel that King Tarq's forces had discovered their hiding place. According to Ferrel, the avoidance spell Sindelar had set was weakening.

"So that means that the Tal is somewhere near. And where the Tal is, so is the King." Ferrel was a dark, handsome young boy of sixteen. "King Tarq isn't really all that bad," Ferrel confided to Mark, "But he's being forced to fight for his crown again. It's bound to have a bad affect on his ability to keep peace."

"I really don't see," Mark answered, "why you are all fighting. You told me that everyone knows the Princess' father was crazy, and you even admit Tarq isn't bad. So why fight?"

"Old loyalties die hard," Ferrel replied miserably. "Well, we'd better get on with your weapons practice. You're learning swordplay well. On light arrows, though, you need a lot of work."

"I still don't see why you just don't bring guns along the paths," grumbled Mark.

"They're forbidden! The Gods themselves would destroy any fool who tried to bring them through. They are not part of our world and never have been. So it's prohibited for them to be introduced." Ferrel smiled at Mark's skeptical expression. "Whether you believe it or not, the last idiot who tried to bring explosives through was disintegrated as he left the path. The place where I was exiled had them. I saw a man killed from forty yards, his head blown away. It was awful. At least here with a

74

blade or an arrow you confront your enemy at close range. It's not so… impersonal. You feel each death, and that's what the Gods expect."

"How old were you when you were exiled?" Mark asked quietly.

"I was eleven," Ferrel sighed. "My father was a leader in the Olenteas' faction. He raised three thousand soldiers to fight the King. My mother was Pyramus and she refused to rebel, so she left my father and returned to her own lands. My brothers, sisters, and I stayed with my mother during the revolt, but after it was over, when King Tarq exiled my father and my oldest brother Merrick — even though he hadn't fought — I had to go too. I was really close to my father and couldn't stand the thought of him going into exile without me. My mother gave me the choice of being disowned by going with my father or staying with her. I chose my father.

"When he and Merrick were sentenced, we petitioned the King and he allowed me to go too as a favor to my Pyramus clan relationship. My aunt Carr intervened and Tarq allowed me to go with them. My father died four years ago, and since neither Merrick nor I were pathfinders, we weren't able to come home. That is until Sindelar's maelstrom path found us," Ferrel paused, looking down, "if Merrick hadn't been there, I would have died alone in exile."

"Is Merrick a soldier?"

"No, not quite. He's vanished so I guess he must have found a way to Tarq. I hope." Ferrel sighed.

"As a recruit? But he exiled you." Mark was puzzled.

"No," said Ferrel sadly, "Merrick's a spy. If Tarq's people find out about him, they'll kill him."

"Oh," Mark blinked, a bit sorry for bringing the subject up. For a moment he was silent, then he added, choosing his words carefully, "You aren't happy that he's spying?"

"It's not that. The King is a good man. If he'd been the one to find us, we'd have joined his forces at once. Only Sindelar found us instead and he's holding me to force Merrick to work for him. You may not have noticed, but all my movements outside this tent are carefully watched." Ferrel's voice became softer, but bitter.

"What about the rest of your family?"

"When I joined my father, like I said, we were formally disowned by our mother. She wanted no traitor sons. There's no welcome in Dal Ryeas for us." Ferrel said bleakly. "She never wants to see either of us again." Forcing a smile, he slapped his knees and rose. "Let's go practice. Too much talk makes a soul weak and a body lazy."

Mark followed him. It was a beautiful morning. The sun was half-risen in a cloudless azure sky, the trees a lush green. People were hurrying all over the camp, looking busy and serious. As the two young men proceeded to the practice field his new friend's handling of adversity suddenly awed Mark. Ferrel was incredibly brave. To have gone so young and so bravely into exile with his father was an astounding choice for a young boy. Mark tried to imagine himself having to make such a choice. But you are in exile, a small voice said inside him. But he answered himself "Ferrel made the choice to go, I didn't get the chance. Events just pulled me along."

"Ferrel," Mark spoke up as they walked. "When…"

Ferrel turned. "When what?"

Suddenly shy, Mark said, "Nothing. It's not important."

Mark carefully scrutinized his friend. He was four years older than Ferrel; yet somehow the younger boy seemed more mature. Looking for outward manifestations of Ferrell's courage, all Mark saw was a lanky sixteen-year old with long dark brown hair that brushed his shoulders. Though he often smiled his eyes hinted at the turbulence of his young life. Only when Ferrel spoke of Merrick did the wariness leave his eyes.

Before beginning his own practice, Mark watched Ferrel commence his session with the sword mistress. Slender and tall, Ferrel did not seem to be a warrior, yet his thin body was tautly muscled. Even a novice like Mark realized how good the younger boy was. He wondered, briefly, if he could ever learn.

Turning from the duelists, Mark started his own work with the light arrows. The bow, unlike the bows of his world, was a cross between a long bow and a rifle. Aim was through a sighting mechanism. The arrows were long, nearly three feet, with curly barbed heads. The weapon loaded the arrow along a barrel. Knocking the arrow and sighting along the shaft, a pull trigger yanked back the string to eye level, and releasing the trigger shot the arrow. Unlike a crossbow, the light arrows were full- shafted and feathered, not a short quarrel. The arrows used in battle were anointed with a type of glowing ointment that burned the target, be it flesh or stone.

Mark's proficiency with the bow gun was increasing. Ferrel, an excellent teacher, arranged equal practice with sword. Working hard, neither young man noted the passing of the morning, until the sword mistress called a halt.

"Come, even young warriors need to eat," she said smiling. "Why don't you join me?"

Gratefully, the two young men did so. They were so engrossed in the assessments of the sword mistress over their respective styles that they never saw the ornately-dressed girl standing at the edge of the field.

"Mark," Lisa called imperiously. "I wish to speak with you."

"Oh God." Mark groaned. He dreaded his meetings with Lisa. Her ardent admiration of the Princess was already affecting her manners in all ways. He wearily glanced at Ferrel, who indicated he should attend to whatever Lisa wanted this time. They both knew that ignoring Lisa's demands only brought Mark trouble. An encounter he was able to avoid earlier in the week had led him to be chastised by Sindelar himself for his insensitivity.

Ferrel watched with a troubled expression as Mark left their little group and approached his tyrannical little sister.

"I do not appreciate being made to wait," Lisa began in her best imitation Killia-voice, which made Mark inwardly shudder. There was something distasteful to him about anything concerning the Princess.

"I'm sorry Lisa. I didn't see you standing there." Mark said wearily. "I was practicing."

"So I noticed," Lisa frowned, and then abruptly dropped her haughty façade, "Mark, why are you avoiding me?"

"I'm not, Leese. I just don't live in the royal tents." He said this without any emphasis, trying not to upset her. Lisa's temper, always quick, was even more erratic in the two weeks they had been in the camp. Mark worriedly considered what toll this world, in fact this whole situation, would have on her state of mind.

"I dreamed about Mom last night," she said in her small voice. "And Daddy and everybody. Sometimes I don't think of them for days." She looked at the mixture of compassion and love on her brother's face. "Mark, how long have we been here?"

"About two weeks, maybe a bit more." he answered her carefully.

"Do you think Diana got in touch with them about what happened to us?"

"I'm certain of it." Mark reassured her soothingly. "But remember, all Di knows is that we vanished in the backyard."

"Are we ever going home?" Lisa turned from him looking towards the trees.

"I don't know. I hope so." Mark went on without thinking. "I think they could send us back now, but for some reason they don't."

"Sindelar says he needs the Tal to pinpoint accuracy," Lisa replied primly.

"Oh hell, Lisa, they can send us back to our world and I'll figure out a way to get us home."

"They can't, I asked. Killia told me that all of Sindelar's crystals are focused to bringing everyone here to Dal Ryeas. To reverse even one path opening takes tremendous energy, and he can't afford to do this since Tarq is so close." She whispered close to him, "I even heard that Tarq's wizard, Carr, is trying to force a breach in the protective wards."

"Well, you certainly hear a lot in the royal pavilion. And you're learning so much." Mark answered, being careful with his words.

"Princess Killia is training me to be a lady-in-waiting. She's even promised me a title and an estate when she comes into her own."

"But they're going to send us home I thought." Mark insisted.

"If they can." Lisa replied airily, her thoughts of home vanishing in an instant. It infuriated Mark that she could change her attitude so quickly.

"You know, I think you're really so enmeshed with the Princess that you've forgotten something." Mark snapped at her. "You've just flip-flopped. One minute you want to go home, the next you want to stay here on Dal Ryeas. You've managed to forget that this isn't our fight. We don't know what's really going on. You've chosen the Princess, fine, but you aren't of this place and, honey, we're a long way from home. Maybe you're happy doing nothing, being pampered, and spoiled, but remember these people are preparing for a war. And that's no place for a little girl from Cleveland Heights to find herself."

Lisa was furious. "You... you turd! These people have been wonderful! You're just jealous, like you always are. First, when Diana and I became so close, then when Lauren was so nice to me; and now because the Princess prefers me to you. And why not? All you ever do is complain and make nasty remarks about my friends! I hate you! I never want to see you again!" She spun away, beginning to cry.

"Lisa!" Mark exclaimed, trying to reach for her, but she shook away from his grasp. She ran to the waiting arms of Princess Killia who, with Captain Volta, stood at the edge of the practice field. Mark wondered how long they had been there and how much Killia heard. Mark's eyes met Killia's and he knew by the triumphant set of her head and the gentle caress of her hand as she stroked the weeping girl's flaming curls that she heard all of it. With a sudden clarity, Mark knew that Killia would use his new breach with Lisa to strengthen her hold on the girl.

After a moment, Killia turned and gently escorted Lisa back to the Royal tents, leaving Volta to watch Mark speculatively.

Rhea Volta broke the silence. "Watch your step, young Mark. The Princess is not noted for her kindness to traitors." Then Volta turned and followed Killia and Lisa.

"How can I be a traitor?" Mark turned to Ferrel when the trio was out of hearing range. "I'm not even one of her subjects!"

Ferrel, with a worried expression, watched the retreating figures a moment before he answered. "Be careful, Mark. No one knows what Killia's capable of doing."

Chapter 7

"Carr," Diana asked for the third time before she managed to command the sorceress' attention. "Yes?" Carr looked up from the cloth she was avidly studying.

"The barrier they found. Are Mark and Lisa behind it?"

"Yes Diana, along with an army of incalculable size. That is why we are trying to penetrate the area." Carr smiled wearily. Her once smooth and ruddy brown skin was ashen from sleeplessness. She was thin and drawn from exhaustion, and her temper was worsening daily.

"Is that why Lauren spends so much time near the barrier?"

"She gives Alaeric the first reports." Carr was always uncommunicative whenever Lauren's name came up. She retained certain doubts concerning the Olenteas Princess' loyalties, but knew better than to voice them to Diana or even the King.

"How are your studies coming along?" She asked, leaning back in her chair tiredly. "We haven't had much time for review this last week."

"Today I was able to put a freeze on Maril Zan for an entire minute." Diana responded excitedly. "And I got Alaeric's sword to summon a breeze. I used the green crystals."

"Well done. You're doing quite well for one so new to the field. I see fine potential for crystal manipulation in general."

"Carr, are we ever going home?" Diana knew that her parents must be frantic by now. They must have been home three weeks.

"Tarq can send you today if you like."

"But without Lisa and Mark, right?" Diana said sadly. "I can't do that. We have to get them back. I don't suppose that time is passing more slowly there than here is it?"

"No Diana, it's the same."

"So it's really been a month?"

"That's right." Carr smiled placidly.

"I don't understand something, Carr," Diana was hesitant to voice her doubts. Sensing this reluctance, Carr reached out and placed a comforting hand on her protégé's shoulder. Encouraged, Diana continued, "Why are you and King Tarq here and not in Tadia?"

"He has gone back a number of times since your arrival. But to do so he has to use the Tal and take it with him. Only Tarq can fully use it and right now it keeps Sindelar from strengthening the barriers. For the rest of us to use the Tal, Tarq has to be here to release the power."

"I don't get it," Diana was puzzled. "I keep hearing about this Tal, but I never really get a straight answer as to what it is and what it does. All I know is that magic is harder to do without it."

"The Tal is a stone containing enormous power. It is a conduit for all the King's needs. It can pinpoint a path and translate its bearer and his or her chosen to an exact location. It can enhance the power of the other lesser crystals and increase the scope and purpose of spells. At the coronation ceremony the ruler is consecrated to a Tal and its total array of powers are revealed to him or her. While others can use a Tal to the upper limits of their abilities and enhance their powers somewhat, only one consecrated to a Tal can tap its total potential.

"In our case, that's King Tarq. Each world has a Tal. It's a gift of the Gods. Some Tals are in use, others lost, still others not yet found. But all of them contain immense sources of power. Dal Ryeas' Tal is old and focused. Through the King's bounty, Dal Ryean sorcerers can share in its power. So the Tal is the foundation for all our power. Because Tarq is generous with sharing that power, Dal Ryean wizards have been able to increase their skills. Other places and even other rulers in Dal Ryeas history, keep the power solely for personal uses."

"What if it's never found?" Diana asked. "I mean, you said that there were places where a Tal has never been found."

"Then a vast power exists for the taking of whoever finds it,"

Carr smiled. "But not to worry, as long as Tarq holds Dal Ryeas' Tal, we're fairly safe."

"What if Sindelar were to find a Tal or somehow steal Dal Ryeas' Tal?"

"Then we're all in a lot of trouble. Sindelar learned much from King Philos on using a Tal. He could effectively cut us off from Tadia, even without a consecration of the stone to Killia." Carr smiled and got up. "It's late. Let's eat some supper and then see what the captains have to report."

Carr and Diana arrived at the King's pavilion, where only the King and Prince Alaeric were present. There was evidence of a hurried meal, pushed half-eaten to the side of the table, while the two men poured over a map of the area. The map was a scaled drawing of the northwest quadrant. A barrier was been drawn and on the far side of the barrier, Sindelar's camp was depicted in full detail.

Alaeric and the King were quietly arguing the best strategies to breach the barrier and take the camp. They broke off their conversation as the King focused his attention on Diana.

"I'm glad you are here, Mistress Diana. It is to you that I particularly wish to speak." The King is very formal tonight, Diana thought, this can only mean trouble.

"We are on the verge of battle," Tarq continued, indicating the map, "and I cannot ensure your safety. Therefore, I wish to send you home."

Diana gasped, but having sensed this was coming, had her answer prepared. "I'm sorry, sir," she
said, "but I can't go home without Mark and Lisa. My family would never forgive me."

"And we'd never forgive ourselves if anything were to happen to you," rumbled Alaeric, "We are very fond of you and we want you safe."

"Not without them," Diana objected. "My parents—"

"Exactly. Your parents, they must be sick with dread by now. It's been weeks."

"Only one, sir," Diana interrupted. "They just got home. Maybe they haven't even noticed." Alaeric looked at her in disbelief.

"I cannot deprive them of all their children. I must send you back."

"With all due respect, sir, I can't go home without Mark and Lisa. I'd rather be here in battle with you than try to explain to my folks that I left them here to some ghastly fate. They'd never believe me."

"If you are worried about being believed, Carr will accompany you to show your parents the veracity of your claims. Although," he looked at her softly, "You'd be surprised what they'll believe."

"Even more reason for me not to abandon them," Diana was near tears. "I was raised to stand by our own. Mark has always been there for me. When we were young, Mark defended me against anyone who would've bothered me. As long as he's in danger or being held against his will, I can't leave him."

"And Lisa?

"She's my baby sister," Diana brushed her eyes, "And I've always taken care of her. She may be spoiled and somewhat cocky, but to leave her here, to abandon her or Mark, I can't. Even if I never go home again, I can't leave them…"

Tarq looked at Alaeric and motioned for his war leader to say something. Before he could say anything, a new voice entered the discussion.

"Very eloquent, Diana," Everyone turned to see Lauren still dressed in her midnight blue scouting leathers, leaning against the front tent post. "I'm glad to see that you are realizing your responsibility. It's important to understand this."

Tarq stood up and tried to sound casual, "We did not expect you back so soon, Lauren. Come in. Tell us how you are faring in the forest."

Smiling, Lauren strolled across the tent. Diana was reminded of the elegant movements of a wild cat as she approached. She realized suddenly that this woman was not the same as the one who had lived next door to them on the edgeworld. Even her smile, which once was so wistful and sad, now radiated confidence and triumph.

Diana understood that this side of Lauren was the one that she always hid at home. This was the true Lauren - the suppressed one, the mysterious one. The Lauren of the junk food suppers, the games, and the fancy costumes was only a facade. Instead she was a sleek, powerful woman of authority and wisdom. Seeing Diana's troubled expression, the old Lauren, who was only a tiny facet of the regal woman before her, smiled and gently patted her shoulder. This familiar gesture lightened the girl's expression although her words did not.

"Although I agree, she should be sent home," she said, pretending not to notice Diana's mutinous look. "I don't think we can afford the luxury. Sindelar has been waiting for Tarq to use the Tal so he can order a sneak attack and steal it."

"How did you learn this?" Alaeric demanded.

"Oh, well, we are now in possession of a double agent." She replied, a little uneasily.

"Who?"

"Merrick Dracos Olenteas."

"Merrick?" said Alaeric. "But his father is one of our father's loyalists."

"Was. The father died in exile four years ago. Merrick and his younger brother, Ferrel, were with him. One of Sindelar's rift winds trapped them about two years ago at Morsea. When Sindelar came here, he brought them along. Merrick doesn't know why. But Sindelar holds Ferrel as surety for Merrick's behavior and loyalty. Ferrel now shares a tent with Mark. Lisa has been 'adopted' as a pet to Killia. According to Merrick, it amuses her to have a living doll and it keeps her from active interference with Sindelar's activities. He says Killia is beginning to deteriorate, so his guess is that Sindelar will have to move quickly."

"How can we believe him?" Carr asked amazed with the amount of information Lauren had obtained.

"You mean you don't trust your own nephew, enchantress?" Lauren replied snidely. "He gave me his blood-oath. Merrick is now mine, and will do my bidding." She smiled at Carr.

Carr gave Lauren a cold look. "So what. That may be of some benefit to you but since we are not certain of your loyalties, what benefit is it to us?"

"Enough!" Tarq shouted, startling everyone, especially Carr. "You made me doubt Lauren's loyalty to the crown once, but you'll never be able to do so again. I know of Merrick Olenteas' oath and have given my approval."

Carr squirmed uncomfortably under the angry gaze of the King.

Alaeric grinned, raising his glass and saluting his cousin as she continued her report as if the entire interchange with Carr had not occurred.

"He will try to get word to Mark and Lisa that you're here, Diana, and that they should try to come to us. I only wish he could get Ferrel out as well. Maybe he can."

Even without his assertion that he knew of the agent, it was apparent none of this was news to the King. On the very night she had sworn Merrick Olenteas to the cause, Lauren came to his tent, well after midnight, not for the reasons he would have preferred, but to tell him of this new spy. It was a triumph for her. Not only had she turned a traitor's son into an unquestioning ally, and found the missing pair's location, but she had gained a spy in Sindelar's camp.

Thus, she had performed her duty to her Kingdom and had proved her loyalty to the crown. But the cool, formal way in which she had delivered her news to him, even in the dead of night, had dampened his excitement over her presence in his tent and had effectively thwarted his hopes of discussing other matters closer to his heart.

"Why are you trusting this man?"' Diana asked, still upset. "You said he was working for Sindelar."

"Under duress, Diana. They are holding his brother hostage."

"Well, he could be lying, right?"

"Not if he willingly gave Lauren an Olenteas blood-oath," Tarq interjected.

"I don't get it." Diana declared. "Why should he swear on blood and not be lying?"

"Olenteas' is the only clan who uses this oath," Tarq explained, "and it is given only when there is no choice." He looked at Lauren steadily as he spoke. *She seems so pleased with herself,* he thought, *I have not seen her smile like this in so long.* "What else does Merrick report?"

"There seems to be an unusual type of activity near the barriers. It is not ours—and certainly not Sindelar's work. Whoever is there is very good at placing barriers within barriers."

"Wonderful, now we have an unknown to deal with," Tarq grumbled.

"Don't worry, my King"'" Lauren answered blithely. "It can't be any worse than the known."

Chapter 8

"Come, young Lisa," Princess Killia smiled, "I have an errand for you to run. And you'd love to escape practice, I suspect."

Lisa, dutifully trying to learn to play the siganhar, a small harp-shaped instrument that seemed like a cross between an autoharp and a balalaika, looked up gratefully at the excuse of exercise. She enjoyed being with the Princess, but felt much of the freedom she was used to disappearing as she took on more duties for her Highness.

Even though she had spent much of her time alone at home, there were many more distractions there than here. She discovered the few occasions she tried to learn some of the bow work or sword play that seemed so engrossing to Mark, the Princess became annoyed. Killia wanted her ladies available and compliant. After a few feeble attempts of asserting her independence, Lisa fell smartly into line and earned only the Princess' praise. She enjoyed being cosseted, but it was with relief that she learned of her errand, freeing her for awhile from Killia's stultifying regulations.

"Lord Sindelar sent word of a trouble spot near the barrier. He has gone to investigate this. I have, however, an urgent message for him, so I'm sending you to him. You will be accompanied by the soldiers waiting outside." The Princess smiled, handing her a sealed envelope. "You'd better hurry. It's very important."

Lisa awkwardly curtsied and left the tent. She found the troop waiting and with Sergeant Orado in the lead they immediately left for their destination.

Mark was once again on the practice grounds with the sword mistress and Ferrel when the Princess' summons came. The two young men exchanged worried looks as Mark put up his sword. Ferrel looked at his friend, "What do you think she wants?"

"Nothing good, I expect." Mark grimaced. "As soon as I find out, I'll tell you."

Ferrel touched his friend's arm. "Be careful. Merrick says not to trust her."

"Funny advice from a spy," Mark said, trying for a momentary lightness but quickly became serious, "I'm scared, Ferrel, believe me..." Then clapping Ferrel's shoulder, he hurried towards the Princess' tents.

He could hear her wails of distress before he even entered the tent. Hesitant, he knocked lightly on the tent post. Rhea Volta, looking grim and somber, pulled the pavilion's flap open and bid him to enter.

Killia, looking distraught, was leaning on her arm in a pose of utter dejection. Her hair was loosened and falling in a tangle down her back. Her clothing, usually crisply formal, was limp and hanging awkwardly about her. Her carefully applied cosmetics slashed by tear stains and her eyes red-rimmed from weeping.

When she saw Mark, she began to weep wildly. Her ladies fluttered about her helplessly like directionless chickens, trying to comfort her. Captain Volta, leaving Mark's side, strode through the ineffectual maids and patted the Princess awkwardly.

"Oh Rhea," Killia said in a low voice throbbing with emotion. "I cannot tell him. You must do this for me."

"Yes, my Queen." Volta stated quietly.

Throughout the entire exchange, Mark felt himself observing an elaborate staging. Although everything seemed based in reality, there was a sense of mendacity permeating the whole performance. With Volta's next words, Mark felt himself drawn unwillingly into the play.

"Princess Killia received what she believed was a real communiqué from Lord Sindelar. He requested that one of her ladies come to him with a valuable crystal to aid in strengthening the barrier between us and the enemy."

Killia groaned. "I only sent her because she was so bored. I thought the fresh air and an adventure to the borders would cheer her up." Killia's tears began anew.

Captain Volta, standing stiffly by the Princess, patted her shoulders awkwardly. "There, there your Highness, how were you to know the message was false?"

"What happened? Is it Lisa?" Mark still suspected a ruse, but felt he had to ask.

"Be brave, young Mark," Volta said seriously. "We fear Lisa has been taken by Tarq's spies."

"What? How?" Mark exclaimed. "I thought we were protected from them by this much vaunted barrier."

"We fear infiltration. Not an hour since your sister left with the crystal did we receive word that Lord Sindelar will be here within the hour. The Princess scryed a crystal and there was no sign of Lisa."

"How long has she been gone? Why didn't you send me with her?"

"I'm sorry. I didn't think it would be dangerous." Killia sobbed. "I thought she'd enjoy it."

"Not dangerous? We're in the middle of a war, not a garden party. And why the hell would they take her?"

"It wasn't Lisa they wanted, but the crystal," Volta spoke up, "They would've seized whoever took it. Lisa's capture was incidental."

"What can we do?"

"I'm leaving in a few moments to attempt to track them and rescue her. Why don't you come with me? She may need you after her ordeal." She gave him a smile that chilled him to the bone.

"I'll go get my things," Mark said gruffly. "I want my sister back."

"Hurry boy," Volta said as he left. "I'll be at your tent in ten minutes."

As Mark left the pavilion, Killia's expression changed suddenly, scrunching into a masque of hatred. "Remember, Volta," she said through clenched teeth, "I want him dead before dusk..."

The young man rushed from the pavilion and raced headlong through the camp to his tent. Ferrel was still outside. Mark still felt uneasy about the situation and knew the Princess and her Captain were lying about something. "What if they're telling the truth?" he thought, "What if something did happen? She's your responsibility. You have to find out."

Against his better judgment, he decided he had to accompany the Captain. Being a cautious young man, however, he quickly wrote a note to Ferrel.

'The Princess told me Lisa has been kidnapped by Tarq's men, which if true is probably not a bad thing. But if she is in trouble she may need me. I have gone with Volta to find her. I don't trust this, Ferrel. It seems too convenient. It's too easy to get rid of us both but I think they want me out of the way... If I don't come back, find out what really happened, please. Take care of Lisa for me please. In spite of everything, I do love her and want her to be safe and happy. — Mark

Frantically Mark searched for a place to put the where Ferrel could find it, but would remain hidden from any other prying eyes. Hearing Volta outside the tent, he thrust the note under Ferrel's pillow with a tiny end sticking out.

When Volta entered, she found Mark calmly strapping on a knife and picking up his crossbow and quarrels. Before she could scan the room, Mark blocked her view by walking up in front of her. "I'm ready Captain. Shall we go?"

Not able to think of a reason to stay, Volta nodded and led the way out to the horses.

Mark still felt awkward on horseback, but better than his first ride a month earlier. Volta impatiently rode ahead of him trying to keep her feisty horse from bolting.

Just as Mark was getting his mount under control, Ferrel came around the corner. He tried to wave Mark down, but Volta's imperious command stopped him. "Ride, Harrison, there will be time for your friends after we rescue your sister." Ferrel looked askance at her tone.

Catching Ferrel's eye, Mark mouthed, "Pillow." Volta, unable to hear with he said, angrily tried to block Ferrel's view of Mark with her horse. The younger boy smiled and nodded in understanding and Mark felt a little better. Volta rode off and he followed her with a quick wave to his friend.

Ferrel watched them disappear into the woods, and then he turned and entered the tent where he found the note thrust under his pillow. He was still sitting on his cot a half hour later, staring at the note and trying to figure out what to do, when Merrick entered

"Hey little brother," Merrick said, smiling. "Why the sad face?"

"Merrick!" Ferrel cried joyfully, looking up. "You're all right?"

"Just fine." Merrick grinned and hugged the boy, sprawling out beside him on the cot. "What's wrong? You look gloomier than when you got bad grades in school."

"Merrick...," Ferrel hesitated.

"Yes?" Merrick smiled reassuringly. Since Ferrel was a boy, throughout their exile he had confided in him. Merrick knew that since their father had died, he was Ferrel's only emotional support. All of his own actions were to ensure Ferrel's safety. Sensing his brother's reluctance, Merrick decided to encourage his confidence.

"Before you tell me what's troubling you, Ferrel, I want you to know something," he began casually. Walking to the door of the tent, he looked out to see if anyone was near. "I've sworn a blood-oath to Lauren Olenteas. I am now bonded to Tarq's cause."

"Oh Gods," whispered Ferrel. "Then you are spying for Tarq. I thought so!"

"I'm going to try and get you out of here as soon as I can." Merrick approached his brother and sat down beside him, placing a hand on his shoulder. "I don't trust this wizard or his Princess. And I think maybe they don't trust me either." Merrick chuckled. "With some justification, I suppose, I've always had my doubts as to their cause. Pyramus has ruled justly. Father was wrong not to change his allegiance." Merrick worried how Ferrel would react to this obvious slur on his cherished memories.

"I know. I've been doing a lot of thinking while you've been away. There's something not quite right going on here."

"What is it?" Merrick had come to respect Ferrel's assessments. During their years wandering the edgeworlds, he had always been able to determine if a situation was really what it appeared, or if there were something not quite right about it. On more than a few occasions, the younger Dracos kept his older brother safe from harm.

"Everything is wrong about this. It's as if... Killia has taken someone essentially wise and noble, like Sindelar, and made him come down to her level. I like the wizard, but there is something not quite right about this whole place. All Princess Killia cares about is having her own way. Like with Mark. I know she is trying to hurt him, but I am not certain what she means to do."

"Mark - the boy who shares this tent?" Merrick sat up.

"Uh-huh. He and his sister sort of arrived in the forest," Ferrel explained, ""They got caught in a path maelstrom and were drawn here during Sindelar's spell. And now I think Mark is in danger because Killia wants to keep Lisa. And the Princess wants no other influence on the girl than her own."

"What do you mean?" Merrick asked.

Ferrel explained the scene he had witnessed with Mark and Volta earlier. "And when I came back here I found his note, Mark was already gone. But Merrick, I saw his sister, Lisa riding out with Sergeant Orado and a couple other of Volta's crew about half an hour before. I was coming from the practice fields and they were going in the opposite direction than where Volta took Mark."

Merrick picked up the note, scanning it over. "I think your friend is in deep trouble. I'll try to track them." He rose from the cot. "Whatever you do, don't let on to them you suspect anything. You're a hostage to my good behavior."

"When do we get out of here?" Ferrel asked. "I hate this place. I wish we were still in the edges."

"I don't know. Lauren wants me to try and find out when Sindelar plans to move." Merrick grimaced. "We'd better find your friend and his sister and take them to Tarq. His other sister is there waiting."

"What do you mean?" Ferrel was confused. "Mark's sister, Diana? Mark told me about her. But what is she doing in the King's camp?"

"Well, it seems that they were friends of Lauren and Alaeric in exile. Alaeric marked the path with blood and followed Mark and Lisa when they traveled across the maelstrom. Diana came with them to help." Merrick went on to explain what he promised Lauren.

"I think Lauren wants to reunite them and send them home before all hell breaks loose. I was supposed to get news of this to Mark." Merrick frowned and turned to the tent flap. "Alright, I have to report to Sindelar. Be careful, don't let on that you suspect anything, and destroy that note."

When Merrick had gone, Ferrel felt suddenly chilled. He crossed his arms and began to pace. Instead of burning the note, he hid it in the hollow of his boot heel. He knew Lisa and she was the type who would only heed concrete evidence. Sudden fears for Merrick replaced the ones he had for Mark. He felt trapped in an untenable situation and saw no way to his freedom.

"Well, anyway," he said aloud to his tent walls. "At least I'll try to look after the girl."

Mark rode in worried silence beside Rhea Volta. He did not trust this woman. Even though she was the first person he had met on this world, her relationship to the Princess gave him inexplicable reasons to fear her. He held her partly responsible for driving the wedge between Lisa and him.

"Captain," he said after an hour or so of hard riding. "Aren't we closer to them?"

"I think so. Here, let's get down and check the ground." She got off her horse and knelt by the path side.

Mark dismounted and began to look around. The path ran along the edge of a steep tree-filled ravine. Even in his anxiety, he wondered at the ability of trees to sprout from the side of a cliff. A stream was gently flowing at the ravine's bottom. The woods around him seemed unnaturally quiet. He half turned to where Volta had stood and realized that she had silently moved and was now behind him. She had a long knife drawn in her hand. Its edge reflected the sunlight streaming through the trees and shone directly in his eyes. The glare was enough to blind him.

Mark started to back away, but she was too quick for him. She grabbed him around the neck with one arm, while stabbing him brutally in the side. He cried out in agony, as she pulled the blade out and stabbed again. With another cry, he broke her hold and staggered to the edge of the ravine.

Volta stalked him, knife held low. He glanced behind him, his fingers clutching at his wounds, blood pouring down his clothing. Volta's menacing form was coming nearer. Closing his eyes, he stepped back, over the edge of the ravine.

As his foot slipped, a wave of pain shot through him. He never felt himself falling until he struck a tree and the direction of his fall took a turn towards the stream. His last sight was that of

Volta, dispassionately watching him fall as she stood at the edge of the ravine. Then he felt the cool water of the stream against him and finally nothing.

Lisa accompanied Lord Sindelar back to camp. She was confused as to why she had to deliver a crystal to him when he was obviously on his way back, but then at times she thought that the Princess' demands seemed silly. Lisa quickly learned that thwarting Killia brought on temper tantrums and sulks that made everything unbearable. She was embarrassed at times, because it reminded herself of her own fits when involved in fights with her brother.

Sindelar was also confused by Lisa's errand. Killia's urgent message and delivery was incomprehensible. He felt a vague sense of foreboding as his entourage entered the encampment. Everything seemed normal. Yet… why was Ferrel seated on the edge of the practice field watching their arrival, staring at Lisa in open amazement? Glancing at the girl by his side, Sindelar could see she was oblivious to Ferrel's scrutiny. Scanning the area quickly, his senses tingling in mild anger,

Sindelar searched for Mark. Not seeing him anywhere, he instinctively knew something was wrong and it concerned Lisa's brother.

"Damn that woman," he muttered under his breath and spurred his horse into a canter leaving a puzzled Lisa and entourage behind. When he reached the Princess' pavilion, he flung himself from the saddle and strode angrily into the tent.

"What have you done?" he roared at the startled Princess and her favorite guard, who were sitting casually at tea.

"What do you mean?" the Princess whined in surprise.

"Tell me quickly before the girl arrives!" the wizard was furious. "What have you done?"

"I've rid us of her brother," the Princess retorted smugly.

"You fool!" snarled the wizard. 'The girl—"

"The girl is mine, Sindelar," Killia asserted. 'Without her brother, she becomes even more my own. Nothing will distract her now. She will want to stay here forever!" Killia was inordinately pleased with herself.

Rhea Volta leaned against the Princess, subtly taunting the sorcerer, "Why worry, my Lord, the Princess knows what she

93

wants."

"And when she tires of the child?" Sindelar asked. "What becomes of her then?"

"That is not my concern." Volta replied airily and took another biscuit.

"Then whose—" But before the magician could complete the thought, the sound of Lisa's horse was heard stopping outside the tent. She was laughing as she dismounted.

"Are you with me?" hissed the Princess, beginning to shed false tears. Morosely the wizard nodded, seeing no alternative.

By the time Lisa entered the pavilion; Killia had worked herself into hysterics and was weeping wildly. Volta was pretending to comfort her, as Sindelar stood nearby, arms folded and scowling.

Lisa, seeing the Princess' distress, rushed to her side and fell to her knees beside her. "My lady, what is wrong? Please let me help you!" Lisa cried out earnestly.

Killia looked up, saw Lisa, and clutched her in a fierce embrace. "Oh my child, how can I tell you?" Killia wailed. "How can I be the one to tell you?"

"Tell me what?" Lisa was suddenly frightened.

"It's your brother..." Killia began to weep again.

"What about Mark?" Lisa was thinking that somehow Mark had gotten into trouble and that now she about to be sent away.

"He... He" the Princess, unable to continue, pointed to Volta.

Captain Volta, very formally and distantly announced, "We regret that we must inform you that your brother, Mark Harrison, has met with a tragic accident and subsequently has died."

"No," Lisa choked back tears, "Th-that's not true." She looked around her wildly.

Killia, still holding her tightly, said in a broken voice. "He was lured away by an enemy. Volta tried to save him, but she was too late. He fell down a deep ravine, so she couldn't even bring him back."

"You left him there? You just... left him?" Lisa broke from the Princess' embrace and launched herself at Volta. The Captain caught her by the wrists and nearly lost her as she fiercely struggled, crying hysterically, "Mark, oh Mark! No!"

Killia briefly regretted her actions as she watched the weeping girl. Then she rapidly put the thoughts aside. Lisa would get over this and be more her creation than before.

Finally, disgusted with the entire drama played before him and out of pity for the child, Sindelar came forward. Volta was holding Lisa's hands away from her eyes and trying to control the girl physically when Sindelar put his hand on the girl's forehead.

"Sleep. Forget for a little while."

Lisa slumped in Volta's arms weakly. Gently, the wizard took her from the Captain and lifted her up into his arms. Without a word to the Princess, he carried her from the tent.

Ferrel was waiting outside the Princess' tent. "Sir, may I help?" the boy said diffidently. "Why, young Ferrel?" Sindelar paused. "What concern is this girl of yours?"

"Her brother shares my tent and..." he began, not sure how to continue.

"No longer. The enemy lured him away and murdered him. Captain Volta followed, but was unable to save him."

"Mark... dead, sir?" Ferrel whispered in horror.

The wizard looked at the unconscious girl in his arms still shedding tears even in her induced sleep. He turned with her towards his own tent. "Yes. Now go. I need to attend to her." Sindelar turned back and said, "Oh and Ferrel when next you see Merrick, tell him from me that his reports must come to me first, before he gives them to Volta or the Princess. Do you understand?"

"Y-yes, sir." Alarmed at Sindelar's implications, he watched as the wizard carried Lisa into his tent. For long moments he stood standing by the Princess' tent. He had seen Volta and Mark leave together, but would Volta let Mark go off by himself? Moreover, would Mark, still so timid of his new surroundings, want to leave Volta's side to explore? He had never felt so helpless in his entire life. He slowly walked away from the pavilions and returned to his own small tent, fervently praying for Merrick's safe return and his own escape.

Chapter 9

Diana was happy. For the first time she felt unique and not part of a crowd. She was finally separate of the hodge-podge of half siblings like Alexis or Joe or her full siblings like Mark and Lisa. Each of her siblings rightfully received attention from their parents, only there never seemed to be enough time for any individual concern for anyone. But here, in King Tarq's camp amidst his soldiers and advisors, she felt special. She was part of the King's inner circle, due to her friendship with Lauren and Alaeric. She was also Sorceress Carr's newest apprentice, learning the intricacies of magic.

In some ways she realized she was a living amulet for the King's forces and a signal of his victory. Her need had returned their invincible War leader to them. When it spread through the camp that both Warleader Alaeric and the King were overseeing her weapons training, old veterans gave her helpful advice as to how to fight to her best advantage.

The scouts taught her wood-craft, while Tarq's personal guards gave her lessons in Dal Ryean games of luck. She had even made friends with a young officer named Maril Zan, and whenever the two young women were free from other duties, they shared secrets and laughed together like childhood friends. She was enjoying herself immensely. Even her concern for Mark and Lisa did not interfere in the pleasure she had in her situation.

One day as she sat outside her tent with Lauren, she mused. "There are times when I never want to go home…"

"Oh?" said Lauren, surprised. "Why is that, Diana?"

"Because I feel special here," she sighed and looked around her.

"Diana, that's silly. You're special wherever you are."

"I don't mean... What I mean is that I feel right, as if this were more my home than home is." Diana smiled. "I guess I'm angling for an invitation to stay forever."

"Wouldn't you miss your family?" Lauren frowned.

"I don't really know. I mean, you can always visit home. But there comes a time to leave anyway, right?" Diana was warming up to her subject. "The early settlers and immigrants left everyone behind and they never went back."

"Diana, this place is not home. This is just an unsettled part of the Dal Ryean sub-continent. We are a long way from Tadia." Lauren frowned and knelt down in front of her. "I'm glad you're enjoying your stay with us. I was concerned about you when the days lengthened to weeks and we were no closer to rescuing Mark and Lisa, but you've adjusted beautifully to all this. Someday, the King will have to force the issue and then a battle will begin from which we cannot retreat. Right now, Tarq is ruling in absentia, through his council and occasional forays home. But he can't stay away from Tadia forever, so we're going to have to force Killia and Sindelar to make a move. And then it will get ugly."

"I understand all that Lauren. But don't you see I've found somewhere to feel loyal. I was just drifting along dating guys, trying to decide what college to go to, being uninvolved. If someone fell down in front of me, sure I'd help him up, but would I really care? No way. But suddenly I'm here and I'm truly a part of this. I care. I want to study with Carr. She was telling me of the University of Tadia and that it was devoted to the study of magic. I want to go there. I'm really alive here and when I am practicing the spells Carr is teaching me, I never want to lose this feeling again." Diana's earnest plea was accompanied by emphatic arm gestures, one of which nearly struck Lauren.

"So I see." Lauren grinned wryly. 'Well, there's a long road ahead of us, and we know where it leads." She hesitated for a moment, watching Diana through half-closed eyes. Finally she spoke again. "I probably shouldn't tell you this, but it may help you to understand why you have these feelings about Dal Ryeas."

"What? Tell me?" Diana listened intently.

"Didn't you ever wonder why of all the empty houses in the world, Alaeric and I chose the one next door to you?"

"Because it was for sale?" Diana said.

"No, silly," Lauren laughed, heartily. Diana laughed in spite of herself. Not only had she adjusted well to this place, but also she was equally pleased to see Lauren so happy.

"Because your mother arranged for us to acquire it." Lauren smiled and winked at her.

"My mother?" Diana was confused. "Why would she have anything..." her voice trailed away, realization dawning in her eyes already.

"How many relatives do you know on your mother's side of the family?"

"Wh— just Aunt —, no she's dad's cousin. Well, none, I guess."

Lauren grinned, "Do you remember when I was telling you about the first revolt, the one thirty years ago? Well, your mother is of the Olenteas clan and she chose to leave Dal Ryeas rather than betray her clan or her friend, who was Tarq's father Prince Tyrmandos. She was unable to swear loyalty to Tyrmandos' father without betraying her own father, so she chose to leave instead of being forced into a terrible bind. Our family wizard located her years ago, and when Alaeric and I went into exile; he got word to us where she was. I suppose so we wouldn't feel entirely alone." Lauren chuckled, "We're distant cousins, you and I, Diana."

"Wh-why didn't she ever tell us?"

"Would you have believed her?"

"Well, no, I guess not." Diana grew pensive. "Do you think Mark and Lisa feel the same way about this place?"

"According to Merrick, your brother is unhappy, while your sister is the pet of the Princess. She is probably very happy."

"Poor Lisa. She always has to be somebody's pet. Even when we were little, Alexis and I used to baby her. She loves that kind of attention." Diana laughed bitterly. "It used to drive Mark crazy. Joe and Alexis always took Lisa's side and it made Mark feel awful. Lisa never really cared for Mark". Diana paused, "Joe and Alexis are the children of my father's first marriage, you know, and they always made Mark feel like an outsider.

"So Mark was essentially isolated, except for me. He and I were close but Lisa hated it when I paid attention to Mark, and she made certain that we all knew it. Her voice could be very penetrating and her tantrums unbelievable. Sometimes it was just better to ignore Mark than have to deal with Lisa. It was all very difficult. And now Lisa's with Mark. What a joke!"

"I hope she doesn't try to be assertive or spoiled," Lauren frowned, "Killia has a very short attention span and a low tolerance for anyone other than herself getting attention. When she came to Dal Ryeas for her father's funeral, she was so arrogant and unbearable that we all tried to avoid her. Except poor Tarq, who as the host was stuck entertaining her." Lauren laughed.

Lauren rose suddenly. "Enough of this. Why I looked you up this morning is to ask if you want to come out today. One of the scouts thinks that you might be able to breach the barrier from this side."

"Why?" Diana asked curiously.

"You aren't of our world – entirely."

"Is that why Merrick can come and go?" Diana casually brought up his name. Two days earlier she had met Merrick Dracos Olenteas when he reported in to Lauren. She liked him. He seemed so hurt and alone. She had an urge to ease that loneliness. Merrick's long dark hair, his sad but handsome face, tanned skin, and his shadowed brown eyes had haunted her dreams the last two nights. She found herself musing about him whenever she was alone.

She had once tried to ask Carr questions about him, but received only short answers stating that she and Merrick's mother were half-sisters and not close. Merrick, she relented finally, was a kind, loyal boy with a strong sense of family. Diana liked that quality a lot.

"Merrick," Lauren said, smiling knowingly at Diana's blush at the mention of his name, "was specially enchanted by Sindelar to be able to avoid the barrier spell. Carr tries to study him whenever he is here to discover what's allowing him to let him pass unscathed.

Diana inwardly melted, thinking how lucky Carr was to be so close to him.

"But it's a very delicate operation because we don't want

99

Sindelar to suspect tampering."

"What's he like, this Sindelar?" For weeks this magician had kept everything at a standstill. Tarq was unable to penetrate the spell, even with the Tal enhancing Carr's powers.

"In a word, brilliant. He's probably the most talented enchanter of our age. They say when he was born the goddess, Sarama, personally blessed him with a visitation. Within days of his birth, the King took him away from his parents and had him raised with his own son, Philos."

"He was given the best teachers, and by the time Sindelar was fifteen, he was the brightest star of at the University. Even our Carr was in awe of him. He was on his way to being the best wizard of all the path worlds. It was at this time, however, that Prince Philos, Sindelar's foster brother, began to show signs of his instability and Sindelar stayed with him. Even when the King was beginning his excesses, Sindelar tried to save Philos from the worst of them.

"He managed to spirit the King away from Leas Pyramus and arranged for him to marry an exiled Dal Ryean girl and father a child. Then he cared for him until the King died raving. What more can I say? He is now our most fearsome enemy, as well as being loyal, noble, and talented. It's such a waste." Lauren smiled sadly, shaking her head at the injustice of the universes. "We'd better go. I promised to meet one of the scouts before noon."

Diana followed the Princess, thinking about all she had been told. There was a gnawing fear for her brother and sister captive in the hands of the brilliant Sindelar, but a growing anxiety for Merrick beginning as well. She really felt drawn to the man and wanted to learn more about him.

"Let's try to breach this magician's barrier," Diana said suddenly as they were walking, feeling very brave and confident. She earned a grin from Lauren and an arm put around her shoulders, briefly.

The forest seemed preternaturally silent around the barrier. Now that they were aware of it, Tarq's scouts were amazed that they had missed it. In attempts to misdirect Sindelar's spies from them, only a small number of Tarq's personnel were in the area at any time. Lauren was primarily responsible for this barrier work, carefully keeping a decoy scouting force searching the rest of the forest. Merrick reported that other spies were content that the barrier remained inviolate and were focusing their efforts on other areas of concern to Sindelar. Merrick identified them all and a campaign of misdirection was underway.

Diana nervously looked at what seemed to be a regular portion of the forest. She felt an aversion to the dark looming trees around her and started to turn back. But Lauren's arm on her shoulders stopped her.

"It's the spell. It will pass." Lauren said reassuringly. "You'll feel all right in a few minutes."

"That's the barrier?" Diana asked wonderingly.

"Yes. Merrick is due to cross through in a little while." Lauren saw Diana's cheeks color again and inwardly smiled. "When Merrick comes, I want you to try to cross over with him. I figure if he's holding you, then you'll have a better than average chance of success. Try to remember, the way Carr taught you, how you feel as you pass through. It may give us a hint of the composition."

"Alright." Diana was a bit skeptical. Holding Merrick's hand as they passed through might very well mix her feelings into a jumble, but she didn't dare say this aloud to Lauren. Instead she did a quick mental review of the sensation exercises that Carr had taught her. *"In order to understand how to create, it is necessary to understand the already created. Sight, sound, touch, taste, smell, as well as an intrinsic understanding of the composition beyond are all fundamental lessons in the nature of the universes. Everything is different and you must learn how it relates to the forces within you, and then how to manipulate it."* Diana could hear Carr's voice repeating the lessons. She smiled wryly at the recollection and turned her attention to Lauren.

A faint shimmer broke through the shadows of the forest, and then Merrick was there. He seemed surprised and saddened with Diana's presence. He smiled bleakly at them and approached.

"My Lady," he said, bowing to Lauren, and then turned to Diana. "Greetings, Diana," he said, awkwardly. "Princess, may I speak with you? Alone?"

"Of course. Excuse us, Diana." She drew Merrick to one side by some trees. "Alright, what's wrong?"

"Lauren, Ferrel told me that Mark Harrison was murdered two days ago by Killia's henchwoman, Volta, and that they've convinced the girl Lisa, that we were responsible."

"Oh… gods," Lauren put a hand to her mouth, tears welling already. "That poor boy, he never had a chance against that butcher." She glanced over at Diana. "Come Merrick, help me tell her. Oh, the poor girl…"

Diana immediately sensed something wrong. As Lauren and Merrick returned to her, a flash of insight told her something was the matter with Mark. Before either spoke she said, "Something's happened to Mark, hasn't it?"

Lauren put her arm around the girl's shoulder. "I'm sorry, Diana. I'm so sorry. Mark's been killed by Killia."

"No… " Diana said in a low passionate voice."He's not dead…"

"My brother, Ferrel, was told by Lord Sindelar himself that Mark was dead," Merrick replied uncomfortably, "Sindelar, said that we had done it, but Ferrel saw Mark ride away with Princess Killia's personal assassin, Rhea Volta, and only Volta returned."

"No, I'm telling you that Mark isn't dead," Diana declared with unshakable certainty. "He may be hurt or hiding or even unconscious, but he isn't dead. I'd know it."

Lauren asked her. "Are you certain? Is this wishful thinking or do you actually know this?"

Earnestly, Diana tried to explain. "There are times – there have always been times when I feel them – my family, and nothing has changed. Mark is still there, same as Lisa. Carr taught me how to do this. Please believe me. He's not dead. I'd know it!"

Merrick spoke slowly. "Volta did not bring back the body. We really have no proof. Mistress Diana, I believe you. I'll try to find him for you."

Lauren spoke sharply. "Merrick, you cannot do everything yourself. You'll endanger all of us. Engage Ferrel in the search." Merrick looked startled.

Suddenly very much a princess, Lauren continued. "We must try to breach this barrier soon. Maybe whomever we sensed hiding behind this wall is aiding Mark or Mark is wandering around wounded in the lost places of this forest. Diana, are you willing to try? Time grows ever more precious."

Without answering, Diana walked over to Merrick and took his hand. "Take me through, Merrick. Let's see if we can end this."

Merrick stared at the slight young woman standing beside him. Her large blue eyes captured his. For the first time in years he felt warmth and admiration for someone other than kin. He began to imagine a future when he was home on Dal Ryeas and able to court this independent and intelligent young woman freely and openly.

Diana, in her scrutiny of Merrick, saw the hidden pain and strength, the overwhelming sense of honesty and nobility and *really* wanted to get to know him. She too had a fleeting image of a future, free of stress, where they could grow towards intimacy.

"Do you think we could try to do this today?" Lauren's voice interrupted their mutual reverie.

Merrick smiled. "Shall we?"

Diana nodded nervously.

They warily approached the barrier, Diana tightly clutching Merrick's hand. Slightly ahead, Merrick walked through backwards while gently pulling Diana with him. Holding both her hands and staring directly into her eyes, they both penetrated the barrier. After a moment's hesitation Diana followed, seeming to flow through on a cloud.

Lauren watched them disappear and felt a surge of relief. There was a way. Then she sat down to wait. She figured from what she had seen earlier, they were going to spend some time "getting acquainted".

"I wish I had brought a book," she muttered as she settled herself comfortably against a tree trunk for a long afternoon's wait.

Quite a while later they reappeared. Diana appeared somewhat disheveled and Merrick flushed and breathless.

"I hate to break this up, but I've got to get Diana back to Carr to interpret what happened." Lauren couldn't help the wicked grin.

"And I have to get back to Ferrel. My brother and I will try to find out what really happened to Mark." Merrick bowed to Lauren, softly kissed Diana's hand, then turned and crossed through the barrier.

"He... very nice." Diana said, shyly.

"Oh yes, he is," Lauren giggled. "Come, let's return to camp. Carr will want to hear our report."

Chapter 10

"Welcome back to the land of the living..." a gentle voice said quietly.

Mark, his eyes unfocussed and weary, tried to assess where he was. His forehead felt cool, and severe pains shot up and down his right side and back. He tried to move and found himself wrapped tightly in a blanket.

"Lie still. I don't want those cuts opening again."

"Where am I? Who are you?" Mark was surprised at how raspy and weak he sounded. A woman brushed his hair from his eyes.

"You're safe. Your attacker thinks you're dead." the woman soothed.

"Lisa!" Mark began to struggle weakly against the covers.

"Lie still!" the woman said sharply. "Now, who is Lisa?"

"My little sister," Mark gasped. "She's with Killia's army. I have to get back to her."

"Killia?" the woman questioned. "What is she doing there? You're not Dal Ryean?"

"No. We were sucked here from one of Sindelar's maelstroms. Killia liked Lisa. It was a trap." Mark was becoming overwrought and incoherent.

"Stop. Nothing you can do right now. When you are better, we shall evaluate how to rescue your sister. She is in no danger if the Princess likes her." The woman smiled at him. She was a small woman about Lauren's age with long blonde hair and dark green eyes. Her clothing was simple but in a style unlike anything from

104

his world or this one. The embroidery on her dark blue tunic was very unusual and elaborate. Her voice was calm and soothing but there was an edge underneath it, one of command. Mark also noticed her entire demeanor seemed tainted with sadness.

"Now," she was saying, "tell me your name and the name of your world."

"Mark Harrison and my world is an edgeworld we call Earth."

"Earth?" the woman's voice had suppressed excitement. "An edgeworld? Tell me, Mark Harrison, did you know anyone named Alaeric or Laurenthalia Olenteas?" the woman leaned towards him eagerly.

"I knew Ric and Lauren Olenteas," Mark answered carefully, a bit afraid of the woman's intensity.

"Ric? Yes, that would work," she muttered. "Was he a big blonde man, well over six feet, built um…heroically?"

"Muscles coming out of his muscles?" Mark asked.

The woman laughed, "Good description."

"He lived next door with his cousin." Mark was feeling confused and tired. "Do you know him?" "Fairly well. I'm his wife." She smiled widely, "I'm Tayaela Pyramus of Dal Ryeas."

"King Tarq's sister? But, Ferrel said you disappeared."

"And who is Ferrel?"

"He's my tent mate. Sindelar is keeping him as hostage for his brother Merrick's good behavior."

"Merrick Dracos-Olenteas?" the Princess smiled as Mark nodded. "I saw him the other day. Sindelar has given him the ability to cross the barrier."

"Merrick is one of Sindelar's spies to Tarq's camp. But Ferrel thinks he's doing work for the King as well. Anyway whenever he goes across the barriers, he comes back with news of the King's forces and attempts to breach the barrier."

"Tarq?" the Princess was excited. "Are you certain he's beyond the barrier?"

"That's what Sindelar says," Mark replied drowsily. He felt the pain receding in waves and all he wanted to do was fall into oblivion.

"Sleep now, Mark. We'll talk more, later." Tayaela slowly passed her hand across his face and he slumped into full sleep.

Mark woke again when light began to shine in his eyes. As he grew accustomed to it, he realized he was in a dry cave and that the 'bed' he was lying on was a large sack stuffed with leaves. Another smaller sack served as a pillow for his head. He was covered with a long plush velvet cloak, tucked in all around him. His chest and back were carefully bandaged and he felt numb from his chest down. When he tried to move, he found his body refused to obey. He thought about calling out, but he was too weary to worry about it. It hurt him to breathe.

He turned his head and surveyed the rest of the cave. To his left and above his head a small fire burned, while at its side was a cooking pot steaming merrily. Another pallet lay beyond the fire and this was where he assumed Tayaela stayed. As he looked towards the cave mouth he was startled to see a huge cat staring benignly at him. There was no sign of Tayaela.

Mark realized that he was naked except for the bandages and cloak. Embarrassed, he tried to determine how long he had been ill. He felt leaden and was worried how seriously he was hurt.

He did not know how long he had lain there awake and fretting before Tayaela returned. She was carrying a brace of small game birds and a wicked-looking cross bow and quarrels. She smiled when she saw him awake, but her first words were to the cat.

"Off guard, Maikai," she commanded and the large animal rose, stretched, and wandered outside. "Good hunting." she called after it softly laughing. Then she turned to Mark. "I'll have these cooking soon, and we'll see if you can eat something. I'm going to make some broth first." She competently plucked and cleaned the birds as she spoke. "These are excellent for healing."

"How long have I been ill?" Mark was still shocked by the rasping hoarse sound of his voice.

"It's been about a week now." she replied, "But I think we're past most of the crisis."

"A week? But..." Mark was completely mortified at the thought of this strange woman caring for his unconscious body.

Sensing his distress, Tayaela said quietly. "You are not the first wounded man I've cared for. Even in your worst delirium, which you'll remember eventually, you were able to help me." She grinned.

"Why can't I remember?" Mark asked nervously.

"Shock, pain, and the fact that I've suppressed most of it. You were a very sick young man, Mark. But, you'll be fine." She smiled at him and continued to work.

"Why can't I feel my legs?" His voice sounded frightened now.

"Because I've had to numb you from the chest down so you wouldn't tear yourself open. Your wounds are knitting quite well, however, until I get you to a regular physician, I won't feel comfortable about any internal injuries which you might have." She came over and eased him to a sitting position, putting a bolster behind his back. "Your back wound wasn't as deep as the side," she added conversationally.

"Uh—and wh-where are my clothes?"

"I've washed and mended them. Here are your trousers." Tayaela handed him his jeans. "I had to throw away your under clothes. They were too blood stained."

"Oh. I need to go to the... uh... go outside."

"Do you want some help?"

"I'm not sure. Let me try it alone."

Tayaela smiled and gestured. "I'll be here. Just tell me when you're ready." She muttered some words in an unintelligible language and Mark felt his lower body again.

It was quite a struggle but after a few tries, Mark was able to get his jeans back on. When he tried to rise though, he immediately felt dizzy, short of breath and unable to stand on his own. He called to Tayaela who silently helped him to stand. His legs were so weak that he collapsed against her. Small though she was, she was strong and was anticipating his weight. She carefully led him outside to a small thicket.

Mark did what needed done for so long, and then she returned for him. Instead of leading him inside though, she threw a cloak over him and arranged a seat for him outside the cave.

"Fresh air will do you good." she smiled as she returned inside to her task of preparing food.

Mark was too tired at first to talk and contently dozed in the warm afternoon sun. After a while, he felt refreshed, the urge to learn more about this capable Princess getting him slowly to his feet again, and he leaned against the cave mouth. "Princess Tayaela?"

"Yes, Mark," was the kind reply.

"When Ferrel told me how you went into exile because Tarq had banished your husband, I always wondered why you didn't just go with him."

"It's not that simple, Mark. Tarq did not banish my husband. Alaeric chose to accompany his cousin into exile because he disagreed with our position. He believed completely in Lauren's innocence since he was innocent himself. But there was enough evidence presented to me and to the King that raised doubts about Lauren being as innocent as her cousin is. Tarq agreed to allow Alaeric to protect the honor of his family and accompany Lauren into exile. I reluctantly agreed. After all, how could I stop my husband from following his beliefs? I was acting on mine. I even toyed with the idea of going too, but I felt obliged to stay and assist Tarq in getting things back in order. When I went to follow the trail a year later, I could not locate the exact path they took." She paused and sighed sadly.

"Why didn't you ask someone?"

"The only people who knew what world they would pick were the Olenteas Lords. It seemed like the Olenteas had a special world on the edges picked out for their exiles, and the King decided that although Lauren was going into exile, she could still go to the world where she had some kin.

"With all the turmoil of the exile, I never thought to ask what path they were going to follow and by the time I remembered they were gone. I could have asked Alaeric's family, but since the Lords are locked up in the Crimson Fortress, and that includes my father-in-law, I really doubt they would have told me. After all, I am the King's sister, who was one of the people who locked them up in the first place. I think that they would rather die than confide the coordinates of the path they used to send their children into exile.

"So I started to wander, at first for a few days and paths at a time and then I finally decided to just go and search without coming home. It became a bad habit. For the last two months or so I have been staying in an uninhabited place. It was a beautiful world and I could sense that there was an unaligned Tal. I was trying to find it so that I could have it consecrated to me and locate Alaeric when the maelstrom on the path caught me."

"What about Tarq?" Mark asked, "Why didn't he help you find Ric? How come he didn't use the what- do you call it - the Tal?"

"Tarq is the King, and he bears a special relationship to both the Tal and the people. As such, he always sacrifices his own interests to the common good. The Kingdom must come first. It's his sacred responsibility and his burden. If I had asked him to use the Tal to locate Alaeric, then he would have located Lauren. That would have placed too great a strain on him. I mean, I knew that he had the will power not to use the Tal for his own selfish reasons, but if I had asked him, he would have done it, no matter how much it hurt. I couldn't do that to him. Then it would have driven him nuts to know where she was and not be able to go to her.

"I guess Lauren knew all of this too, but still resented that Tarq felt he had to exile her. She thought that their love should give him some leeway, but the kingdom's safety was tantamount. Her exile caused the rebellion to end and peace to reign. Even though the evidence against her was never very strong, it was based on her reluctance to set a wedding date and some minor things; he had to do what he did. He will never stop feeling deeply about her. I don't know about her, but Tarq is like me, once he has given his love he will never give it again."

"I'd like to meet him," Mark said. "Sindelar and Killia hate him, but seem to respect him. They want the Tal, of course, but I think Killia wants Tarq too."

"Of course they do! So they've created a stalemate. For months the two forces are stalemated. Sindelar can't go to Tadia and Tarq can't break the barrier. So everyone is stuck. And we're stuck on the wrong side of the spell. I can't try to break it without giving away our position and I refuse to be a pawn in Sindelar's hands. That would be all that Tarq needed!"

"How can we get to the King?"

"One of two ways. We must find the way to break the spell or if that is not possible we must go to another world, find a Tal and bring it here, then we can shift anywhere on this world."

"Another Tal?"

"Every world has one, even the edgeworlds. All you have to do is be able to recognize it." Tayaela frowned. "I can send you home without it, you know," she said seriously. "I'm a path forger."

"I can't leave. I still have to rescue Lisa." Mark answered, inwardly torn by a fierce urge to go home and a stronger sense of loyalty to his sister. "She may be a pill, but she's still my responsibility."

"I had a feeling you'd say that. So our first priority is to get you well." Tayaela said briskly, finishing the preparations for Mark's first meal in a while. "Then we'll figure out what to do next. Somehow we have to breach that barrier!"

Chapter 11

Sindelar was concerned about Lisa and even Princess Killia felt a slight remorse over her actions. For over a week, Lisa was unable to deal on her own with Mark's death. Every time the wizard lifted the spells that eased her grief, the girl was disoriented and worked herself into hysteria.

Killia, with a wholehearted effort, tried to divert the girl's mind, even going so far as to allow her to walk through camp with Ferrel. Captain Volta viewed this action with disfavor but refrained from comment since Ferrel seemed the only one who was able to keep the girl's grief at bay for even a little.

"She cannot go on like this," the Princess complained to her wizard, agitated. "She has lost that buoyancy which made her so attractive. You have to do something."

"Highness," replied the wizard, "it's natural for her to grieve. Her mind is confused. She can't wholly believe he's dead. She never saw her brother's body. It will take time for her to heal, but she is very young and her true nature will assert itself eventually, and the hurt will go away."

"She is always crying." Killia said peevishly. She hated to acknowledge her own culpability in the situation. She wanted to forget that the murder was at her instigation. "Can't you keep the spells on her for a longer time?"

"Not if you ever want her to return to normal!" Sindelar snapped at her, his patience at an end, "What did you think would happen to her when you had that she-wolf kill her brother? Did you think the girl would be overjoyed? Did you even think at

111

all?"

"I thought," replied Killia haughtily, "that she would turn to me. Not to that boy!" Killia came closer to the wizard. "Don't be angry with me, Sindelar". She smiled winsomely, putting her arms around his neck and leaning seductively against him. Sindelar resisted the desire to take her in his arms and kiss her passionately.

"Ferrel was Mark's friend, while you were barely civil to him. Of course she would gravitate to him. It's all she has left of her brother."

"Well, I want her to be dependent on me," the Princess broke from their embrace. She turned from him and returned to her tent. "Do it!" she snapped as she flung the tent flap behind her.

Sindelar remained standing before his tent. There were times when he regretted his love for his foster brother's daughter. He knew she was unstable, that she had no sense of right and wrong, but her beauty had won him long before. Even without the oaths he had given Philos, his loyalty now belonged solely to her. It was a powerful combination, a master wizard's love and loyalty.

Sometimes he wondered if he ignored his foster brother and pursued his true interest in theoretical sorcery, if his life would have been more meaningful. He even thought regretfully about his lost affair with Tarq's sorceress, Carr, and how much they had started to feel for each other. But always his loyalty to Philos and his cause came before his personal life. So many regrets and roads not taken, he thought sadly. So much time wasted.

In the distance he saw Lisa walking with Ferrel. The boy with his arm around her shoulders was listening intently to her. Finally the girl turned to the boy and wept on his chest. Sindelar watched as Ferrel awkwardly put both his arms about her, wondering what the boy might be saying to her.

"Easy, Lisa…" Ferrel held her tightly as sobs wracked her body. He had tried earlier to let her know his suspicions concerning Mark's death, but every time he tried to tell her about the note and what he had seen, she became even more upset. She refused to believe that the Princess was implicated. In her mind, King Tarq's men had done this heinous deed.

Ferrel pleaded again for her trust, but all she wanted was his comfort. Dreading to wait for a better time, Ferrel held her until the storm of her emotions eased. Feeling drained and powerless, he walked her back to Sindelar who was waiting for them before his tent. The wizard touched the girl lightly on the forehead and told her to go lie down. Obeying woodenly, Lisa entered the tent.

Sindelar turned back to Ferrel. "Merrick was here the other night. I see you gave him my message."

"Yes sir," Ferrel replied meekly. He was uncomfortable with the wizard and longed to escape to the privacy of his own tent.

"You don't like me very much do you, Ferrel?" Sindelar asked, in a conversational tone.

Startled, the boy blushed and looked about him wildly. There was no one in view and he realized that he had to be very careful in his answer. The wizard could dispose of him so easily and no one but Merrick would notice. "It's not that I dislike you, sir," he responded carefully. "It's just that, well, you are Sindelar, the Lord wizard, and I'm a sixteen-year-old boy who has spent five years in exile. I'm just not…used to such exalted people. You, uh, make me, uh, nervous."

"Candidly said, Ferrel," Sindelar laughed softly, "Who are you loyal to, my boy?"

"My friends, sir, my brother, and my father." Ferrel answered.

"What of me? And the Princess?"

"I am here, Lord. I am trying to help with Lady Lisa. What more can I do?" Ferrel asked hesitantly. "I never really thought about to whom I should be loyal, besides Merrick."

"What of Merrick? Is he loyal?"

"If he weren't, sir, why do you have him spy for you?"

"He spies, but does he tell me everything?" the wizard muttered.

"You do have me, sir."

"Ah, you understand your role then in our scheme of things?"

"Yes, Lord. I've always known." Ferrel answered grimly.

"Then, you don't approve?" The wizard caught his tone.

"You shouldn't have to buy loyalty with threats because the loyalty lasts only as long as the threat is effective." Ferrel spoke up, determined that compromising truth or his feelings was only more dangerous to him now.

"But, I hold you and as long as I do, Merrick remains loyal. He's very special, your brother Merrick. He's intelligent, observant, and courageous. That's a rare combination and I like having it in my control. So if I have to control you to keep it, I will. So tell me", Sindelar shifted the topic quickly, "what was your exile like?" He liked this boy. He had a refreshing sense of honesty that was missing from the wizard's life.

"At first, my father kept us isolated. He expected to come home within weeks. When he wasn't summoned home, he began to fail. The wounds he received in battle never really healed and he lost the will to live. Merrick tried everything, but nothing worked. He died when I turned twelve. After that, Merrick got me involved in the Phrygan society. He sent me to schools and he went to work." Ferrel smiled briefly, remembering the rough Phrygan mining town and some of his wilder friends. There were times he actually enjoyed his life there.

"There are mines in Phryga, and Merrick worked them sixteen hours a day, so that I would have what I needed. I worked after school too and we were able to live comfortably. When your maelstrom path found us, Merrick was on his way to the night shift. When we landed here, I was confused and frightened, but Merrick managed to locate you and everything was all right again."

"Merrick is very important to you." Sindelar said gently.

"He's my brother." Ferrel replied warily. "He's all that I have."

"And how is Lisa?" Sindelar again changed the subject, feeling an overwhelming appreciation of Ferrel's love for his brother. It bothered him that he was using this boy for his selfish ends. This child needed a home, a family, and security. Instead he had wasted his youth to the vagaries of politics and war.

"Distraught, angry and confused." As quickly as Sindelar changed topics, Ferrel proved himself adaptable and able to take the wizard's thoughts in stride.

"I appreciate your concern for her. This is a very hard time in her life, her first experience with death."

"Her brother was my friend. It's the least I could do." Ferrel seemed wary. "Do you want me to stop?

"On the contrary, you are doing her good!" Sindelar clapped the boy on the shoulder. "But, a word to the wise," he turned the boy to face him. "Stay away from the Princess. She is jealous of your influence on Lisa." The wizard smiled and left the boy standing alone.

Ferrel was torn. He could almost like the wizard, but he feared the awesome power at his command and he did not trust him. Hurriedly, he fled to his tent to pray for Merrick to come and save him.

Lisa awoke, her heart beating wildly. She was in that in-between state, when dreams become reality and true life fades. Everything was perfectly clear in her mind for the first time in a week. She had to find a way home. She wanted her mother. She wanted to be held and told that everything was fine, that it was all an evil dream. She longed for her father to protect her from all the horror. She wanted to go home. And she had to find Mark.

She got out of bed and unwittingly put on her own clothes, ignoring the rich gowns Killia had left strewn about for her pleasure. She crept from the tent and quietly began to move in the direction she was told Mark had gone. No one saw her leave.

For hours the young girl wandered in the forest lost, weeping, and searching for Mark. Woodenly, oblivious to the dangers inherent in the forest, she made her way towards the barrier. Unmolested by the forest beasts, Lisa, bruised and scraped, searched in single-minded determination for Mark and the way back to her family.

It was late morning when Merrick, coming across the barrier, found her. She was crying and only half-conscious of the man who suddenly materialized before her.

"I can't find him. I can't find him. I want to go home. I want my mother!" the frightened child cried repeatedly.

Merrick, compassion overcoming his good sense, crouched down beside her as she sat on the ground and wept. He gently pulled the twigs and leaves from her hair. "Hush, Lisa. It'll be all right. I'll take you where you will get help." He hugged her against him and thought for a moment what to do. He knew that the King's plans included rescuing Lisa, but it was imperative for him to return to Killia's camp with his latest mission.

He argued with himself for a few minutes and decided not

to return her to Sindelar even though he risked his credibility by taking the girl to Tarq. He only hoped that his compassion was rewarded someday. "My Aunt Carr will help you." He told the girl soothingly.

Carefully, Merrick lifted the girl in his arms. She put her head on his shoulder and her arms around his neck. She was completely unaware of her surroundings and never felt the sensation of flowing through the barrier.

Strong as he was, Merrick was forced to rest periodically as he carried his young charge towards Tarq's camp. It was late afternoon when he arrived. Ignoring the guards he immediately strode with the now-sleeping Lisa to the King's tent.

Alaeric, seated in his customary chair before the pavilion, called inside and the King emerged to see Merrick approaching with Lisa.

"Well, I see you've brought us a pleasant surprise, Merrick." Alaeric remarked.

"I found her wandering." Merrick replied shortly. "She has fallen asleep, poor child. She's been hysterical all day weeping and struggling. She's exhausted."

"Put her on my bed." The King stood aside to allow Merrick to enter his tent. The sleeping quarters, in the rear of the tent, were curtained-off from the rest of the area. Merrick smiled at the stark, simple tent. A bed and a small table were all the furniture in the sleeping room, with the front room set as a conference area with folding chairs and tables.

Tarq, seeing Merrick's smile said, "We prefer to travel lightly. There's nothing here we can't abandon at a moment's notice."

"Princess Killia should take lessons from you, sir." Merrick grinned as he placed Lisa on the cot. As he straightened up, her arms tightened around his neck, and he gently disentangled himself from her grip. She resumed her fitful sleep.

Tarq motioned him out of the tent. "We are very pleased with your progress, Merrick."

"Thank you, Sire."

"Lord Alaeric has sent a courier for Diana. Why don't you wait here and see her? I'm sure she would like to thank you for returning her sister." The King smiled softly. Lauren had told him of the attraction between Merrick and Diana.

"Thank you, sire. It was a long walk. I could use the rest." Merrick felt pleased knowing he was soon to see Diana again.

A cook brought some food and drink. The King and his two companions fell to eating. Discussions ranged from favorite games they had all enjoyed as children to the niceties of women and the hunt. For a short while they forgot the grim tasks ahead of them.

Diana, with Lauren and Carr in tow, arrived breathlessly. "Did you really rescue her?" she asked eagerly. "Oh, Merrick!" Diana grabbed him in a strong embrace.

Merrick blushed and muttered. "It was nothing, really." The King and Lauren exchanged a knowing look and stifled a laugh.

"May I see her, Sire?" Diana asked excitedly. The King himself led Diana into the tent.

"She's sleeping, as you can see." Tarq said, opening the inner tent flap to the sleeping section and allowed Diana to enter. She stood for a while by Lisa's bed crying quietly. Carr, following, reassured her with a hug, that the girl was well and that her sleep was quite natural.

"It's the best thing for her right now." Carr smiled.

Diana bent over, kissed the sleeping girl and left.

Merrick was waiting outside the tent. "Diana, would you care to walk with me?" He seemed shyly diffident, very different from the confident agent he usually was.

Alaeric, drinking, choked. "Haven't you done enough walking today, cousin?" He grinned wickedly at Merrick and then winked at Diana.

Ignoring him, Diana answered. "I'd love to, Merrick." And hand-in-hand they walked away from the King's pavilion towards the privacy of her own tent, set closer to the woods.

Lauren nodded approvingly after them. "I think that will go very well."

Tarq watched them as their arms slipped around each other's waists. "I hope they're not rushing things."

"Like you did?" Lauren said bitingly, her good mood suddenly gone. "With your permission, I'll take my leave."

The King sighed. "Very well. Come back after supper though. We need to confer on strategy. I grow weary of this stalemate. We need to determine our next move. It's time to take action." Lauren bowed and walked away.

Tarq turned to his brother-in-law. "Is she ever going to let me past her guard?"

"She needs time, Tarq. She doesn't know what she wants." Alaeric answered.

Tarq smirked, "Thanks, you are a world of help."

"I try." Alaeric grinned.

Chapter 12

Angry voices jolted Lisa rudely awake. For the first time in a week she awoke to full consciousness. Even this brief time away from Sindelar had weakened her spell-induced daze. A chill of fear crept down her spine when she realized that this was not the Princess' camp. Cautiously she sat up on the cot and listened to the arguing voices outside the tent.

"He will be back soon and then we can plan," a woman's voice said sharply. "He has an excellent idea of what's going on over there."

"Just because he is your bondsman doesn't mean that I have to include him in all my plans," a man's voice retorted sharply.

"I'm so sorry, Your Majesty, but I thought he had proven his loyalty beyond doubt!" the woman was bitingly civil and near shouting.

"Well, my Lady, he hasn't. Sindelar still has his brother and as long as he does, I'm not revealing everything to him!" the man's voice icily replied, also rising in volume.

"By the Twins, stop your arguing!" a third voice, another man's, interrupted. "This gets us nowhere. He brought the girl. Now we have to help him free his brother." To Lisa, the deep faintly-accented voice sounded hauntingly familiar. "Tarq, I also think," the voice continued reasonably, "we should go to my tent, so as not to wake the girl."

"Right as always, brother-in-law," the Tarq voice chuckled. "I'll look in on our sleeping beauty and then we'll go."

Lisa quickly lay down and shut her eyes. She felt rather than

119

saw the movement of the curtain. She knew where she was: in the enemy camp and right before her, if she opened her eyes, stood King Tarq himself.

"She's still asleep. Let's go." the voice was so close to her that she nearly jumped. She heard the sounds of their departure as the King ordered a guard posted at the door of the tent. She saw the shadows of the King and his party leaving and that of the guard standing outside. The tent fell eerily silent.

For a long time she waited, feigning sleep, trying to control the rising fear that threatened to overwhelm her. Lisa began to think of her deepest desires. She wanted to be home, with everyone all right and not stuck in the tent of her brother's killers. She wanted her mother. As she quietly cried a thought occurred to her. Why had Ferrel's brother brought her to these people? She thought he was the Princess' man and Sindelar's. Perhaps he had no choice. She only vaguely recalled the trip to the camp. Merrick probably had an excellent reason. For some time, as the outside camp settled for the night, she tried to decide what that reason was.

In a flash she realized the significance of where she was. Merrick had brought her to Tarq's camp. Tarq was the King, the enemy, but he possessed the one item in the world that could aid the Princess and Lord Sindelar. Merrick could not steal it, but she could. It would be her revenge for Mark and she knew beyond any doubt that she could find the Tal and take it to Sindelar.

She remembered Sindelar's description of the stone. She thought of the reverence with which everyone spoke of this talisman. She had to find it and this was her only chance.

Silently, she rose from the cot and began a careful search of Tarq's sleeping quarters. There weren't many places to hide such an item, but Lisa looked everywhere: under the cot, through his clothing, some papers on the chair, in the dirt. Finally in frustration she sat down on the cot again and glanced over at a small table next to her. There in an open lacquered box was a purple jewel with dark green fire wrapped in silver wire. The Tal sat, nestled on a velvet cushion, out in the open. Lisa felt a momentary qualm about taking it, but this soon passed as she reached out and grasped the Tal.

Its warmth surprised her. She thought that it would be cold. She gazed at it, mesmerized by the deep purple and green lights shining in its depths as they created patterns of incredible complexity. Stealthily she crept from the rear of the tent moving as silently as she could so as not to alert the guard of her actions. With the Tal grasped firmly in her hand, she unerringly walked in the direction of Sindelar's camp.

The Tal reacted as a homing beacon for her directional senses and even though she was unaware of it, she went in the proper direction without problem, creating an internal path leading her directly to the barrier in the forest. Because she was ignorant of its uses, the Tal reacted only to her surface desires. Lisa's yearning to leave the King's camp and safely return to the Princess superseded her deeper desire to go home to her parents. And the Tal of Dal Ryeas responded to this.

Unseen by the sentries, lulled into oblivion by the Tal's power, Lisa walked past them and into the deep forest. Untroubled, she walked unceasingly through Sindelar's barrier. Again the power of the Tal blinded sentries to her presence.

It was dawn when she found herself at the entrance of the wizard's tent. For a moment she hesitated to enter, a small part of her concerned for King Tarq's unsuspecting army. But the thought of Mark gave her courage to continue her mission.

Sindelar leapt to his feet as the young girl came towards his bed. Always a nervous sleeper, the least sound woke him instantly. He watched the girl approach his bed, feigning a casualness he did not feel. At first he thought it might be Killia, coming for love and reassurance of her destiny. Then he realized it was Lisa. Somehow she looked different, harder, and colder, more like the Princess. He silently watched her as she reached him and held out her hand.

Lying in her palm, as beautiful as morning, glowed the Tal. Deep purple lights flowed around it and changed to green periodically. Sindelar's startled glance turned from the Tal to the girl. She was disheveled but obviously unharmed and awake from his spells. Sindelar felt a strange pity for her then, as if the gift she offered him was robbing her of her last freedom.

"Here. Take this. I stole it. Send me home now." Lisa demanded.

"Are you all right, child?" Sindelar mentally probed the girl for signs of any tampering with her mind. He found nothing.

What fools, he thought.

"I'm fine." she replied, looking bleakly into his eyes.

She knows, he thought, and someday it will be her tragedy.

"Where have you been?" he asked, concern dripping from his voice. "The Princess and I have been so worried."

"I went to find Mark. Only he was gone. So I looked for his body. Then I wandered for hours, I don't know where, when a man found me. He took me to Tarq's camp." She frowned, pausing, unable to remember her time at Tarq's clearly.

"And?" prompted the wizard, intensely curious.

"And then they put me to bed, I guess. Anyway, I woke up to an argument. Some of the people sounded familiar. I even think I dreamed about Diana." Lisa looked puzzled for a moment. "Anyway, I woke up and knew what to do. You told me what the Tal looked like and it was just sitting there, so I took it and came back. They'll pay for Mark's death," she concluded fiercely. "They'll suffer for what they did to him."

"Yes, my child, they will," he chuckled, holding the Tal aloft. Killia's plot had at least this redeeming aspect.

The dawn was breaking and light began to filter through the open tent flap. It caught on the Tal and the stone blazed radiant in the morning light. Sindelar was overjoyed. He held the final key to the conquering of Dal Ryeas. With the Tal he could travel to any location on Dal Ryeas and Tarq was unable to stop him. With the power of the King, no inter-world travel was forbidden to him. Tarq was virtually helpless now. He could close off the city to Tarq, stranding him here. Even if Tarq could get to the Kingdom and the clans, without a Tal the City of Tadia would remain impervious to his magic and weapons.

"Once Killia and I hold Tadia, we will hold the Kingdom," he thought. His mind began to plan, oblivious to Lisa's continuing requests that he send her home. The magician strode from the tent issuing orders to begin breaking camp.

Forgotten, Lisa stood in the center of his tent.

Chapter 13

Tarq spent the night on an extra cot in Alaeric's tent, so as not to disturb Lisa. After Lauren returned to her tent and the others dispersed, Tarq sat talking long into the night with Alaeric. It was a welcome relief to confide in someone again. For five years he had hardly spoken to anyone except in his capacity as King.

Friendship was vital to Tarq and usually unattainable because of his position, first as Prince, then as King. He was unable to approach persons who interested him. He really had no ability to make friends, merely acquaintances. Trained from an early age to know that everyone wanted something from him, Tarq found it extremely difficult to trust anyone. As a child, he only trusted his sister, Tayaela.

When Alaeric and Lauren came to live at Tadia Castle he was able to find some release in friendship with them. These three were the only ones who ever saw Tarq carefree and relaxed. He grew dependent on his sense of their mutual trust. The civil war that tore them asunder had effectively obliterated his youth. He forced himself to exile his lover for the good of the realm, no matter what his own desires dictated. His best friend followed her into exile to protest his decision and then his sister had deserted him. Truly alone, he ruled his kingdom in a self-imposed emotional isolation.

"I am a just King," he confided to Alaeric, "but I leave it to Carr to determine mercy." He stared at his hands, his long blonde hair obscuring his eyes.

"Why can't you accept that what you did was necessary? Tarq, forgive yourself." Alaeric was sprawled across his bed.

"I can't," Tarq lowered his head into his hands. "I should have found another way. Lauren doesn't forgive me."

"Of course she does! She understands!"

"Then why? Why does she treat me like this?"

Alaeric thought carefully before replying. "It's not that she doesn't love you. I think she does. I know that she used to cry herself to sleep every night when we were first exiled. She had dreams about you all the time. There were times when she couldn't mention your name without tears springing to her eyes. Then she stopped. She couldn't remember because we had to survive on that edgeworld."

"What happened? What was it like?" Tarq looked at his friend. Alaeric refused to meet his eyes.

"We began to enjoy a freedom never permitted us at home." Alaeric grimaced. "The edgeworld is a very different place, you see. It has no commerce with any other places or even knowledge of their existence. It exists in a splendid isolation we at first found hard to understand. It can be a very lethal place and for awhile, most of our time was spent trying to survive.

"Then when we had mastered that part of it, we discovered that the restrictions, under which we labored at home, being Prince Alaeric or Princess Lauren, didn't apply. It was exhilarating, a heady experience, and frankly, we liked it." Alaeric sighed. "If Tayaela and you had been with us, I think we would have been content to stay there forever. As it was…"

"You know that's impossible." Tarq interrupted harshly, not looking at him.

"Yes, I know." Alaeric swung his legs onto the floor. "We'd better get some sleep. I want to talk to the girl in the morning about Killia's condition. If she's been close to the woman, she might have some insight."

"But will she cooperate?" Tarq took off his leather jacket and his shirt.

"We can but hope." Alaeric said. "She always liked me on the edgeworld maybe that will help here and now."

Tarq once again realized how alone he was. "If she wants to go back," he said into the darkness after Alaeric had doused the lamp, "I won't try to interfere."

He had been sleeping peacefully for five hours, when Sindelar's hand grasped the Tal. A scream tore through him, shattering the silence of the dawn.

Clutching his side as his symbiosis with the Tal was severed, Tarq ran from the tent with Alaeric close behind. From beyond the edge of the clearing, Lauren appeared with Carr while Diana and Merrick ran from the direction of the deep forest. Others gathered as the King, stumbling and sobbing in pain, raced to his tent.

Tarq entered alone. Nervously, Diana clutched Merrick's hand while Lauren and Alaeric stood barring the entrance. The sounds of rage, furniture being overturned and incoherent cries of anger ripped through the tent walls.

Lauren, after a quick look at Alaeric, entered the tent.

Tarq was in the back, his cot overturned, and everything scattered. He was on his knees searching the floor, his face red with rage and unimaginable pain.

"Where's Lisa?" Lauren asked, although she was afraid she already knew.

"Gone, and the little bitch has stolen the Tal."

"What?!"

"It's gone and I felt Sindelar's hand gather its power."

"Oh Creator, grant us aid." Lauren prayed.

"That's not going to help!" the King shouted brutally.

"What are we going to do?"

"Do? We're going to try to get it back. Get the others, the full council with all the field commanders. Bring that spy of yours and the girl. Report here at once!"

"It's not Diana's fault," asserted Lauren.

"I never said it was. But she may be able to tell us why." Tarq growled. "Go!"

Lauren hurried from the tent, her face pale and her manner agitated, and conveyed the King's word to his councilors and commanders. Within a half hour of the King's discovery of the theft everyone concerned with the problem had gathered at the royal tent. Lauren came in last with Diana and Merrick.

Diana was visibly distraught and Merrick had his arm around her shoulders, trying to comfort her. Troop commanders stood around the tent nervously waiting.

The King was brief. "As you know, Sindelar has gained possession of the Tal. With it in his possession, he has effectively cut off our way back to Tadia. In order to get home again we're going to have to travel a circuitous route through other worlds. I fear that he will act at once to take the city, and block our way in. It is imperative that I send you into hiding before he and his madwoman try to get their hands on you."

"Why, Sire?" A commander asked.

"To keep you free. If we move too many to the area around Tadia, we will be caught. We have to move you back quietly to the outlying clan holds and then move slowly, in pairs and threes towards the city. Too precipitous a movement will alert Sindelar and Killia to our arrival and cripple us." The King paused. "As long as I held the Tal, Tadia was safe, now not only the capital is in danger but the other cities and holds. Now..." His voice trailed away and he looked down at the ground.

Reality came crashing in on all sides. Tadia was the least of his worries, and everyone knew it. Dal Ryeas was merely an obstacle on the path of destruction Sindelar was capable of starting. The safety of whole worlds was in jeopardy.

Tarq sighed deeply and faced them all again. "While you are on these other worlds and at the clan holds, awaiting recall, I also charge you to seek for unaligned Tals. Those of you especially on the edgeworlds have a better chance of finding them."

Carr broke in clearly, "Pardon, Sire, but the commanders should know that a Tal not being used or focused can be used only by one who has been in symbiosis with another."

"I thought each Tal was unique to its own world?" a captain asked.

"True enough, but those never used can easily be tapped for power by one attuned. So, even an industrial world's Tal can be used to focus magic on a world like ours."

The King spoke up again, "Carr and I have determined that we have at least six months before Killia can be consecrated to the Tal, since certain conditions must be met for the ceremony. This buys us some time."

"Why don't we stand and fight?" a voice called.

"By now Sindelar must have used the Tal to close off Tadia and huge path movements will be seen in the colors of the Tal.

We have to move in a few at a time over a period of months. Then although he'll suspect, he won't be able to trace us."

"Sire, what next?"

"I want you all to pack. They'll try to sneak attack here, after they have secured the city. I want you all hidden. Carr and her assistants will open paths for you and give you means of communications. She will remain here in hiding to co-ordinate all messengers from the edges. Now go! Time is more valuable than curiosity."

The King dismissed his commanders who immediately gathered outside the tent with Carr. She completed instructing them and set up lines of communication. Although realistically there were days remaining before Sindelar could attack the camp, the King was determined to have the first troops shifted to the other cores and edges by evening.

"Merrick?" Tarq said moodily when all had followed Carr except his inner circle.

"Sire?" Merrick released Diana and went to the King.

"I need you to go back in. Try to rescue the girl. Find out what's going on in Tadia. Spread the word that I will return." Tarq clapped him on the shoulder and smiled softly. "Set up a resistance. Your family excels at that. I should warn you that you'll only be able to send information out to us, since Sindelar will have blocked all incoming communication. Essentially you will be working blind, but we need you there, we have to know what is happening in the city. And we especially need you to continue your double game. It is more important than ever now. Carr will give you a crystal and you are to report as often as you can. And we will try to find some means of getting word to you of our progress."

"Yes, Sire. I'll do whatever I can." Merrick turned to Diana and took her into his arms, holding her close to him.

"Take me with you…,"the girl begged. "I need to find Lisa. I have to know why she did this."

"No," Lauren's voice harshly cut through their intimacy. "I have to have at least one of you when I take Tarq through."

"What?" Diana peered over Merrick's arm at her friend.

"I'm taking you home. Your parents are not going to be thrilled to know that Mark is dead or missing, and that Lisa is under thrall to Killia. I'll need at least one of you."

Diana was about to protest, but the unyielding expression on Lauren's face made her refrain.

"I'll take care of Lisa," Merrick promised Diana. "Ferrel will help too. We'll get her to come to her senses." He kissed her softly, hugging around her once more.

"Please be careful," she whispered into his ear.

The embrace lengthened considerably, neither wanting to let go before Tarq gently spoke up, clearing his throat. "Go, Merrick, or they'll leave without you. Good luck."

Embarrassed Diana and Merrick broke awkwardly apart. With a shaky bow, Merrick sprinted from the tent. He spoke briefly to Carr, received a crystal, and within a few minutes disappeared into the forest.

Alaeric put a comforting arm around Diana. "Well, we'd better make plans."

"It's going to take days to shift all our troops." Tarq said.

"Sire, we must get you to the edgeworld as soon as we can."

"I'm not leaving until the army is hidden."

"Don't be stubborn, Tarq!" Alaeric surprised everyone with his loud retort. "You're the one Sindelar wants. I'll stay here and assist Carr. If they find you it won't matter how many armies you've hidden. All will be lost!"

"I'm not so irresponsible as to trust my army's future safety to underlings!" Tarq shot back angrily.

"Underlings?" Alaeric raged. "I've been War leader trained and I'm more capable than you at this juncture because I'm not a target to all enemy snipers. How do you know Sindelar won't leave troops behind to assassinate you, knowing full well that you won't leave your army?"

"Oh, and if you think you know so much on how Sindelar thinks, perhaps you can-"

"Knock it off!" Lauren intervened, screaming louder than either combatant. Both men were stunned that Lauren could raise her voice so vehemently.

"Sire, you are coming with me to my edgeworld!" Lauren declared her eyes filled with fire. "Alaeric is right and you know it! You are too valuable and vulnerable to stay here. He will stay with Carr and when the troops have been moved, you can join us."

Alaeric nodded, amused at Lauren's sudden authority. She sounds so much like a Princess again, he thought to himself.

"While we are on Earth, you and I will seek Earth's Tal. I don't think it's focused. Since one is attuned to you, you ought to be able to locate another." Lauren's highhanded pronouncements had created a vast silence in the tent. All eyes were on the King, whose usual even temper was reaching its detonation point.

Tarq's angry blue eyes met Lauren's cold brown ones. She calmly waited for him to regain control of himself. Then she said softly, "Come, Your Majesty. Diana, we must to prepare to leave."

With a sigh, the anger released itself and the King, in a final voice tinged with deep sorrow said, 'Very well, I will go into exile with you."

PART TWO

Chapter 14

Tayaela felt the fluctuations presaging a mag or shift in the paths and tried to decide whether to wake Mark. Although much improved, he was still weak and slept heavily. She moved swiftly to his side and created a small oasis within the tremendous forces building around her. Mark awoke to find a heavy darkness surrounding them and the walls of the cave gone.

Mark cried out in surprise, but the gentle pressure of Tayaela's hand kept him lying still. She smiled at him reassuringly.

"Where are we? What's going on?" he whispered in a frightened voice.

"I've moved us to a place where we won't be whisked away where we don't wish to go." She patted his shoulder gently.

"What?" Mark was genuinely puzzled. "I don't understand you."

"Someone is using the Tal and it's not Tarq, ergo, it is someone we wish to avoid, probably Sindelar." Tayaela responded.

"How do you know this?"

"Until Tarq marries and has a child, I'm his heir. Since one of the primary duties of a Dal Ryean ruler is to distribute the power of the Tal, it takes some training. Since I'm heir, I have some training too. I can sense a Tal, especially a focused one, and I recognize a user's touch. Tarq's is distinctive, and what I felt today was definitely not Tarq's."

"Oh." Mark understood vaguely.

"Anyway, I really don't want to be in Sindelar's control, so I moved us." Tayaela finished.

"So where are we now?" Mark felt agitated. His body still felt as if a hundred pins were constantly sticking him all over.

"In a pocket." Tayaela explained patiently.

"A pocket?"

"It's a sort of bulge between paths," Tayaela grinned. "Path forgers can make this. It's one of our special talents. Finders can travel anywhere, but Forgers are best at hiding. That's why when I don't wish to be found, I'm not," she finished proudly.

"Oh." Mark could think of no other reply.

Tayaela laughed merrily. "Oh Mark, you should see your face. It's a classic of non-expression."

"How long will we be here?" Mark changed the subject, blushing a bit. He liked Tayaela's cool, yet kind nature, and hearing her laugh was like music to him.

"I don't know. Probably a while. It will take even Sindelar some time to send everyone through. So why don't you rest?" Tayaela patted his shoulder and looked away into the darkness.

Mark looked up at her profile and once again forgot she was married. He imagined that it was a typical night and that instead of a cave floor hidden in a pocket between the universes, they were in their own place, and she was his exclusively. In all, this feeling lasted for only an instant, but the warmth and affection it engendered stayed with him.

"Go to sleep, Mark," Tayaela said, as if reading his thoughts, "You need all your strength to get well."

Merrick arrived at Sindelar's tent at mid-morning. The entire camp was bustling. Inwardly Merrick shuddered; knowing that unsuspecting Tadia was doomed to fall to this half-crazed army before long and after Tadia, the rest of Dal Ryeas would follow unless he stopped it.

Unlike Tarq's camp where desperation prevailed, the soldiers at Killia's camp were boldly declaring complete victory before the month was out. Everywhere soldiers were joking and boasting of an easy conquest, how once Sindelar broke through the shields on the other side, Dal Ryeas was theirs.

Sindelar was sequestered in his tent making final preparations for the transference of his army to Tadia. Merrick, knowing how futile it was to try a frontal assault of stealing the Tal back again, wildly considered the idea for a moment. It would create the requisite chaos if he were to boldly march into the wizard's tent and seize the crystal. Only he had absolutely no idea how to use the thing. Ruefully smiling to himself as he approached the tent, he muttered, "I should have studied crystal magic harder at school."

Captain Volta stood before Sindelar's tent. "I'm sorry, Lord Merrick, but the Princess has left strict orders that no one is to disturb Lord Sindelar today. He must marshal his strength to move into Tadia." She was obviously pleased to boast of her access to the Princess to one of the wizard's subordinates. Volta's monumental self-conceit caused her to distrust anyone but herself for sensitive matters. It was at once her greatest strength and her most prevalent weakness. By trusting no one except Killia, she left herself open to treachery and hatred. *In my case of course*, Merrick thought, *she's absolutely right.* It gave him a secret pleasure to know that he was putting one over on Volta.

With a smile and a honey-sweet voice, Merrick asked her, "What should I be doing? I just returned from the enemy camp. All is chaotic." He reminded her ever so gently of his own role in the scheme of events. He knew she hated the idea of anyone else contributing to Killia's victory.

"Prepare to move." Volta growled viciously. "We will be leaving tomorrow." She then turned her back as Merrick sketched a mocking half-bow to her.

Pleased with himself, Merrick then made his way through camp to Ferrel's tent. It took him four detours because of the camp's intense activity to reach the edge of camp where Ferrel's tent was located. By the time he got there, he was alarmed at the efficiency and absolute sense of victory that prevailed in all sectors of the army. There was no way to warn Tarq of this situation. He knew his duty.

Merrick saw the boy sitting cross-legged on the ground, struggling to lock a strap on his pack. "Ferrel," he called, grinning.

Ferrel looked up, saw Merrick, and jumped to his feet. Joyfully, he ran over to his brother and capered after him like a puppy once they exchanged a quick embrace. "Oh gods, Merrick, I never thought you'd get back. I mean, when Lisa came here with the

Tal. How did she get it? Sindelar made a fuss over her but I don't think she's too happy. She came here earlier. All she wants to do is go home, and he won't send her. I tried to tell her he was lying but she wouldn't listen to me!"

"Slow down, slow down!" Merrick laughed. "I can't keep it straight. Start at the beginning."

"Lisa is unhappy. The wizard won't send her home. Before when we tried, Mark and me, to tell her that she was a prisoner here like us, that Sindelar could have returned her home at any time, she refused to listen. All she said was that he needed the Tal to do this. I mean, what does she know about paths? Only now he has told her she has to wait. I think she's getting the idea everyone's lying to her. She's very nervous."

"Diana, her sister, warned me she might be getting edgy. I guess that's how she reacts to things." Merrick said. Smiling, he added, "You'll like Diana, Ferrel. She's beautiful and talented and kind. Aunt Carr is teaching her the various ways of the wizards."

"So you're in love, huh? And I thought it was just duty." Ferrel grinned as Merrick blushed. The two brothers wrestled for a few moments to ease Merrick's embarrassment. "Hey Merrick, I'm happy for you." Ferrel said, and then after looking around he lowered his voice, "What of the King? What's going to happen now?"

"Don't worry, we'll figure some way to help-"

Just then, Lisa, accompanied by one of Captain Volta's elite guard, Sergeant Orado, sauntered over to the brothers. "Hello, Ferrel," she said shyly, smiling at the boy.

Merrick could tell instantly that the girl was interested in his younger brother. It must run in the family, he thought and grinned.

"Lady Lisa," Ferrel answered her with a bow and flourish. "I see you brought a pet." He blithely indicated a furious Orado.

"Oh, Lord Sindelar insists that I have to be accompanied by a guard. He fears retaliation by one of Tarq's spies." Lisa excused herself warily.

"Oh, I'm sure that won't happen." Ferrel answered quickly. "Won't you come inside?" He gestured to the tent. "The cots are still up." They entered the tent, leaving Orado outside fuming.

"Oh, Lady Lisa, may I present you to my brother, Lord Merrick Dracos Olenteas."

"I know you! You're the man who found me in the forest!" Lisa exclaimed.

Merrick guardedly replied. "Yes, and took you to King Tarq's camp. But please, don't mention this to anyone. They might not understand."

"Oh, I won't." Lisa assured him. She put it from her mind. Now that she recognized him, she merely assumed that he had been acting on secret orders as she had suspected.

Ferrel deftly switched the conversation to the coming events and Mark watched as his brother teased and cajoled her into a tranquil state of mind. The earlier part of the conversation was forgotten in tales of Dal Ryeas.

A pleasant hour was spent before Sergeant Orado entered and diffidently reminded Lisa that her attendance upon the Princess was required. Lisa reluctantly accompanied the guard, but turned back to wave cheerfully at the brothers as they watched her wend her way back to the center of camp.

"A nice girl." Merrick remarked. "She doesn't understand what's going on, though. And I just don't feel as if we can tell her."

"Maybe we should." said Ferrel. "She might be an asset, being so close to the Princess."

"I don't know. I think she'd bring danger to us as well as herself. She's not exactly circumspect and her entire outlook has been formed by Killia."

Ferrel frowned. "Ever since Mark died though, she's been coming here and depending on me. I think we could trust her."

"Let's not worry about that now. We'll see how things shape up in Dal Ryeas. We're going to have a lot of work to do. Let's finish your packing."

"Merrick?" Ferrel said after a long quiet time. "Do you think we'll see Mother?"

"Don't get your hopes up, Ferrel. She doesn't want us around."

"Why are she and Aunt Carr so different?"

"Different mothers. Aunt Carr's mother was a wonderful person who truly loved grandfather. She died when Aunt Carr was quite little, even before she started wizard training. Our grandmother just never really knew how to bring up children. She left Carr alone and neglected our mother. Carr cared for her little sister as well as she could, but when she started wizard training, Mother was deserted. Although she still loves Aunt Carr she has never been able to get over her sense of betrayal. It's made her a very bitter person. When we chose to go with father even after she revealed the plot against the King to Carr and had guaranteed our safety, she saw it as another desertion. So she closed herself to us."

"But she's our Mother!"

"So? She has problems. Look, we're lucky. We've had a father, we have each other, and Aunt Carr truly cares, you'll see! Let's forget about Mother. She's a bitter woman, old before her time, jealous of her sister's prominence and she sees us as rejecting her."

"But we didn't!" Ferrel complained.

"I know. But by rejecting us first, she thinks to avoid being rejected. It's a vicious cycle. Come on, we've work to do."

Merrick turned back to the packing. For a moment, Ferrel watched him. Inwardly he thanked the Twins for Merrick. He swore to himself that whatever Merrick needed, even if it meant his life, Ferrel would be there just as Merrick was there for him.

Diana nervously watched as Tarq and Lauren fought over every item. She wondered how they were going to act with each other when they were alone on earth. Without Alaeric, whose good humor and excellent advice buffered their sharpest attacks, she wondered if they would end up killing each other. I can see the headlines now, she thought.

She reflected on the two and a half months she had spent in this untamed forest. Things she never believed existed were reality. Mythology sprang to life, magic worked. Although she knew that the camp was warded against the predators of this continent, she had seen them in her travels with Lauren. Carr's teachings had given her insight into the vast realm of magic, and the more she learned, the more she wanted to know.

Vaguely she wondered if, when the war ended and Tarq returned to power, she might attend the university in Tadia. What would her parents think?

At the thought of her parents, she grew anxious. They ought to be home by now. Even though Lauren assured her of her mother's acquaintance with the concepts of path finding, Diana was vastly perturbed with the whole idea. Her mother was a nice American lady with a good income, fine house, and five kids – two step kids and three of her own. She was entirely normal, nothing magical about her. How could she be from the same place? She did not seem even remotely related to the events of the summer. How could she be?

At last, Lauren stopped arguing with Tarq and they were ready to go. Diana gathered her things and carried them over to where the King was standing. He smiled reassuringly at her, but she sensed a deep sadness in him. It occurred to her that Tarq thought he was going into barren exile forever: his Kingdom was lost; his only love a distant cold woman willing to save his life but not to share it. Diana found herself admiring the courageous front he was showing. Always somewhat shy around the King, now in the face of his fortitude, all she felt was awe.

Carr was talking softly to him, "As soon as we find anything, we'll contact you. Don't worry, please. Sindelar will be too busy trying to consolidate his position. Our people will not be that complacent. There should be insurrection. And it will take the priests a goodly time to find auspicious dates for transference."

"Carr, do not summon any other world beasts," Tarq ordered. "Just because they have done so does not mean we must stoop to their level. I won't have my people caught between. There are enough beasts wandering in Tadia as it stands. We'll have to find other methods."

"But my liege, it's a very effective way of sabotage," Carr protested. "Look at the havoc the griffs wreaked. Not to mention the dragons."

"I said no." He touched his chest lightly, tracing the lines of his scars. "I will not have my people victimized. We'll be fighting those things for years as it is!"

"As you wish, Sire." Carr agreed.

"We should be going, my Lord," Lauren said in a surprisingly gentle tone. Tarq stared at her, perplexed and confused at the change in her tone. He saw the pity on her face and turned from it. He reached for his pack and got his wayward feelings under control.

Diana and Tarq stood together, Lauren's hands lightly resting on the girl's shoulders, packs slung over their feet as Lauren summoned her path. It manifested slowly at her feet and spread before them, a yawning black road into oblivion.

Carr looked at her King and vowed to restore him to power as Alaeric stood beside her and lifted his sword in a salute. Mist swirled around them, obscuring the trio from view. When it was gone, Alaeric and Carr were alone in the night.

A moment of darkness as the winds of the gods whirled around them and then they landed in the back garden of the Harrison's property. Both houses looked abandoned. The grass was overgrown and unkempt. Lisa's vegetable garden resembled a jungle, while the Olenteas' garden was dry and withered. For a moment, Diana was certain that no one was at home and that their entry into the edgeworld would be unnoticed. Or worse, they arrived in another time, perhaps months, or years into the future.

As they began to get their bearings after the transition, Diana's hopes were lifted when the back porch light flickered on and her father's voice called, "Who's there?"

"Daddy?" Diana said shyly, a sudden rush of emotion overwhelming her. She was truly home. "Diana...?" And the Ron Harrison was out the door and across the lawn in seconds, grabbing her up in a jubilant bone-crushing hug. "Honey, are you all right? Where have you been?"

"Oh yes. Oh, Daddy, I've got so much to tell you..." She was crying in his arms.

"Where are Mark and Lisa?" Ron refused to let her go.

"Uh... that's part of what I have to tell you..." Diana replied hesitantly, breaking his hold.

Lila Harrison came outside then. When she saw her daughter standing there, obviously healthy, a small frown creased her mouth. "Well Diana," she said, embracing the girl tightly. "So how do you like my side of the family?"

"Well, they are exciting!" Diana said, hugging back and almost crying.

"You seem to have misplaced your brother and sister." Mrs. Harrison remarked casually, looking around. With her arm around her daughter's shoulders, she looked at Tarq with interest.

"It's a long story, Mom. But before we even get into it, um, I'd… like to present you to His Majesty, King Tarq Antonas Pyramus," and Diana stumbled over the formal name of the King, "of Dal Ryeas."

To her husband's great surprise, Lila Harrison sank into a deep formal curtsy.

Tarq gently took her arm, raising her again. "Lady Lila. I long ago heard of your beauty and grace. My father spoke of you often. He remembered you with great fondness and respect. All reports were unexaggerated."

"Your father was my good friend," Lila smiled. "Circumstances being what they were, we still never let our political differences come between us. Welcome." She turned to her husband. "Sire, this is my husband, Ron," she smiled, presenting a bemused man to the strangers that had manifested in his back yard.

Ron exchanged brief greetings with Tarq and Lauren before demanding again, "Where are Mark and Lisa?"

Lauren, who had remained silent up until then, said, "We should discuss this inside. There is much to tell you. Not all of it pleasant."

The group entered the Harrison kitchen where Diana helped her mother prepare a midnight snack, and Lauren briefly explained the events of the last few months. Only when she mentioned the rumor of Mark's death did Ron start violently to protest their lack of action. But Lila reassured him that she would know if Mark was killed, and she had no such feeling. Diana, amazed at her mother's calm and father's acceptance of her word during the telling of the possible death of her brother, suddenly saw them in a new light. She was anxious to get them alone for a long talk. There was a lot she needed to know.

The only time Lauren hesitated in her story was when she reached the part concerning Lisa's theft of the Tal. Sensing Lauren's reluctance to tell her kinswoman of her daughter's iniquity, Diana took up the tale.

"Lisa, after being rescued by Lord Merrick, turned around and stole the Tal from us and gave it to Sindelar. The wizard broke Tarq's barriers to Tadia and cut us off. The King sent all the troops into hiding where they await either the recovery of the Tal or the

141

discovery of a new one. Everyone is on alert. But Merrick is going to try and steal it back." Diana finished confidently.

Lauren looked astonished. "He is? He'll be caught. Sindelar can't possibly trust him, especially after he learns that Merrick brought Lisa to us."

Diana paled. "I never thought of that. And she will betray him. Oh, Merrick…"

"Merrick will be careful, I'm certain." Lauren reassured the girl quickly with a hand.

"Who is Merrick?" asked Ron, having switched instantly to the usual "protective-father" mode. And a new round of explanations began. The discussion continued until sunrise when Ron finally said, "We'll continue all this later. Everyone needs sleep. You must be exhausted. Do you want to stay here or go back to your place? Lila has kept it ready but it still might be somewhat musty."

Lauren answered, "No, thank you. We'll go back to my house." Tarq rose and followed Lauren.

Just before they left, Lila said reluctantly to the exiled King, "For what it is worth, the reason we settled here in this city, is because I could vaguely sense the presence of this world's Tal. Only it's an unfocussed one and I could not pinpoint its location."

Tarq's eyes grew sharp and keen. For the first time since their arrival he had begun to show an interest in his new surroundings. "An unfocussed Tal…interesting."

Chapter 15

Daylight came as a surprise. Mark had fallen asleep during the long darkness while Tayaela shifted them back into the forest during his slumber. Groggily, he pulled himself to a sitting position and looked around the cave. The cat was sitting at the foot of his bed watching him with interest. The animal's sleek black fur and white chest patch gave him a formal appearance. His large yellow-green eyes held an understanding and a knowledge that was disconcerting.

"Good morning Maikai," he said to the animal who responded in a silent mew. "I don't suppose you know where breakfast is kept do you?"

Maikai came over to him and forced his head under Mark's hand. When he responded by stroking his head, the animal turned over on his back, paws in the air, and enticingly demanded a stomach rub. Mark cheerfully complied, although bending hurt his side somewhat, and it was in this way that Tayaela found them.

She stood in the entrance for some time before she cleared her throat and said, "Aren't you both glad I'm not an enemy?"

Mark and the cat both looked up ruefully. "I thought they were all gone?"

"Lucky for you they are!" she exclaimed. "Maikai, I'm ashamed of you."

The cat hung his head, and then bounded to her. He stood on his hind legs, paws reaching near her waist and rubbing his head against her leg, as she laughingly protested.

"Alright, I'm glad to see you too! Get off me, you behemoth. No jumping." Tayaela failed to sound stern and the cat tried to jump into her arms. "You are not a kitten anymore and I can't hold you for long."

Maikai's rapture subsided eventually and Tayaela, her hand still caressing his head, asked Mark, "Do you feel up to moving around a bit? I want to make certain they've all left."

"I think so," Mark answered gamely, "We'll never know unless I try. When do you want to get started?"

"After breakfast. I've been doing some scouting and so far we're clear. I've been thinking that if everything is all right we'll take a path back to a world where I spent some time. It's an uninhabited place, so surely its Tal is clear." Tayaela frowned. "Only, before I go making paths to spots unknown, I need to check for traps. Sindelar is powerful; he may have left spells to send unwitting travelers to their doom. If we're alert, we'll feel them. We'll use this as a base and move out from here. Don't worry. I'll attune you to the things to search for."

"So how do we look?" Mark asked. "What's a trap like?"

Tayaela crouched down, a stick in her hand. "We start from here. We move out, say a mile or so, and then come back in a star pattern. This way we'll cover a lot of the area and examine thoroughly."

"How will we know it?"

"If he's used the Tal to fix a path to nowhere, various stones will glow an iridescent green. They might be a cairn or a small outcropping but the green will burn. Sometimes an unfocussed Tal will have the same glow, but since there's only one to a world and Dal Ryeas' is found, any of these glows will be traps laid by Sindelar and his Tal."

"Where are they usually found?"

"It can be anywhere. So just look carefully."

"You mean it could just…"

"Be sitting on a tree stump, yes. One thing, it won't be buried. It's impossible for it to be buried otherwise the trap won't spring. Oh, and no other stone even resembling the trap will be near."

"Why is that?"

"The power of the Tal sort of moves things." Tayaela, sensing his confusion, relented in her oblique explanations. "You see,

Mark, the power of the Tal is so extraordinary that even items infused with its essence become like it. Crystal magic is a difficult science, but it's the foundation of all sorcery on Dal Ryeas. It all leads back to the Tal. I mean, other magic is possible of course, but it takes someone with exceptional skill to work the greater magic without the power of the Tal. Communications crystals or the story crystals are simple and can be used even between worlds, but to heal or to conjure from nothing, that power belongs to the Tal, and only the King, the keeper of the crystal, can dispense it. That's why the King is the head of the College of wizards. Only he can disperse the requisite power."

"Is it always a King?" Mark asked, imagining Tayaela as a powerful Queen on a golden throne.

"Oh no, it's just the birthright of the first born King or Queen."

"Oh," Mark spoke lamely.

"If we don't find any traps in a few days, I'll assume there are none and we'll forge a path to the place I was telling you about. Now, I know you're not totally well, so take it slow and search carefully." Tayaela turned to the cat. "Maikai, you'll stay with Mark at all times."

The huge cat swished its tail like a happy kitten and butted his head under Mark's hand. Mark had the feeling he had just acquired a friend for life.

They set out at a moderate pace, Tayaela keeping watchful eye on Mark so as not to tire him.

The first two days the three rested often, but as they continued the search, Mark's strength gradually returned, and they were able to travel further distances. Even as they sought possible dangers, Mark realized what a lush, beautiful place the forest was.

For his first months, his incarceration at Sindelar's camp and his concern for Lisa kept him from appreciating his surroundings, but now his search with Tayaela and Maikai gave him an opportunity to revel in the deep greens and purples of the forest. The vegetation, similar to his home, yet different, fascinated him just as the animals they encountered mesmerized him. He felt strangely at peace and happy, somehow never wanting the idyllic journey to end.

On the fifth day of their search, Tayaela found two horses.

The animals were tethered in a grassy meadow. Water was within reach and they seemed very content to wander on their leads. Tayaela was overjoyed to discover tack, somewhat weathered but useful nearby on the ground.

"Mark," she called, "come help me."

As he joined her, Mark felt a relief as transportation appeared. Even as weak a rider as he was, he preferred the idea of riding to walking. Eagerly, he helped Tayaela as they saddled the animals.

"Now we can cover more ground during the day and shelter in the cave at night. We'll be able to path forge soon!" she said excitedly.

Mark happily nodded. As much as he was enjoying his time with Tayaela, the press of events was beginning to intrude upon his consciousness. He wanted to find Lisa and get her home.

Tayaela was also enjoying her time in the woods. It gave her a respite from her unending despair over Alaeric. She felt as if she were actively involved in searching for him. For with a Tal, she could provide freedom to Tadia and find her brother. She could find her love.

During her exile on her uninhabited place she searched for the Tal, slowly narrowing her area of search. Each day she felt closer to discovery, closer to reunion. Never wavering in her belief in its existence, she had started each day's search eagerly. Always optimistic, Tayaela knew her efforts were being rewarded, if not now, then soon. Now, once she was certain that no hidden dangers awaited them; Tayaela eagerly anticipated her return to her world and the discovery of its Tal.

Late on the eighth day, as they were turning their steeds to return to the cave for the night, they heard new sounds. Not the gentle sounds of the wind, or the cries of animals, but the sound of people on horseback, and close behind them. Tayaela, turning to face Mark, caught a glimpse of a cloak behind them as it flashed through the sunlit trees. Beckoning to Mark, she silently gestured to him to take shelter beneath a stand of trees.

As they reached safety, she whispered, "I think I'd rather see who they are before we hail them. Sindelar may have left human traps as well."

Chapter 16

The fall of Tadia, the massive capital of Tarq's far-flung kingdom, was violent, swift, and demoralizing. Sindelar's attack came unexpectedly, hidden from the vigilance of the faculty of wizards at the University by the very presence of the stolen Tal. With it, the renegade wizard was able to block all communications from the King to his regents who might warn them of the imminent danger.

Sindelar then, under the cover of night with the shielding of the Tal, opened a path directly into the city and led his troops in personally. Accompanied by Rhea Volta and her vanguard of elite fighters, the wizard proceeded to order the arrest and imprisonment of all sorcerers. These he found by their links to the Tal that Princess Killia, even though unconsecrated to the stone, could feel.

Many fled in the first nights of chaos, aided by a fearful and angry citizenry; many were taken to the Crimson Fortress and imprisoned. The city expected the wizard and the Princess would release Prince Kir'san and Prince Ertlan Olenteas and their families, but the Princess refused, saying that as long as any of Olenteas blood was bound to Pyramus, the mountain clans were not to be trusted.

Many Olenteans and others felt confused by this attitude until they remembered that Alaeric Olenteas was married to Princess Tayaela. Sindelar tried to convince the Princess she erred in her decision to continue the imprisonment of the Olenteas Princes, but she laughed in a near hysterical way and declared, "I only want those around me who are pure. Olenteas blood is tainted. I'll have none of them. They brought me to defeat by their treachery once, but never again. If Lauren Olenteas had never been born, I would have married Tarq and this entire situation would not have occurred!"

Merrick, standing guard in the Princess tent, overheard the remark, and stored it away in his memory for later use. Sindelar, painfully aware that the Olenteas lords were allies in the previous rebellion, and that Merrick's father had chosen exile rather than betray his loyalty to Tadiak, looked apologetically at the young man. Merrick returned the look with such indifference that the wizard thought that the young Olenteas kinsman had not heard the Princess' remark.

Trying to control the situation as much as possible, Sindelar persuaded Killia to place the Olenteas Lords under palace arrest with her private troops acting as honor guards. Killia conceded to allowing this but insisted that the Lords were to be located in cells in the lower level of the Tadia Palace.

This news leaked into the city and increased the resistance met by Sindelar's troops. After thirty years of peace and prosperity under Pyramus rule, the citizens of Tadia had no wish to return to the excesses of a Tadiak dynasty. They remembered the screams in the night, the terror by day. Many wealthy Tadains attempted to flee the city for the clan holds of their families; however, Rhea Volta's troops intercepted most of these Tadains as they ran and held them as hostages to ensure cooperation from remaining family members.

It was a time of great fear and sorrow. The only positive outcome of the coup was the healing of the long-standing breach between Olenteas and Pyramus. When it became apparent in the very first days that the Tadiak Queen held no trust for the Olenteas clans, older clan leaders residing in Tadia recalled that when the Pyramus revolution occurred, none of the rank-and-file Tadiak clan folk were ever detained. Killia made enemies of her former allies in one swift instant.

Olenteas remained loyal, based upon pledges from eons of mutual trust with Tadiak. Even though their own children had forsaken ancient alliances, the Olenteas Princes remained true to their word – through imprisonment and exile from their mountain strongholds. And in one day, Killia had betrayed them and broken her own liege oath. In the minds of the Olenteas princes, who had thought much about the futility of their cause in their five years at the Crimson Fortress, Killia's choice had freed them from their obligations.

From their prison cells, the Olenteas lords smuggled word to their kin residing in town to give succor and any other type of assistance necessary to the clan Pyramus. Not really needing any authority from their absent lords, Olenteas kin were already hiding their Pyramus friends and smuggling them from the city. Tadains united by hiding the unfortunate from Volta's troops, as Olenteas' traders smuggled as many as they could to Chaldia, the home city of Pyramus and to the Mountain Fortress city of Olen itself. Many brave acts by Olenteas clan folk secured the safety of their former enemies and old wounds and mistrust healed. The warring of the Olenteas and Pyramus born of envy and greed ended in deeds of bravery and honor. Long after this war, these acts were remembered and new alliances were forged between the clans.

Now the other Dal Ryean cities waited in fear for Sindelar's next move. Many of Tarq's troops removed their uniforms and blended into the general populace. Others engaged in sorties against Killia's army and still others fought in the outlying areas against the raging other world beasts. However, while the underground leadership was forming, the resistance was sporadic and weak. They were waiting for Alaeric and the King to return.

Only the great temple of the Twins, Saevirg and Sarama, openly defied Sindelar and Killia. The High Priestess refused to budge on any of her prerogatives. She refused to yield to Volta's troops any of the Pyramus or Olenteas clergy or guards. In front of a hostile silent crowd, The High Priestess politely but firmly turned Rhea Volta away, threatening her with excommunication from entering the temple precincts or harming any of her priesthood.

Vowing revenge against the insult, Volta rode through the sullen city to the camp where Killia was staying until Sindelar was certain Tadia was ready for her royal arrival. Killia tried to comfort her with creative inventions of future tortures for the Priestess.

The defiance of the Priestess brought a tiny ray of optimism to the beleaguered city. Quickly, citizens began to whisper the name of Tarq. Hope for their King's swift return kept the city from complete despair. They were prepared to aid him any way possible.

Ruthlessly, Sindelar squelched any form of resistance.

His troops patrolled the streets of Tadia causing the once noisy thriving city to conduct its business in a subdued, unnatural silence. Strict curfews were enforced and free speech curtailed. Almost every family had someone taken as hostage. Yet, the wizard still had doubts as to the efficiency of his policies.

There were still areas not responding to the regime. Even though unconvinced about the safety of Tadia, Sindelar felt obligated to bring Killia into the city. He could only hope her presence and beauty would begin to restore tranquility. He immediately began to doubt his wisdom in this as he escorted her through the streets. A moody populace watched as the sorcerer, dressed in dull yellow, escorted Killia, gowned in vibrant green, to her castle. Surrounded by soldiers and greeted by silence was not the way Killia envisioned her triumphal entry into Tadia. Her displeasure showed in a narrowing of her lips.

A woman, standing next to her neighbor, was heard by Captain Volta to say, "She has a sullen mouth, surely a mean disposition." Volta thereupon dispatched two soldiers who beat the woman senseless and left her lying on the ground. As word of the incident spread through the city, the moody silence swiftly changed to a still, angry waiting. By the time Killia and her wizard reached the castle, the tension was at near-riot level. Sindelar dispatched more troops to patrol the streets. He was worried about the palpable hatred he had felt directed at Killia. In a rage, Killia dismounted from her palfrey and stalked into the castle.

"What is the meaning of this!" she demanded in a high pitched shriek as her attendants hurried after her. "How dare they behave in such a way!" she stamped her foot. "They shall not treat me as a pariah!"

Her attendants, Lisa, and another girl Mara, paled at the Princess' irrational anger. They knew once she began her tirades, only exhaustion would stop her. Hopelessly, they looked to Sindelar to aid them in calming the Princess.

"They don't know what is happening, my Lady," he began,

and then a sly smile crossed his face, "and they are awed by your beauty. Perhaps they felt it irreverent to cheer at such loveliness for fear of marring it." He flattered her outrageously.

"I am beautiful, aren't I?" Killia said, her long hands playing with her hair. "I'll be the most beautiful queen the world has ever seen. All of them will worship me!" Killia laughed and twirled around, all anger forgotten. "When will the Priestess set the date for my bonding with the Tal?" Killia slipped her arm through Sindelar's and permitted him to escort her around the castle.

"Quite a stable person, exactly the sort of person we want as a ruler." a voice behind Lisa said quietly. It was Ferrel with his brother, Merrick, watching as the future Queen looked over her new possessions.

"Hello," she said shyly. She really liked Ferrel and thought Merrick quite romantic and heroic. Killia and Sindelar reached a set of great doors. Before they opened, the wizard held his hand up for silence.

"Today returns the Tadiak heir to the Throne of Dal Ryeas. We mark this auspicious occasion to welcome thee, Killia Tadiak to Tadia Castle, the center of your empire. We wait only on the auguries of the High Priestess of the Twins to set the date of your sealing with the Tal, making you at one with your people." Sindelar's voice rang through the castle, leaving behind a strange emptiness where joy should have been. Realizing that the castle residents were uncertain as to their roles, he began a cheer himself. Volta followed and soon the cheering of her own troops cancelled the silence of Killia's arrival.

"The priestess will only be able to hold them off for six months or so," Merrick quietly said from behind them.

"Why, Merrick?" Ferrel asked urgently. He forgot for a moment that Lisa was not privy to Tarq's secrets and in fact was cause of their current problems.

"Because in six months comes the Year's End. Auguries are rampant then and all the bards from the Kingdom will gather for their annual blessing. Somehow, Sindelar will make the Priestess declare this the time for the consecration and coronation. But maybe…" Merrick's voice trailed away. He fingered a small crystal sphere that hung on a chain around his neck. "Look Ferrel, I'll be back later. I have something to do. Goodbye, Lisa."

He left the pair gaping after him as he hurried from the castle.

Merrick watched in grim amusement as Leda, the daughter of the Arras Tavern's proprietors, for the third time in as many days, managed to distract the attention of the soldier Rhea Volta had put on him as a shadow. The poor boy, Merrick thought of the soldier, will never understand what hit him.

In his earlier briefings with Carr, Merrick discovered that the sorceress had close ties with Vida, the proprietress. They were friends of long standing and on many an occasion the tavern keeper and her husband Dirk, assisted in clandestine government activities.

Five years earlier, Vida discovered the Tadiak-Olenteas plot to stage a coup and accordingly warned the King of the event. Vida was a Lynteas and her husband a Cynthean so loyalty to Pyramus, Tadiak, or Olenteas was not an issue. When Merrick made his first contact with the taverners, they were already involved in assisting Pyramus and Olenteas to escape Tadia for the hinterlands. It was very simple for Merrick to convert an already established network for Tarq's purposes.

Merrick's first contact with the Arras Tavern came within the first days of the conquest. He skillfully managed to make his way unseen to the back door following Carr's instructions. Vida and Dirk greeted him enthusiastically. Diligently, the three began to lay the foundation for Tarq's return. Safe havens were located and a series of rumors circulated.

Merrick was in the unique position of knowing Sindelar's agents. He identified these spies to his captains and through a set of careful maneuvers was able to isolate them. Information carefully leaked to the agents, and the conflicting stories soon had the Sindelar's secret service in chaos. Sindelar could only trust his own personal resources, one of whom was Merrick. After all, Merrick was vulnerable and the wizard held his vulnerability in thrall.

Early on, Merrick brought Sindelar to the Arras Tavern. In the guise of an evening out on the town, the young agent convinced the sorcerer (who was heavily disguised, if unconvincingly) that this establishment was a perfect location for heading their clandestine activities. It was so innocuous. Vida, Dirk, and Leda all worked very hard at appearing diligent taverners without a political concern in the world. Whenever Sindelar, who was dressed as Biltean caravanserai, tried to complain about the new regime, Dirk cut him off saying, "Politics was fine to discuss among friends, but he would have none of it treasonous." This pleased the magician immensely, and he agreed to Merrick's plan for an alternate spy headquarters.

Until Killia's entry into Tadia, Merrick operated autonomously. His creative rumor mill kept the populace of Tadia quietly seething. All appeared calm on the surface, but it was part of a massive deception. The silence that greeted the Princess' entry was the first indication that the city was dissatisfied with the new order.

On that first day, Volta, always sensing treachery, assigned a soldier to follow Merrick. He did so and followed Merrick at once to the Arras. There Merrick entertained a diverse number of guests and became roaring drunk. After passing out, Dirk put him to bed in a back room. When the soldier tried to follow, Leda made her first move on him. Time passed and the soldier, weary of waiting for Merrick, returned to Volta with the tale that the young lord had returned home to bed.

She set him to following Merrick daily. On this third day, Merrick led him on a tantalizing journey through the marketplace, followed by a pious trip to the Temple of the Twins. The soldier could not follow here and was completely unaware that his quarry was meeting with the High Priestess on behalf of Tarq. After the Temple, Merrick returned to the castle where he spent some hours with his brother. At dusk, the soldier then followed Merrick, who was very careful not to lose him, to the Arras once again.

Leda was waiting and almost before Merrick could sit down and watch her machinations, she had the soldier's complete attention. Vida, also watching her daughter with amusement, said to Merrick. "It's all in the name of duty."

"Quite." answered Merrick. "I think he's distracted." Merrick rose and went towards the back room.

"For the duration." Vida replied softly.

"Well, let's go create some problems." The grim young man grinned evilly at his hostess as she led him to the private chamber where his leaders awaited their next set of instructions.

153

Chapter 17

On the third morning after their arrival, Lauren decided to re-establish her connections to her edgeworld. She quietly looked in on Tarq, who was sprawled across Alaeric's bed, sleeping. She was glad, since she knew that his first two nights had been restless. She suppressed the urge to go to the bed and stroke the tousled blonde hair back from his face. Instead, she tiptoed to the night table and left a note prominently displayed telling him that she was going shopping.

For a time, she watched him sleeping, his face smooth, almost boy-like, and serene. She dreaded seeing him awake, when the trouble and pain marred his face and knowing there was nothing she could do. Her own face, she knew, was for the moment, nakedly expressing her own emotional turmoil. If Tarq awakened, Lauren knew she could never explain why tears were in her eyes as she looked at him. But he remained asleep and the haunted, dark-eyed princess quietly left him to his rest.

Lauren gathered her jacket, a shoulder bag, and car keys and left the house as soon as she could. It was a bright August morning. A fine mist settled on everything and sparkled like diamonds in the sun. Looking next door, she decided to ask Diana to join her for a shopping spree. She knew the girl needed to return to normal life after months in an alien environment. Shopping was just the thing!

Crossing through the hedge, Lauren sauntered towards the back door. There she found Diana and her mother sharing a mid-morning snack.

154

"Good morning." she said cheerfully through the screen.

"Oh Lauren," Lila exclaimed. "Come in. Would you like a cup of tea?"

"Yes, that would be lovely." Lauren smiled as she sat down in one of the comfortable kitchen chairs. "Diana, have you settled in all right?"

"It's a little hard being here and not knowing what's going on back on Dal Ryeas." The girl confessed.

"We should hear from Carr soon. Merrick will report to her as to what's happening on Dal Ryeas. We do know the attack is in full force against the city."

"What about Mark?" Lila Harrison asked bluntly.

"Well, since you both," Lauren looked at Diana and Lila, "insist he's alive, I expect he'll either turn up somewhere in the forest or he was taken with the others to Tadia. If he's in the woods, Alaeric will find him, and Merrick's keeping an eye out for him in the city."

"Is Merrick going to be all right?" Diana asked in a tight little voice.

Lauren considered evading the question, but then determined honesty should prevail. "What Merrick is doing is extremely hazardous. I can't guarantee his safety. He is aware of the risks." She looked at the girl who had gone rather pale. "I know you feel very strongly about him, but there are no guarantees. I know he'll be careful and that for your sake, he'll try to protect Lisa as well as Ferrel. And that's all I can say."

Diana nodded and quickly wiped a tear from her eye.

"What I came here for though," Lauren continued briskly, ignoring the impending waterworks from Diana, "was to see if you want to go shopping."

"Shopping?" Diana was puzzled.

"Yeah, you know, go to the mall, shop? I need some clothes and I have to get Tarq some. He can wear Alaeric's shirts, but the trousers are going to be huge."

"Oh." Diana looked at her mother who nodded. "Sure, let me get my purse."

Within minutes, Lauren and Diana seated in Alaeric's red SUV, drove to the mall. The day was warm, the late morning sun burning brightly in the clear blue sky. The morning haze, burned away, was a vague memory as the two young women sped through the half-deserted streets of the city on their way to the local shopping center.

For a time, they forgot their concerns and merely appreciated the finely tuned engine as it sped its way along the highway, with their favorite songs vying for airtime. For a while they were untroubled, cheerful young women participating in a ritual of modern society.

They parked the car in a slightly giddy state and entered the mall. Lauren felt some trepidation as she walked under the glowing skylights amidst the profusion of shapes, a feeling that her presence was an anomaly. This passed, however, as the plethora of goods and shops assailed her senses.

"Oh look!" she exclaimed, pointing out a men's store. "They've got a sale going. I'm going to get some clothes for Tarq."

As they entered, Diana asked, "How is he? I looked for him yesterday, but he never came outside."

"He's having a hard time adjusting." Lauren sighed. "I know what he's going through and it's going to take a while. Clothes will help and then I'll try to get him out. He hasn't left his room for three days." She finished worriedly.

Diana, whose innate courtesy sensed that Lauren did not want to discuss the King, began exclaiming over new styles of clothing. Before long, Lauren joined her and they selected a number of outfits. As Lauren was charging them, Diana wandered to the store entrance.

"Hey Diana!" a voice called. It was her friend, Jill. "When did you get back?" Jill asked in an accusatory tone.

"Oh, a couple of days ago." Diana felt curiously distant from her once closest friend.

"Why didn't you tell me you were leaving home? I came by your house and it was all dark. Some friend." Jill playfully punched Diana's arm. It took all her control to stop herself from responding as if the punch were a threat.

"It was an unexpected trip," Diana said uncomfortably. "We had to go away with relatives on a wilderness survival course."

"I take it your mom had second thoughts about leaving you with Mark." Jill had a fixation on Mark and brought him into every conversation. "Is he home too? Can I come over?" Jill eagerly asked.

"No, uh, Mark and Lisa are staying with the relatives for the rest of the summer. Maybe fall too." The conversation with Jill brought back her fears and worries of her siblings' condition, and she realized she needed to devise an acceptable story about her absence around the sad, haunted look on her face. She turned to leave but Jill stopped her again.

"So, have you called Jim?" Jill asked. "He's been completely depressed all summer. You could've sent a postcard."

"Jim?" Diana asked blankly. And then it hit her like a falling tree that she had forgotten Jim, her boyfriend of two years. Things were worse than she realized.

"Oh, no. I uh- haven't had..." her voice trailed off.

Just then, Lauren emerged from the store, laughing and laden with bags. "Diana, help!"

Grateful for the diversion, Diana rushed to her and took some packages. "What did you do, buy out the whole store?" she asked, laughing.

"Nearly," Lauren grinned. "Who's your friend?"

"Lauren, this is Jill Freeman. Jill, this is my cousin Lauren." Diana felt oddly formal. She realized that her months with Carr had begun to instill a sense of protocol foreign to a twenty-first century American girl.

Giving Diana an odd look, Jill said. "Pleased to meet you, Lauren."

"So now where, Diana?" Lauren said after replying to Jill. "I want to get some new jeans and some sweaters."

"The *Roundtree* has new stuff for school." Jill volunteered.

"School?" Diana said blankly.

"You know, senior year? High school less than a month?" Jill said. "Hello Diana?" she gently tapped Diana's forehead. "Where's your brain wandering?"

"Oh," Diana's laugh was stilted. "A dimension away."

The three women laughed, and Jill was invited to accompany them. They shopped for the remainder of the morning, making inconsequential chatter as Jill's presence inhibited Lauren and Diana from discussing their deepest concerns, which was fine by them. After a special lunch at the mall's best restaurant, to which Lauren included the excited Jill, Diana's friend departed leaving

Diana and Lauren free to speak.

"Do you think we'll go back soon?" Diana asked. "Do you think Merrick's all right?"

"I don't know," Lauren replied honestly to both questions. "Do you want to go back?"

"More than anything..." Diana searched for words. "On Dal Ryeas I felt really important, that I wasn't just some kid, but an integral part of the campaign. Here I'm just Diana Harrison; there I'm Carr's apprentice."

"Really, or is it only Merrick?" Lauren asked shrewdly.

"No. It's home. Even if Merrick's... not there. I want to make a life there. As long as I can come home occasionally to shop." Diana grinned.

"Of course." Lauren agreed solemnly. Both young women began to laugh and were able to complete their excursion in a positive mood, which they hoped would strengthen them in the days ahead.

Staring blankly at night-shrouded walls, the King, lost in his endless self-recriminations sought the comfort of the darkness. Since his arrival on this bizarre, incomprehensible edgeworld he had stayed in the room Lauren had given him, except for brief forays to the kitchen for food. The room, which had been Alaeric's in this foul world, was an odd mixture of Earth and Dal Ryeas.

Familiar Dal Ryean objects - like Alaeric's favorite story crystal - stood in a room of intricate plumbing and luxurious scents, right off the sleeping quarters. In idle, lighter moments Tarq discovered how the strange plumbing worked. It used water, not crystals, and whirled down a hole very readily. He wondered if this could be adapted for his own home. And then when the reality of this world struck, with its noises and smells, its technological reveling and its primitive self-interest, the thought terrified him.

Since the night of their arrival, he had been assailed, unprepared, by the utter strangeness of this edgeworld. It bothered him that Lauren fit in so easily to the aura of the place. Diana, he could understand, it was her birthright, and she took for granted the wonders that disturbed him. But Lauren, not only utilized the marvels of this edgeworld for her own purpose, but she delighted in them.

The day before, she had come to his room. Tarq kept repeating the scene in his mind, as he watched the blank wall. Her outfit was of this edgeworld, not of home. He felt awkward in her presence, aware that his shirt and leathers seemed vastly inappropriate when compared to her own. She wore a leather jacket but it closed with decorative snaps as opposed to having laces. Her trousers were the same blue of Diana's. She looked casually natural as she leaned in his doorway.

He felt himself flush again as her words returned to haunt him in the dark.

"I'm going shopping, my liege," she had said, looking at him. "I forgot something the first time." "Where are the shops?" he had asked, for lack of anything else to say.

"The mall is about a fifteen-minute drive."

"You're going in one of those vehicles then, correct?" He had never felt so foolish, or been so aware of his ignorance. As a boy, when he occasionally visited core and edgeworlds dominated by science and not magic, he arrogantly assumed that he would never have to understand the other way of living.

"A car, right," she had replied. She had then paused before continuing. "I forgot to buy you the proper underclothing. Alaeric's would be far too large for you."

"Thank you," he had said simply, hating the thought of her charity.

"Don't worry, Sire, I'll charge it, and by the time the bill comes due, you'll be able to repay me." Lauren had responded blithely. Then she added, "Are you going to be all right here alone?"

"I was before, wasn't I?" he had replied stiffly before turning his back on her and staring out the window.

He covered his face with his hands, remembering her worried look and the casual shrug as she left him. He felt inadequate and humiliated. When she had returned she brought him the underwear and left as quickly as she had come. He had then dressed himself fully. The edgeworld's clothing was a perfect fit and very comfortable. I'm still an alien here, he had thought. And I always will be.

"But so is she." he whispered to the night black room now. "I will abide here, somehow. I can be no less successful with my exile than Lauren was with hers," he added in resolution. He then lay back on the bed and attempted to sleep.

He remembered long before when he was trying to get Lauren to set the date for their wedding, how fascinated she was about the other worlds. He knew her her desire to marry him or to have the freedom to explore the paths of the universes was tearing her apart. At the time he resented her desires and the amount of time she spent listening to the different bards when they returned from their travels.

He winced as he recalled how often he accused her of caring more for adventure than for him. Even as he had made the painful decision to banish Lauren from Dal Ryeas, a small part of him resented that she was finally getting her wish to explore the edges and without him. If only he could get past her guard long enough to tell her the hope he still felt about their eventually exploring together.

Before he could continue this new line of reasoning, Carr contacted him and he became mentally engrossed in the news of the war effort. Thoughts of Lauren put carefully in the back of his mind as the King once more concentrated on his duty.

Carr's voice projected itself into his mind clearly. "Sire, the deployment of your troops and the plans to infiltrate Tadia are underway."

"Any word on the search for Tals?"

"None yet, but I am confident that one of my agents will be able to locate an unfocussed Tal eventually, provided that our time limit still is at least five to six months." She went on to share with him the news that the Olenteas clans were spiriting Pyramus clan folk and soldiers out of Tadia, hiding them from Sindelar. She also indicated that the Olenteas Princes were still imprisoned and that this was brewing discontent among clans.

Even though he was reluctant to believe her, Tarq felt better than he had for days. At least his own side was not as idle as their King was. He still resented that he had to be away from the fray, but he understood the necessity. It was like chess. Protect the King. He wondered if this world played the game. So many others did. Before he finally slept, the King made a personal vow to accept whatever fate had in store for him with calm and equanimity.

When he awoke later in the morning, he dressed himself in the strange, unfamiliar clothing and sauntered downstairs to the kitchen where Lauren was preparing breakfast. He felt slightly inclined to swagger in his new clothing, but determined it was a singularly inappropriate way for a supplicant to behave.

Instead, he quietly entered the kitchen and waited until Lauren saw him. The sight of her brought back a host of memories, Lauren standing up to him over an apparent injustice, or slaying him with her biting wit. He recalled the first day when he realized that he loved her. She had been to the mountains to attend the funeral of an ancient relative and was gone for over a month. He had wandered through the castle and his duties sullenly. He was sitting in his study when he heard her voice outside the door.

Suddenly the depression lifted from him and he hurried to the door. Even though the weather was gloomy and cold, Tarq felt warmth transfuse him. As he greeted Lauren, pulling her into the room, he knew that for the last month his misery was caused by her absence. The usually taciturn Tarq pulled her into his arms and kissed her passionately. In between kisses, he spoke of his feelings and of his need, only stopping when Lauren aroused by his passion matched his and confessed her own feelings. By supper that night their engagement was officially announced.

"My Lord!" she exclaimed, surprised at his silent entrance, and jolting him back to the present. She was evidently pleased at his decision to come out of seclusion although her shock caused her to drop the bowl of eggs she was mixing.

As they cleaned up the liquid from the floor, Tarq took a deep breath and asked, "Is it possible for you to be a little less formal?"

"How do you want me to be?" Lauren asked her gaze direct and yet a trifle guarded. "I want us to be as we were," he replied casually, "But at least friends."

"I've always been your friend." Lauren said quietly. She scooped up the remaining liquid and threw her sodden paper towels away. When she turned back to him, her face was as closed and distant as ever. Inwardly he sighed. Someday perhaps.

Lauren, briskly going to the stove, asked again, "What do you want for breakfast, Tarq?" Astounded and very pleased at her use of his name, the King replied in a rushed stammer. "I don't... really... whatever you care to prepare."

Lauren continued, smiling, "I think I'll make you hot cakes, sausage, and tea. That ought to hold you. Today I'm taking you out of this house and showing you some of this world also."

Tarq smiled, "I'd like that. What are hot cakes?"

Lauren laughed softly, "They're good. You'll like them." And she proceeded to bustle around the kitchen making her preparations for breakfast. She poured Tarq a cup of tea from a ceramic pot that was steeping on the counter. He stared curiously at the mug that had the slogan: **eat, drink, and be merry for tomorrow you may diet.**

"What does this mean?" he looked very confused.

"It's part of the American obsession with weight control," Lauren explained as she cooked. "American? I thought this country was the United States?" he asked, confused.

"It is, but the people are called American. The continent is North America. Look, I have some books and maps, and there's a show on PBS on history tonight. You can watch that and get oriented. Then I'll teach you about the Internet, kindles and cell phone apps and texting."

Lauren said quickly as she spattered water across the griddle. It danced in little droplets and she poured batter from her Tupperware container onto the pan.

Tarq stared in amazement at the plastic, "What is that stuff? What are you talking about?" He was utterly confused.

"Plastic. It's made from fossil oil. And the only way I can explain the television is to show you." Lauren walked over to the counter and turned on the small plasma television Alaeric had placed there. She then handed Tarq the remote, gave him brief instructions on its use, and returned to her cooking. When she had finished his plate, she turned back to find him mesmerized at the screen.

"This is better than tale crystals," Tarq remarked, referring to a peculiar stone which when warmed in a fire, re-enacted a story which had been spelled into it. "You can only watch those a few times before they disintegrate, this thing can be watched all the time?"

"It also creates a sense of community," Lauren answered, sitting down.

"How so?" He seemed interested in this.

"The same stories or programs can be watched simultaneously in different households."

"Really. What a thought. When I get home, I'm going to have to tell Carr to try and develop something like this." Tarq was excited. "It's even better than bards."

"News disseminates faster," Lauren replied enthusiastically and inwardly giggled. She was glad he seemed so interested and the thought of Dal Ryeas with television was just too much. Couch Potato Tarq, they would call him, she laughed to herself.

"So, when are you going to take me out in the . . . car?"

"You're awfully chipper this morning."

"Lauren, I'm here. I can't do anything for the time being on Dal Ryeas. Carr reported that she has the troops hidden. She also reported that Killia has managed to alienate your father and uncle already, so they are helping us from prison. So I can either spend my time like I did this past week, brooding, or I can see if something on this world gives me any inspirations as to how I can regain my own again."

Lauren was pleased with Tarq's ambition. She remembered her own first days, when she and Alaeric were thrust into this world of mechanical complexities. She had been terrified. Tarq seemed to be adjusting better than she thought.

Feeling encouraged, Lauren was almost warm when she replied. "Let's go after breakfast. I'll show you — well, you'll see."

They rapidly finished their meal and Tarq complimented Lauren extravagantly on her acquired cooking skills. He recalled to her how in the past she could burn water. As they laughingly cleared the table, Lauren felt an ache for Tarq's well-hidden sorrow. It was there, hidden beneath his assumed demeanor of contentment, ever present and painful. His eyes, caught off guard, were haunted, and she longed to comfort him. Fearing a misinterpretation of any actions, Lauren pointedly maintained her own cheerful aura and led him to the car.

Slightly apprehensive, Tarq hesitated at the door and then gamely opened the door and slid into the seat, mimicking Lauren's movements. The car was a sleek late-model Corvette, black with black interior. To Tarq it seemed like a beast waiting to pounce.

Lauren demonstrated seat belts, and with a mocking grin started the car. Only the warrior training in Tarq kept him from bolting from the door. The roar of the engine sounded as if a herd of dragons were chasing him for breakfast. He smiled wanly at Lauren who seemed lost in thought.

"I think I'm going to take you to the airport first." Lauren mused. "I might as well break you in with a vengeance."

Chapter 18

Alaeric spent days searching the area vacated by Sindelar's troops following faint emanations of the Tal that had passed through the area. For hours he rode in ever-increasing circles through the heavily wooded areas. His search, hot and frustrating, brought him into numerous contacts with the indigenous wild life. For the most part, the animals were vegetarians, however occasionally a predator would see him or force him to fight. These were mostly animals that Sindelar had brought through.

Alaeric disliked killing. Although he was larger, stronger, and more skillful than any number of his contemporaries, his interest in weaponry and warfare was very divorced from killing. It was the skill and challenge that mattered. His skills were legendary even was a boy.

At fifteen, he defeated an entire troop of rebelling soldiers with minimal injuries. At twenty, he single-handedly outwitted a band of brigands, catching them in a cleverly crafted trap and hurting no one. Tarq, appreciating his insights and care, had made him War leader.

Alaeric rode on, thinking of his past and searching for his future. Inwardly, he felt that if anyone discovered an unfocussed Tal then perhaps he could use it to find Tayaela.

Wincing from the pain caused by his recollections of his wife, Alaeric tried very hard to face his fear that she might be wandering the paths forever. "Oh, Tayaela," he said aloud to the trees. In his anger he whacked a huge gash into a tree beside him, causing his sword to become stuck. "Damn!" he exclaimed as he tried to work it loose. "You know," he said conversationally to the air, "if you were going to go into exile, why the hell," he grunted as he pulled the sword loose, "didn't you come to me?"

Panting slightly over his exertion in pulling the sword free, Alaeric resumed both his search and his musing. Tayaela was his best friend and probably the only woman he was likely to love. He missed her as much after five years as he did his first night in exile. He remembered that night. Lauren and he arrived on the strange world with its technical monstrosities. A vague Olenteas connection had met them and taken them to a house, somewhere in England.

Lauren was walking in a daze, while he was trying to maintain a calm demeanor, a sense of dignity in impossible circumstances. It was fine until the relative left them alone. Lauren fell asleep on the sofa as he sprawled across the bed. Defenses finally lowered, he began to weep: to weep for Tayaela, for his lost home. Lauren awoke and tried to comfort him. But, his defenses shattered, all the effect that her gentle touch had caused him to weep the harder. She stayed there with him throughout the night, lending him her strength and her kindness. It got him through the hardest night of his life.

By morning, Lauren and he had created an unbreakable bond of friendship that transcended even their family ties. But every night he wept for Tayaela.

Lost in his morose thoughts, Alaeric deviated from his concentric path. Unaware of his deviation, he wandered deeper into the forest than he intended. He came upon a glen where the sun was shining on a field of bright purple flowers. He stood quite still, transfixed by their beauty. So bemused by the beauty and tired from his long ride, he was unaware of a man entering the meadow across from him. He was itching to have his paint kit to capture the beauty he saw before him.

Alaeric saw the man only after he had begun to walk towards the center of the field. There was something very familiar about the man. Then the young man paused and turned his head half-cocked towards the direction he had come. Alaeric had seen the same motion in Diana.

Suddenly he realized who the youth was. "All my gods," he

muttered softly to himself. "Mark…" Then he drew breath and shouted, "MARK!"

The young man turned, bow in hand, half-notched. Alaeric throwing caution to the gods, stepped out from the protecting valance of the trees.

Mark raised the bow, took aim, and then recognized his former neighbor. For an instant he almost pretended that he did not know the man. But the thought of Tayaela's loneliness and despair caused him to lower his bow. As he did so, he also became aware of another stronger emotion; the joy at meeting this man again.

"Alaeric?" he said hesitantly. Dropping the bow and quiver he loped towards the big man. "Alaeric?"

They embraced roughly and Alaeric said in a harsh, gruff voice. "Your sister was right. Volta didn't manage to kill you!"

"Naw. I'm too mean to die." Mark grinned fully. Both men laughed, and then Mark asked. "Is Diana with you?"

"No. She went to your edgeworld with Lauren and Tarq." Alaeric was uncertain at first how much to reveal, then decided the truth was his alternative. "Lisa stole the Tal from our camp and gave it to Sindelar. As far as we can tell, she was under the impression that we had killed you and she wanted to strike us a crippling blow. She succeeded."

Mark whistled. "That idiot! So she is still with Sindelar?"

"Merrick has reported that she is in the Princess' train. Ferrel, I believe, is trying to contact her and tell her the truth. It's very dangerous in Tadia right now. But what of you? How is it you managed to survive Volta's attack?"

"I had help." Mark answered. "Come with me and I'll introduce you." Mark turned away but was unable to hide his widening grin from Alaeric.

Puzzled, Alaeric obediently followed Mark, leading his horse from the meadow. He sensed something about the younger man that seemed like suppressed glee, but he put it down to Mark's enthusiasm of meeting with an old friend again.

They had walked for a quarter of an hour as Alaeric's great horse wanted to stop and nibble at every tree, when they came to a small, hilly clearing. A huge cat sat in the doorway of a cave, and from inside came the sound of singing.

Alaeric stopped in suspicious silence. Mark, after a glance at him, whistled three short notes. The cat that was half dozing woke and saw Alaeric. The cat meowed with happy recognition.

"Maikai?" Alaeric called, half-afraid of him. Confirming the truth, the cat bounded down the small slope and launched himself at Alaeric. Arms and legs and happy cat kisses followed in a tangled mess.

When Alaeric finally disengaged from his frantic cat, he looked up and saw her there, standing silhouetted in the cave entrance. Mark, a smile beaming, grabbed the cat who wanted to follow his master up the hill. "Um...we'll be back in a few hours. Come on, Maikai." He grinned as he led the cat back, murmuring.

Alaeric nodded absently as he strode up the hill. Tayaela remained motionless in the entrance watching his approach with hungry eyes. He stopped a few feet from her. Staring, unable to speak, he held out his hand.

"Am I forgiven?" he asked, humbly. Tayaela did not answer. Her look of confusion worried him. He wanted her reassurances.

Then she spoke, her low voice exactly as he had dreamed it for five long, empty years.

"Somehow when I daydreamed our reunion, I never expected the first words from your mouth to be 'am I forgiven?' 'Hello Tayaela, long time no see,' or 'Have you missed me?' or even 'By the gods, Tayaela, you've put on weight,' but never 'Am I forgiven.' What do I have to forgive you for?"

Alaeric laughed. "For not taking you with me."

"Oh. Well, yes then, there is that." Tayaela responded. "Do you forgive me?"

"What for?"

"For allowing you to be exiled, then not coming along."

"Tarq did what he had to, and I knew you had to stay and help." Alaeric answered her.

"Well, so we're forgiven," Tayaela, stated stroking the cave mouth slowly. "What now?" She was still ten feet from him and not certain what to do. For a moment longer Alaeric hesitated, and then closed the gap until he was right in front of her.

She reached up and gently put her hand on his chest. "You really are here," she whispered excitedly. "You're not another daydream."

"I'm here," he sighed, just here mere touch lighting a fire deep within him. "May I kiss you to assure myself that you're not an apparition set to vanish the moment I touch you?"

"I think that can be arranged." she said, almost primly. But then her arms were around his neck as he grabbed her behind the back and for a long time they locked in a passionate embrace.

When they finally broke apart, trembling from the ferocity of their reactions to their reunion, Tayaela said in a shaking voice. "Well, at least I'm not imagining you."

"Or I you," Alaeric bent and buried his head in her hair. "Or I you," he repeated. "I think I'd like

to carry you into the cave right now and begin to make inroads into five years separation."

"That would be nice," she smiled. So without further hesitation, Tayaela allowed him to carry her into the cave. Alaeric banged his head twice on the way, reducing Tayaela to happy giggles. "I don't think it's so funny." he complained, but was laughing too.

"Romantic gestures never seem to work for us. Remember the time we made love on the seashore and the tide washed our clothes away?" Tayaela reminded him, laughing. "Or when the hay loft in my father's barn fell in?"

Alaeric was also laughing hard by now and the two were lovingly reunited. He softly caressed her shoulder, gently pulling her shirt away from her body. His huge hands cupped her breast in a gesture both familiar and yet so distant that she found her body responding like a shy virgin.

That didn't last for long as she felt the hardness between his legs press against her. Her own passion ignited and she grabbed for his chest, feeling the strength of the huge muscles rippling as he moved against her in pleasure. The tide of their lovemaking ebbed and flowed like the sea, at first calm then crashing in thunderous waves against each other. Five years of waiting captured like a butterfly in amber dissolved at once, in their reunion. Five years of longing, tears and grief washed away in the all-consuming desires they awakened in each other.

When their lovemaking was finally over, Tayaela laying her head against his shoulder, Alaeric felt complete once more. For so long, his emotions had been carefully disengaged. All his energies were devoted to other, more destructive forms of amusement.

Even his artwork had seemed uninspired and sullen. All this caused by his separation from this lithe woman beside him.

"No one will ever separate us again," he declared, stroking her shoulder.

"Never," she agreed solemnly, putting her hand to his cheek as if reassuring herself once again of his reality. "Much as I wish to lie here forever, though love, Mark will be back soon. He'll be tired."

"Has he told you how he got here?"

"He's told me his whole story. But even though it's been nearly two months since his stabbing, he's not that well. I think that part of the blade is still in him. He gets weak suddenly. It worries me."

"In the morning we'll take him to Carr. She'll be able to help him."

"Carr? Is she here? Good. So what else is happening?"

As they dressed, Alaeric apprised Tayaela of the whole situation.

"We'll combine our searches for a Tal," Tayaela replied, "I spent much time on an uninhabited place and I think we could locate a Tal fairly quickly if we are both looking." She pulled on her boots. "In fact, with all of us looking, we ought to locate it fairly soon. I mean, all those agents, us, Tarq, and Lauren looking, somebody ought to find something!" She said enthusiastically and grinned, "And then we'll show that bitch and her wizard what it means to mess with us."

Alaeric grinned back. "You never change. Oh Tayaela, I do love you." She flowed into his arms again, and for a moment each was eager once more to undress and make love again. A howling meow interrupted them. Looking at one another curiously, they emerged from the cave into the growing twilight, hearing Maikai's howl once more, a distress call.

Mark was lying at the foot of the hill, near the stream, panting rapidly. Maikai stood over him meowing and howling in concern. In a few moments, Tayaela and Alaeric had rushed to his side. "I'm all right," Mark tried to reassure Tayaela as she admonished him. "I'm just a little tired."

Tayaela had Alaeric assist Mark up the hill to the cave. "We'll stay here tonight," she said, as she settled Mark onto his pallet and brought him some game bird soup. "And then tomorrow, we'll go to Carr. I've let you do too much."

"Come on, Princess," Mark said. "I just overdid it. Don't blame yourself. I'm a grown man. I ought to know better."

"Right. You should know better," she said sarcastically.

Mark blushed and shot an appealing glance at Alaeric, who laughed saying. "I'm not about to thwart my wife after five years Mark. This is your fight." His grin was so infectious that soon all three were relaxed and Tayaela was able to cajole three cups of soup into the boy.

After dinner, they built up the fire and began to tell each other of the years spent apart. Mark, exhausted, fell asleep soon after full dark but Alaeric and Tayaela talked long into the night.

The next day Mark woke first and saw his companions entwined in each other's arms and legs. The utter peacefulness of their expressions brought a lump in his throat. He felt moved to tears. Quietly he rose and took the water pot outside to fill.

Musing on the love he had witnessed, Mark hoped that one day he would have something akin to it. He suspected that the girls on his world paled in comparison to the women of Dal Ryeas. Somehow in those quiet moments before Alaeric and Tayaela awoke, Mark realized that while he wanted to see his family again, his future was not on Earth.

"I want to stay," he said softly to the cat. "I want to be Dal Ryean." Maikai meowed approvingly and purred Mark stroked his head.

Breakfast and packing took most of the morning, but before noon, Alaeric, Tayaela, Mark, and the cat were on their way back to Carr.

The trip, which normally would have taken two to three hours, took much longer due to Mark's condition. As the day wore on, his energy flagged, and his ability to recuperate after a rest break diminished hourly. By the time they reached the hidden camp, Alaeric was helping to steady Mark as he rode.

But even though he was exhausted, he was cheerful about it and Alaeric was impressed by his fortitude. On Earth, Mark had never seemed courageous or even cheerful. He was always sullen and detached a sarcastic remark never far from his lips. Now he seemed merely self-deprecating but willing to go on. His wound was serious, Tayaela had told him, but Mark never made a fuss and remained cheerful and resolute. Alaeric's opinion of him rose with each passing mile.

Tayaela, watching Mark's energy fade, was thankful when they reached Carr. The enchantress and the small troop of soldiers who had remained with her were gathered before a central fire eating supper.

"Lady Carr! Look who I found!" Alaeric cheerfully called out as he brought Tayaela and Mark into the light. Recognizing the King's sister, the soldiers struggled to their feet as Tayaela tried to make them remain seated.

"Please, don't get up!" she exclaimed uselessly. Finally they all reseated themselves and Tayaela was able to talk to Carr. Quickly she related to the sorceress all that had befallen Mark and her own diagnosis. Carr nodded and signaled two men to escort Mark to her tent.

"You two eat. I'll take care of him."

Relieved of her charge, Tayaela sat down thankfully next to her husband.

"You like him?" Alaeric asked, pointing with a knife to Carr's tent.

"He's a nice boy," Tayaela answered, smiling. "I think he'll be a terrific bowman someday."

"He's a lot like Diana." Alaeric was eating quickly, apparently ravenous from the journey to camp. "I think his..."

Before he could finish, Carr summoned Tayaela to her tent.

"There's no blade in him." Carr reported. "But I have found traces of anathema in his blood."

"What?" Tayaela gasped, and felt a cold chill shiver down her spine. Anathema was Dal Ryeas most deadly poison. How had he survived?

"That's what's making him so weak, the wounds were not so bad, and you did a fine initial healing on them. By rights, he ought to be further along than this. Volta's knife must have been coated with the poison." Carr frowned. "Only his father's blood has let him survive this long. If he were one of us, he'd have died within hours without the antidote."

"Can you save him?" Tayaela asked, worried.

"I think so. I'll dose him tonight and retest him tomorrow. He'll have to rest a few days."

"Oh gods," moaned Tayaela, "I've had him out wandering and practicing with the bow and exercising constantly."

"That probably saved his life." Carr replied, touching Tayaela's shoulder soothingly. "Anathema needs a sedentary time to work properly. That's why it's so dangerous. When you're wounded, you usually have to lie still, and if the poison's undetected, it will kill you. Only after the antidote is administered does the body require rest." Carr smiled. "Don't you panic Tayaela, I'll save the boy."

"Good," breathed Tayaela, "I'll go back to Alaeric and let him know how Mark is."

Tayaela began walking back to the fire when the enchantress called after her. "By the way, highness, it's awfully good to have you back."

Tayaela grinned, "It's nice to be had..." She ignored the puzzled look from Carr and returned to the fire to snuggle with her husband.

Chapter 19

Lauren entered the kitchen late one morning to find Tarq gallantly attempting to prepare breakfast. She moved very quietly, being still half-asleep, and leaned into the doorjamb, observing the King. Except for occasional forays to show him the world - houses, museums, shopping malls and other indigenous cultural institutions - she tended to avoid him when they were in the house alone together. Except for meals and sometimes explaining a film to him, Lauren left Tarq to his own amusements.

He was often on Internet sites, researching other kings in exile. Often she found him reading the histories of the edgeworld. King Charles II of England fascinated him, probably because his King spent ten years in exile before his people recalled him to his throne. Lauren assumed this filled a deep-seated desire in Tarq, the wish tor the recall home. She understood it totally.

During meals they often spoke of the progress Carr and Alaeric were having on the empty continent. They conjectured as to the success of the troops in hiding, the resistance movement at home and discussed possible strategies for retaking Tadia. They even joked about Tarq's acclamation to Earth culture. Lauren taught him to cook and drive. Tarq was an apt pupil, showing an astounding degree of flexibility that surprised Lauren.

After she had gotten his false papers from the same exiled source that had gotten hers, he used the drivers license to travel around the town. He loved driving the Corvette. She even reopened her shop and felt comfortable for him to drive her there and then use the car for the rest of the day.

She never realized how adaptable he was. He was far better at adjusting than she was in similar circumstances. She told him of this and they joked about this newly acquired skill. But they never discussed their own situation. They never removed the self-imposed barriers that kept them from comforting one another. They remained intimate strangers, sharing their past but never looking towards their future.

Lauren, leaning against the doorjamb, reflected on this strange intimacy. Sometimes feeling that the first move should be hers, she never knew where to begin. She sighed over her own inadequacy and Tarq turned to face the direction of the sound.

"Good morning," he said cheerfully. "And how did you sleep?"

"I didn't," Lauren replied grumpily. "I was trying to come up with a way to infiltrate the palace. Any news from Alaeric and Carr?"

"No luck finding a Tal." Tarq frowned. "But, there is some excellent news. Tayaela was the one you and Merrick suspected of hiding behind the barrier. Better yet, she found Mark Harrison and nursed him to health. They're with Alaeric and Carr right now. And my sister spent her time on an uninhabited world and she sensed a Tal — an unfocused one. She and Alaeric are going to search there for it."

"Oh, that's wonderful!" exclaimed Lauren. "Just when you think there is no hope, something like this happens to lift your spirits. You'll be home in no time."

"We should inform the Harrisons." Tarq mused, smiling wryly at her sudden good humor.

"Let's go now." Lauren grinned. She grabbed their jackets and thrust his at him then pulled on her own as she opened the back door.

For a brief time they were in accord. Tarq wished it were always like this as they stepped through the door into the brisk October air. Feeling the cold seeping into their bones, they hurried across the well-worn path between the hedges and bounded up to the Harrison's door. They knocked simultaneously and started laughing as Lila Harrison opened the inner door.

"Lauren, Tarq!" she smiled with a curtsy, which looked

incongruous in her housecoat and flip-flop slippers. "What brings you out so early? Come in, come in."

Tarq followed Lauren into the brightly lit kitchen. Ron Harrison was seated at the table and Diana was getting milk from the refrigerator. They both greeted the excited pair warily. Ron began to rise, when Tarq motioned him to remain seated.

"Please, don't get up. Eat your breakfast," the King said insistently. "We only came to give you the wonderful news that Mark has been found! He was badly hurt but my sister, it appears, was on the spot or near it and nursed him to health. Tayaela and he have joined with Alaeric and Carr in the effort to free Dal Ryeas."

Diana and Lila Harrison began to weep quietly and Lauren went to them and they all hugged tightly. Ron, grinning widely, offered his hand to Tarq who took it and drew the older man into a rough embrace. Overcome by their happiness, the Harrisons tried to calm down by offering breakfast to Lauren and the King. For the first time in weeks a sense of optimism lightened their spirits. The meal turned into a feast where the future was discussed with joy and optimism. It was the finest days Tarq had spent for months.

After leaving the Harrison's, Lauren and Tarq commenced upon their daily routine. They separated for hours, Lauren going to a small art shop she owned and worked at, when the mood struck, part-time, and Tarq continuing his study of earth and its history and mostly its technology. This filled their days and kept them from dwelling on what their nights could be. Even though the war news was good and the fact that Mark and Tayaela were safe, there still remained a wall between them. They avoided each other for the next week, meeting only at meals and during other necessary times.

One night Lauren was fetching her laptop from the living room when she saw Tarq pouring intently over a map of Tadia on the dining room table. As always, he remained oblivious to her presence and she was able to watch him. An inner voice, which she usually chose to ignore, began to chide her and she fell to arguing with herself.

"There is a void in me," she thought. "Why can't I fill it? I know I love him, I know he needs me, but I can't seem to give him what he wants. You're afraid to give. You think he'll send you away again, so you're sending him away."

"This is ridiculous!" Lauren exclaimed aloud, startling Tarq.

"What?" he asked concerned.

She glared at him and stalked from the room.

Tarq stared after her in puzzlement but had no time to wonder. He was trying to coordinate his attack on Tadia. He was prepared to move as soon as an active Tal was in his possession. His latest communication from Carr was frustrating, but the search continued and he was trying to maintain hope.

He felt the time constraint. Merrick's news that the temple might not be able to delay Killia's coronation much longer gave him very little time in which to maneuver. Once Killia was crowned and anointed, it would be harder to dislodge her from power.

Later after school, Diana went with him to the mall to shop for clothes. While they were waiting for their packages, Tarq found himself musing on his first days on earth. Then it struck him. Why hadn't he thought of it before?

He turned to Diana and said, "What was it your mother said that first night?"

"About what?" Diana was taken aback by his abruptness.

"About this world's Tal. That they moved here because your mother suspected that the Tal was located in the vicinity?"

She stared at him in shock, realization dawning. "Do you really mean here? In the mall?"

"No, not in the mall, but I think here in town. It's nagging me, pulling me to it!" Tarq looked at her seriously. "Are you willing to help me find it?"

"Absolutely, but how?"

"I'm attuned to the very special emanations of a Tal, any world's Tal, more strongly than most people. Everyone who has ever been in contact with one will feel the pull somewhat. Your mother, for one. Only a few know what it means. But since I was a child, I've been trained to recognize the power at once. Your mother felt compelled to settle near it so she could maintain her unconscious link with it. It brings a great deal of comfort to the troubled."

"My mother has links to a Tal?" Diana asked suspiciously, as she thanked the salesperson and took their packages. It sounded preposterous. Her mother was so…normal.

As they walked towards the exit and their car, Tarq further explained.

"Most people feel something if they try. Few have the inherent ability to manipulate the powers though. Tayaela and I have the skill, Carr too. She used it for years and has developed considerable powers in creating other smaller Tal-like crystals that can do various aspects of what the main one can. She has healing crystals, communicating ones, advanced tale ones. I try to encourage this research because one never knows when the Tal will be unavailable."

"But only one linked by the ceremony in the Twin's House can become truly in complete symbiosis with the Tal and tap its powers. That's why I have to get to Killia before she's consecrated. It would create quite a rift if we both try to use it at once." Tarq smiled ruefully. "It could destroy the entire world. If I can find one to use, I'll be able to fight with equal and opposing force and maybe be able to tap into the power of my original Tal."

"Well, what should it look like?" Diana said, looking around anxiously.

"I'll know it when I see it." Tarq declared. "When we get home, I am going to open myself up to the emanations and try to locate it. I'll do some Internet searches too, and see if there are any places around that display unusual stones. Once I do, no matter what, I'll take it and we can fight on an equal level."

As soon as Diana went home, Tarq locked himself into his room and began to summon his waning powers to help him locate the Earth Tal. He stayed there for hours until he felt hungry. Through his efforts he narrowed the location to within five miles. When he checked Google maps, he noticed that his focus was located in an area dominated by cultural landmarks.

He was tempted to tell Lauren about his discovery. He quietly went towards her room and stood outside her door. He knew that she was there and he could sense that she was waiting for him to make a move. Just as he was about to open the door, he heard the kitchen door open and Diana's cheerful voice call out, "Tarq, Lauren, are you home?"

"Up here, Diana," Tarq answered, almost a growl. For an

instant, he wanted to strangle the girl. Lauren opened her door then and looked at him. Before he could summon his courage to speak, Diana ran up the stairs.

She was in a happy mood and never sensed the tension between her friends. "Hi! My mother wants to know if you would come for dinner?"

"Actually, I have a bad headache," Lauren replied as they made their way downstairs. "I think I'm just going to sleep. What about you, Sire?"

"I'd be happy to join you." Tarq spoke up.

"Oh good!" Diana smiled. "My mother was ecstatic when I told her about the Tal. Do you really think that you can find it?"

"What?" Lauren said sharply, looking at the King's back as he preceded her into the kitchen. He avoided looking at her as Diana continued chattering.

"Today at the mall, Tarq felt that he could locate the Tal here on this world by opening himself up to it. He agrees that my mother did feel it and that it was nearby. She was thrilled to know her feelings were right. My dad wasn't so excited. I think he wants my mother to forget she was ever from another place. This whole thing has upset him."

Diana poked her head in the refrigerator as they entered the kitchen, still talking. "I think he's better though, now that he knows Mark is all right."

"That's good." Lauren replied absently. Something in her tone made Diana emerge from the refrigerator to stare at her friends. Lauren was half-sitting on the table, one leg slung over the side swinging, the other firmly planted on the ground. Her arms were crossed and her eyes, hard as brown topaz, stared straight at the King.

Tarq was trying to appear nonchalant and failing miserably as he shifted his feet in the doorway. "So you think you can find it?" Lauren's voice was edged with shaved ice. "Were you planning to tell me or was it going to be a surprise?"

"I haven't decided what I'm going to do yet," he replied loftily. "I had planned to tell you when I had done eventually. I am still trying to locate it though."

Pointedly, Lauren turned to Diana. "So how's school?" she asked, abruptly changing the subject. Diana replied hesitantly, looking from her to Tarq. "It's all right, I guess, but well, there is something missing."

"What do you mean?" Lauren encouraged her gently to continue, never looking at the squirming, uncomfortable King.

"All summer, when we were gone, I felt special. Carr made me her student. I was in your confidence. Merrick treated me like a woman. And now…" Her voice trailed away.

"Now?" prompted Lauren.

"Now I'm a kid again. A high school senior. All my friends talk about are guys or clothes or what college they're going to attend next year. And me… I care nothing about that. What I care about is so removed from them. I see them as thoughtless, careless, irresponsible girls. Even when they talk about last summer it's all giggles and airiness. Not a serious thought among them. And the boys… they're just as bad or worse. My ex-boyfriend, Jim, thinks only about sex and how to get it. I went out with him and a bunch of the others and if he wasn't trying to get his hand down my shirt, he was boasting of his summer conquests to make me jealous. I hate it. I hate them all."

Tarq groaned. "Oh Diana, what have we done to you? You should be a kid; you should be having fun with your friends. Not be so involved with us that your life here is meaningless."

"But I believe in you and your fight. It's part of me." Diana said hotly.

"But so is being young," the King replied evenly, "You belong here. You are part of this world as well as part of mine. Don't lose your youth. Enjoy it."

Lauren smiled sadly. "We love your loyalty to our cause. But who knows how long it will be before we return. The King is speaking from experience. Our youth was cut short by assassination, revolution and the onset of very sudden adulthood." Shrewdly she glanced at the girl. "And I don't think Merrick wants you to be lonely."

Diana blushed. "It's true, I do care about Merrick and what he thinks a lot, but I understand how dangerous his assignment is and" her eyes filled with tears but she refused to allow them to flow, "that I may never see him again. But it's not only that, I believe in the entire cause. I'm so thankful that Mark is alright, but I'm worried about Lisa."

"We are too. Merrick reports that Lisa is still well and that Ferrel has kept contact with her. We hope he'll have her out soon. It depends on Lisa. Ferrel is doing his best to guide her to our side."

"That's good." Diana rose. "Are you coming over for dinner then? We'll be eating soon."

Lauren decided to join them and they ended their conversation by trooping over to a convivial dinner at the Harrisons.

Later that night, Lauren knocked on Tarq's door. When he answered, dressed only in his jeans, his muscles and scars gleaming in the soft hallway light, she almost forgot why she had knocked. Quickly recovering herself, she asked bluntly. "What are you planning?"

With a secretive smile he answered, "Don't buy anything on a long term credit arrangement. You might not be able to make all the payments."

"What?" she exclaimed, exasperated.

He grinned. "You'll see."

Chapter 20

Merrick never saw the shadowy figure detach itself from the darkened doorway and signal to other lurking shadows. He was preoccupied when he left the Arras Tavern. His official shadow was still enthralled in the wild embraces of Leda and never noted his target's departure. Unwilling to wait any longer, Merrick decided to leave the young soldier to his own devices.

For months Merrick had lived a double life, ostensibly consolidating Sindelar's position in the city, while he actually sowed discontent and recruited fighters and safe houses for his King's cause. Since communications were necessarily one-sided between Carr and Merrick due to his proximity to the Dal Ryean Tal, Merrick could only report his activities in full. He knew that even if captured there was not much he could tell under torture. It was for the best, he supposed, but he nonetheless felt isolated and vulnerable. He also felt fearful about the safety of Lisa and especially Ferrel.

Trying to establish an escape plan for this pair kept at the castle, Merrick was less than vigilant as he walked slowly to his quarters at the castle. For once, he was unaware that earlier in the evening another of Volta's spies had stopped in at the Arras, and had observed the young soldier's distraction with Leda. Reporting to his Captain of the shadow's inattention caused Killia's chief enforcer to send a team of her best expert guards after Merrick.

A light tenor voice broke through his reverie, "Out late again, Lord Merrick?"

Merrick stopped, a long knife halfway drawn from the belt at his waist.

"I don't think that would be wise." Sergeant Orado, Volta's personal henchman, stepped from the shadows into the silvery moonlight.

"Good evening, Sergeant," Merrick said politely but warily. "Troubled times." He said apologetically, indicating his knife hand.

"Oh, that's all right," the Sergeant sneered, "It would only have hurried the inevitable."

"What do you mean?" Merrick asked suspiciously.

"The Princess would like to have a little talk with you, Merrick."

"I'm Lord Sindelar's man," Merrick replied stiffly, knowing the implications of Killia's "little talks" all too well.

"We're all on the same side," Orado grinned nastily, "Aren't we? The Princess likes to be kept informed of how her affairs are being conducted."

Merrick, suppressing the rising tide of panic within him, mentally began to prepare himself for his inevitable confrontation with Killia and the sadistic Volta. While maintaining a calm demeanor, he replied, "We all like being informed, Orado."

Frantically, he invoked a spell that Carr had provided him against the chance of capture. He was certain that the precaution was necessary. Rumors of Volta's tortures indicated he needed all the aid he could get. Briefly, he hoped that the spell worked against pain as well as blocking his ability to reveal secrets.

Orado, surprised at Merrick's pleasant acceptance of what would prove his final ordeal, wondered if this was an error. No one but an innocent would agree to meet with Killia and Volta.

The shadowy guards materialized around Merrick and escorted him to the castle. Orado, after trying to initiate a conversation, lapsed into silence when Merrick did not respond. He was quite annoyed that his prisoner refused to be goaded into anger. It left him frustrated.

Merrick, for his part, felt the effects of Carr's spell begin. His fear vanished and a kind of induced serenity took its place. He was able to view his fate objectively. He knew beyond doubt his ability to protect the secrets of the King.

He regretted not being able to free Lisa for Diana's sake, or completing his bonded duty to Lauren. He daydreamed briefly about Diana, remembering her smile, her caress of his face, and her laughter before he carefully put her from his mind. He needed no distractions. His concern for Ferrel was more intense.

As the small troop entered the south gate of the castle, Merrick looked up towards the corridor where his brother and he shared rooms. "Oh Saevirg, Sarama," he invoked softly to the twin gods, "keep him safe and free from harm. Let him be able to escape with the girl, Lisa, and find the freedom he needs to prosper. Let his mother receive him once more." And with that small prayer, Merrick delivered himself and his brother into the Gods' hands. Steeling himself for his coming ordeal, Merrick followed his escort through a small door on the ground floor of the castle.

By the time Merrick was escorted to a small stark cell on the lowest level of the castle, he was completely in control of all his thoughts and actions. Carr's spell and his own indomitable will ensured that while he was physically incarcerated, he nevertheless would remain mentally free. As Sergeant Orado chained his leg and arm to a wall, Merrick wondered about the other prisoners. Were the Olenteas Lords chained as well?

In the dark, Merrick waited. Dawn came and noisily streamed through his windows. Somberly he waited for his captors and their inquisition.

Orado crept along the upper corridors to Rhea Volta's apartments. Only a sergeant, he was forbidden from entering the inner reaches of the palace that were reserved for officers and courtiers after dark. Orado enjoyed a heady sense of power as he flaunted regulations to reach his lover. If they only knew…

Volta answered the door to her chambers on his first soft knock. The tall dark haired woman was dressed for special company. Orado smiled when he saw her, his dark eyes glowing in the candlelight. She had discarded her severe uniform for a robe of silver tissue with a silk gown beneath that showed off her usually camouflaged curves.

After kissing him teasingly, Volta turned from Orado and walked back into the room. From the corner of his eye, Orado saw that the bed covers turned back and that a tray with wine and food stood on the night table. He smiled at her preparations, knowing she was in an excellent mood and anticipating the night.

"Well," she asked, "Did you get him?"

"Merrick Olenteas is now a guest of Her majesty's prison." Orado replied with a broad grin.

"Good." Volta sinuously embraced him. "This will cripple Sindelar's operations and control in the city. I've already convinced Killia that the wizard harbors disloyal thoughts and isn't as powerful as he appears."

"And she believes you?" Orado asked, nipping lightly at her earlobe.

"Of course she does! She believes anything I tell her and I make her think it's her idea." Volta shivered in his arms, "I have to try this on her. She'll melt like ice in the sun."

Orado continued his seduction for a while longer before he asked, "So what is next?"

"Next we torture Dracos. I'll take the Princess with me, since she will enjoy it. By the time we are through with him, she'll have total doubts about the wizard's loyalty. And Sindelar will never know why! You know, just yesterday he suggested that Killia ask the High Priestess for a public blessing. I mean it's actually a very good idea because it gives the Princess an appearance of sanctity, but Killia avoids the temple and even though he knows this, Sindelar kept trying to convince her. Killia began to shriek and only I could intercede and soothe her. I escorted the wizard from her presence and if looks could kill I'd be deader than a stuffed dog."

Volta twirled away from his arms and sat on the bed. "Come here," she motioned, "By the day after the coronation, I'll be first minister and you'll be head of the army. We will control Dal Ryeas between us!"

Orado laughed, "It'll be worth it. So what are we going to do with the wizard?"

"Kill him. If we let him live, he'll try to undermine us. He's served his usefulness."

Orado yawned, "Enough of politics. The night is fading and I have other things on my mind." He leaped onto the bed and nothing more was said concerning Dal Ryeas' future for the remainder of the night.

Princess Killia and Rhea Volta arrived to visit Merrick

Olenteas in the late morning. The Princess, tall, beautiful, and fastidious, looked askance at the stark unadorned cell. Wrinkling her nose in distaste, she regally seated herself on the only chair. Volta paced the small confined area in five short steps. Without a word to the prisoner, Volta signaled to three guards waiting in the corridor. They entered the cell, unchained Merrick, and began systematically beating him.

Watching critically, Volta allowed the beating to continue for five minutes. Then she dismissed the guards and told one to summon Sergeant Orado.

Merrick was thrown on the metal-framed cot gasping and panting. Blood was flowing from a cut lip and his nose. His left eye was swelling shut and he could feel that one of his ribs was broken. Carr's spell held, though, and he found that it did help in suppressing pain. With an almost contemptuous gaze he looked at the two women who were watching him.

"Do you think he'll talk now, Rhea?" the Princess asked naughtily.

In a hoarse rasping voice, he asked, "What do you want?"

"To have a chat." the Princess replied primly, "We really haven't communicated for quite some time. I feel it incumbent upon a ruler to understand and communicate with her people after all."

"This is a novel approach to effective communications skills." Merrick said wryly, as he shook blood from his eyes.

"Enough!" roared Volta, her always-short temper flaring. "Tell us what Sindelar is planning." Inwardly, Merrick felt a great sense of first relief and then confusion. Although the pain was breaking through the edges of the spell and dulling his senses, he realized that Killia and Volta suspected his activities solely for the wizard, not the King at all. Killia's basic paranoia caused her to miss the greater danger of Tarq in her fear of Sindelar.

"What do you mean?" he gasped softly, still out of breath, "The wizard is your loyal subject, Highness."

"Certainly," the Princess sneered. "And that's why you've been taken into his service. What recruiting have you done at the Arras? I know you took him there. Is he going to stage another coup?"

Merrick said with an air of innocence. "I'm not recruiting

anyone. I go out to get away from the castle. The Arras was my father's favorite place. He always talked about it. So, where else can I go? I've been in exile for five years."

Killia laughed. "I think we'll be going now. A few days here might make you open up and talk to us."

Volta opened the door for the Princess after reattaching Merrick's chains. "Expect a visit from Orado later. He always enjoys his work."

Merrick smiled wanly. "Thanks."

It was midnight when Orado returned. Merrick had fallen into an uneasy sleep anticipating the encounter. A crippling blow to his solar plexus awakened him. Merrick realized that when taken by surprise, Carr's spell took a while to begin working. I bet he waited until he was certain I was asleep, thought Merrick, before he came for his little visit.

"Don't we have a unique wake-up call?" Merrick was writhing in pain.

"I hate small talk…" Orado said as he proceeded systematically to bruise every muscle in Merrick's body. For ten excruciating minutes, Merrick endured the agony in silence. When he was finished, Orado grudgingly said, "You certainly have strength."

Silently, Merrick glared as the brutal Sergeant left the cell. It took all of his resolve not to cry out until the spell was able to alleviate some of the pain. But he refused to give his torturer the pleasure of his work.

In the week that followed, Merrick's torture continued at Orado's whim. Killia and Volta paid him visits daily and tried to elicit information concerning Sindelar. Eventually only the spell Carr had given him enabled him to withstand the torture and not reveal the truth.

On the eighth morning, about halfway through his interrogation, a timid knock on the cell door interrupted the proceedings.

Volta called out in her harsh voice, "Enter!", and the door hesitantly opened.

Merrick rested a moment with his eyes shut trying to hold together the ravaged remains of the spell and did not realize that Lisa had entered the cell until he heard her cry out in shock. Recognizing her voice he opened his eyes alarmed. Since the

Princess and Volta were facing Lisa's direction as she stared in horror at Merrick's battered face, the tortured man chanced to meet her eyes and slowly shake his head, his eyes begging her not to betray him. Inwardly stealing herself, Lisa delivered her message.

"I'm sorry to disturb you, Highness, but Lady Audra sent me to get you. Lord Sindelar is on his way to your apartments and I gather he is very unhappy." Lisa's voice quivered slightly as she spoke.

"I'm sorry you had to see this, child," the Princess said smoothly. "But sometimes we must be cruel to be kind. Come now."

Lisa, with a last look at Merrick, began to follow the Princess and Volta from the cell. As she turned Merrick realized that her body was blocking Volta and the Princess' view of him. Merrick took the chance to exaggeratedly mouth, "Ferrel". Lisa nodded in understanding and followed the Princess as Volta closed the door.

Ferrel was near breaking. Isolated by his precarious position as a hostage and his relationship to Merrick, the boy spent most his days alone. Occasionally Lisa was able to sneak away from her duties to the Princess and be with him, but for the most part he wandered the back corridors of Castle Tadia trying to gather information for Merrick. He was so quiet and unobtrusive that most denizens of the castle never even realized when he was there.

In the first days, he found in the library a compilation of Dal Ryean literature and the personal papers of the Tadiak and Pyramus rulers. There were maps and he carefully passed these and other important documents to Merrick. He overheard conversations and remembered scraps of seemingly useless trivia as well. He provided Merrick an accurate assessment of the mood of the castle since the coup by the Princess and her sorcerer.

He felt proud that he was helping Merrick in organizing King Tarq's return. His information was providing a vital link between castle and city. He was under orders by his brother to pass on his data to Vida, proprietress of Arras Tavern, whenever Merrick was away. Ferrel did this diligently for a week until both he and the taverners realized that there was something unusual in Merrick's absence. Ferrel was frantic with worry.

On the eighth day after Merrick's disappearance, he gathered his courage and gingerly decided to approach Sindelar regarding his brother. He found the wizard contemplating the city from one of the roof gardens. Tadia was beautiful in the bright morning light. It spread below the castle like a gleaming jewel, the bright white sun reflected off the multi-colored buildings and the three great rivers flowing through the city to the harbor. The beauty below him temporarily dazzled Ferrel. Only when the wizard cleared his throat did he remember his mission.

"My Lord," he blurted out, his concern for his brother blotting out his fear of the wizard, "Where is Merrick? Is he on a mission for you?"

"What do you mean, boy?" The wizard was astonished at Ferrel's question.

"I haven't seen him for seven days..."

"I haven't seen him either. But he sent a note that he'd gone to see your mother." Sindelar said soothingly.

"Oh, no sir," Ferrel said stoutly. "My mother has disowned us both. Merrick would have told me if there was a change."

"Maybe he's trying to have that change." Sindelar replied gently, his heart filled with pity at the boy's loneliness.

"He would have told me. Sir." Ferrel was adamant. "It was a trick to get you off guard. Something's happened to him, I feel it."

"And whom do you suspect, young Ferrel," Sindelar chuckled "of nefariously spiriting away your brother?"

"Captain Volta." Ferrel maintained enough sense not to name the Princess. Sindelar was a reasonable being but he had a blind spot where Killia was concerned.

"You might be right," agreed the wizard, suddenly seeing a solution to a puzzle. Sindelar rose swiftly. "Come with me. Guard, take a message to the Princess that I am attending on her directly."

As they neared the Princess' apartments the wizard turned to Ferrel and said. "Wait here. I don't want her enmity to fall on you."

The youth obeyed. Nervously, he waited as the wizard entered the Princess' quarters. Seating himself in a wall niche unobserved, he saw the Princess, Volta and Lisa arrive. Lisa was casually dismissed as the Princess and her bodyguard entered the royal chambers.

Ferrel heard shouting begin between the Princess and Sindelar as the door closed. Lisa, standing outside the door, looked distraught. He jumped down from his niche and called her name, softly.

She whirled to face him. Realizing it was Ferrel, she ran to meet him, grabbing his arms in a tight hold. "Oh Ferrel, Thank God!" she cried, looking around frantically. "We can't talk here, come on." She grabbed his hand and pulled him down the corridor to her rooms. Bemused, Ferrel followed.

Lisa opened her door, pulled him in, and locked the door behind her. "Come to the window. No one will hear us there."

"What's wrong, Lisa?" Ferrel was growing fearful of her distress.

"It's so awful. She enjoys this. I never realized. She loves to see suffering. I want to go home." Lisa burst into tears.

"What is it?" Ferrel awkwardly put his arm around the weeping girl.

Gulping a sob, Lisa narrated. "When the messenger from the wizard came, Lady Audra sent me to fetch the Princess. She and the Captain were on level one. So I went. Sergeant Orado showed me. He even smiled. I knocked, went in, and found them talking to a man. Only I didn't recognize him. Not till the end. It was Merrick. They've beaten him. His face is bruised and . . . he looks half dead." she finished in a whisper.

"Merrick? A prisoner?" Ferrel nearly shouted.

"Hush, we'll be heard!" Lisa desperately tried to remain calm.

"So how do you like your Princess now, Lisa?" Ferrel asked scornfully. "First, she has Mark killed by her bitch-in-waiting and now she's killing Merrick."

"Mark?" Lisa whispered.

"You don't really believe that Tarq's men infiltrated a spell-guarded camp that had withstood siege for months and killed an unsuspecting boy do you?" Ferrel's scorn was almost laughter. "Mark was told you were captured by spies and even though he realized it was probably a trap, he went with Volta to find you. I saw them leave together and later Volta returned alone."

Lisa blinked and began to weep quietly at the thought of her dead brother's betrayal. "Why didn't you tell me before?" she asked through her tears.

"Would you have believed me?" Ferrel asked bitterly. He reached down to the hidden compartment in the heel of his boot. He opened it, removed the note from Mark, and handed it to Lisa.

"Mark…" Lisa said in a small voice, acknowledging the truth as she read the note.

"At least you are honest." Ferrel said grudgingly. He began to remove his arm from around her shoulder, but she caught his hand and kept it there. He half-smiled; for all her faults he always rather liked her.

"So what do we do? We can't let Merrick die." Lisa stated emphatically.

"Can you find the cell again?" Ferrel began to plan.

Lisa nodded, "Sure. It wasn't hard. And I saw where the keys were. They're on a hook outside the guard station."

"Easy to get to?"

"Yeah. There were only two guards and they were at the other post. Only Orado uses the station room."

"Orado. He's a problem." Ferrel mused.

"I could distract him." Lisa volunteered.

"How?" Ferrel was suspicious.

"Well, he was one of the people who found Mark and me. Today was the first time I saw him since we came to Tadia. He used to guard me at the camps sometimes. It would be natural for me to go have a chat with him. I can pretend he's my friend and I miss him. You know the stuff."

"You're willing to do this?" Ferrel was excited.

"Yes." Lisa said, silently promising to hold accountable everyone involved with Mark's death.

Ferrel, overcome with excitement, grabbed her and kissed her. Instantly both were overwhelmed with confusion and embarrassment. After trying to frame an apology for his impetuous act and failing miserably, Ferrel tried to change the subject.

"So I can be assured you've switched to our side now?"

Lisa, still a bit shy from her first kiss and all it promised, said,

"Yes. What side is that?"

"King Tarq's and Lauren Olenteas and your sister, Diana."

"Diana?"

"Merrick likes her a lot." Ferrel said eagerly, trying to secure Lisa more fully to his cause. "He met her when she was with Lauren and Alaeric at the King's camp."

"Lauren? Alaeric? You mean our neighbors?" Lisa was stunned. "Oh my. I have been out of touch."

"That's because you became so close to the Princess."

Lisa was unhappy. She felt she had betrayed everyone.

Ferrel, sensing this, hastened to reassure her. "Actually, in your position you could really help us."

"How?"

For the next hour or so they discussed how her proximity to Killia could aid the King's cause. With the wholehearted enthusiasm of youth, Lisa immediately grasped her new role eagerly. She saw it as reparation for her earlier transgressions and the death of her brother.

Evening was finally coming. Lisa sent for a large meal that Ferrel and she shared in her chambers. Since Killia never sent for her in the evenings, her time was her own. All day she had avoided the Princess, staying locked in her room with Ferrel, lest she inadvertently betray their plans.

At full dark, shortly after the day guards gave over to the night guards, Ferrel and Lisa made their way to the first level cell block.

"Why don't they have dungeons?" she whispered.

"They did but Tarq had them converted to wine cellars. Actually, the first floor rooms are guard quarters. Only Killia's using them as cells until she clears the dungeons." Ferrel explained, nervously looking about him.

"Oh!" Lisa was anxiously holding Ferrel's hand and felt her palms begin to sweat as they proceeded down the corridor.

They reached the cellblock and Ferrel gave her a quick kiss and a squeeze on her shoulder. Squaring her shoulders and tossing her hair over her shoulders, Lisa proceeded to the doorway and stood in the middle of the arch. Ferrel sneaked past her as she said in a clear voice to cover his passage.

"Hello, Sergeant Orado."

Orado gasped in surprise.

"Oh dear." Lisa exclaimed as Ferrel lifted the keys. "Did I startle you?"

"Mistress Lisa," Orado said gallantly. "How delightful. I'm sorry to say the Princess is not here."

"I came to see you actually." Lisa said nervously. An inexperienced thirteen-year old knows to be wary of a brutal, lecherous man. "You see, I don't have anyone to talk to, with my brother dead. And when I saw you today I thought — I remembered about the day you found us. So I came to visit."

"Please come in." Orado wiped a seat, and escorted Lisa to it.

Lisa decided her best course was to babble continuously. She told him her whole life story as he sat watching her. Occasionally he tried to ask her questions and guide the conversation, but this only started her on more inconsequential anecdotes and rapid thoughts.

A glassy-eyed stare became his expression as she babbled. Orado tried to appear interested, but was started to fade into a half-trance. Lisa was certain that she could finish her 'chat' soon and that the others would be safely away.

Ferrel was appalled at Merrick's condition. His brother was battered almost beyond recognition. Merrick tried to reassure Ferrel that he was all right.

"At least I still have all my teeth," Merrick joked weakly as Ferrel tried to find the right key for the leg chains. As he worked, Ferrel related to Merrick everything he knew. Sindelar's actions, Lisa's aid, everything he had overheard in the past week.

Merrick using a memory trick learned from Carr, memorized all of it for assimilation and later analysis. He hurt too much to do it now.

Ferrel tried rubbing some circulation into his brother's legs. "We have to go. Lisa can't hold out much longer."

"Help me up," Merrick grasped Ferrel's shoulder and pulled himself upright. His legs, weakened and bruised, were unable to hold his weight. He fell against the bed. The crash resounded through the hall.

"Run Ferrel! Save yourself!" Merrick cried in anguish.

"Not without you!" Ferrel answered frantically, pulling Merrick from the cell.

Orado pushed Lisa aside and raced down the hall, his drawn dagger gleaming in the torchlight. Lisa was close behind him, trying to impede his progress. Merrick stood leaning against the wall. Ferrel, sword drawn, stood in front of him.

"Ferrel, no!" cried Merrick as the boy moved forward to protect him.

Orado flung his dagger, catching Ferrel in the stomach. The boy collapsed at his feet. Merrick heard Lisa's scream and somehow found the last vestige of strength in his battered, bleeding body to move away from the wall and confront Orado before the guard gave Ferrel the killing strike.

"I'll kill you!" Merrick snarled.

Orado laughed. "You can hardly stand…"

Both men forgot Lisa. Warily she made her way to Ferrel. He was still conscious, but bleeding profusely, having pulled the dagger from his wound with his failing strength.

"Lisa," he whispered, "get this to Merrick, please…"

Grasping the dagger gingerly, Lisa carefully moved into Merrick's line of sight. He saw the dagger held out to him, Ferrel's sword under her foot, and edged towards her in an attempt to arm himself.

Orado, a talkative fighter, was stating. "Of course you know that the dagger was forged with anathema. It's deadly every time. Your little brother is dead, Olenteas. Pity, he's so young."

With a savage cry, Merrick closed the final distance between the dagger and himself. He grabbed the knife from Lisa and with an accuracy born of desperation, threw it at Orado. It struck the guard low in the chest and embedded to the hilt.

Orado collapsed, screaming. Lisa grabbed her handkerchief and stuffed it in his mouth. The stricken man tried to grab her skirt, but she pulled it away and hurried to Ferrel.

Near collapse himself, Merrick fell to his knees and took Ferrel in his arms. Lisa knelt beside him, holding the boy's hand. Already the poison was working through his bloodstream. Unlike Mark Harrison, Ferrel had no otherworld blood to stave off the effects of the anathema until a healer could be found. Death came within a half-hour unless a healer caught it within moments of its introduction into the body.

Ferrel tried to speak, "Merrick, I'm sorry…"

"For what, little brother?" Merrick's eyes were filled with unshed tears.

"Not finding you sooner..." Ferrel began to cry.

"Hush, child," Merrick stroked his hair. "You found me and saved me. It was soon enough."

"Lisa..." Ferrel looked at her. "You'll help us now?"

Wordlessly, the tears flowing down her cheeks, the girl nodded. She had been privy to discussions in the Princess retinue on the importance of anathema as a political tool. She never thought to see its effects.

"I'm scared, Merrick..." Ferrel said.

"I'm here, I have you." Merrick's voice was firm, confident. Lisa looked at him and realized the effort this sorely wounded man was making to ease his brother's passing.

Ferrel's breath became short and shallow. "I can't feel anything...," he whispered."Merrick, where's momma? Where's father?"

"Father's waiting for you, Ferrel." Merrick said softly. "Do you remember the story I used to tell you when you were little, and when father died?"

"About the fields of the Gods..." Ferrel smiled faintly. "Tell me Merrick. Tell me again."

"In the everlasting halls of the Creator, there is the garden of Divine Wisdom, the Queen of all Heavens and Mother to all the young Gods. There in the garden the Queen allows all her favorites to gather. She is beautiful and kind and wise beyond the comprehension of men. Her flowers are beauty, her wells are ideas, and her trees are thoughts. And in her bounty, she shares with us all. For it was here in her garden that all the young gods and goddesses grew and learned. And the Queen gave of her seedling to all the worlds, for she is bountiful. But her greatest gift is her love..."

Merrick looked down into Ferrel's peaceful blank eyes. He was weeping openly now, for his brother had returned to his bounteous mother. *"For in her love,"* he continued, his voice breaking, *"she takes us to her garden when we die, there to rest and wait for our loved ones or to prepare for our next adventure..."*

Gently Merrick closed Ferrel's eyes, and kissed him on his forehead. Lisa was weeping bitterly, holding the dead boy's hand. Merrick replaced his living hand for Ferrel's lax one in her grasp and squeezed tightly. He lowered Ferrel to the floor and crossed his hands across his chest. Once more he looked at his brother, so young and brave, and he could not hold back his grief.

He began to weep; huge wrenching sobs that came from the depths of his soul. Lisa, never having heard a grown man cry before, felt helpless. Nonetheless, she crept to his side and put her arms about him. Together they wept until the first storm of their grief subsided.

Merrick recovered first and held the girl as she too wept, for Ferrel and for Mark and her own bitter lessons of truth. Finally, he said, "I have to go, or Ferrel's death is in vain. Come."

A harsh voice came from one of the other cells. "No. The Guard will change soon. Put Orado in your cell, Merrick Dracos Olenteas, and hide the boy over by the wall, in the shadows."

"Who are you?" Merrick asked.

"Don't you know your own Lord?" The voice asked sarcastically. "And here I've been told you're my daughter's bonded."

"Prince Kir'san?" Merrick said in surprise. "This is where she's keeping you? We thought you were in the Crimson Fortress! How did you know?"

"About your bond? I can feel my daughter's delicate touch across continents let alone a corridor. Look at you, man. You're standing on borrowed strength."

Merrick staggered over to the door of the cell. Lauren's father, Prince Kir'san, stood at the door. "The strength is mine and my brother's."

Prince Kir'san indicated the cell next to his where the other Olenteas Prince, Ertlan was held. "As my daughter's bonded, we have a moral obligation to you, let alone our own natural inclination to see the bitch fail in her attempt to steal the throne. Once blind, now we can see her for what she is."

"You're with us?"

"As much as we can be from here," The Prince indicated his walls.

"I have the keys." Merrick held them out to the Olenteas Lords.

"No. Then they'll hunt our people even harder. We'll coordinate with you from here. Tell your Aunt Carr to contact us in the family way. She'll know what that means."

"As you wish, my Lord." Merrick tried to sketch a bow, but was brought up sharply by the pain. "You'd better hurry. That spell's going to wear off soon and we can only give you so much protection when you are away from here."

Merrick nodded and was preparing to go when Prince Ertlan said, "Be proud of your brother, Merrick. His loyalty was beyond price. We will ensure nothing bad happens to his body."

"My thanks, Lord," Merrick said in a husky voice and began to move Ferrel closer to the Lords' cells. Lisa moved to help him and Prince Kir'san reached out from the bars and gently patted her head.

"You have done well, young one. Lauren has had contact with you as well. Take your lord's blessing for what it's worth." He smiled at her, a young Olenteas from so far away. Somehow it pleased Lord Kir'san that his blood lines flowed on other worlds.

Lisa stared in wonder at the captive prince. She could feel a sense of calm come over her. For the moment she felt invincible and in that instant she decided what to do.

"Come Lisa. After we finish here, we have to go." Merrick said.

Surprisingly, Lisa said, "No. I can help best if I stay here. I'll feed you information like...like Ferrel did."

"It's too dangerous."

"Please Merrick, let me... I have to do this...to make up, even if only in part... for everything."

"Alright. I don't have time to argue." Merrick felt his strength ebbing.

"Good," grinned Prince Kir'san. "You need someone inside you can trust and she'll be able to carry instructions from us to you for our clansmen." He smiled at the girl. "You will come and visit us won't you young lady?"

"Thank you for your confidence in me." She curtseyed to the Olenteas Princes.

Merrick approached Orado, making certain he was quite dead. He removed the handkerchief and pocketed it. "We mustn't leave any evidence," he told the girl grimly. Then Lisa and he dragged the guard to Merrick's cell and closed the door on him. "That'll delay them."

With one last look at Ferrel, they left the corridor. Lisa was subdued but enthusiastic to help as they established a signal system. As they reached a postern gate on the wall, she looked critically at Merrick. In a voice older than her thirteen years, she stated. "You'll never make it. I'll help you."

"You'll get lost coming back," Merrick protested.

"No I won't and I want you to live. Please Merrick. You're the only friend I have here."

He agreed. After an hour, she got him safely to the Arras Tavern. Vida took one look at him and hurried him into a clean, soft bed. While the doctor came and attended to Merrick's wounds, the girl related the whole story to the kindly tavern keeper and was comforted in her strong arms. Vida's own daughter would barely have survived the harrowing night. After the weeping subsided, Lisa was fed, and cosseted. Then Vida escorted Lisa back to the castle walls.

"I'll come by tomorrow," Lisa promised as she entered the postern gate. "I have to see how he is doing."

"Be careful, child," Vida said. "Don't do anything foolish."

"Take care of Merrick," Lisa said shyly.

"We'll cure his body, but only time will heal his grief," Vida replied, "or yours." She hugged her.

Lisa, feeling tears again, returned the embrace and hurried away without a backward glance to her room, fearing to stay any longer. Stripping off her clothes, she fell into bed. Crying herself to sleep, she was rudely awakened by shouting and running in the halls. A knock on her door and a peremptory entrance found her in bed, clutching the covers.

"Beg pardon, miss. We have an escaped prisoner. We're checking all rooms."

"Escaped?"

"And dangerous. Killed the Sergeant and another man as well."

"Oh my. Well, please search. I'll feel better." Lisa was amazed to hear these words coming from her mouth so calmly.

"Sorry to bother you, Miss." the guard said again and then left.

Alone in the dark, Lisa lay staring at the ceiling. "Oh Ferrel..." she said aloud, and began to weep anew.

Chapter 21

Carr's concealed her anxiety over Mark's failing strength beneath a cheerful bedside manner. Each day as Alaeric and Tayaela followed the path to find Tayaela's world's Tal, Carr attempted to find a working antidote for the anathema that was slowly killing the boy. None of the regular ones used on Dal Ryeas seemed to work. She used a spell that slowed the progress of the poison, but it was only a temporary respite.

Whenever she was unoccupied with maintaining communications with all the force leaders scattered throughout the edges, she studied the ancient texts and spell books that made up her traveling reference library. She cursed herself for not bringing more with her. She spent long hours, her beautiful face lined with worry, trying to find a cure.

Mark was content to rest. Most mornings it was difficult for him to rise or dress unaided. He was frustrated and frightened of weakness. He spoke little but thought much about it. He knew he was dying. He wanted to be brave, but the fear in him kept growing. One evening, as Carr fed him her latest healing potion, he began to talk.

"Am I dying?" he asked her bluntly, searching her face for comfort.

Without meeting his eyes, Carr answered honestly, "I'm trying to save you but I don't know if I can. I'm doing everything I know how."

"How long do I have?" Mark asked quietly.

"I don't know. Anathema is a deadly poison to Dal Ryeans. It usually kills within minutes. The only way to cure it is to catch it at once, then the healer gives the person poisoned the potion of curative herbs and calls on the power of the Tal to imbue them with power. I gave you a potion when you came but it only slowed the progress of the anathema to a crawl. It didn't cure it. Without a Tal within my power's reach, I'm not sure what else to do. So every day I study the old texts and the more obscure theories to see what I can find."

"Why am I still alive, if this poison is so deadly? It's been weeks."

"You are only half Dal Ryean. We figure your father's blood protected you from the anathema's full effects." Carr looked at him. "How do you feel?" she asked as she pushed his unruly hair away from his eyes.

"Tired. Like I want to sleep forever."

She smiled sadly. "Well, I'll try to keep that from happening. But you had better get some rest now."

"Carr? Will Alaeric and Tayaela find a Tal?"

"I hope so, and soon. If we have a Tal available, we can use it to reverse what's happening to you."

"I still don't understand. How can a rock cure me?"

"It's more than a rock. It's many things. It's the focus of a world's power; it's the wild magic within us. Anyone trained can tap into its power source, which is the universe itself. In the hands of a wizard, its magical properties come forth. In the hands of a scholar new forms of knowledge are developed. But, in the hands of the one consecrated, the Tal becomes the protection of the people. It is the basic security of a world and through the ruler all share its power. It enhances even the weakest of us and keeps us united."

As she spoke, Carr helped Mark get into bed. When he was lying down she quickly scanned his vital signs. The strain of his illness was aging him. There were lines on his face, hollows in his cheeks. He no longer resembled a carefree boy, but a man courageously striving against his own mortality. If courage alone could cure him, Carr thought, he would be quite well.

As she was leaving his tent to return to her research, he asked, "Carr, what is the news from Merrick? How are Ferrel and Lisa?"

200

Carr carefully turned her face away from the light.

"Merrick is in hiding, but he has organized an underground awaiting our arrival. Now all we need is a Tal and the way is set for Tarq's return."

"What of the others?" Mark was insistent.

"Lisa is on our side now. She's sending Merrick bulletins from the castle." Carr kept her face carefully hidden in the shadows.

"Good. What about Ferrel?" Mark asked again.

Carr was silent.

"Ferrel's dead, isn't he?" He placed his hand over his eyes.

Shocked, Carr turned to face him. "How did you know?"

"Besides your silence? Maybe it was that. Or because I am so near death too, and I could almost hear you thinking, 'how do I tell him'? Am I right?"

"Yes. Ferrel's dead. He died while he and Lisa were rescuing Merrick. Killia and Volta had imprisoned Merrick and tortured him. The children found out, and broke him free. Ferrel was fatally wounded, and died in Merrick's arms. Lisa got Merrick to a safe house and then returned to the castle to spy for us on Killia."

"Oh, Ferrel," Mark said softly in remembrance. Then catching himself up, he said. "He was my only friend there." He struggled to a sitting position. "Carr, that spell? Can it be done without the Tal?"

"Yes, but it's very dangerous."

"We must do it, soon." Mark was insistent.

"Mark, calm yourself. Please. It could fail without the Tal as a base."

He was agitatedly running his hands through his hair. "No. I need to be upset. I was giving up on life. I was trying to become used to the idea of dying, but I can't. Ferrel's dead, and I have to avenge him. Volta and the serpent Princess are responsible. I won't die. You have to try it. Tal or not!"

"It could kill you!"

"So?" Mark said coldly. "I'm already dead."

"Rest now," Carr said, tears in her eyes again. "No matter what, we'll try it tomorrow night. And Mark, thank you for caring so much about my nephew."

With that, she left him alone with his grief for his friend.

Chapter 22

Diana woke before dawn feeling both exhilarated and terrified. Today was the day when her life as a law-abiding citizen ended. Now that she had practiced and planned the heist, she found that all she could do was think about what could go wrong. For an hour before anyone stirred, she reviewed the past two weeks over in her mind.

Tarq had determined an approximate location for the Tal. He sensed it was located in the Arts District. He decided that they would look for it in each of the galleries and museums that were part of this area. Since Lauren's shop was located in the middle of the district, it became their operational headquarters as the king planned to locate the elusive world stone. Diana knew that the princess was not happy with the idea of the theft and was trying to discourage any attempt at robbery.

"What are you planning?" Lauren demanded of Tarq.

"Nothing. I just want to locate the thing in case we need it to protect this world," he answered her innocently.

"You're going to steal it," she mused, "but how?"

"What makes you think that?" Tarq asked, marking off the locations that he and Diana had already visited.

"I know you."

"You may think so, lady," Tarq's arrogant tone stunned Lauren for a moment. "You only know what I permit to be known."

Lauren stormed into the back room and Tarq grabbed a surprised Diana wordlessly, hustling her from the shop before she returned. He knew that she was angry and hurt and whenever

Lauren was angry it was better to get out of her way.

Once outside, he declared. "Today we go to the Museum of Natural History."

Diana nodded and followed the King warily. He was in a strange mood and it worried her.

They arrived at the museum just after the busloads of tourists on field trips retired to the cafeteria for lunch. It was an unusually hot day for fall and the museums air conditioning felt wonderful. They wandered around for a while and Diana mused to herself that even if they didn't find the Tal, she was enjoying her time with the King. She looked forward to their daily excursions after school.

He was more relaxed and friendly these days. His humor had become wicked and his take on their world quite refreshing. Even if he never went home, she thought, he could become a really cool writer or commentator.

Then she saw his face. It had paled, except for a red flush on his cheeks. He was staring at a floor case that held a display of what appeared to be volcanic rock.

He reached out his hand and Diana grabbed it. "Tarq, don't... there are too many people around. And museum robbery makes the news! We don't want that."

Tarq looked at Diana with unseeing eyes for a moment. "That's it. That's my way home," he muttered. He felt Diana's incessant tug on his hand and focused on her. "Don't look so concerned Di, I am not going to smash and grab."

Then he sat down on a bench and began staring at the stone. He sat motionless, oblivious to the stares and whisperings of the other museum patrons. Diana watched in concern as the guards began to hover around the tall, intense blond haired man as he sat before the dark non-descript volcanic dross.

They were so intent on watching him that they failed to notice that the rock located on the right side of the display began to glow, and iridescent green striations began to etch themselves into the monochromatic black of the rock. Diana felt a shiver of fear as she saw a guard approach Tarq after an hour.

"Sir, are you all right? You've been sitting here for quite some time and we're concerned about your-" The guard touched the King's shoulder.

Tarq, startled by the interruption, looking dazed as his focus on the stone was broken. "I am fine. I just ....uh... needed to rest a while. Has it really been so long?" he answered in a faltering voice.

Diana approached the pair and said in a cheerful voice "Oh, hi Uncle Tony. I'm back. Are you feeling better?"

Tarq looked at Diana and grinned. "Hi. I am feeling much better. Did you enjoy yourself?"

Diana sparkled. "Oh yes, we are going to have to come back before you go home."

Tarq turned to the guard. "I am sorry if my sitting here bothered you. I was rather exhausted, I only arrived last night, and my niece here took me to the doctor this morning. I am somewhat under the weather. Then she wanted to come here to see an exhibit and I just couldn't go on."

Diana dragged the King from the museum before he could tell more lies to the incredulous guards.

Once they were in the SUV, Tarq began to hit the dashboard in frustration. "I almost had it. Five more minutes and the stone would have focused to me. Did you see the streaks of green orange? My Tal is purple green; I've never used the orange spectrum before. I wonder if there is a world with two Tals." He turned to Diana. "Why would a place with such potential ignore the power of that Tal?"

Diana considered his question for a moment. "Perhaps it's better this way. Knowing us, the Tal would fall into the wrong hands, you know like a Hitler-wannabe and we'd be in real trouble!"

Tarq barely heard her. "How well does magic work here? I know that Lauren can summon paths and com-crystals, and entertainment cubes work here. But what kind of higher spells function here? Can we try a few spells? I need to know what we have to work with."

As soon as they reached home, Diana ran to her room and found the practice spell book Carr had given her. She shoved it down the back of her pants and nonchalantly strolled past her mother in the kitchen. Lila looked at her daughter but said nothing, continuing with her dinner preparations. As Diana opened the back door, she said, "Dinner is at 7. Try to be here."

Diana grinned and waved.

Tarq was standing in the yard watching Lauren weed a flowerbed. He was frowning and when he saw Diana, he shook his head. Immediately Diana sensed that they were not going to involve Lauren in their plot.

A stray thought wafted through her head that it was wrong to rob a museum, but she quickly suppressed it as she recalled the Machiavellian axiom: the ends justify the means. Diana felt that a walk on her wild side would do her a world of good.

Smiling casually at Lauren, she approached the King. "Did you want to go to the park now? I've got the baseball gear."

Tarq nodded and strolled off with his accomplice. At the last minute, he turned and asked Lauren, "Do you want to come with us?"

Lauren smiled, "No thanks, I need to finish this. You guys go ahead. Want to take my Vette?"

Tarq smiled, "As long as I can drive." He reached up and grabbed the keys she tossed in his general direction. "Thanks. See you in an hour or so."

Barring any police intervention, Diana thought amusingly.

As Tarq backed the Corvette out of the drive, Diana asked, "What kind of spell are we looking for?"

"I am not sure. We want to make this robbery as painless to the museum as possible. We are going to have to plan this very carefully." Tarq took a corner with ease and drove the car into the huge park. He maneuvered down a path to a picnic area that was rarely used and hidden from regular park goers. "It shouldn't be too complicated; you are only a beginner after all."

Diana muttered, "Thanks..."

They parked the car and walked behind some camouflaging rocks. Tarq sat down and smiled. "Show me what you can do."

Diana opened her notebook. "I can make things invisible, but I am not sure how big an object I can control." She flipped the pages to find other appropriate spells that would serve the King's needs. "I can knock things over from a distance. Copy the appearance of small object to another. I can make people oblivious to my presence, and I can cause stomach aches."

Tarq rolled his eyes, "What else can you do?"

"Not much. I can hide troops if there is another enchanter

there, I can heal small cuts, and I can program an entertainment cube. I am just a beginner, after all."

"How big an item can you make invisible?" he asked, an idea forming in his head.

"Let's see." Diana pointed to a boulder and murmured the incantation. Nothing happened. She then pointed to a rock about six inches in diameter and tried again. Again nothing occurred. Finally she pointed to a small three-inch rock and it vanished from sight. When she reached out to touch it, it was still there. She smiled sadly at the King.

"I don't think I am going to be much help."

Instead of looking disappointed, Tarq grabbed her and began to dance her around hugging her tightly. "It's perfect! I know exactly how we are going to get this Tal!" he exclaimed, laughing. "What time does the museum close? We have to go now. Do you think that Lauren still has that old digital camera in the glove box?"

Tarq grabbed Diana's hand and dragged her back to the car, talking all the way. "It's going to work. I feel it and this isn't just some sort of wish fulfillment fantasy. I have a true vision going here!"

They reached the museum with an hour left until closing. Fearing the guards would recognize him, Tarq sent Diana inside to take pictures of the display, the unfocused Tal, and the guards' locations. She returned in ten minutes and they hurried on their way, Tarq carefully pocketing USB drive with all the shots. On the way, Tarq outlined his plan.

Diana went down to breakfast the next morning, feeling as if it was going to be her last meal in freedom. It was a Saturday. For the past several days, Tarq had come for her at precisely 10 AM, and they would spend the day as tourists wandering around galleries and museums until evening. This day would be no different.

Tarq arrived and was cheerfully greeted by Lila, "It's going to be quite a scorcher." She handed him a cup of iced tea, "I can't believe this is October."

Tarq smiled, "I wouldn't know, although the weather channel said it was a result of something called 'La Nina'. Anyway we are going to be spending it mostly inside."

"Are you having any luck finding the Earth Tal? You and

Diana have been going at it for days."

"I think we are getting closer. At lease it gives me something active to pursue while Carr and Alaeric plan my attack." Tarq carefully looked at his teacup, not meeting Lila's eyes.

Diana felt his tension and stood up. "We'd better get going, time's a wasting."

Tarq followed Diana out of the kitchen. "Times' a wasting?"

"Let's go. I want to get this over with," Diana declared over her shoulder. "I want my one foray into felony over by lunchtime."

Tarq smiled as they walked to the car. "I am so sorry, Diana. If I could do this alone, I would. But at this point you are the only person with the right skills who can help me return to my home and kingdom."

When they were in the SUV and away from prying eyes, Tarq reviewed the order of events. "Do you have the rock?"

"Yes and before I made it invisible I changed it, so that I will only have to do one spell at the site."

"Good. Well, let's go." Tarq started the car and then just sat.

"What's wrong?" Diana asked

"Nothing. I've always upheld the law before. Hell, I've *been* the law." He put the car into reverse. "Let's do this before I find a reason not to."

They reached the museum at noon, after spending the morning in a number of galleries to establish themselves as sight-seers. Diana carried bags from the gallery across the street from the museum. Carefully she and the King made their way to the display case where the Earth Tal stood.

Diana was amazed at the King's performance. Gone were all traces of the cool aloof king she had grown to respect. Instead, Tarq chattered and made friends at each display. He was laughing and joking, commenting on the objects and charming everyone; tourists, guards, and tour guides. All attention focused on him. Diana found herself wondering if Lauren ever saw this side of the King. She knew there was tension between them and hoped that that they could work things out.

Diana took the opportunity to mutter her oblivion spell that would make people overlook her. Tarq nodded to her and strolled over to the volcanic display case, the girl following at a discreet distance. Other people wandered over, drawn by the King's presence.

Once there was a crowd of persons gathered, Tarq suddenly grabbed his head, shook it as if trying to clear cobwebs, and then staggered in the direction of the case. His outstretched hands, seeking balance, pushed against the case. Muttering a spell of his own, the king's strength toppled the case, scattering the exhibit across the floor. Tarq lay motionless in the middle of the broken glass and splintered wood. The rocks rolled across the floor, but no one was paying any attention to them as they rushed to help the stricken man.

Diana quickly located the Tal and muttered her invisibility spell over it. Before she put it in her tote bag, she removed the other disguised rock from her bag, made it visible, and placed it on the ground. She transferred the Tal into the bag, keeping it invisible. The she rose and joined the crowd around Tarq.

"Let me through!" She declared, breaking the spell of oblivion. "He's my uncle!"

The crowd parted and Diana approached the sprawled King. "Uncle Tony. Are you all right?" she cried hysterically. It was the signal that the switch was made.

As soon as he heard her voice, Tarq started to come around. "What happened?"

"You fainted again. We have to get you to the doctor."

"EMS is on its way, miss," A guard told them.

"Oh, thank you, he has been doing too much. He isn't all that well, but he does insist that he can do more." Diana babbled as the guard helped Tarq rise as Diana retrieved her museum bags and followed the staggering Tarq and his escort over to a bench.

The ambulance team arrived and Tarq explained that he was suffering from sunstroke, was under doctor's care and that he was quite all right. They checked him out, made certain that his eyes tracked and bandaged some cuts on his hands from the glass before releasing him.

Before leaving the museum, Tarq insisted on paying for the exhibit. He gave them several thousand dollars in traveler's checks. The museum director himself escorted them to the door and waved to them as they left.

"Well, that's done," he said as Diana drove the SUV away from the parking lot.

"I almost died when EMS wanted to take you to the hospital!" Diana laughed, feeling that her breathing was coming back to normal. "And then when you insisted on paying for the exhibit!"

"If I had been robbing the museum, I wouldn't have felt so contrite," Tarq answered evenly, smiling himself, "This way they will remember only an embarrassed man and his niece. Besides, you replaced the stone, so as far as they know it was an accident. I feel as if I had recompensed them in some way, so we didn't completely steal the Tal."

Diana opened her bag and made the Tal visible. She looked at its black base with the iridescent green and orange etchings. It was beautiful. Tarq's recovering his kingdom and her ticket back to Dal Ryeas. Overall, it had been a really good day.

When they got home, Lauren and Lila were waiting outside for them in the Harrison's yard. News of Tarq's mishap had been on the noon news, since a camera team was at the museum for another reason and taped the accident. Diana had not even seen them.

"So what were you two doing today, exactly?"

Diana quietly handed the stolen Tal to the King and took her mother's arm. "I'll see you later, Lauren. Come on Mom, I'll tell you all about it!" She smiled at the King, receiving a smile back and a nod, and took her mother inside the house.

Tarq started walking towards Lauren's house. The Tal felt heavy in his hand and it was beginning to pulsate. This was a good time to focus it to his will. It wouldn't be the same as being consecrated to a Tal, but it would be enough to give him the edge in regaining his own.

Lauren followed and watched him as he sat at the kitchen table with the small black stone in front of him, seemingly oblivious to her presence. She felt her anger begin to rise. Days earlier he had implied she had no knowledge of him and it had been festering inside her since. She was furious and decided that if she stayed in the room she would say things that were unforgivable.

"I did not give you permission to withdraw," Tarq said coolly as she started to walk out, "There are things we must discuss. This Tal changes everything."

Her face flushed, her movements sloppy and agitated, Lauren turned to the King. "I don't need your permission to do anything.

I never have and I never will. You are not on Dal Ryeas now, Tarq. You are in exile, just like me and I'd say that puts us on an equal footing for once!"

Tarq's eyes blazed. "That's it, isn't it? You're glad I'm being defeated!"

"Don't be absurd!" Lauren snapped. "I've done my best, always, to keep you secure on your throne. Even six years ago, when I betrayed my own family, it was for you. And what did it get me? Exile - exile forever from my family, from my home world and from you! And what thanks have I ever gotten? I'm vilified, watched, and not trusted. Alaeric returns and he's immediately in your confidence!"

Lauren came back and sat down roughly, still shouting at the surprised Tarq. "No one suspects Alaeric of ever being less than noble. Head high, he went into exile for the honor of his King. I'm sure the bards throughout Dal Ryeas sing melancholy lays about the sundering of noble Lord Alaeric from his beloved Princess Tayaela. But as for the other one, Laurenthalia, the King is well to be rid of that Olenteas bitch. He'd be better off married to Killia. Then there would be peace. I'm no fool, Tarq. I've spent time with the bards back home – a lot of time, I was even a part-time student at the bardic school. Most never knew who I was and they spoke freely to a young woman with no apparent rank. I heard their messages."

Her voice rose to a high falsetto, "A woman who will betray her father will kill her husband. The evil Olenteas Princess is simply a plant, a fail-safe if the rebellion goes awry. I'd beware if I were the King about the scorpion I took to bed. At least Killia would nullify any opposition to the throne and she's so much lovelier. I wouldn't trust that Olenteas woman as far as I could throw her."

Tarq gaped at her, aghast at what she was recounting. "Why didn't you tell me this before?" he shouted angrily.

"You were busy and it was my fight." Lauren answered shortly.

"Isn't that just like you! First you blame me for not trusting you and then you don't trust me!" The King's own long-held anger broke in a tidal wave of rage. "You want me to be perfect, well I'm not! I'm just a man who's lost his throne, his people, and his love! I don't understand most of it and I'm trying to muddle through the best I know how!"

"You're the King," Lauren said quietly in the wake of his fury. "You're the only one."

"I'm a lonely man, who can't afford to be vulnerable. I was raised in a castle of treachery. Even my best friends were, albeit unknown to them, part of the treachery against my house. Pyramus and Olenteas were forever allies, partners, until Tadiak fell and betrayal became the norm. And it's all still falling apart and somehow, with your help, or without it, I've got to put it all right again." Tarq slumped into a chair and buried his face in his hands.

Lauren watched him for a moment in silence. "Do you know what I like about this place?" her voice was light and casual again. "It's that you don't have to be responsible for anyone else. You don't have to be a royal. You can be free to do whatever you want. Having had this freedom," she continued, oblivious of the effect her words were having on Tarq, "it may be impossible to be as I used to be."

"Don't you want to come home?" he asked, making certain she could not see his face.

"I want you restored to your rightful position." she replied evasively.

"Damn it, Lauren. What do you want?" Tarq rose from the chair, angry once more. "In the last ten minutes you complained bitterly that I exiled you and now when I ask you to come back, you avoid my question. What do you want?"

"I don't know!" she shouted back. "If I knew it would be easy, I could give you an answer, but I can't. I don't know if I want to return to that life. I like this life. I like this place. But I love Dal Ryeas and I'm loyal to you. I do want you restored. So right now, that's all I'm focusing on!" She was only a foot away from him, standing up, and hands arrogantly clenched at her hips. Her hair was loose and flowing wildly down her back. Her face was flushed and rosy.

Tarq, unable to stop himself, placed his hands on her shoulders. "I'll never try to stop you from having what you truly desire. Just be certain it's what you want. If it isn't, please don't be too proud to let me know. I can't stand it when you are unhappy. I lo-"

She stopped him from saying what was in his heart by placing

211

a finger on his lips. "Don't," she said softly, "Don't say it. We might both regret it later." She moved closer to him. "Kiss me, Tarq, now," Her voice was nothing but a whisper, "As if there were nothing beyond tonight. Make love to me for now only. And we'll always have a night of happiness to sustain us in the days to come…"

She pulled his head down to her and kissed his lips, savoring the touch of him, the taste of him. His arms closed around her and their embrace yielded to the passions locked away from the world for many weary years.

Lauren's hands wrapped around Tarq's back, his hands caressing her sides. The wildness of their kisses forced them against the wall, with Tarq leaning into Lauren. Slowly her nails raked gently up his back and stroked his hair. Her kisses became harder and more serious. He felt her body tremble against his and he pressed harder. Her leg slid up and down his, arousing his passion to a new level. He gripped her tighter and bruised her mouth with his lips. She bit his lower lip lightly and laughed.

He pulled back from her a moment and stared into her deep brown eyes. They were warm and trusting for a change. He smiled and was rewarded with the genuine smile that made her so beautiful. He softly brushed the long dark hair away from her eyes and then gently ran a finger down the side of her face. She turned her head and kissed the palm of his hand. Then she playfully licked his wrist and laughed at his expression. He scowled and tickled her side and they fell to the floor giggling like children.

Tarq got up and held out his hand for Lauren. She rose and then ran from the kitchen. He chased her and they started an impromptu game of tag. Finally exhausted they collapsed onto the sofa and began their lovemaking again.

Neither remembered how they got upstairs to Lauren's bed, but each could recall for the rest of their lives their reunion; this exquisite, almost sad, intense lovemaking. How they explored each other and memorized each other, as if this was their only night together in all eternity.

Finally, after hours, spent and exhausted from their efforts they were content to lay together, their limbs intertwined and their long blonde and dark hair mixed, they drifted into sleep.

Just as he entered twilight sleep, still aware but unable to move, Tarq heard Lauren murmur softly to his chest, "Tomorrow we figure out how to return that Tal to the museum, alright?" He was smiling as sleep overcame him. Lauren snuggled against his side, eyes closed, breathing in his warmth, and storing it in her memory forever.

Chapter 23

"Do you think Mark will die?" Alaeric asked Tayaela as they rode through her world seeking its Tal.

Tayaela exclaimed. "What a morbid thought! And on such a beautiful day."

"Well, he doesn't seem to be getting any better. In fact, yesterday I thought he actually looked translucent." Alaeric was concerned for Mark, but ever a realist he was trying to prepare her for sorrow. His own life had been such that sorrow was a constant, hidden companion. It was his way of seeing the world, while Tayaela saw happiness as the universal force. It was one of their great differences; she was always surprised by sadness, he by happiness.

"Well, then we'd better locate this damn stone," snapped Tayaela, "It'll increase his chances, for Carr can only do so much with her own resources."

"You know, maybe we're going about this the wrong way." Alaeric reined in his horse suddenly. Tayaela stopped also and turned in her saddle to stare at him. "We're so busy trying to find the Tal that we haven't let it find us. You said it. We can only do so much with our own resources."

"You've lost me…"

"We're trying to track something we've never seen, never touched. We've used our skills from our world but we've never allowed the resources of this world to… to control us!" Alaeric was excited, in the grips of his idea. "What is the power of Dal Ryeas' Tal? What does it do?"

"It increases power. It serves the King." Tayaela answered, confused. "It aids the wizard. It protects Dal Ryeas. It-"

"Exactly. Well this place has no king. So how can it serve him?"

"I don't know." Tayaela was perplexed.

"There is no indigenous intelligent population here."

"Right."

"So there is no one to use the Tal. So maybe instead of searching in a prescribed manner, we ought to follow tendrils of...um..."

"The Tal's emanations!" Tayaela finished for him excitedly. "Of course! We're assuming that it has the same focus as Dal Ryeas' Tal. But it can't because we're talking about a virgin Tal from a virgin world! How stupid! I landed here because somehow this world's Tal seemed to promise me a haven. So it can't be far from us!"

"So we follow the emanations," concluded Alaeric.

Tayaela felt inordinately pleased with her husband. She was convinced he was right as she began to look at him speculatively. In that moment she could just-

"Tayaela," Alaeric interrupted her budding salacious thoughts. "There's no time for that now. If you were at home, how would you communicate to the Tal?"

"That won't work. Dal Ryeas' Tal focused and channeled for a thousand years, maybe more is a different type of stone. No. I think I'm going to have to open myself up completely to the undercurrents of this Tal, the ones which call on an emotional level."

Alaeric nodded and dismounted. "We'll camp here tonight. No sense in going back until we find something."

After an agreeable hour or so lighting a fire, eating a meal and making love under the blue-gray, twilight sky, they watched the moon rise.

"Somehow," Tayaela sighed. "I wish this could go on forever."

"So do I, love." Alaeric replied softly, kissing her hair as it rested on his shoulders.

"But it can't." Tayaela briskly rose and began preparations for the night. She fed the horses and spread out bedrolls. She saw Alaeric's eyebrow rise as she separated their bedrolls by the campfire between them.

"I don't need distractions," she said apologetically.

"Oh, I'm just a distraction then, am I?" Alaeric said in a hurt voice.

"Now don't be hurt," Tayaela came over to him, "please." She reached out to touch his shoulder.

Alaeric, with lightening speed, grabbed her and began to tickle her unmercifully. Tayaela gasped and tried to break his iron hold, but soon, too spent with laughter to struggle any more, gave up and surrendered meekly to his embrace. Alaeric, certain of victory, released his grip on her wrists and she immediately dove beneath his guard and began an assault on his most sensitive areas.

They grew weak with laughter eventually and lay panting, side-by-side on the forest floor, their small rock-ringed fire burning cheerfully in the gathering night. Then it came to Tayaela, like a faint breath of music on the wind or a far distant smile, that feeling not quite human but not alien, of warmth, of affection, and underneath it all, of power, benign unaligned power.

Wordlessly, she rose, with only a beckoning glance at Alaeric. He followed, trusting her instincts. It wasn't a hum but merely a whisper, the hint of a seductive power. But she knew it for what it was and she followed it.

After half a night's walk with Alaeric leading the horses behind her, Tayaela suddenly stopped. Alaeric was startled to find them being bathed in a red glow. It was warm but not unpleasant, although he was hesitant to accept it until Tayaela spoke.

"We found it! Or rather, it found us. We're its first intelligent life force and it's giving us access to its power!"

"You talk like it's alive." Alaeric said, uncertain.

"No, it's only a power source. It increases and focuses power, and it gives its user incredible abilities, but it's not living."

"So how does it know us?"

"We're human, we're intelligent. Everyday animals see this ritual and go on their way. But we stopped. We looked. Now, we're attuned!"

"Oh." Alaeric considered the implications. "So a Tal will work for anyone?"

"A new one like this will," Tayaela replied. "Dal Ryeas' Tal is so surrounded by spells and safeguards that only the consecrated rightful ruler can fully use it. Sindelar himself can only tap part of its potential. He's probably trying to break the safeguards somehow."

"What about Killia?"

"Until she is anointed, only Tarq can really use it to full capacity."

"Why are we discussing this?" Alaeric snapped. "I know all this. Let's get this back to Mark!"

Tayaela plucked the small basalt stone, un-cut, and unpolished, and put it in her pouch. Eventually its carnelian fire subsided and the new Tal waited for its powers to be touched again.

"Let's go." Tayaela finished her bedroll and mounted her horse. Alaeric led their return to camp. She concentrated for a long moment, visualizing her destination on the far side of Dal Ryeas. Before her, like the wisp of the wind, a breeze upon time, a path opened. Alaeric passed over it and through to the campsite. Wistfully Tayaela looked around her and remembered her sense of safety in the place.

"Don't worry, I'll bring you back." She promised the Tal. Then softly she closed the door upon her world.

Chapter 24

Mark lay listlessly on his cot. The cat, Maikai, on the bed beside him, kept butting his head under his adopted master's hand in a bid for attention. The young man tried to pet the cat but the effort seemed too much for him. All he wanted to do was sleep. As his eyes closed involuntarily, his hand fell away from the cat's head and hung over the side of the bed. He was too weak to raise it.

His breathing began to slow, each ragged breath becoming an effort in survival. The cat, nudging him, tried to get his attention. Sensing something wrong, Maikai began to meow wildly. Even the loud harsh noise was unable to raise the unconscious man.

Fortunately, Maril Zan, on duty near the tent, heard the cat's frantic meows. She entered the tent to find the cat half on the cot, trying to lick Mark awake. Maril Zan and the other remaining vanguard knew of Mark's wound and were all on guard against the day when the anathema would overpower the youth's other-world resilience and kill him. Someone was always near the tent in case help was needed. Mark's cheerful courage impressed these warriors and they rallied to his aid.

Realizing how close to death Mark was, Maril Zan wrote a note, tied it to the cat's collar, and sent Maikai to fetch Carr. Then she sat next to Mark and, in a low gentle voice, kept talking to him, trying to bring him around. She expertly massaged his chest, easing the strain of his breathing. There was little else she could do but wait.

The cat returned moments later bringing the sorceress with

him at a run. In her hand Carr clutched an ancient volume of healing spells. On its cover, a mosaic representation of the Dal Ryean Tal, the book announced that its prowess depended on the availability of a Tal to enhance the spells' powers.

Carr, after a quick examination of Mark, muttered. "It's the only way." She began her simple preparations. "Otherwise I'll lose him and I hate giving up without a fight." Carr was murmuring soothing phrases to Mark who was half-awake now.

Maril Zan looked shocked. "Lady, you can't do this without a Tal. I mean that's what the book says. Even I know that!"

"If I allow him to die because I don't have a stone to enhance my skills, then I'm not much of an enchantress." Carr snapped back. "I've always felt that our dependence on the Tal has stunted our independent development. So now I'm going to find out. Besides, maybe he won't need it as much as a full-blooded Dal Ryean does. He's stayed alive this long."

"It's too dangerous. What if the forces are too much for you and we lose you?" Maril Zan was adamant. "What's this one life compared to our cause?"

Carr replied, "If I can't help one individual to life, then I don't deserve to lead any cause. I'm sure Tarq will understand if I fail. But at least I'll have tried! And that's what I have to do! Look at the bright side, there are twin full moons, Maril Zan, and there is power there. I'll use it or anything else I can get my hands on. I don't need any hindrances. This will be hard enough. Now, unless you want to help, leave."

Maril Zan looked at Mark lying in agony. He was not much younger than she was, but the pain had etched years onto his face. She knew that without help he would be dead before morning. She hated wasted lives and was revered for her caution by her troops. But she also knew when it was imperative to risk everything on a single throw.

"I'll help," she declared.

Carr smiled, "Good. Now sit behind him and support him. He can't rise unaided." She rapidly completed her preparations.

Maril Zan lifted Mark's body gently, supporting him in a seated position. Her arms were under his chest, his head on her shoulder and she shifted him to ease his breathing. The cat sat on the bed next to the young man and laid a paw on his leg.

Carr sat on the floor below them and softly began to chant a litany of spells. As her concentration increased, her cross-legged form began to rise in the first manifestation of her power. She opened her eyes, changed from a deep earth brown to a vibrant gold. Her skin, a smooth deep brown, began to give off an aura of blues and reds. A nimbus of green light played about her hands.

As her voice rose, chanting the spell, and repeating the ancient formula, the light began to grow between her hands until she held a triangle of green fire. It spread and she moved her hands over Mark's chest. The triangle became a pyramid, its base spread over Mark's heart, its point controlled in Carr's hands.

Maril Zan, afraid to move, felt the warmth of the triangle on her own hands. Mark's heart fluttered and stopped his ragged choking breath suddenly silent. Maril Zan looked in horror as she felt the boy die in her arms.

And then the pyramid changed.

The green turned a dull pulsating brown, shot with streaks of black, and the red of dried wounds. Mark's heart suddenly lurched, and began to beat in a strong steady rhythm. His eyes opened, his body strained, as he gasped for air. The air filled his lungs as a newborn's and he cried out, his flung hand meeting Carr's sure, steady finger. Her kind eyes, brown once again, met his and she smiled.

"I feel..." he started to say and stopped, amazed at the strength of his voice.

"Yes?" Carr prompted, signaling Maril Zan to release him. The soldier rose, and quietly left the tent. In bemused amazement she went to her companions at once and told them of Carr's triumph.

Mark, sitting on his own for the first time in days, marveled at the strength coursing through him. Carr kept the spell on him, green light flowing once again, in an effort to rebuild much of his lost health. She sat before him, hovering in the air, as the green light encompassed them.

The spell enclosed them in the tent for the remainder of the day. Carr was reluctant to allow the magic to dissipate, fearing that once it did, Mark would relapse and die. Ruefully, she wondered how long she could keep hovering there. Because of the spell's inherent noise, the pair was completely unaware of the excitement outside the glowing tent.

They never heard Alaeric's shout or see Tayaela's smile, but suddenly in their green midst, a warm carnelian light began to glow, and there in Alaeric's hand the Tal of Tayaela's world shared its power for the first time. Once more, the surge of powers coursed through Mark and Carr and replenished them.

After a time, the lights began to fade, returning to the hidden dimensions of magic until needed again.

"It's over," breathed Carr, uncrossing her legs and standing once more. "That was just too close a call." She sat down next to Mark and grabbed him in a light embrace.

Mark shivered, "I was dead. I could feel it, the world was fading around me, and I could see the beyond and then you called me back." He tightly returned the sorceress' embrace. "You've given me two gifts this night."

"Two?" Carr was amused. "And what are they?" She ruffled his hair.

"My life and you've taken away my fear of dying. When the time comes again and I hope it won't be for awhile, I'll be able to face it bravely."

"You already have done that, Mark," Alaeric replied gruffly, moved by the night's events. Mark seemed so much older to him than the callow nineteen-year old he had first met so long ago.

Tayaela, sensing an emotional deluge, decided to channel the energies constructively. "So, now we have the Tal, Mark is well and Carr has just become the most powerful sorceress in the world – possibly several sorcery based worlds."

"That's going to be hard to live up to." Carr grinned wryly.

"Well, you know what I mean!" Tayaela replied airily with a wave of her hand. "So what's next?"

They laughed heartily at Tayaela's sudden air of fragility. It was so untypical of her, this imitation of Killia's airs, that it provided them a healthy release. Mark realized, now that it was over, how worried everyone had been over him. He admitted to himself at last that each night he feared that he would never see another morning. For the rest of his life, he would strive to greet each new day with a deep abiding joy, a glorious appreciation of merely living.

"Now what?" Alaeric repeated, when the laughter subsided.

He was sprawled across Mark's cot, his long legs stretched before him. Mark sat on the floor, with Maikai's head in his lap, happily reunited with his savior. Tayaela and Carr seated on camp chairs, Tayaela, sitting with her legs propped up on Alaeric's, and Carr more primly with her hands folded in her lap. No one presently seeing the sedate, well-dressed enchantress could ever imagine the wild power that earlier had coursed through her.

"Now, we begin to recall the troops," Carr spoke finally. "Killia is bound to set the date soon."

"No," Tayaela declared. "First we get the King. He has to be involved from the beginning. Everything must be his way."

"I think we should go through tonight then," said Alaeric. "I feel a great sense of urgency. She's going to force the Temple to anoint her before years' end. I want us ready."

"Can you contact Merrick?" Tayaela asked Carr. "Tell him what we're doing?"

"Maybe. I've been having trouble. His emotional state is interfering." Carr had a troubled look on her face.

"When we reach Tarq, we'll have Lauren try. They're bonded." Alaeric remarked. "She ought to be able to talk to him and comfort him."

"Good thinking." Tayaela exclaimed. "Alright, we meet back in an hour to leave."

"Carr, will Mark be all right?" Alaeric wanted to know.

"As long as you use the Tal to ease the passage," Carr replied. "Besides we can't leave him here. I plan to send the vanguard to Chaldia. You can force a path near there and over the next few days, they can drift in. I want them ready."

"Why Chaldia?"

"It's nearest to Tadia. They'll have to be close by when we make our move."

Tayaela hurriedly packed, then met with the vanguard captains. She explained their trip and gave them assignments to recruit as many as they could at Chaldia.

Once crystals exchanged and orders given, Tayaela joined the others, preparing to return to Mark's edgeworld. Alaeric and Carr refused to let Mark help with anything. He sat on the ground, patting the cat. All around him there was furious activity.

Tayaela laughed and met Mark's dejected look. Whenever he tried to move or help anyone, she smiled and shook her finger at him. "You sit there! We don't want to have to go through your healing all over again!" She called gaily to her husband and Carr. "Are you ready yet? It's going to be late enough when we get there."

"Have you given all the orders? Does everyone know what to do?" Carr asked anxiously. "Yes. Let's go!"

Finally everyone got into formation. Tayaela, personally, thought that her own path-making was smooth enough but decided if Carr wanted to test the new Tal then that was her business. Tayaela stood in the center of the formation and the others grouped around her.

Carr held Mark's arm as he held onto the cat. Alaeric, holding a large pack with all the weapons on his back, linked his arm through Carr's elbow. Tayaela held the Tal in one hand and Alaeric's arm in the other. She then invoked the power of the King and the Tal. Like a whisper of perfume, the ever-shifting paths slowed and opened before the pathforger, leading them through.

A moment of void, a feeling of empty night and they were in the middle of the Harrison's garden.

Chapter 25

Once it was discovered that Ferrel Olenteas had died breaking his brother Merrick out of prison, Princess Killia used all of her wiles to force the High Priestess of the temple of the twin Gods to set the date for her coronation.

Fearing to displease the woman who seemed firmly in control of the capital for much longer than the High Priestess thought, she reluctantly announced that the Gods blessed the middle day of Year's End, the annual Dal Ryean festival marking the rebirth. It was a time of merriment and much travel throughout the Kingdom. The priestess, knowing that the date would infuriate the wizard, nevertheless stuck by her decision and the coronation was set for two months away.

It was a well known secret in the King's loyal forces that the High Priestess was daily praying for the King's safe return and had told Tarq's agents of the date before she announced it to Killia. She was trying to assist her King in every way she could. After she made the announcement, the city held its breath to see what would happen. There was a sense that the world was about to change forever and the citizens of Tadia wondered just what their fate would be.

Throughout the city plans were made, rumors spread and questions asked. Where was the King? Was he deserting the Kingdom to the whims of Killia? Was he alive? Had the Olenteas bitch betrayed him again?

From the back room of the Arras Tavern, Merrick kept a flurry of innuendo and speculative rumors traveling the city. The wilder the tale, the more it spread so that no one except the force leaders really knew the actual plans. These stories kept both Sindelar's and Killia's agents scurrying around trying to determine fact from fiction, and left the way open for Tarq's loyalists to have easier access to the city. Everything was beginning to fall into place.

Princess Killia, lulled into a false sense of security by the apparent calm acceptance of her coup, began to feel that Tarq would never strike.

"He is such a coward," she would chirp to her chosen companions. "He could not even remain in possession of the Tal. Look at it!" She would then point to the purple-green stone, where it hung on its silken cord nestled in its silver wire, which was never far from the malachite throne of the Kings.

Killia spent most of her days in the throne room studying the stone. "Do you realize that by Year's End he will not even have a chance? Tadiak will regain fully what was stolen from our clan. And I am Tadiak!" In her mind, she would soon crow exultantly over the downfall of her enemies.

Lisa would listen to this unseemly and vulgar arrogance and recall with an inward shudder the Princess' reactions to the discovery of Ferrel's death. Killia's first reaction had been to throw the boy's body to the fierce guard dogs that guarded her stables. This shocked the court into a fearful silence as the full range of her cruelty was revealed to them for the first time.

While most were the Princess' loyal followers, Ferrel's deed had reminded them of the higher loyalty to one's family and most had admired the brave youth's action in freeing his brother. They were appalled by the Princess' declaration and a few older loyalists remembered grimly the excesses of the Princess' father in his last years as King.

Only Sindelar, who possessed a genuine fondness for Ferrel, expressed his outrage openly. He took the boy's body from the Princess' henchmen and prepared the boy for a proper burial. Lisa found out when Sindelar was holding the ceremony and defiantly appeared at the funeral. Sindelar, who had paid little heed to the girl after her theft of the Tal, was surprised at her presence. He believed her a complete sycophant to the Princess.

When he questioned the girl about her attendance, Lisa realized that if she were not careful with her answer he would become suspicious of her motives. "No matter what he did," she said haltingly, "he was my friend when my brother died. And I can never forget that." Lisa confessed in truth to the sorcerer.

Sindelar, whose own loyalty to his friend King Philos, who had led him to this rebellion, felt a surge of warmth for the girl who braved Killia's anger to honor a friend. For Sindelar, friendship and loyalty were his guiding principles even as they led him along dark and dangerous paths. He felt a growing fondness for the girl.

Together they stood beside Ferrel's' body and mourned the life that was so short and sad. Sindelar even put a comforting arm around Lisa as she wept while the Twin's priest sent Ferrel to the purifying flames of the Creator and on his way to the Garden of Holy Wisdom.

As the days passed, Sindelar remembered the girl and found he encouraged her to come to him with her problems. He liked her and tried to make her feel at ease. What he never knew was that Merrick Olenteas was encouraging Lisa to accept this guise of friendship with the man she feared most in two worlds to further the cause of his King.

As the time of Killia's coronation approached, Lisa's sense of isolation and fear grew. Her position as the petted favorite eroded as Dal Ryean girls who fawned upon the Princess supplanted her in Killia's regard. Her service was curtailed and she had much time to wander the huge palace at Tadia.

In many ways it was a relief to find herself with Sindelar rather than with the Princess. After witnessing first-hand the Princess' cruelty, Lisa found it difficult to pretend loyalty. Although she feared the wizard, he was not as cruel and demanding as the Princess. The Princess required unswerving, unquestioning obedience, such as that given to her by Rhea Volta. She had no patience for the company of fourteen-year old girls with incessant curiosity and a fine, if lately developed, sense of conscience.

Ferrel's death had shaken Lisa to her very soul. He was always her friend, and he had given the girl her first kiss. Ferrel never treated her as a stupid child, but gave her the courtesy of respecting her budding adulthood. His death was the first time she had seen someone die. Even Mark's death was an event that had occurred off stage, the results presented to her and his body never seen. Every time she closed her eyes, or heard the Princess' high-pitched laugh, she saw an image of Merrick, tears coursing down his battered, bruised face, holding Ferrel's body, rocking him gently, stroking his hair and saying goodbye.

She wanted to go home, but she was trapped. Only by helping Merrick, could she ever escape. Merrick, Lisa thought, was remarkable. Barely able to stand, he managed to come to the castle gate each night to hear her reports and give her much needed reassurance. In his quiet way, he taught her how to be unobtrusive. "Never seem to hide, be there in the open," he once told her. "If anyone asks you to leave, do so cheerfully, without apology. Seem like you belong."

And it worked. Even when she was near Sindelar, who was far more astute than Killia, her obvious presence soon became an accustomed sight. Plans and secrets were spoken freely before her. Even Sindelar forgot her presence or ignored it, counting on her loyalty.

She reported everything to Merrick. In the course of the first week, she was able to tell him of troop movements to other cities in Dal Ryeas, especially those shipping out to Chaldia, the port city nearest the capital, troop deployment for the week preceding the coronation and when the crackdown on insurgents would occur.

Merrick, utilizing her data, was then able to minimize dangers to his organization. He found her invaluable and told her so.

"You know, young Lisa," he said quietly to her late one night after her report, "you have quite a gift for this." he smiled. "Even Ferrel was unable to provide me with such pertinent information."

Lisa winced at mention of Ferrel's name. Merrick noticed and said, "I know it's hard to think about him, but we can't let his death make us forget what a wonderful boy he was." Merrick's eyes were bright. "Ferrel liked you and now that I know you, so do I. We make an excellent team."

Lisa, unable to suppress a sob, found comforting arms around her. "Oh Merrick, it's all my fault. Everything!"

"Shh. No it isn't. Mark and Ferrel died because they were trapped by wickedness. Killia is the fault, not you. She is mad and she has no sense of right or wrong. But her madness is insidious, even a fairly decent man like Sindelar is taken in. And if a powerful wizard succumbs, how could you avoid it?" Merrick explained in a low even tone that did much to lessen the girl's crying.

"But I could have resisted."

"How?"

"I don't know."

"Lisa, don't thrash yourself needlessly. You're resisting now. That's what's important."

"But Ferrel… and Mark… are still dead!" she cried again.

"And we go on. King Tarq, Princess Lauren and Prince Alaeric, my Aunt Carr, and your sister Diana are alive, and they're counting on us. A frightened fourteen-year old girl and a battered twenty-six year old man to pave the way for their return. It boils down to us. We have to be strong and we have to survive." Merrick lifted her chin. "You're doing wonderfully."

"You mean it?" Lisa whispered, huddling in the circle of his arm, her eyes on his face.

"Absolutely." Merrick smiled at her.

"It kind of rests on us," she said gravely. "So I'd better get back and find out more stuff."

"Good girl. I promise you'll be safe." Merrick silently swore to the twins and the Creator to keep at least this child from all harm.

"OK. I'll see you tomorrow night." Lisa declared, wiping her eyes.

"I'll be here." Merrick gave her a final hug and watched her march back to the castle. He knew how terrified she was and as he saw her pull herself straight and tall as she entered the gate, he felt inordinately proud of her. "That is one tough young girl," he said, admiringly to himself before he returned to other tasks.

On the following day, Lisa presented herself to the Princess for her regular shift as an attendant. Killia was in a foul mood, cursing everyone in sight. Throwing tantrums and making outrageous demands seemed to be a natural outlet for the Princess. Eventually reducing her ladies to nervous hysteria, Killia's mood would swing to gaiety suddenly and she would demand music and laughter from her followers. It drove her ladies to distraction and many fled to their clan holds to avoid her service.

On this day Lisa managed to remain unnoticed and therefore in the Princess' good graces. She was the only lady still in attendance upon the Princess when Sindelar came to see her. Quietly, she remained seated on a small footstool behind the Princess' chair as the wizard paced the room restlessly.

"I'm bringing the Olenteas' lords up from the cells and installing them in their traditional rooms in the palace," Sindelar announced abruptly, "I've ordered their release from their confinement."

"Oh, good." the Princess said in a bored tone.

"They are reluctant to appear. So I'm sending the remainder of their immediate families to the Fortress."

"That's a nice touch," Killia replied, examining her jeweled cloak. "I wonder what ever happened to Lauren and Alaeric."

"As far as we can tell they wander lost in the edgeworlds."

"Do you think she'll ever marry him?" the Princess asked, fiddling with the fringe of her gold weave shawl.

"Who?" asked Sindelar.

"Lauren. You know, the Olenteas Princess set to marry Tarq. He should have married me you know. Then none of this would have ever happened." Killia stood up and preened before a mirror.

"Please not again," Sindelar groaned. "He didn't marry you and that's the end of it."

"Well, he should have," Killia continued, obstinately. "She's such a bitch, that Lauren. I remember meeting her a few times when we were here for my father's funeral. She has no beauty at all, nothing to recommend her and that hulking cousin of hers - I wonder how Tayaela could stand to bed him." Killia shuddered. "No, Tarq would have been much better off with me." She was silent a moment then asked, "Have you any idea where Tarq is?"

"No. Merrick Olenteas was on his path when he vanished." Sindelar said carefully. Killia had yet to reveal to him why she had imprisoned Merrick and the wizard kept trying to find her reasons. "Well, that is a pity!" Killia was all innocence. "Merrick was such a good man."

"Yes, wasn't he..." Sindelar said dryly.

The conversation then turned to coronation plans and Lisa quietly sneaked from the room. It was nearly time for her meeting with Merrick.

"What does it mean?" she asked the young man, after reporting about the release of the Olenteas Lords.

"It means Lauren and Alaeric's fathers are now hostages to their good behavior. He's a cunning one, that wizard. He has effectively neutralized them." Merrick sighed. "At least we know they'll be at the pre-coronation events. Whatever you do, don't mention to anyone that you've ever met Lauren and Alaeric. That'll only get you into trouble."

"I haven't yet!" Lisa declared indignantly, and then amended, "The subject never came up, I mean."

Merrick grinned at her, "Oh, good. If you can possibly do it without arousing suspicion, try to see if you can visit either of the Lords in their chambers. It'll be harder than before, but if we can get some word out or to them, it may help their plans."

Lisa nodded. She was able to visit Lords Ertlan and Kir'san a few times over the past weeks since Ferrell had died. She took messages between them and Merrick, extra food that she hid in the voluminous skirts Killia made her wear and books. In turn the Olenteas Lords had started teaching her ways of being invisible and the history of Dal Ryeas.

In a quiet voice Lisa asked, "Do you think the King will win?"

"I honestly don't know," he replied honestly "It'll depend on a number of factors. How powerful my aunt is, what support the King has, and the element of surprise. "

"We can only hope then."

"Hope and plan and have faith in the Creator," Merrick smiled. "Good night, young Lisa."

"Merrick, are you in love with Diana?" Lisa wanted to delay his departure for a while. She was lonely and talking about her sister made her feel better.

Merrick laughed. "I'm very fond of her. But until this is over, I'm not thinking of love. I am too…

"Well, I hope you are." Lisa remarked. "You're by far the most interesting person she's ever been involved with!"

With a bow and a flourish, Merrick replied, "Thank you, milady. Now, go inside."

Lisa shyly stood on tiptoe and kissed his cheek. "Good night, Merrick, see you tomorrow."

Merrick smiled and watched the girl carefully make her way into the castle. Tomorrow, he would make a final report. The coronation was less than a month away. It was time for the King to move.

Chapter 26

"Will you look at all that hair!" a voice exclaimed, "You could keep the wig makers of Phryga employed for months!"

Lauren, who was sleeping, her head nestled on Tarq's shoulder, came instantly awake, her hand grasping a long dagger she kept under her pillow. Tarq reached for an unsheathed long sword hidden at the side of the bed, poised to leap into battle.

"I'm glad you two at least sleep partially clothed." Alaeric was leaning casually in the doorway, Tayaela grinning wickedly behind him.

"What the hell are you doing here?" Tarq recovered first and demanded.

Lauren carefully sheathed her dagger and climbed out of bed. Her jeans, tossed recklessly on the floor, were nearby and she pulled them on, oblivious to the amused looks of her cousin.

Tarq regally drew on his trousers and turned to face his grinning sister. A haughty arrogant expression was quickly replaced by a look of genuine delight as he embraced his younger sister for the first time in years. "Tayaela," he murmured into her hair.

Their embrace lasted for a long while and when they emerged they were misty-eyed and shaken. Alaeric and Lauren looked on, sentimentally amused.

"In answer to your question, we have found an unfocussed Tal on the place Tayaela found during her exile, my liege, and it is all yours."

"Are you serious?" Tarq asked eagerly "we have the unfocused Tal from this world! We should compare them! Who has it?"

"Carr has it; Mark and she are at the Harrisons', but will be joining us directly. Right now they are experiencing a rapturous welcome."

"How is Mark?" asked Lauren.

"Cured. It seems our esteemed enchantress is even more powerful than we thought. She used a Tal spell without the Tal, and…"

"And succeeded?" Tarq was amazed. "That's wonderful!"

"Yes. It may begin a whole new school of sorcery, independent of the crown."

Tarq laughed a full-hearted laugh. "Suddenly I feel really positive. We are going to win. We'll soon be home!"

Lauren smiled. "Ah, I hate to put a damper on such enthusiasm, but don't we have to return the Tal that Diana and you stole from the museum before we leave?"

Alaeric's eyebrows raised but Tarq gave him a smoking look before he could make any wry comments about wrongdoings or a blot on his kingship.

"I suppose so. I don't want to leave any bad, what's it called… um…karma here. And we can't deny this edgeworld's protection by the Tal." Tarq sighed in mock regret. He was too excited to be distracted by restitution for his earlier theft. "Well, it's no use repining. We have a coup to plan – and a Tal to return."

"Nice choice of words," muttered Lauren. As conversation with Tayaela and Alaeric continued, she felt the barriers erected between herself and Tarq once more. Even their intimacy of the night before did not lessen the profound nature of the choice facing her.

Tarq looked at her quizzically. His expression told her that he knew about her dilemma. A question formed in his eyes and on his lips, but he turned from her before he allowed himself to ask it.

"Let's go downstairs." said the King. "We have to determine our course of action." He turned from Lauren and led the way from the room. Alaeric and Tayaela followed, leaving Lauren behind, locked in her unending struggle against herself and her desires.

Before he left the room, Alaeric turned to his cousin and said one word, "Duty."

"When have I ever neglected my duty?" Lauren said furiously, glaring after him.

After they had gone, Lauren tried to put her problem from her mind. It was destroying her effectiveness as a force leader. She looked into the mirror and stared at her large haunted brown eyes. She saw two people in her mirror. Laurenthalia Olenteas, Princess of the Clan, and Lauren Olenteas, resident of the edgeworld Earth. It was getting harder to differentiate between the two. More often than not the arrogant haughty Princess was sublimated into the casual earth woman. And she found that she liked being that latter person. Vaguely she wondered if she could change into that person permanently.

As she stood before her mirror lost in her impossible problem, the voices of the other wafted up to her. It was apparent that Carr, Mark, and Diana had joined the war council. Only she was missing.

"We need to storm the castle!" Alaeric's voice boomed.

"Are you crazy?" Tayaela's voice interjected, "No one storms Tadia. The place is huge and well fortified."

"Carr was saying something about using her magic..."

"No, you'll need it to confront Sindelar," Tarq replied. "Any other use will exhaust you." Wild ideas sprang from everyone. The main idea was to continue sending troops to Chaldia, and infiltrate the vanguard into Tadia. As she stood alone outside the door an idea occurred to Lauren that seemed so audacious that it might work.

When she entered the family room everyone was sprawled on the furniture listening to Tarq state his position adamantly.

"I want to commit all the troops at once. The efforts need perfect timing. I either win back my crown in one attack or die trying. I won't have the country so polarized by a civil war that it never recovers. It took too long before and I'd rather Tadiak regain the crown than lose my people in battle."

"We'll never be able to do it." Alaeric objected. "Not in one battle. The castle is much too strong and could withstand a siege for years. Without the castle we can't take the city and we can't take the castle in one pitched battle."

"That's where you're wrong," Lauren said from the doorway. Bestowing a warm smile and welcoming hug upon Mark, she continued. "What you need are people inside the castle ready to signal you. And I have a plan."

"What is it?" Tarq asked suspiciously.

"Who gets into places no one else can approach?"

"Who?"

"Bards," Lauren smiled. "And the best part is that no one even checks their bone fides. What I propose is to appear at the castle in bardic colors, instruments and apprentice in hand, for the pre-coronation Supplicant's Feast. It's always open to bards the night before the anointing and everyone —all the clan lords, their households are obligated to be there."

"You're not exactly unknown though." Tarq protested.

"If I wear a wig and have Diana with me I can be disguised. As far as they know, Laurenthalia is a far distant exile and a Princess. They won't be looking for me – Lauren a shabby bard."

"They're going to be looking for anything suspicious, anything unusual, any sign of trouble." Tarq protested. "They have to know that we are coming!"

"They've already announced traditional coronation events. People will be pouring into the city for both it and Year's End. So will our people."

"And they know that," Tayaela pointed out, "This is what they are waiting for us to do. We can never get into the castle. We're all a little too well known..."

"Not," interrupted Alaeric, "if we provide a proper diversion."

"Meaning what?" asked Mark.

"Under my very obvious leadership, we make a feint at, say, taking control of Chaldia, with shock troops. What I mean is I make the attack in Tarq's name. With Tayaela by my side and the regulars Merrick reports are in place at Chaldia, it will appear that we are the King's main strike force. If we are convincing enough then we divert attention from the castle where the rest of you are attacking."

Carr added, "I could even perform a spell that would make it appear to casual observers that Tayaela is the King. They look enough alike. It would confuse the issue even more and possibly take Sindelar off guard. Our best weapons are that no one knows that Tayaela is back and or that Lauren and Tarq are reunited. Secrecy is quite powerful. It lets us operate in the dark."

"In the meantime," Lauren continued, "we get the vanguard to drift into Tadia for the festivities. Merrick's people can hide them. And when the royal party is on display during the Supplicant's Feast…"

"The supplicants will be the vanguard." the King smiled broadly.

"The important thing, my King, is to get you to the Tal. Once you have it, all the rest of us will have to do is clean up the mess."

"True," said the King. "Alaeric, can you make it seem that you are going to move from Chaldia to Megra, maybe appear on the run? That will distract more attention away from the Tadia. Once they have relaxed because of Alaeric's apparent defeat, they will not look for us any more at the castle. Sindelar has no idea about Tayaela's Tal. He thinks I will be cut off from the city and can't get in. He already assumes that we are powerless but as Carr has shown, even without a Tal miracles can happen." Tarq smiled at Mark, who was petting Maikai as the cat sprawled on the table in their midst.

"Fine, we create the diversion then," Alaeric said with finality. "Carr, I am going to need a major shift to Chaldia. We have to figure out how to hide so many soldiers until the right time."

"We could assemble them on the new world. No one is there and only I know how to create the paths from there to Chaldia," Tayaela suggested. "That way we can shift the troops a little at a time and with all the preparations for the consecration, no one will notice paths going to an empty world. Or if Sindelar does, he will just think it is Pyramus loyalists going into exile."

"Good thinking, Tay," said her brother. "We are going to have very little leeway for error. The sooner we move the better. We have a little less than a month to get everything in place."

"True." Carr smiled. She pulled out a velvet bag from a pocket in her coat. From it she took out a number of communication crystals. She handed one to Tayaela and attuned it to her. She then handed and attuned crystals to each of the others in order to ease communications.

Alaeric spoke quietly to the King for a moment while the others continued to discuss Lauren's plan to infiltrate the feast.

"The King and Merrick can sneak into the castle the night before the feast. Merrick should be able to arrange this," Carr continued. "Mark and I will go in with the general populace and the vanguard. This will enable us to get close to the head table and Sindelar. Since Killia has to come out and show herself, I expect Sindelar will come, too. When they let everyone in to the feast, I'll make my way over to the dais below the wizard's table."

"In the meantime, I'll be entertaining, and making my way towards the Princess," Lauren said. "Diana will spot Lisa and try to get to her."

"What if you're recognized? Merrick said your father will be there under duress."

"I've been avoiding my father for years. I've had a lot of practice. Besides," Lauren grinned, "don't underestimate Prince Kir'san's poker face. He always looks as if he swallowed something that disagreed with him, and Uncle Ertlan always looks oblivious to the world around him. He's practiced that for years." Alaric heard her and laughed, nodding in agreement about his father

Tarq and Alaeric were done with their conversation and listening. "Merrick and I," said the King, "will come from behind the throne. While the focus is on you, Lauren, I will retake the Tal. I know Tadia castle and I can always find a back route to any spot in it."

The King turned to Carr. "Send someone to contact Merrick, and have him prepare for our people to infiltrate the crowds. I want a minimum of bloodletting. These are my people."

"Pyramus always has soft cores." Lauren remarked to Alaeric, who laughed at an old family joke. Tarq, smiling sweetly, got in his own dig. "That's because we don't have rocks in our skulls masquerading as brains, like Olenteas."

"No, you have clammy seaweed for hearts," Lauren sneered.

"Enough!" exclaimed Carr. "This is futile and childish." But she was grinning too.

"True," the King conceded as Lauren gave a short laugh. "But it's so satisfying."

The intimacy between Tarq and Lauren resurrected itself for an instant, as if their barriers were down, before going up stronger and higher than ever. Their lovemaking was a memory only to be recalled sometime in the distant future when the pain of proximity was no longer a problem.

Lauren, still reluctant to commit her life to Dal Ryeas, refused to analyze her emotions for Tarq. While the King stubbornly refused to request Lauren to stay with him, he felt she ought to know how he felt without words. He felt that if he asked, she would accept out of pity for his loneliness and forsake her true desires. He refused pity, but for one brief moment they could share another's lives.

So the planning continued. By the end of the night, Carr was prepared to shift Tayaela and Alaeric to Chaldia.

As he was leaving, Alaeric called out, "By this time a month hence we'll be feasting in Tadia!"

As they vanished onto the path toward Chaldia and their part of the attack on Killia, Tarq gloomily murmured, "Or will we be the feast?"

Lauren, looking up from her discussion with Diana of appropriate bardic behavior, wisely refrained from comment. Instead, she said in a placid voice, "My liege, I think the signal to commence the attack should be a song from this world. Diana and I will sing it, when everyone is in place, and we are set to begin."

"What song is that?"

"It's a really old song called "Bad Company," Diana replied with a laugh.

"Bad Company, hmm…how appropriate."

Lauren carefully began to hum the tune and then sing, "Rebel souls, deserters we are called…" By the end of the song the King was visibly amused.

"Yes, that's perfect. When you reach the end of the third refrain 'Bad Company, I won't deny', the attack will commence. Carr, try to work it so that few civilians are hurt."

"I'll try," Carr sighed, "but I expect Sindelar will be a bit of a problem for me. He's awfully good."

"I'll distract him hopefully." the King assured her. "I'm going directly for the Tal. He'll try to keep me away from it."

"My responsibility will be the civilians," Mark declared. "I am more of an archer than a swordsman so I will get the innocent away."

"Good, then I leave that to you." Tarq was inwardly pleased with the boy. Despite nearly dying, he was determined to assist in any way. "We will get some soldiers with bows under your command. Once I have my hand on the Tal the symbiosis will commence. It will take a moment for the stone's full power to enter me. That's when I will be most vulnerable, so you'll have to guard my back. Once the symbiosis is restored, I'll combine it with the power of the new stone and we should be able to control the forces against us. We ought to be able to neutralize anything the wizard can bring against us. We can even open a path inside the castle for Alaeric and Tayaela to come through."

Tarq turned to face them all, speaking in serious tones, "I don't think I need to remind you that our work for the next two to three weeks must be done in extreme secrecy. I don't want to scare Killia into trying for consecration before we're ready. The High Priestess can only hold out for so long. I've already shielded Alaeric and Tayaela as well as I can with the new Tal, but its power has less focus than our own, so haste is of the essence. Be very careful especially when we get to Tadia. We will start infiltrating now, and get the vanguard in place. The rest of us will shift between the staging world and here. Fluctuations in the paths won't be so noticeable here. Then at the last week, we will shift ourselves to Dal Ryeas and make our final preparations. Are we ready?

"We will be, Tarq," Lauren assured him. "Now how are we going to return this world's Tal to the museum?"

"We aren't." Tarq replied absently.

Before he could continue Lauren screeched. "What? Are you that selfish and greedy that you have to have three Tals? The Creator will never allow that. You will doom us from the start!"

"Take it easy, Lauren," Tarq smiled. "Boy, you really don't know me do you? What I meant was that Diana's replica is so good, why return the original to the museum where it will be encased in glass. I want us to place it in the park or somewhere where it is free to spread its powers.

"Oh," said Lauren meekly. "Sorry."

Tarq grinned. "That's ok. Now then, let's plan our revolution."

Chapter 27

A few days later during the final days of preparation for the transition to Dal Ryeas, Lauren and Diana, accompanied by Carr, went to a costume shop and bought wigs, one purple spiked and the other fluorescent green. Carr taught them a simple spell to adhere the hair to their heads while intertwining their own hair through it. They bought black leather jackets and trousers with violet blouses that gave them a rakish medieval look. They also bought a guitar for Diana.

"I can't play this very well," she protested.

Carr smiled and muttered a few words, "Now you can. It'll hold for about two months."

"Thanks!" Diana was pleased with her new-found skill and serenaded Carr and Lauren all the way home. They arrived to find the King and Mark preparing to leave. Staring in shock at Lauren's purple spikes, the King's speechlessness reduced Lauren's to helpless giggles. She finished her packing, chuckling at the King's discomfort.

Diana and Mark went home to say goodbye to their parents. The Harrisons, especially Ron, were reluctant to allow them to return to Dal Ryeas and the dangers facing them. Mark was nearly grown and although his decision to continue his education in Dal Ryeas dismayed them, they were really unable to stop him. Diana, on the other hand, had to promise to return at least to finish high school. Then she could make her choice. Eager to go, she agreed to the condition.

Lila Harrison felt torn between her own loyalty to Dal Ryeas and her fear for her children. As long as her youngest child was hostage to Sindelar, Lila felt any action to free her was imperative. She convinced her husband that Mark and Diana were Lisa's best insurance and Ron eventually agreed.

Before the situation at the Harrisons reduced Mark and Diana to emotional wrecks, Lauren and the King went to the rescue.

"Don't worry, Lila," Lauren said cheerfully. "I'll bring both girls home to you!" She never saw the stricken look in Tarq's eyes at her statement. Before she could turn towards him, he had resumed his usual aloof expression. Only Diana saw the pain cross his face.

"Are we ready?" asked the King as they finally assembled. He stood in the middle of the group. Diana and Mark, with Maikai draped around his shoulders, flanked him as he raised the unfocussed Tal. Lauren stood behind him, sword drawn at the ready, while Carr knelt before him sharing her power with him and the Tal. A shimmering path yawned before them. "Next stop, Chaldia!"

The Harrisons watched as the path spiraled skyward slowly as Tarq manipulated the Tal to hide their passage. He called up a wind much like the one Sindelar used to gather his forces. The King and his companions crossed the path quickly to the Pyramus hold of Chaldia, leaving the Harrisons to watch empty space.

Chaldia was crowded and awash with rumors concerning the return of King Tarq. Spies were unable to determine truth from carefully concocted lies. All they were able to report were the inordinate numbers of old soldiers coming to the city daily, unemployed, and frustrated. Sindelar, upon receiving these reports assessed that Chaldia was the focal point for Tarq's eventual counterrevolution. He focused much of his attention and committed many of his troops not far from the city.

Chaldia, in its turn, fully expected annihilation once Killia was enthroned. It was far too close to Tadia to escape the Princess' notice, and Chaldia had been the first place to declare Leas Pyramus as King. It was a Pyramus stronghold and Killia was not likely to forgive this treachery. Rumors of her hostility to even Pyramus-born priests caused all Chaldia to prepare for the worst. They were grateful that the soldiers were pouring into the city, even if the local populace remained uninformed of the King's plans.

Both Sindelar and the Chaldians expected the arrival of Prince Alaeric. When Alaeric called for troops in the King's name, the unemployed soldiers and citizens alike swarmed to his banner.

With all the attention and rumors focused upon Alaeric and his incognito companion which rumor declared would be Tarq, Sindelar's spies in Chaldia never noticed the arrival of two men and a woman. Mark, Carr, and Tarq were able to quietly enter Chaldia and take the road to Tadia along with other travelers unobserved. Meanwhile Alaeric reclaimed Chaldia in Tarq's name, and a panicked Killia, against the advice of her wizard, sent her best troops to meet his challenge.

Sindelar, knowing that to postpone the coronation through fear of Alaeric would be a fatal error, allowed the Princess to dispatch the troops. Killia would never permit him to leave Tadia so close to the anointment, so the wizard was forced to rely on his best Captains to contain the menace in Chaldia. He stressed that no battle was to be fought and that the Queen's troops were to delay engaging the enemy until after the coronation. Killia sent orders that the army was to try to destroy Alaeric's forces immediately. This set of contradictory orders was the first public breach between the Princess and the wizard and it disturbed many courtiers who saw it as a sign of internal dissention.

As the armies gathered around Chaldia, thousands of Dal Ryeans poured into Tadia over the next fortnight. Every clan hold, hostelry, private house, any one with extra rooms to let, were bulging with the extra population. Inwardly the wizard cursed the High Priestess for setting the coronation date during Year's End, but there was little he could say, since the date took on the aura of holy writ. The holiday brought thousands, even entire small towns to the great city to celebrate every year.

With the added attraction of the coronation, Dal Ryeans who normally would have remained at home came to see if the event was really going to occur. Bookmakers were growing rich on the odds and the Bards spread each set of rumors blithely along with the truth.

"Damn those bards," Sindelar was heard to mutter as each rumor brought more people into Tadia. He even complained to the Chief Bard that the traveling minstrels were undermining the authority of the government. The Lord of the Bardic College politely told the irate wizard that it was incumbent upon his guild to disseminate news as it was told to them. The lord then blamed modern sorcery with its crystal transmitters for trying to shut the bards out of their traditional tasks.

Before the argument could blossom into an age-old debate between tradition and modern sorcery, Sindelar wisely dismissed the Bard. He refused to dwell on distractions while the city was awash in massive crowds. Out there he knew there was trouble, but it was so carefully shielded that even when he tapped the power of the Tal, he was unable to locate its source.

He even tried to dissuade the Princess from the traditional pre-coronation appearance and feast but found her adamant in her observances. She defied him and challenged his authority again before witnesses, causing him to suppress succumbing to a towering rage in her presence. He adroitly withdrew and left her, barely maintaining his near legendary calm. He realized that his control was slipping and a shiver of fear for the future coursed through him.

"You're not crowned yet," the wizard snarled to himself in his rock garden. "And until you are, my girl, I'd be well advised to take caution."

Knowing that the rocks in the garden were more inclined to listen than the Princess, Sindelar permitted himself the luxury of telling them all his concerns. What he told no one, not even the rocks, were his own private preparations for whatever the future would bring. Whoever won, he was doomed, he thought morosely.

Lauren and Diana presented themselves to the Entertainments Master a week before the feast. Not trusting her own musical talents, Lauren had Carr create a slight manipulation spell. When she sensed that no one was near who could sense the spell, Lauren whispered it before the audition in front of the master of ceremonies. As expected, their beauty and the unusual repertoire of the edgeworlds enthralled the Master. They sang a repertoire of strange songs and were applauded by the audition committee.

The Entertainments Master was thrilled that he had something new for the feast and he gladly gave the final approval for their appearance at the Supplicant's feast. He found their looks and style refreshing and different. "You spent your time in the edgeworlds well. We look forward to hearing you at the feast!"

Lauren thanked him profusely and guided a nervous Diana away from the castle. They would return there only on the morning of the feast.

"Well, that's taken care of." Lauren exclaimed once out of range of the castle.

"Now what?"

"We wait." Lauren smiled. "According to one of the songs we sang, the waiting is the hardest part."

"I think we'd better practice." Diana suggested.

"We're that bad?" Lauren laughed. "I thought we were improving!"

"We are, but I think we'd better practice." Diana insisted.

Lauren laughed at Diana's earnest request. The two young women felt light-hearted in the bright winter sunlight. They almost forgot their mission. It was a beautiful day and Tadia was bustling with holiday shoppers.

"Let's take the long way back to the Bard Hall," Lauren suggested. "I haven't been in Tadia for years. It's always such an interesting place. I'll show you some of it. It's all decked out for Year's End and the market is in session. It's like a huge mall!"

"Maybe I can get Merrick something," Diana sighed. "He's so sad."

Lauren nodded sympathetically.

The reunion of Merrick and Diana had been subdued. Diana was shocked by his half-healed cuts and yellowing bruises, but more so by the intensity of his grief. She did not know if she loved him, but she did care greatly about him. Knowing she was too young to make a lifetime commitment to any man, she did make herself a promise to see him through this hardest time.

"You're doing him a lot of good," Lauren said approvingly. "He's my bonded and I'm very concerned about him."

"Once you win, will he still be bonded?"

"Uh-huh. Always." Lauren looked over the city. "I was almost Queen here once," she said wistfully.

"You'll be Queen when Tarq regains power."

"I don't know. Freedom is a very hard thing to give up." Lauren mused. "Come on; let's go to the Bard Hall. There are some very nice artisan stalls there. We'll get news and a gift for Merrick."

"When will the others get here?" Diana asked

"Tonight..." Lauren fell silent.

Shouldering their instruments and packs, they returned to the Bard Hall. The Hall was a series of connecting buildings on three-fourths of a large square. The fourth side of the square was part of the Artist's guild, with shops to display their wares.

The Bard Hall was caught in anticipation, like much of the rest of the city. Even though the holidays were coming, Killia's incipient coronation was beginning to frighten the people of Tadia. Erosion in the belief that the King would return to save them from the mad Tadiak was reflected in the grim popular mood. The days to Killia's anointment were closing fast and the only sign of resistance was at Chaldia, where the King's forces seemed to be losing.

The bards in residence were hesitant to share news with one so outlandishly attired as Lauren, but once she showed her credentials, which Carr had thoughtfully provided, they told her the latest news: Killia's troops had the King's forces on the run.

"Do you think Tarq will come back?" Lauren asked an older bard.

The bard shuddered, "If he doesn't rally his forces and make his move before she is anointed he will be forced to fight a crowned Queen. It could create a dilemma in the Tal and destroy it. All those opposing forces surging through the thing..."

"But he's a crowned and anointed King," Lauren pointed out.

"But he doesn't have Sindelar," the bard crooned. "I hope he acts soon. We need him. This woman is a hazard. She doesn't even know how to rule."

Lauren walked away. In four days, if all went well, Tarq would regain his throne, and her role in his life would be over. Once upon his throne, he had no further need of her. It was better for him to contract an alliance with someone more suitable to be his Queen. Once her obligation to him was complete and he was restored to power, Lauren decided she was returning to her exile and out of his life.

Having finally made her decision, she felt relief and a sense of infinite sadness. She determinedly put it from her mind until the time to act upon it was at hand and turned her attention back to Diana.

The girl was purchasing a small statue for Merrick. It was of a young man and young woman holding a small globe between them. They were looking at each other, their expressions mixing of mischief and happiness. The pair made her feel quite good. The young man's face reminded her of Merrick and somehow she thought that their everlasting camaraderie would ease his underlying and perpetual sorrow.

When Lauren saw it, she exclaimed in delight. "How perfect! A statue of the Twin Gods will be invaluable! The male is Saevirg and the female Sarama, and that is the world they created. It is one of the nicest I've seen!"

The young women returned to the Arras Inn by suppertime. Their spirits were high and infectious after a day of wandering around the festive city and making frivolous purchases. Lauren bought a new leather jacket and some sweets while Diana bought a book of Dal Ryean poetry. When they burst happily into the back room they found Merrick, Mark, Carr, and the King discussing the events.

Since only Merrick had been present to greet the King and his companions, everyone exchanged greetings and news. While Lauren was telling the King of the success of her mission, Diana pulled Merrick aside and gave him his gift. He was delighted with it and one of his rare heart-felt smiles transformed his scarred face.

Lauren, from the corner of her eyes, saw this and felt relief that he was on way his towards healing. "Good girl, Diana," she whispered to the King. Tarq nodded in accordance. Merrick was a valuable ally and the thought of his being emotionally crippled bothered Tarq. He liked the man and wanted to ensure that he was on the mend in a spiritual sense.

"I feel like we are just sitting around doing nothing when everyone else is out there taking risks." Mark stated. "I hate the idea that Lisa is in that castle without any protection. Are you certain that we can't get her out before the battle?"

The King shook his head. "I understand your frustration Mark. It's killing me to have Alaeric and Tayaela creating a diversion while I skulk here. But if we take Lisa out of the palace, they'll know something is up."

"Besides," Merrick added, smiling at Mark. "I think Lisa would fight tooth and nail to stay there. She has discovered that she is doing important work for us and she wants to make amends for stealing the Tal in the first place. There is nothing like a convert, for loyalty and fierce devotion to a cause." He paused. "Besides the Olenteas Lords have been giving her lessons in subterfuge and I think Lord Ertlan used a hiding spell on her in an effort to keep her safe too." Merrick looked at Lauren. "It seems your father and uncle have a young protégé." Lauren grinned and shook her head.

Carr was looking at Mark critically. "I think we are going to have to outfit you properly. We don't want anyone to recognize you at the feast before we are ready to attack." She smiled and took Mark with her. "Come with me. I need to buy us some supplicant clothing. We'll see you later."

When they left, the others settled down to wait. Lauren pulled out her long knife and began to whet it on a pocket stone. Merrick told Diana myths concerning the Twin Gods and the King.

Tarq simply waited.

Chapter 28

Princess Tayaela watched as Alaeric roused the troops from their tents. In the middle of Chaldia's public square a makeshift army camp had sprouted. Tayaela, for all appearances, looked like Tarq from a distance and the populace of Chaldia, the Pyramus home city, swarmed around their army with food, drink, and tents. Chaldians knew that the minute Killia was crowned they were doomed.

The daily skirmishes between the troops were starting to demoralize them but on the other hand the presence of Alaeric allayed those fears. His great battle prowess had been proved as a young boy when he led a campaign against brigands in the Olenteas highlands and won almost single-handedly. Just knowing that Alaeric was there allowed Chaldians to prepare happily for Year's End and be thankful that there was an army between them and Killia's troops outside the city.

The troops, rousted out of bed in the pre-dawn hours, were anxious to hear what their commander wanted. They waited as their officers met with Alaeric and the person they assumed was Tarq.

"We have had word from our people in that Killia's troops are on their way into the city." Alaeric stated. "Knowing Sindelar, he will send them along a path that is obscured to us. He thinks that he has our main force here at Chaldia and that Tarq is with us. All those skirmishes, the feints towards Megra have all been to lure her best troops here. "

Alaeric smiled and spoke a few words under his breath.

Tayaela, standing in the corner and looking like a man obscured by a cloak, was revealed to all the captains as the Princess and not the King. There was a hush in the crowd of officers for a moment and then they spontaneously began applauding.

One young officer looked puzzled as the veterans were laughing. In a moment she understood that they were a feint to pull Sindelar's troops away from Tadia and that the King himself was going to seize back the throne from within the capital itself. Once she grasped this, the young woman enthusiastically joined in the applause and laughter.

Alaeric and Tayaela let the amusement continue for a moment and then began to announce their battle plan. "Sindelar thinks that the King is making his stand from here and we are going to continue that illusion. Tayaela will resume her disguise and ride at the head of the troops here in the square. I want the First, Second and Third Centuries surrounding her and making it look as if this was the central massing area and that except for the Fifth Century patrolling the walls, these are all the soldiers we have.

"I will take the eleventh, the twenty-third, and the irregulars and fade into the city. We will be scattered around the square and along the walls. As soon as we determine the exact location of the attack – which we predict will be the square, but we don't want to take any chances — we will all converge at the attack point. The fifth will stay at the periphery in order to mop up stragglers and in case they launch a second front from the troops outside.

"Tayaela's group will engage their attention and defend themselves in a siege formation. Once we are certain the path is closed, my troops will attack from behind, and we will squeeze them in the middle. Try to disarm them and take them prisoner, since they are still Dal Ryeans and many are our kin, but by no means allow your men to undertake any undue risks to take prisoners. Any questions?"

"Sir, do we have an escape route?"

"I am glad you asked that. Once we have contained the battle, we are shifting to Tayaela's world. Try to maneuver all fighting towards the main tent. The Princess has forged a one-way path to her world. Once we know that the battle is going our way, she will cross to the new world and await your coming. We already have holding cells and guards standing by to take your prisoners.

Then we will all retreat there and when we get word from the King, they will forge a path to Tadia inside the castle and we assist in retaking the city. Now go back and get ready. We will have some stragglers appear to be fleeing to Megra and beyond to lull them those outside. We expect the army here within the next two hours."

Alaeric then accompanied his officers to where the assembled troops were waiting and reviewed them. Within minutes the fifth century was patrolling the city, Tayaela's troops were setting themselves in for a short siege in the center of town, and Alaeric's soldiers were fading away from sight.

Word was sent to the citizens of Chaldia that a battle was imminent and they should barricade themselves in their homes to await the outcome. A strange quiet descended upon the city as they waited for Killia's army to arrive.

When the sun was turning to late morning, a maelstrom wind swirled in the middle of the square and under the protection of magic, Killia's troops emerged from a path ready to battle. It was the morning of the Supplicant's Feast and they were determined to crush the King's army before nightfall and be home for the Queen's coronation in the morning.

Chapter 29

On the day of the Supplicant's feast, Lisa awoke at dawn. The night before, Merrick had told her of the plans and her role in them. She was to stay as close to Killia and Sindelar as possible. Diana would be near with Lauren and Mark. When she found out Mark was alive, she began to weep with joy. It was almost too hard to hide the happiness she felt from the prying eyes of Killia.

Mark and Carr would be in the crowd with the soldiers. The King and Merrick would be coming up from the rear. Her job was to keep the wizard from realizing that there was a rearguard attack coming. All she had to do was stand in front of the panel where Tarq and Merrick were hiding. Upon their signal she was to move aside and try to reach Diana. The King and Merrick would burst out and go directly for the Tal.

She was terrified. At any time during the last few days she was afraid that an inadvertent slip of her tongue would give away the entire plan. She knew Volta was watching her closely, but she tried to convince herself that Volta was watching everyone closely. She tried to put the Captain from her mind but whenever she managed to do this, she found Volta's cold eyes looking in her direction again. Ever since Orado died, the Captain watched her suspiciously.

Sindelar was acting strangely too. He kept seeking her company and he had begun to wear the Tal tied on its leather thong around his neck. Lisa knew he would have to give it to Killia at the coronation and that it had to be on display at the feast in its traditional stand at the side of the ruler's chair. But ever since Ferrel's death he had kept it close by him.

"Maybe to keep it from being stolen," she said aloud, wincing at the remembrance of her own theft. "If I hadn't done that, Ferrel would still be alive." She remembered her friend every day and the vivid recollection of his death reminded her how serious everything was.

Lost in her thoughts, Lisa missed the first sight of the dawn. By the time the bell sounded for the second hour though, she rose and dressed. Under her voluminous skirt, she put on her own jeans and shoes. This way when the fight started, she could tear off the skirt and be able to run. It was going to be an endless day.

After briefing Lisa on her part in the following day's events, Tarq and Merrick had crept into the castle. The King, who had spent many happy childhood hours exploring the secrets of Tadia Castle, led his spy to a specially constructed room behind a third floor reception area. Unless someone was familiar with the castle, this room remained always hidden.

It was the assignation room of a distant Tadiak Queen, who would hide her activities from an extremely jealous consort. Her lover hid in the back room whenever the Prince Consort sought the Queen out. She always appeared that she was hard at work on her malachite throne, and that nothing was going on.

It drove the consort crazy, but he could never prove that his wife was cheating on him with a young lover since whenever he checked the room known to be behind the throne, it was always empty. The lover was hiding in a room beneath the first room and it was only accessible by a hidden door and stair. The story was lost in the fables of the castle, but the young Tarq always took the legends at face value and found the hidden spaces. It proved very convenient for hiding as a child and even more so now as an adult.

Barring the door from the inside, the two young men prepared for their night in the 'Lover's Room'. Being trained warriors they knew how to set aside their anxieties. Sleep was vital and the next day's events would decide the fate of more than just the Kingdom.

Before drifting off, Tarq said, "I can't thank you enough, Merrick, for everything that you have done. I admit that I was reluctant to trust you at first. Only Lauren's confidence in you kept me from ordering your arrest. That would have been a tragic mistake for all of us." Tarq paused, knowing that his next words would cause Merrick pain.

"I cannot express my gratitude or my sorrow strongly enough. Your brother's sacrifice is a debt I can never repay. I hope when this is over you will continue to work with me in making Dal Ryeas the kind of place where we can all live in harmony and freedom. I know you are bonded to Lauren, but everything you've done for our cause far exceeds any bonding. You are my ally and I hope you will become my friend." Tarq finished shyly, staring at the darkened ceiling above him. He was unused to confiding in anyone but Lauren, Alaeric, and Tayaela.

"Thank you, my King," Merrick said, fingering the figurine Diana had given him. He was honored by the King's growing trust. With the loss of Ferrel, whom he had guarded for years, Merrick was himself lost as to what his future held. He had no plans after tomorrow, but now the King was offering him a future, a goal for the next years of his life. He also sensed that Tarq understood how lost he was feeling and was concerned. A warm gratitude suffused him and the last vestiges of his father's loyalty to Tadiak evaporated in the King's honesty.

"Friendship with you is something I will cherish always." Merrick said simply.

"Let's get through tomorrow first," Tarq said wryly.

Both men fell silent, and soon were asleep. Morning would soon be upon them.

Mark and Carr joined Tarq's disguised vanguard at the castle gate. Merrick's agents had effectively informed most native Tadains that there might be trouble at the Feast. Only a few hundred had ventured forth. Mark and some of the Maril Zan's troopers were subtly trying to herd these civilians into a group that could be protected later in the day. Most of the citizens refused to cooperate however, and Mark found the task frustrating.

Returning to Carr's side after an hour he pointed out, "These people don't want protection. They want to be here and participate in history. I just hope no one gets hurt."

"Well, you've done your best," Carr reassured him. Just then a troop of guards in Killia's uniforms pushed their way through the crowd. They were escorting two men dressed in black. Neither man looked happy. Arrogantly ignoring their escort, the men strode towards the castle doors without looking about at the crowd around them.

"That was close!" exclaimed Carr.

"What do you mean?" asked Mark.

"I was afraid they might recognize us and expect us to release them!"

"Who were they?" Mark was looking after the troop as they entered the courtyard.

"Prince Kir'san and Prince Ertlan Olenteas. The Olenteas Lords. I wonder where they've been, since we know that Sindelar had them in their quarters in the castle. They looked pretty furious."

"Will they recognize Lauren?"

"Probably, but they won't willingly betray her," Carr frowned. "But if they had recognized me, then by many of our oaths I would be required to release them. All I hope is that they can control their tempers until we are in place. From the look on Kir'san's face, I think they are ready to explode. I hope that they watch out for Lisa at least."

"Do you know them?"

"Oh, yes, we grew up together. We're cousins."

"That's right! You're related to my mother too. I am glad that we are family," Mark was still confused over the nuances of their strange ties.

Before Carr could answer, the castle gates opened and the Supplicant crowd was admitted to the courtyard of the Great Hall. Mark decided that they would work out the family details later. He gave Carr a brief hug, squared his shoulders, and moved forward with the crowd. Beyond the gate he could see huge trestle tables leading from the Malachite Hall.

"Here we go," muttered Carr and they entered the castle.

Lauren and Diana were the last to reach the castle. An hour before the Princess' appearance, Carr and her troops were settling themselves strategically at various tables. They sauntered to a side entrance and presented their passes. They were the only ones to do so openly. No one could have penetrated their disguises unless they had an intimate knowledge of the women.

Lauren was dressed in the leather trousers and white top she had purchased on the edgeworld. Over this she had thrown a long black velvet cloak that had once belonged to her mother. Her long dark hair was skillfully intermingled with the purple wig as Carr had shown her and she wore heavy theatrical makeup. Diana was also dressed in leather; however she wore the short blue cape of an apprentice. Her hair was stiffly spiked and its ends were touched with green fluorescent spray – she had decided the wig was too much to handle. Her own make-up was less garish than Lauren's but still heavy for the norm in Dal Ryeas.

Casually the two women made their way to where the other musicians were unpacking their instruments. Taking her siganhar from its case, Lauren also slipped her sword into a deep holster inside the cape. Briefly she wondered if her mother found this feature useful as well. Diana, armed only with a long knife, had some protective spells she learned from Carr for her armament. She started tuning her guitar.

Lauren whispered to her companion, "Remember, when the fighting starts get to Lisa and stay away from the battle. And be careful."

Diana smiled at Lauren's motherly concern. "You be careful too!"

Lauren nodded, suddenly preoccupied with the tuning of her harp.

A voluntary trumpet announced the arrival of some of the lesser courtiers to the head tables. Lauren signaled to Diana and they took their places in the feasting hall. Once they were near the dais, they began to circulate singing their off-world songs and entertaining the assembled guests. Carr and Lauren exchanged a glance and a nod as the Princess's personal entourage entered to the sounds of cymbals trumpets and drums. It was time.

Tayaela and Alaeric, some hundred miles away, opened the path for their army to escape to into Tayaela's world. Killia's army was squeezed between the fighters on the square, who were retreating towards the main tent, and the rearguard that seemed to come from nowhere.

The fighting was fierce and almost one-sided. Alaeric's soldiers fought grimly and skillfully, disarming their opponents more often than wounding them. Killia's troops sensed that there were no reinforcements coming since the maelstrom fizzled as soon as the path was withdrawn. No other one appeared and they realized that they were on their own. As soon as this realization spread through the army, the heart went from them and they allowed themselves to be herded towards the center of the square, where Tayaela's path was awaiting them.

The final humiliation for Killia's army came when they realized that behind Alaeric's troops the citizens of Chaldia were blocking any avenue of escape.

It was an eerily silent moment, except for the groans of the wounded and dying, when Alaeric strode forward and held out his hand for Killia's commander's sword. He held it aloft and it burst into flames.

The citizens of Chaldia began to cheer. It swelled into a roar of triumph as Tayaela appeared from the tent as herself and everyone – soldiers, citizens, exiles, and Killia's army – realized that a ruse had been perpetrated on them. The King was not in Chaldia and everyone knew that meant he was in Tadia. The Year's End celebrations started a day early in Chaldia that year, and from then on the holiday was extended by a day to commemorate Alaeric's and Tayaela's victory

With the sound of their defeat ringing in their ears, Killia's disheartened army was sent along the path to Tayaela's world and out of the struggle for the throne. As soon as the last of her troops were across the path to her world Tayaela blocked the pathway.

"Now we wait," Tayaela said, ministering to a large number of cuts Alaeric had received. They were watching as their troops escorted Killia's into a large holding area. Her cooks were preparing meals for both armies and her troops were passing out water and medical treatment. Killia's army seemed stunned that Tayaela and Alaeric cared about their well-being. For most, their years in exile had conditioned them to think of anything related to Pyramus and even Olenteas as just this side of evil. Kindness was the last thing they expected.

"If he wins, we go home. If not," grumbled Alaeric wincing at his wife's attempts at nursing, "we start a colony here."

"We could do that anyway." Tayaela grinned. "Let's survey the troops about this. And don't be such a baby, you're going to be alright!" She exclaimed as Alaeric reacted to the antiseptic.

Cheerfully planning their future, Alaeric and Tayaela set off to talk their troops into immigrating to a newly formed colony under their leadership. It was a pleasant way to spend the anxious waiting time until they knew if the King was restored to his own again or not.

Chapter 30

For the first time in weeks the Princess and the wizard were in complete accord. At noon the Princess, with Sindelar close behind, made her appearance in the royal court, which opened onto the courtyard. A thousand supplicants were waiting to be presented to her.

"My people," she intoned ritually, "Tomorrow, I become your queen. Today I bid you feast with me." She signaled for the doors to be thrown open and the food to be brought for the feast. A cheer went up from the crowd.

Bards and other entertainers wandered the hall as the servers began to pass huge platters of food. Storytellers sat at tables spinning myths of the gods and showing their crystals. No one noticed that more than half of the supplicants never touched the food set before them.

The Princess, with Sindelar and other important lords and ladies, sat at a long table at the center of the courtyard. This was placed on a raised dais so that all could see her. Killia was at her sparkling best, laughing and joking with the wizard, looking triumphant. All her plans were coming to completion in the morning and she would be the rightful Queen, regaining her throne after years of adversity. She looked longingly at the Tal as it stood upon its traditional stand next to her chair. Tomorrow it would be hers, forever.

Lauren and Diana strolled towards the table. Lauren was deftly playing the siganhar and singing a medley of earth folk songs. The regular supplicants were enthralled and threw money in her direction. Diana, in her role as apprentice, stooped to pick it up. This gave her a chance to survey the room and notice where everyone was stationed.

Almost at once Diana noticed that Lisa stood behind the Princess leaning against a malachite panel. She was so busy looking at her sister that she did not see the look exchanged between Lauren and Prince Kir'san. Guards surrounded Kir'san and Ertlan monitoring their every move, but the Prince still managed to acknowledge his daughter and nod approvingly at her. Lauren, with tears in her eyes, smiled back at the father whom she thought had abandoned her. She felt a strange sense of relief knowing they were absolutely and finally on the same side.

Inexorably the feast wore on. Each supplicant approached the Princess and presented her with a request. Courtesy demanded that she listen and record each request. They were supposed to be the very first acts of her reign. The guards were justifiably nervous as each supplicant approached the Princess, fearing assassination attempts or other trouble, however as no incidents occurred, they began to relax.

Carr and Mark were at a table just below Sindelar. Mark kept his hood up to avoid recognition. He was nervous and kept fingering his bow. Carr was concentrating on maintaining a disguise with a minimal use of perceptible magic. She did not want to alert Sindelar of her presence. She carefully watched to see if the soldiers were prepared for the signal. Catching the eye of Maril Zan, Carr nodded and was acknowledged by Maril's slight bow.

Lauren, seeing Lisa move away from the panel against which she was leaning, cautiously made her way to the front table. She looked for signs of Tarq and Merrick. Then she saw the panel move slightly. They were in place behind the dais and Lisa had unlocked the door. As soon as she was certain everyone was in place, Lauren took center stage and focused all eyes upon her.

"My Princess, lords, wizards, ladies. I bring you songs from the edges." Lauren said in ringing tones that cut through the chatter of the room.

"Sing them, bard!" Killia exclaimed excitedly. "I love edge music. It reminds me of my childhood!"

Placing her siganhar in front of her, Lauren, with Diana

harmonizing, began singing a medley of songs from the earth edge. She sang for over a half hour. Killia was delighted and the courtiers amused at the variety and scope of her songs.

"After we are crowned," Killia smiled once they had finished a song, "you and your assistant must come to us at court."

"I have a final song for you, Princess." Lauren announced.

"Oh? What is it?" Killia was anxious. "I can't tell you how pleased I am so far, you are both so versatile!"

"More than you know," muttered Lauren to Diana as she tuned her harp. With a quick glance at Carr, who made a slight motion with her hand, Lauren strummed the opening chords of "Bad Company".

"I was born, six-gun in my hand," she sang as Carr amplified her voice to all corners of the hall. "Behind a gun..."

Tarq silently emerged from behind the arras to stand behind the guard.

"—I'll make my final stand..." As she began the chorus, Merrick moved behind Volta. "—Bad Company, I won't deny. Bad company, until the day I die."

The vanguard rose as one and began to stalk the Princess' guard while Mark uncloaked and Carr rose before a stunned Sindelar.

Lauren dropped her harp as Diana dropped her guitar to rush to Lisa. Maril Zan was ordering her troops into position while Mark left Carr's side to try to herd the civilians to safety.

Lauren vaulted onto the table before Killia and the Princess, seeing the faces of her enemies for the first time, broke the tableaux and ran. Battle was engaged and no one saw Lauren chase after her.

The few civilians in the crowd were led to safety. Mark herded them towards the castle gate and a group of Maril Zan's soldiers. The troopers escorted these innocents to freedom outside before returning to the battle inside Tadia Castle. Mark was trying to reassure a young couple that the situation was under control and that there was nothing to worry about when he heard Lisa scream.

Mark whirled toward the dais where he saw his youngest sister caught in an arm-breaking grip by Sindelar. Protected by Volta who was fighting with Merrick, the wizard tried to use the girl as a hostage to evade Tarq's advances. Carr kept trying to cast spells to distract Sindelar into releasing Lisa but the wizard deftly countered each one with the Tal gripped tightly in his left hand. He had grabbed it as soon as he realized an attack had commenced.

Frustrated in her anger, Carr started to lose her concentration. Mark sensed something amiss and raced to her side. Diana crept up behind the wizard, grabbed her sister's arm, and started to pull. The attack was so sudden that Sindelar nearly lost his grip on the girl, however, his powers being so much greater than Diana's nascent ones; he was able to trap her as well.

Merrick, seeing the struggle, turned from his battle with Volta to assist Diana. Volta, seeing the opening, brought her weapon back for a final blow. Diana cried a warning and Merrick leapt away from the slashing blade, receiving a deep gash on his arm.

Volta turned to attack the King, who was battling Sindelar's bodyguard, when Merrick returned to face her. He had tied a scarf around his arm and their battle began in deadly earnest. They were evenly matched and neither was making any headway.

Neither saw Tarq destroy Sindelar's bodyguard and with a flick of his hand call the Tal to him. Nor did the fighters see the Tal fly from Sindelar's grasp, burning a deep brand into his hand or hear him cry out in rage. Volta did not hear Tarq call out to Carr to protect the eyes of all his warriors from the unshielded light of the two Tals.

Neither saw the wizard begin to fight Carr in earnest, nor did they see lights of magic flowing around the new combatants. Merrick never heard Diana and Lisa, released from the wizard's deadly grip, cry out his name in horror as they saw the blood flow from his arm. Nor did they see Prince Kir'san or Prince Ertlan overpower their guards and shield the girls. Only when the light of the Tal in the King's hand burned in response to the Dal Ryeas Tal did they momentarily pause.

Tarq stood, a bloodied sword blazing blue, purple and carnelian lights, in his hand. His blonde hair seemed afire. A circle was cleared about him as he joined the full power of two Tals. Carr, her robes ablaze with blue light, stood arms outstretched reaching for the second Tal in Tarq's hands to give her power. The wizard swathed in white light was writhing between the two forces assaulting him. He never saw the battle being lost around him. He did not hear the cries of the wounded and never saw the youth, whose death his Princess had ordered, come up behind him and hit him with a flat-edged sword.

He only saw the King, blazing in his glorious power, fully restored to the symbiosis that gave him the greatest control of magic in the Kingdom. Never before, not even in the days of his beloved friend Philos, had Sindelar seen the full power of the King. Only Tarq had the control to release the force.

And for once the wizard knew fear.

With the greatest effort he turned to the enchantress, facing him in her implacable wrath. Carr deftly turned his own skills against him as the King channeled power to his sorceress. Suddenly trapped between the inexorable force of the King and the growing anger of the enchantress, Sindelar felt the end of his gambit for the crown of Dal Ryeas.

Calling up the reserves of his own considerable skill, Sindelar opened a path in the midst of the battle and summoned a whirlwind to cover his passage as he stepped onto the path. Carr, realizing his intent, stepped through the vortex to follow. Sindelar closed the gate and suddenly he was gone, escaping to the edgeworlds.

In horror, Tarq watched as the two wizards disappeared. He howled in rage at losing the wizard to the world paths. "Carr! Catch" he cried out, tossing the unfocused Tal at her, as he tried to maintain a thread of contact with his enchantress. Faintly her voice returned, "I'll follow him as long as I can." and then silence.

The battle raged on for another few minutes before the Princess' troops realized that their leaders had both vanished. The ground was strewn with the dead and dying. Tarq's troops were in control of the battle and it was becoming a massacre.

Eventually, order was restored as the King used the power of the Tal to quell the fighting. Only the fierce fighting between Volta and Merrick continued. They were dropping from exhaustion and yet they continued to fight, even as the battle died around them.

Once she realized that Killia had fled and the King had regained possession of the Tal, Volta began to fight for her own cause. She was desperate to kill Merrick. She knew he had killed Orado and hated him. She realized she was doomed and wanted more than anything to take him with her.

Grimly, Merrick fought on and gave her no quarter. Volta was a superb fighter in peak condition while Merrick was wounded and only recently recovered from Volta's and Orado's previous torture sessions. Only his own hatred of this cruel woman kept him standing.

Volta sensed he was tiring and moved in for the kill, her joy at taking him with her complete.

But Mark Harrison also had a score to settle with Rhea Volta. He realized that in the confusion that she had not seen him. So intense was her concentration on Merrick that he was able to maneuver strategically behind the weary fighter. He pulled his hood over his face again and silently prayed to anyone who would listen that this ruse worked.

Dramatically, he threw his hood back. "Rhea Volta!"

Volta dropped her guard, suddenly distracted by the ghost of the man she had killed. Shock, anger, and fear crossed her face and she began to back away from Merrick.

The diversion created by Mark's bizarre apparition gave Merrick the opening he needed. He slid his blade between her ribs and struck her to her heart. Volta, with a look of infinite surprise, toppled off the edge of his blade and crumpled dead to the floor.

"I've been dreaming of this moment for months," said Mark as he walked up to the heavily-panting Merrick. "It seems quite just that she met her death at your hands."

Merrick dropped the bloody blade and drew the younger man into a rough embrace. Only an instant passed before Diana and Lisa joined them. For a long time it seemed as if their emotions entirely overwhelmed them.

Lisa grabbed Mark and buried her head into his shoulder, huge gasping sobs only somewhat muffled by his cloak. He put his arms around her and held her in a tight hug. Diana moved towards them and the three Harrisons were reunited. Their months of separation had forever changed them and forged bonds between them as hard as titanium. Merrick beamed at them until Diana drew him into the embrace. He was forever part of them as well.

At last Merrick broke from the embrace. He wiped his eyes and looked around him. "Where are Lauren and Killia?"

"I don't know," Tarq answered harshly, as he came up to them. "No one does."

A new voice answered him, "Do you think my daughter has deserted you again, young King?" "Prince Kir'san." the King growled, "I know she hasn't. I just don't want her to come to any harm. Killia will be like a trapped beast and... I'd better find her."

Prince Kir'san grinned and pointed towards the back of the castle. "I think that they went that way."

The King sprinted from the hall, followed by his loyal advisors. Close behind followed Princes Kir'san and Ertlan. They were tired of fighting on the wrong side and anxious to see how this ended.

Chapter 31

Lauren knew at once where Killia was going. She could tell by the corridors that the woman chose that she was seeking refuge in the Queen's chambers. Through a long and intimate knowledge of the castle, Lauren ducked into a maze of hidden passages and circumvented her rival's flight.

Arriving seconds before Killia, Lauren found that her sense of irony was still intact. Realizing that the game she was about to play was cruel and somewhat childish; Lauren indulged herself this one time, after years of iron discipline. She seated herself on a royal chaise and waited.

Breathlessly, Killia arrived at the antechamber. Lauren could hear her throw the bolt into the lock and run to the inner chamber. Not seeing Lauren, Killia came into the bedroom and collapsed into the first chair she found, weeping hysterically.

Lauren gave her a few minutes to get the crying out of her system and then spoke. "Think no one will look for you here?"

"Who are you?" Killia screamed in panic, jumping from the chair.

"Why, my dear," Lauren said in a cool, kind voice. "Don't you recognize me?"

"You, you are the bard!" Killia said in surprised recognition. "What are you doing here? Are you hiding from the fighting?"

"I came to get you."

"Are you here to rescue me?" Killia exclaimed hopefully.

Feeling a small tug of sympathy for the distraught, insane woman, Lauren kept her voice calm "Not in the way you mean,

Killia." She smiled softly. "I am Laurenthalia Olenteas."

"Don't be silly," Killia, replied scornfully, "Lauren doesn't have purple hair."

"Oh this? This is nothing." Lauren pulled off the purple wig and shook out her long dark hair. "Is this better?"

"Are-are you going to kill me?" Killia asked, fearfully stepping back.

"Don't be silly. I won't hurt you. But I *am* going to take you to Tarq." Lauren felt that the erstwhile queen was beginning to crumble.

"Tarq! Oh yes, please, take me to Tarq!" Killia began primping and straightening her clothes and wiping her tear-streaked face. "I am certain that once you take me to Tarq he will see how beautiful I am and want to marry me. How could he ever want to marry that Lauren Olenteas? She is so plain! Think of the lovely blond children we will have. Sindelar will arrange it!"

Killia became happily lost in her vision and Lauren realized that her momentary recognition was gone. The poor woman was going mad before her very eyes. "Just think of the beauty our clan would possess, bard. Think of it! Oh please, let's hurry! Please take me to King Tarq." Killia offered Lauren her hand and expected to be led.

"Yes, bard," said the King from the chamber doorway, "Think of the feeble minds those children would inherit."

"When did you get here?" Lauren whirled to face Tarq in surprise.

"You are not the only one who knows the back ways." Tarq replied tartly. He was relieved to see that Lauren was all right.

Lauren, in her turn, was acutely aware that he was holding the Tal in one hand and a long bloody knife in the other. She felt a twinge of guilt that she had left the battle so early.

"Is everyone all right?" she asked.

Tarq nodded, still staring at Killia. "What am I going to do with her?"

"She's mad, you know. Living in her own fantasy Killia-Land." Now that Killia was defeated, Lauren's implacable hated evaporated. "I don't think that you have to kill her." Lauren eyed the naked blade warily.

Insulted, Tarq replied, "I am not in the habit of killing unarmed crazy people. I just didn't have time to clean the thing and I didn't want to put it away all messy!"

Before Lauren could reply, Killia demanded. "Bard, when are you taking me to see the King? He must be in the throne room by now. Let us go at once."

"Go back to the throne room, Tarq. We may as well see this farce to the end." Lauren said wearily, knowing that unless Killia was confronted in the actual throne room, with witnesses, there would be no peace and more rumors would spread concerning her fate. She understood very well the power of rumor and innuendo. Tarq's reign needed to be restored without any distractions or detractions.

"Alright. Let's get this over with already. We can get her the help she needs and be done with her."

Before he left them, Lauren asked, "Why did you come? Why did you follow me?"

Without looking in her direction, he replied. "To see if you needed help. It was the least I could do." He felt his shoulders stiffen as if anticipating her next remark.

"Or were you making sure that I wasn't running away and succoring the enemy? I wouldn't do that to you, you know."

"Don't be stupid!" Tarq snarled savagely. "I trust you more than I do myself." He stalked from the room, leaving Lauren torn between shame and exaltation.

"No matter what I do or say, I manage to hurt him. It is better that I am leaving. Maybe he will find someone more suitable in time." She looked at Killia and sighed. "Come Princess, the King is waiting for you."

Docilely Killia allowed Lauren to lead her from the Queen's chambers. As they walked through the corridors, Killia prattled on how her beauty would win Tarq's heart, just as it had won Sindelar's and Voltas. Lauren said nothing, instead allowing the woman to hold onto her illusions a while longer.

When they reached the court, Lauren found the troops clearing the remnants of battle. Wounded men and women were lying all over the room, groaning in pain and weeping as the healers, doctors, and magi tried to ease the suffering. Killia seemed oblivious to the surrounding sights, her eyes only on Tarq seated on the malachite throne.

"I bring you the usurper Killia, Sire." Lauren said formally.

Tarq beckoned them forward. Killia looked about her with bright unseeing eyes. She did not recognize Lisa, who stood with her brother, or even Mark whom she had ordered killed. Only when she saw the body of Rhea Volta, which was still lying in the room, did she realize something was amiss.

With the wail of a heartbroken child she threw herself over the body. She kissed the dead face and stroked her hair, calling her name over and over. Finally Tarq, moved by pity, ordered the stretcher holding Volta's body removed from the mad Princess' sight.

Hysterically, Killia tried to follow. Only Merrick and Lauren, holding each of her arms, restrained her. Tarq summoned two guards and ordered the Princess taken to the north tower.

"She is to remain there in comfort until I decide her fate," Tarq ordered gently, "She is to be watched from afar so that no harm comes to her, but she is not to be approached until we find help for her."

As she was leaving, Killia turned to the King and coyly smiled, "Do come and see me soon, Tarq. We must discuss our wedding."

The look of disbelief that crossed the King's face never penetrated her addled senses. She blithely accompanied her guards as if they were courtiers escorting her to a ball.

"This was too much for her." Lauren stated quietly.

"For her? How the hell was it for the rest of us?" Tarq exploded. "She's totally insane!" He shuddered at the thought of seeing Killia again.

"Don't you have an announcement to make?" Lauren changed the subject abruptly.

The King nodded and proceeded to declare his return to the throne. He then ordered the prisons emptied of all prisoners taken by Sindelar and Killia. He lifted the exiles and freed the Olenteas from the Crimson Tower, and he ordered a feast of thanksgiving held at the Temple of the Twin Gods in a week's time.

"And now we return to our reign in peace," he concluded. "It is time to heal all wounds." When he turned to speak to Lauren, he found she was gone.

Chapter 32

The day following the Battle of Tadia Castle as the bards had already named it, Prince Alaeric, Princess Tayaela and their army entered the city to the resounding cheers of the populace for their successful diversion. They joined the King in assisting in caring for the wounded and preparing for the Thanksgiving Feast. The casualties were minimal and the city was soon restored to order. There was great anticipation about the Feast and everyone was on edge for the entire week, trying to speculate what Tarq would do.

After the priests had concluded their thanks to the gods, Tarq addressed the city and offered them his own thanks for his restoration. Then in a surprise to even those closest to him, he brought his sister and Alaeric forward and asked them to choose their own reward.

After a quick consultation, Tayaela took a deep breath and asked that she, her beloved Alaeric and any who wanted to follow them, be allowed to settle Tayaela's world as a colony of Dal Ryeas. Tarq smiled and not only granted them a release from their allegiance to him, but the right to begin their own independent country. He called for all intrepid souls to follow his sister and her husband to their new land. By the end of the day, the news of the new Kingdom had spread and thousands petitioned Alaeric and Tayaela to accompany them on their new adventure.

Tarq publicly promised the unfocussed Tal to his sister for her world and her safekeeping. He promised assistance from Dal Ryeas and an everlasting alliance. The High Priestess smiled and decreed the gods happy with this venture. Her announcement was greeted with cheerful applause. The feast then began in earnest and for the rest of the day the citizens of Tadia rejoiced at the return of their king.

That night, Carr returned with Tayaela's Tal.

"I lost him." She said wearily. "He's magnificent. I'd forgotten how good he was. He took paths and created so many diversions that I was completely baffled."

Tarq replied, "Well, we have Killia. Prince Kir'san will take her to the mountain healers to see if they can cure her madness. If the Olenteas can't, no one can."

"Do you trust him?" Carr, ever wary, cautioned. She was still his devil's advocate, even if it were her cousins they were discussing.

"He and Prince Ertlan have sworn blood-oath directly to me." Tarq smirked.

Carr grinned. "Oh, that's all right then." She felt a bit relieved that her enmity with her cousins Kir'san and Ertlan was at an end. She could turn her attention to reconciling her sister with Merrick and resume her training of Diana. And she thought she could relax. Hah.

"Where are the others?"

"Mark, Lisa, and Diana have been inseparable for the past week, playing catch-up and just enjoying some free time here in Tadia. Merrick is helping Lauren pack and Alaeric and Tayaela are planning their colony." Tarq said casually.

"Why is Merrick helping Lauren pack?"

"He's her bond. He is supposed to do these things."

"No, why is she packing?" Carr demanded.

"She is going back," he sighed, "She's taking the girls home and staying there. It's her choice. Mark is staying here. Diana plans to return when she finishes her senior year of high school and they are both planning to attend the university. Diana also wants to come on weekends so she can train with you. I'll explain weekends another time. Lisa is still too young to leave home and I expect that her parents will be watching her carefully for any ill effects of her stay here."

"But…" Carr began.

"I don't wish to discuss it any further." Tarq's voice took on the cool, remote quality that had been so typical for the last five years and had been missing these last few months.

Carr sighed. Maybe Lauren knew what she wanted.

The good-byes the next morning were tearful. Tarq did not come down to the courtyard but said farewell to Lisa and Diana in his private quarters. He never spoke to Lauren.

Carr watched sadly as the girls hugged and swore eternal friendship to Alaeric and Tayaela. Mark, who was going home to get some personal items, was chatting casually to Merrick, who was going along for a visit. Lauren was standing alone, watching all of them. Her eyes met Carr's and she shook her head.

Finally Lauren summoned the well-worn and now familiar path to the Harrison's edgeworld and they were gone. Carr watched the empty space for a moment, hoping that Lauren would return. She felt movement next to her and turned to see that the King was standing there. There were tears in his eyes.

He refused to meet her gaze.

When the very essence of their path was gone from Dal Ryeas, Tarq turned and entered his castle to mount his empty malachite throne.

Epilogue

Contrary to all her expectations, Lauren did not find the haven she sought on her edgeworld. All around her changes occurred as a direct result of the time spent on Dal Ryeas. While Lauren re-opened her shop and spent hours working and reading, at night she returned to an empty house where she often sat in the dark, wondering how Alaeric and Tayaela were faring. She deliberately kept her thoughts away from Tarq and never communicated with Dal Ryeas. It was too painful and she had made her choice. This was her world now. Even her father's communications were short, to the point and upsetting, so she kept those to a minimum, although she was happy to hear from him again.

The six months that remained of high school passed quickly for Diana. Her parents smoothed the way for her to return after her absence on Dal Ryeas. They told the principal of the school that she was away at a funeral. She made up her lost work and soon regained her place at the head of her class.

Somehow, though, it all seemed anticlimactic. Her prom and graduation became special events, since Merrick attended. He was introduced to everyone as her fiancé. Many of her teachers tried to talk her out of an early marriage and she assured them that she was attending university – abroad. There was general relief among the faculty that Diana Harrison was going onto college after all. She had been somewhat odd this past year and they were worried that her relationship with an older man was affecting her good sense. But after all she *was* 18.

On the morning after commencement, Diana cheerfully waved good-bye to her parents, stood in the middle of the yard, surrounded by all her things and Merrick, and returned to Tadia to attend university. She was going to continue studying privately with Carr and some other mages in order to be ready for the new semester. Merrick, cheerfully accompanied her, uncertain of their future, but happy with their present.

Mark and she were going to share a house in the town, not far from where Merrick lived. The cat Maikai, who had adopted Diana as well as Mark, was already in residence with Mark when Diana arrived.

As a reward for the cat's own bravery, Carr had presented him with a special crystal, worn on his collar that allowed him to travel across the paths of the universe to visit the others. Many times he would arrive at Lauren's doorstep, realizing she needed a friend – and the visits were good for a meal and a cuddle always.

He greeted Diana as a long lost friend and was pressing her for food and affection by the time she had dropped her bags. Diana was in love with the house, which was airy and bright. It was built in a square with a large garden courtyard, with a pool in the center. Diana's rooms had doors leading to a private patio and into the courtyard. She was thrilled imagining the many romantic evenings there with Merrick.

With Mark and Diana at Tadia University and Lisa clamoring to visit Dal Ryeas and the court repeatedly, Lila Harrison revived her own pathfinding skills. With some simple instruction from Carr, she was soon able to call up a direct path to Diana's courtyard. Almost each weekend found Lila summoning the path and whisking her family across the dimensions.

Even Ron Harrison agreed to travel the path between the stars to see his children. He enjoyed Dal Ryeas so much he began to think that it might not be a bad place to retire. Weekends and holidays in Tadia or with Alaeric and Tayaela on their new world became the accepted norm for the family. It beat having to buy a country house.

Only Lauren never returned. From the moment she came back from Dal Ryeas, she threw herself into life on earth. She became involved and excited about so many different things – book clubs, cooking classes, museums, fencing, and painting. Diana tried to talk to her about her decision about not returning to Dal Ryeas, but Lauren denied any misgivings about her choice. Instead she bought a new Ferrari.

Diana did notice that she never mentioned Tarq by name, only by title and that bothered her. Lauren refused to acknowledge that she missed Alaeric. She declared that everything was fine and to stop hounding her about Dal Ryeas. Earth was her home now.

In Tadia, it was noted that while the King was as good and generous as ever, he was miserable. The court and his advisors realized that his sorrow was caused by Lauren's absence and it was slowly destroying him. They introduced him to countless women in hopes of distracting him, but none came close to his standards. There were a number of heart-broken young women who did not understand why they couldn't break through his reserve.

Finally his desperate cabinet petitioned Carr, his oldest advisor, to counsel him, but he would not listen to her. Besides Carr was scanning the worlds for signs of Sindelar and had little time for the love life of the King. She was becoming obsessed in finding the wizard and challenging him again.

Finally Merrick, remembering the Tarq's declaration of friendship the night before the battle, took it upon himself to approach the King.

"Tarq, I hate to see you like this." he began.

"Like what?" the King coolly replied.

"You are destroying yourself."

"I am grieving, Merrick."

"I grieve too, sire. A day doesn't go by when I don't remember Ferrel's sacrifice, but I live. I try to adjust and be happy." Merrick said, his face forever scarred by the remains of Killia's tortures.

"At least you are grieving the dead. There's nothing you can do about it." The king snapped, then caught Merrick's look. "I am sorry Merrick that was beastly."

"Right, I am grieving the dead. You are not. Why don't you?"

"What?"

"Do something about it!"

"Like what?"

Merrick looked at Tarq and realized that they were no longer subject and king, but two young men trying to figure out what love was all about. He laughed, drawing a dirty look from his sulking friend.

"Did you ask her to stay?" Merrick already knew the answer, but he wanted to hear what Tarq had to say.

"How could I influence her happiness like that? She would have stayed out of duty!" Tarq was shouting. "I needed her to want me, not the kingdom, not the clan rites, not the sacrifice to her sense of obligation. Her happiness means all the worlds to me!"

"Gods, man. It's your happiness too! I repeat, did you ask her to stay?" Merrick shouted back.

"Uhh...no?" Tarq replied in a low sheepish voice.

"So go ask her. She didn't seem all that thrilled with Earth when I was there for Diana's graduation." Merrick thrust the Tal into Tarq's hand and opened a path. "What have you got to lose? All she can do is say no. But she might say yes!"

Within minutes the King found himself on Lauren's doorstep. It was sunset and the summer flowers were wilting from the terrific heat all around the yard. He drank in the sight of the lush green yard and its foreign flowers. He recalled the months that he had stayed here and felt an inordinate fondness for the place. One part of him realized that Lauren must feel the same way and it almost made him reopen his path and go home.

Instead, he rang the doorbell.

Lauren opened the door with Maikai by her side. There, dressed in full Dal Ryean regalia, stood Tarq, with a bunch of bedraggled flowers – obviously from her own container garden — thrust towards her.

"Come in," she said, more to get him off her porch than to hear what he had to say.

"I want you to marry me," he said without preamble. "I am miserable and I need you."

"So how are you?" she asked, trying to avoid hearing the pain and anguish in his voice. Just seeing him brought all her emotions to the surface. She wanted to throw herself into his arms and kiss him. Inter-dimensional relationships were just too difficult at times.

"I told you, miserable. Please Lauren, I am begging. Marry

275

me. I can't stand the thought of life without you. Do you know, no one ever tells me I am wrong or stupid or even silly? No one tells me jokes. Merrick, finally after months, spoke honestly with me. It felt like a new morning, it was so refreshing to hear the truth."

Lauren petted the cat absently, avoiding Tarq's eyes as she looked down.

"Look Lauren," he sighed softly, "You are the only woman I have ever loved and the only one I ever will love. Ties that no one can understand bind us. I need you to rule with me. I need your laughter and your odd way of seeing things. I need you to remind me that I am human and ground me to reality. I need you to show mercy and love so that I can too. I love you. Please marry me."

"Okay, as long as we can keep this house and escape here sometimes."

"I know that I am not what you… What did you say? Of course we can come here and keep the house! I want to drive the Corvette."

"We have a Ferrari now. I wanted something cooler." Lauren admitted.

"Even better!" Tarq laughed. He felt amazingly free and happy.

He grabbed her in his arms and held her in a tight embrace. After a long time, he finally asked, "What made you change your mind?"

"I missed you. I missed sharing my everyday with you. I love you, Tarq. I always will."

"So you will be my Queen?"

She drew his head down again and kissed him with a passion that matched his own. As the sun set into the west she answered him.

"Well, I'll be your wife, everything else is negotiable…"

Afterword

First I want express my regard to friend, housemate, business partner, & kin, Paul Kraly. Thanks for the advice, the editing, providing outstanding partnership in all the other books and for being the best co-owner, business partner and friend that anyone could have in Scribes Unlimited. Also thank you forever for introducing me to the real Myky and allowing me to share many years with him. (Shout out to Myst, Malkie, and Karma-you have big paws to fill!)

Thanks to Lilly Griveas & Bill & Jason Olszanicky, for all the support, encouragement, and love! Love you guys!

Thank you, Laura Weisberg, and the rest of your family - David, Liana, Julie, Jessica, Danny, Lillian, and Sam for being a great second family to Paul and me.

Love and affection to my Bogas family connections – Steve & Christine, Steve & Amber, Chris, Julie & Nick; Suzanne & Dave; Bill & Kristine, Billy, Halle and godson George; Mara & Tom, Nicholas, Maggie, Jill & Dan, Adam & Tiffany. Dale & Sue, Matt, Brittany; Mary Kay & Randy, Katie, Kyle, Katina; and to all our family gone before too.

A special thanks (again to) Mara and Tom and all the rest of the great Rybak family – your support means a lot. Your acceptance of me as a family connection has always been important to me and I can't tell you how much I appreciate it.

Affection goes to longtime pal and fellow reader and trivia teammate Carolyn Vana for her support and her friendship, and to Kyle Vana for his good humor. I'll never be able to think of

Johannes Guttenberg without thinking of you, Kyle.

My great affection and appreciation to my original trivia teammate and good friend, Siti Fatmah Al Manaf my love and good wishes – always.

I would be nowhere without the support of friends like Athena Sevastos, Michael Janopolis, John Keane, George Chimples, Janet Chimples Kosteas, Vanessa Pasiadis, Priscilla Callos, Cindy Wright Hammond, goddaughter Liz Hammond, Sylvia Seremak, Rick Montonari for being an inspiration, Dave Hall, Phil Hall, Gina Scialla and Ashley Berry, and the list goes on. If I haven't mentioned you, know that I truly do think about you and thank you – it's just my brain is running out of room for names!

Thank you all for your support and encouragement. You've all been inspirational.

Breinigsville, PA USA
05 December 2010
250695BV00001B/38/P